SNOW JOB

WILLIAM DEVERELL

SNOW JOB

McCLELLAND & STEWART

Library and Archives Canada Cataloguing in Publication

Deverell, William, 1937-
    Snow job / William Deverell.

ISBN 978-0-7710-2722-2

    I. Title.

PS8557.E8775S66 2009   C813'.54   C2009-901671-0

We acknowledge the financial support of the Government of Canada through the
Book Publishing Industry Development Program and that of the Government of
Ontario through the Ontario Media Development Corporation's Ontario Book
Initiative. We further acknowledge the support of the Canada Council for the Arts
and the Ontario Arts Council for our publishing program.

Typeset in Scala by M&S, Toronto
Printed and bound in Canada

ANCIENT FOREST
FRIENDLY

McClelland & Stewart Ltd.
75 Sherbourne Street
Toronto, Ontario
M5A 2P9
www.mcclelland.com

1 2 3 4 5   13 12 11 10 09

To the memory of Jim Fulton, 1950–2008,
selfless politician, passionate warrior for this planet

1

___

"**I** am satisfied beyond a reasonable doubt that . . . that thing over there, that statue or whatever you want to call it, is what the Criminal Code calls a disgusting object. Guilty as charged." As Judge Wilkie stammered through this verdict, his unbelieving eyes were fixed – as they'd been through much of the trial – on Exhibit One, a twelve-foot sculpture of a winged, serpent-necked anthropoid with its head halfway up its rear end.

Arthur Beauchamp, Q.C., hadn't expected to hear any brave and stirring tribute to artistic freedom, not from this clubby former small-town practitioner. In all honesty, he himself was repelled by his client's *artificium* – he'd even found himself nodding at the prosecutorial rhetoric: "Is this something you'd allow your five-year-old to see?" Arthur knew he should hold modern, liberal views, but one has to be true to himself, and the hopeless truth was he was a stodgy old fart. Even in his youth he'd been a stodgy old fart.

He was annoyed at losing, of course, but mostly because of the blow to his pride – the judgment had brought his long string of victories, thirty-eight, to an ignoble end. A porno trial. If he were going to end his career at the bar – and he was determined this would be his last case – he'd have preferred to crash in the flames of a good old-fashioned murder.

The venue for this entertainment was Garibaldi Island's unfinished community hall – the framing and siding were done, the roof in place, but windows not. Papers rustled in the balmy breezes from without, a late-September day on warming planet Earth. A few score of the local *mobile vulgus* sat grinning on foldup metal chairs, amid sundry press and international art fanciers.

"Extraordinary." That more satisfactory verdict had been whispered in awed tones by a museum curator during a break. "Breathtaking," said a Boston gallery owner. "Such raw energy," said a buyer for a California collector. Enthusiasts of the bizarre, they'd arrived on Garibaldi like aliens from some planet whose dwellers were required to be outfitted with Armani suits, Rolexes, and Prada bags. Arthur felt like a rube in his comfortable rumpled suit.

"That leaves the matter of sentence, Mr. Beauchamp."

Arthur turned to Hamish McCoy, sitting at his elbow with his leprechaun grin, a pixie mix of Irish and Scots with a Newfoundland brogue. He'd been an artist of middling renown until he unveiled this work two years ago on Ferryboat Knoll. Now, thanks to all the tittering publicity and Internet traffic, he'd been discovered; his pieces, mostly giant mythical creatures, were fetching respectable prices.

McCoy had intended the statue as satire – it was his penance for an earlier crime, a grow-op, two hundred kilograms of Orange Super Skunk, a scheme to pay down his mortgage. Judge Wilkie had granted him a discharge conditional on his erecting a sculpture near the ferry landing, a tourism enhancer. All through the trial, the motions, the arguments, the drone of testimony from art experts, the judge had been in a sulking fury. Out of court, he'd been overheard fulminating about how he'd given McCoy a break only to be mocked.

"A suspended sentence would admirably reflect the gravity of this victimless minor offence," Arthur said.

Wilkie sat back, offended. "A slap on the wrist? For this obscene garbage?" He again fixed his obsessive gaze upon the statue, a study in stilled motion: looped, whorled shapes, a great round belly, a serpentine neck coiled downward and up like an elephant's trunk, a rat's face seeking entry into that most inelegant of orifices. Plaster

2

over forms, rebar, and chicken wire. McCoy's preferred medium was bronze, but that would have been hugely expensive, given this flying rodent's girth and ten-foot wingspan, its humanoid legs with splayed bare feet. Wilkie may have found the tiny penis and testicles especially insulting.

"If it's garbage, it's worthless," Arthur said. "Sentence should be commensurate with that."

"There *are* victims. It is the duty of the courts to protect those who may be morally corrupted by such filthy displays."

That would probably include every man, woman, and child on Garibaldi, given it had been stored in the RCMP's fenced compound, open to view through binoculars on well-tramped Chickadee Ridge. Stoney and Dog, Arthur's occasional handymen, had earned handsome tips guiding tourists there.

Wilkie unhitched his eyes from the sculpture, turned to McCoy. "I ought to send you to jail, that's my first impulse. But I've decided society should not be burdened with the cost of your upkeep. Fifty-thousand-dollar fine, six months in default."

McCoy looked like he was about to blow his top. "Fifty . . ."

Arthur bent low to his client's ear. "Zip it."

"How much time does he need to pay?"

"I suggest fifteen years."

"Payable in six months. Now what do we do with this thing? I don't see anything in the Code about disposing of such items."

"Exactly, Your Honour. It remains the property of the defendant. But maybe not for long." Arthur turned to the gallery. "I understand there's some interest in this unique abstraction."

A pony-tailed gentleman in a double-breasted frock coat: "I represent an interested party."

"Who might that be?" Arthur asked.

"The Shockley Foundation. I hold a certified cheque for eighty thousand dollars."

Up jumped a bejewelled older woman in a chic pantsuit. "Manhattan Contemporary Gallery. Ninety thousand."

Wilkie looked aghast.

"Thank you, I have ninety," Arthur said. "Do I hear a hundred?" A hand was raised, the Armani suit.

"Mr. Beauchamp! This court is in session!"

"I beg forgiveness."

"Please take your business outside."

Arthur bowed solemnly to the judge, motioned to the bidders to join him on the lawn.

"Call the next case," Wilkie said, his voice cracking.

"Regina versus Robert Stonewell. Thirteen counts of operating businesses without a licence, one count of maintaining unsightly premises."

Wilkie blanched as Stoney shuffled forward, holding his tattered copy of the local bylaws. "Not guilty, Your Honour. These here charges deny my fundamental right to earn a livelihood." He was an experienced hand at this, a pettifogging amateur lawyer.

Outside on the grass, under a hot fall sun, Arthur kept the media at bay while bargaining continued, the piece finally fetching a hundred and sixty thousand. McCoy would see a *quantum sufficit* of that, but Arthur wasn't going to let him welsh on the fees this time. He had driven up his stock considerably.

McCoy shook hands with the winning bidder, the Armani suit, a German gallery owner. Arthur accepted a certified cheque for half, scribbled out a contract. As part of the deal, McCoy would enjoy an all-expenses trip to Berlin to oversee installation.

If only out of principle, the conviction would be appealed, but not by Arthur – let the Civil Liberties Association take it. He was at an age when most lawyers were packing it up, retreating to hobby farm and lakeside cottage. He'd undertaken this case only as a reprieve from Ottawa, from which he regularly fled to perform in another scene of this stop-and-go trial. Ottawa was his unhappy home away from home since his beloved wife won a federal by-election thirty months ago. Margaret Blake, diva of the environmental movement, Parliament's sole Green Party member and its leader.

Another bitter Eastern winter looming. The apartment they'd rented was dismal, though well located near the Rideau Canal. But it was four thousand miles from his farm at Blunder Bay, from the gentle, forgiving winters of the Salish Sea.

On his every return to Ottawa, Arthur would endure ribbing from the reporters and politicians he'd befriended. McCoy's *opus foedus* was the subject of much hilarity in the corridors of Parliament, even among normally censorial M.P.s, though they would don pious masks when in the chamber, pretending shock and offence, demanding an end to federal grants for such salacious art.

Arthur wondered if he'd been born with an abhorrence for politics, though likely it had been instilled early by his close-minded, right-wing, iconoclastic parents. He saw politics as a Machiavellian game of clandestine deals and low intrigue. To his dismay, Margaret enjoyed it, enjoyed her underdog role in the Commons, had proved herself agile at it, despite a tart tongue and an impatience with the eco-hypocrisy that pervaded the House.

She'd been isolated by the old boys' club, orphaned to a rear seat on the Opposition side, but she was the poster girl of the Green set, darling of the liberal press, whom she worked with jokes and sound bites. Two decades younger than Arthur, vigorous, trim, and comely. Sort of a political sex object, her gams boldly displayed in that recent *Maclean's* profile. (When had she taken to wearing such short dresses?)

Sauntering from the hall came Robert Stonewell, fresh from beating his bylaw charges. Most of his illegal businesses were auto-related: motor mechanics, a taxi service, and rentals and sales from his sprawling used-car lot, Garibaldi's infamous Centre Road eyesore. But Stoney ran other illegal trades, including a specialty crop called Purple Passion. By now, in late September, his plants will have budded out.

"He finally gave up."

Wilkie, he meant, who'd probably developed one of his migraines trying to deal with Stoney's convolutions. An imminent ferry departure had also played a part: judge, prosecutor, and staff were rushing for their cars, with the local constable, Ernst Pound, escorting them, emergency lights flashing.

"Stoney, I hate to offend you by asking, but when am I going to see my truck again?" Arthur's venerable Fargo had been sitting for a month in the reprobate's yard, awaiting a transplant. It was Blunder Bay's sole vehicle, other than a tractor, Margaret having sold the half-ton diesel. Arthur had been making do by walking or hitching.

"Well, I was gonna surprise you, but you spoiled it by asking. I found a skookum rebuilt trannie in Victoria which I plan to acquire maybe as early as tomorrow. Those babies don't come cheap no more."

The traditional bargaining ceremony followed, one that would not have been out of place in a Cairo souk. Finally, Arthur bowed to the inevitable, greased his palm.

The hall was emptying out. Arthur must get back to the farm. Assuming the caretakers weren't in one of their squabbling modes, he would have a few more days' repose before flying to Ottawa to serve as loyal consort to the member for Cowichan and the Islands.

"Listen, man," Stoney said, "it's that time of year, and a certain individual is in the process of getting his crop off, and this could be a chance to make a advantageous investment. The party I represent needs a little front money."

Arthur looked quickly to his right and left, toward the hall, saw no one close enough to hear this criminal offer.

"Hundred per cent purple Thai, man." Stoney lit a joint, as if in demonstration. "Sweet." The fat rollie gave off an intense aroma.

"Stoney, I do not do drug deals."

"Heaven forbid that I would sully the name of our respectiful . . . respectable town tonsil. In case you ain't aware, Arthur, I am addressing my brother here, my long-time soulmate who has just come into some tall money."

Arthur looked down to see a horny, muscular hand reaching for the joint. Hamish McCoy, a foot shorter than Arthur and below his radar during his lookabout, was right under his beaklike nose.

McCoy took a drag. "Yiss, yiss," he said after a moment, "a fine vintage, b'y."

The two rogues went back to the hall to celebrate and scheme, and Arthur headed off to the trail to Eastshore Way, which led ultimately to Potters Road and home. A two-mile hike, getting his strength up for another snowbound Ottawa winter.

~~~

He was limping as he cut across the high pasture – his feet didn't like these stiff city shoes. Blunder Bay unfurled below, a ridge of arbutus and Douglas fir above a scallop-shaped inlet, a rickety dock with his forty-horse runabout. Greenhouse, barn, deer-fenced garden, goat-milking shed, and two grand old farmhouses. The weary-looking one with the slumping veranda was lived in, and the other was being refurbished: the former home of the neighbour he'd wooed and won.

That was eight years ago, after he'd made a break for freedom, vowing forever to retire from the odious practices of the law. The courtroom had taken a cruel toll: the artifice, the duplicity, the games that he'd despised himself for excelling at. The bloodletting, the acrimony. Dragging the innocent through the mud, painting the brutish client as the angel of innocence.

No one had been surprised as much as Arthur by the prowess he'd displayed in court. A classical scholar, a shy and gentle soul plagued by self-doubt, by an overwhelming sense of inadequacy (blame his merciless parenting), he had magically transformed each time he'd put on his robes.

Maybe it was a dissociative disorder, a double personality. Mild-mannered Arthur Beauchamp becomes his opposite, dons the armour of the Greek and Roman heroes glorified by his beloved Homer and Virgil. He'd astonished himself by winning his first twelve murders, tying Hercules' record of twelve labours, besting the savage Cretan bull that was his own felt impotence.

And then he became a jealous cuckold and a drunk . . .

He carefully closed the gate, manoeuvred around the thick coils of excreta left by Bess, their Jersey milk cow, and Barney, their old stallion, who was grazing by the fence, blind and deaf, only mouth and anus working. In contrast, Homer, their two-year-old border collie, had everything working – he'd seen, heard, and smelled Arthur's coming, was bounding so fast toward him that he over-shot his target by ten feet.

Arthur treated him to a shoulder rub, then ordered him back to work. Homer bounded off to the lower pasture, where the young goat they'd named Papillon had escaped the pen again, was hiding out amid the sheep, trying to look inconspicuous.

Directing this light entertainment was the vivacious Savannah Buckett, eighteen months out of jail for an act of eco-sabotage against a high-end logging operation. She waved, looking a little helpless and flustered – a city woman, a street-smart radical, unused to the travails of country living. As was her partner and fellow parolee, Zachary Flett, who was out there too, sealing a hole in the goat pen.

Arthur paused to look at his flourishing garden, its fattening pumpkins and cabbage heads and wilting potato tops with their promises of bounty below. He will fork some up as soon as he gets out of this sweaty suit and into a uniform more rustic.

Zack had added more solar panels to the roofs of the house and barn – he was a fair hand with green technology. ("We're going to take you off the grid, big boy," Savannah had said, patting his farm-fed belly.) They'd been reviving Margaret's 1920s frame house as well, and planned eventually to move into it.

He mounted the creaking steps to his veranda, sat down on the rocker, kicked off his shoes, massaged his feet, and watched with approval as, with Homer working right point, his caretakers finally arrested the goat while loudly blaming each other for its bolt to freedom.

At first, Arthur hadn't minded sharing his house with this pair. It was spacious, three bedrooms, a large parlour off the living room, funky gingerbread details. But they were constantly at each other over the most trivial transgressions – mislaid toothpaste, underwear and socks lying about, compost not taken out.

Savannah, Zachary, and three other activists of what the press dubbed the Quatsino Five had canoed by night into a log-booming grounds below a hotly debated old-growth clearcut, armed with acetylene sets in backpacks. They'd cut through the boom chains, and by morning several hundred logs were afloat on the Pacific Ocean. Gourmet timber, yellow cedar, forty-thousand dollars per raw log in Japan. Much was salvaged, more pirated by scavengers.

A vicious and ruinous act of eco-terrorism, snarled the judge, getting his headline. He gave each defendant four years, and each served two and a half, unrepentant.

Others had answered Blunder Bay's ad for caretakers, but Margaret made the politically precarious choice of these two newly sprung parolees. She believed in peaceful protest, she assured the press, and disagreed with what they'd done, but they'd paid the price and deserved a chance. Arthur echoed her loyally: rehabilitation not retribution.

Zachary and Savannah were in their early thirties, both from Vancouver, where they'd met and coupled a decade ago. Zack came out of prison wrathful and bitter, but Savannah somehow had taken it in stride, harboured little rancour. In the end, theirs was not a lost cause because half the ancient cloud forest they'd fought to save – a habitat for threatened marbled murrelets – was made a reserve.

"Sometimes a little serious monkeywrenching works," Zack had said. Such musings made Arthur nervous, hinting of anarchist attitudes. He sensed Zack revelled in the role of hero to the more rambunctious elements of the environmental movement.

Though tenderfeet, both were intelligent and industrious, if cynical, and firm subscribers to an organic lifestyle. Neither owned cars, out of principle, relying on bicycles, but Zack seemed adept enough with the tractor and the Fargo, when it was on the road. And it was a break to have someone to talk to other than the layabouts at the General Store. However, they did tend to patronize Arthur, with his square, traditional world view.

Arthur ascended briskly to the second floor, his floor, with its own den, its ample bedroom and bath, its expansive ocean view: the San Juan Islands and the distant snowy Olympics. Might he bring out rods and tackle this evening? Bait some crab pots? So little time, so many things to do.

Clad in rough farm wear, he went down to find Zack barefoot in the kitchen, washing up. Of middling height, gaunt, angular. "Papillon pissed on my boots." He swept a swatch of untrained coal-black hair from his dark sad eyes.

Savannah examined him critically from the doorway. "Jeez, Zack, change your pants while you're at it. Lesson learned. Don't stand behind the livestock."

Arthur picked up a gamy, sweaty smell as she bussed him with pouty lips. A modern woman, brash and tart. Taller than her boyfriend, thick blond curls, a busty, eye-catching figure. Arthur had got used to her nighttime roaming – a sleepwalking disorder had plagued her since childhood.

She continued to scold Zack. "When are you going to get a damn haircut? You look like a palm tree in a hurricane."

"Yeah, right, I'll head right down to the nearest salon."

"You need a weed whacker, pal." She turned to Arthur. "So who won today's battle between good and evil?"

Arthur regaled them with Judge Wilkie's show of dismay as his punitive fine was dwarfed by later, generous ransoms.

"Sounds like the judge we drew," Zack said. "Another guardian of the dying order. Maybe telling him to go to hell was a strategic error. Did Wilkie really think it was a caricature of himself?"

"I'm afraid that's rather typical of the self-absorbed."

"Reminds me of someone else. A pork-bellied flightless ostrich with its head up its patoot – who am I thinking of?"

"Huck Finn," Savannah said.

The Conservative prime minister, she meant, Huck Finnerty. Whom the member for Cowichan and the Islands, in one of her more acidic sound bites, had accused of having his head up his exhaust pipe.

2

———

"Let me guess. They want a handout. Another delegation from another two-bit backwater coming here with their gold teeth and vodka breath and outstretched palms. We can't be filling the beggar's bowl of every Lower Slobovia on the planet while we're in the economic doldrums – got to look after ourselves first." Canada First, that was the horse Huck Finnerty rode to victory at last year's convention. It was his pledge to the nation, and he was sticking by it.

"We come for cultural learnings for make benefit glorious republic of Quackistan." Charley Thiessen, the public safety minister, the official jokester of Finnerty's fractious Privy Council, his inner cabinet. They were meeting in the Round Room, off the horseshoe-shaped lobby of the P.M.'s parliamentary offices.

The foreign minister, Gerry Lafayette, joined politely in the laughter, though he found the humour boorish. He was mystified by Thiessen's popularity in this august conclave. With his bonhomie and his square-chinned film-star looks, he was a vote-getter – but what a *concombre!* How did such a mediocre mind win a law degree? He'd earned his way into Finnerty's cabinet as his tail-wagging poodle.

"What's that place called again?" Finnerty asked.

"Bhashyistan," Lafayette said. "And no, they didn't approach us, we made the overture. It might help, Huck, if you and the ministers were to review the briefing notes from my Central Asian people."

"Better if you just lay it out for us, Gerry." The prime minister fought to maintain his big trademark grin. He wasn't going to betray the slightest hint he was irked by Lafayette, a control freak, an elitist, patronizing everybody with his academic brilliance. Still smarting over losing on the fourth ballot. Never got dirt under his fingernails, never swabbed the deck of a working boat.

Finnerty knew he should have read the briefing notes last night instead of emptying a bottle of CC with a few of the boys from back home. He felt handicapped in this discussion because he had no clear idea where Bhashyistan was. Or *what* it was. One of those former Moscow satellites until the U.S.S.R. imploded. Bolshevik architecture. Pompous statues. Tribal feuds. Donkeys, or maybe camels. Mud wrestling.

"Some of us may be geographically disadvantaged. Show us on the map, Gerry."

Lafayette ordered himself to be patient with this chuckling *colon*, who knew nothing about Central Asia or, for that matter, the entire world beyond the two-hundred-mile fishing zone. He rose from the circular table and directed a pointer at a map on a stand, a mustard-coloured glob – "about the size of New Brunswick, Huck" – bordering Siberia, Mongolia, and Kazakhstan.

"What is now known as the People's Democratic Republic of Bhashyistan can boast of having been subjugated by every tyrant who wandered by, from Alexander, Genghis Khan, and Tamerlane to Empress Alexandra and Josef Stalin. Having been beaten into submission over the eons, the Bhashyistanis apparently find freedom too difficult a concept and have been hard-wired into a state of docility."

Lafayette waited patiently until Finnerty raised his red-rimmed eyes from the briefing notes. The P.M. was a devotee of strong drink and junk food, his concept of haute cuisine a triple patty with a side of fries washed down with a tall rye and ginger. Silhouette of a septic tank.

"This diplomatic breach . . . Remind us, what happened there?"

"Bhashyistan's ex-president – father of the current president – was assassinated fifteen years ago in Vancouver during a stopover on a state visit. I think it was in the newspapers." Too snide, Lafayette was doing it again, showing his impatience with lesser minds. "Boris Mukhamed Ivanovich. Moscow trained, Muscovite wife, an apparatchik sent home to be secretary of the Bhashyistan Communist Party, and who slid into power on the demise of the Soviet Union."

"Right, right, he was shot by a sniper."

"The alleged assassin, Abzal Erzhan, a twenty-two-year-old partisan of the Bhashyistani Democratic Revolutionary Front, had entered Canada under a false Syrian passport as Abu Abdul Khazzam. The case fell apart at trial, and he was acquitted by a Vancouver jury. Bhashyistan took umbrage, recalled its ambassador. Like a maiden scorned, they have not answered our phone calls. Until now."

Here he was, Dr. Gerard Laurier Lafayette, former dean of international studies at the Université de Montréal, lecturing a supposed leader of the free world on basic modern history. Gerry Lafayette, the favourite coming in, every pundit's pick – but he'd fallen fifteen delegates short and lost the ultimate prize to a fat, crackerbarrel sea dog from the Bay of Fundy.

"Help us out a little here, Gerry. We initiated this?"

Lafayette put a Canada First spin on it for him. National interests were at issue. Geologists from Alta International, an aggressive Calgary company, had found extensive fields of oil and natural gas under the deserts of western Bhashyistan. Alta had an inside track on developing these resources. "Alta," he said, "is a friendly."

"They went balls out last go-round." Jack Bodnarchuk, Drumheller–Bow River, Energy and Resources. "Those boys are generous to a fault."

How generous was not discussed. The delicate matter of skirting the $1,100-per-head limit on campaign contributions was discussed only in backrooms.

"Okay," said Finnerty, "so this delegation, they're cabinet-level?"

"All seven of them, yes, high-ranking ministers. Plus an ambassador they want to put in place. A few diplomatic staff will arrive beforehand to assist in arrangements. In due course we will appoint our own ambassador to Bhashyistan."

"So we should welcome these ministers royally."

"They want some sort of apology for the assassin's acquittal — we'll have to manoeuvre around that. Bear in mind we're dealing with a closed, isolated police state."

Finnerty frowned over the briefing notes. "How can that be, Gerry? They're elected parliamentarians."

"Last year's official count of what is laughingly described as the popular vote gave them each about ninety-five per cent. That was after several hundred malcontents had been arrested for unlawful assembly. The president, Igor Muckhali Ivanovich, got an even more resounding mandate. Ninety-nine per cent."

"Surprised he didn't ask for a recount." Charley Thiessen grinned, appreciating the laughter. He enjoyed loosening everyone up, a knack that had made him a cabinet favourite. He'd campaigned hard last year for Huck, but he had no enemies here, he wasn't ambitious for anyone's job.

"Mad Igor, they call him," Lafayette said. "Bastard son of the president who got shot. He has proclaimed himself National Prophet and Ultimate Leader for Life." He let the implications sink in to shuffles of discomfort, chairs squeaking, bodies shifting, groans. The unspoken consensus: cuddling up to Alberta oil interests by extending a royal welcome to emissaries of this police state was not going to attract public applause.

Lafayette felt no need to remind anyone that with the economy in the toilet they'd lost four straight by-elections. Add to that the three *traîtres* who walked the floor after the blown bribery cover-up, and the Conservatives were down to a majority of six.

"Can't we slow things down?" said Bodnarchuk. "Start off with an exchange of trade delegations?"

"I'm afraid nothing will satisfy them but that we feed over-fattened goats at Rideau Hall."

"How low can we sink?" Clara Gracey, the finance minister. "Not with a ten-foot pole, Gerry. That's my attitude."

Lafayette locked eyes with her, the economist from hell. Despite having bedded her at the Montebello Trade Conference – no formidable task – she'd thrown her two hundred votes to Finnerty after bowing out of the leadership race. She was now deputy P.M. A clever woman, with a doctorate from Harvard, but with a feminist edge that rubbed him raw.

"I should also add," he said, "that if Alta doesn't get invited to the ball, a host of others await their chance, including Gazprom, Dutch Shell, and a British-American consortium. But we have an edge: Ultimate Leader for Life Ivanovich distrusts the big powers, with their bad habit of invading Third World countries. He despises the Russians."

"I can't see how we can let our boys down," Bodnarchuk said.

"Our boys?" Clara rolled her eyes. They were talking about affluent oilmen, not combat soldiers. She wondered why Lafayette was pushing this – it was bound to blow up in their faces. But he was always seeking subtle ways to degrade the P.M., enhance his own role. He'd flunked his tryout for the Pierre Trudeau role everyone was demanding of him. Single, soigné, a flair in dress, multi-lingually fluent . . . but the ingredients never jelled as charisma. It was the non-stop arrogance, the narcissism. Showed up in bed.

"I know those guys at Alta International," Bodnarchuk said. "If anyone can step in, anywhere in the world, and do a job, it's them. Their CEO is a real inspiration. A.J. Quilter, I'm proud to know him, he's a can-do kind of guy. And if anyone can tell me how to fund a campaign if the oil patch turns its back on us, let me know."

Bodnarchuk represented a riding full of old dinosaur bones, and in Clara's view he was their living counterpart. He wore ten-gallon hats. Said things like "Howdy-doody."

"Look," she said, "half of these tinpot dictatorships subsist on bribery. It's one of their main engines of commerce. Down that road we do not want to go."

"No bribery." Guy DuWallup, attorney general and justice minister. "Or we call off the wedding." A crony of the P.M., a holier-than-thou Pentecostal, but well regarded, honourable.

"A.J. Quilter doesn't work under the table." Bodnarchuk again.

"Nonetheless, we should caution him," DuWallup said.

Finnerty didn't like the idea of rubbing rear ends with envoys of a megalomaniacal dictator, but Canada First – otherwise, after all his pounding on that theme he'd look like a fool. "Well, folks, my view is that in this dog-eat-dog world we have to think of the home team first. We're not in the business of telling sovereign nations how to run their affairs."

"Well said, Prime Minister," Lafayette said. "A diplomatic breach must be repaired, wounds healed, trade restored. But let us hone the message. We are inviting our Bhashyistani colleagues to see a free society in action. Our goal is to inspire and nurture democracy in this young, emerging state. Bring it into the world, rescue it from isolation."

Applause, table thumping. "Hear, hear."

"Well said yourself, Gerry." Finnerty had to admit to an admiration for Lafayette – how well he played to the cabinet's shifting balances, seeking to seduce allies to his side, always on the move, like a circling buzzard waiting for him to falter. But Gerard Lafayette was never going to be prime minister, *never,* as long as Huck Finnerty had a last breath in him.

He took a show of hands. Some abstainers, only Clara Gracey opposed. She was lying in wait too. Able and thoughtful, but a pink Tory from the Toronto beltway, out of step, hard on guns, soft on abortion.

"Very well," said Lafayette. "I'm sure we can work out terms that will be satisfactory to all parties."

"Except the sacrificial goat," said Thiessen.

"A point of information." Attorney General DuWallup. "This alleged assassin – as I recall, despite his false passport and all sorts of suspicion, some clever lawyer got him off on a failure of identification. No reliable eyewitnesses. Whatever happened to him, Gerry?"

"The government of the time decided, bless their soft hearts, that they couldn't very well deport him to his native land. He was granted a minister's permit, eventually got citizenship under his original name, Abzal Erzhan. He lives in the Montreal area. We intend, with the help of the RCMP, to keep a vigilant eye on him."

"Excellent work, Gerry." Finnerty led a round of applause.

~~~

Dear Hank and the Canora all-girls band,

Hi guys, we had to break away from our tour for two days, but found our roots here (sort of) in the Caucasus in Georgia. I think we located the farm where Great-granddad was born, but maybe that was the local tourist office trying to be nice. No other Svetlikoffs in the neighbourhood, they say Stalin moved all the Doukhobors out. People are nice here. They drink a lot. On to Uzbekistan next.

I hope Mom settled in okay. Hi Mom! Don't let the girls get away with murder. Lockup is ten except weekends. Cassie, Katie, Jessie, don't be making heavy demands on your grandma and dad. Running out of room. Love from me and Auntie Maxine and Cousin Ivy. (I'm still surrounded by girls! Help!)

Jill XOXO

3

——

I t was warm now, at noon, but Arthur had risen to the sparkle of frost on lawns, an unseasonable October cold snap. The maples on Wellington Street had been nipped too, a blood-red spatter on outer leaves. Maybe it wasn't unseasonable – this was Ottawa, the Canadian Shield. In brief but glorious amends for the coming winter, he would have a month of beauty, the famed turning of the leaves, a spectacle denied the West Coast. Today, even the Gothic turrets of the Centre Block and the Peace Tower were shining verdigris bright under the midday sun. But the regal effect of these spires rising from manicured lawns and coddled flowerbeds was marred by the scruffy picketers marching in a loop below the steps.

Arthur guiltily avoided them, the Poverty Action Coalition – he was in a dark suit, they might mistake him for an elected member, harangue him, get pushy: there had been acts of violence as the economy bottomed out and unemployment lines grew. A smaller group of protesters, an environmental group, held signs exhorting "Stop Trawling Now!" and declaring "Finnerty Is a Bottom-Feeder."

The prime minister's family owned a fleet of ocean trawlers. He claimed to have sold his interest but remained a pet target for Greenpeacers and Sea Shepherds. P.M. for not quite a year since his predecessor resigned after being caught covering up bribes by the late, disgraced justice minister. Won the Conservative leadership as everybody's third choice.

Arthur passed through the portals – as an M.P.'s spouse, he had security credentials – and proceeded into the cathedral-like rotunda with its high vaulted ceiling. Clerks, pages, recorders, and interpreters scooted about, priming themselves for the afternoon sitting. He mounted the staircase to the Commons foyer, the scrum zone, where reporters circled like wolves, waiting for prey, a junior minister who might return limping after a kneecapping in Question Period. A couple of M.P.s were being interviewed, others avoiding comment but preening for the cameras as they headed through the members' doorways.

Reporters waved and smiled at Arthur, who was a personage here, a hoary old sage, all the more quotable since the publishing house of McClelland & Stewart announced it had bought the rights to his life and times – a biographer was already on the job. Arthur had given up trying to persuade them his surname was properly pronounced Beechem, as anglicized centuries ago. But here, at the dividing line between French and English Canada, *Beau-champ* reigned, as in beautiful field.

The press had eagerly followed Hamish McCoy's trial, found much hilarity in it. Meanly, during post-trial interviews, Arthur hadn't denied speculation that the sculpture was intended as a sardonic take on the prime minister.

A correspondent for *Le Devoir* sidled up. "Why do we have the honour today, M. Beauchamp?"

Arthur explained that Margaret had got on today's list for Question Period after a Bloc Québécois member gave her his spot. Julien Chambleau, Iberville-Chambly.

"Ah, Julien – I believe he has taken a fancy to Ms. Blake. But not to worry."

Worry? Why should Arthur worry? He'd gotten over all those petty jealousies, a bad habit induced by decades of playing the spineless cuckold to his first wife. It bothered him not at all that

Margaret was regularly surrounded by charming men at cocktail events. Her only affair was with politics.

"And what issue has she chosen?"

"Bhashyistan."

"She must use care duelling with Lafayette."

Arthur continued on up to the Members' Gallery, settled near the front, with a full view of Opposition desks. Including Margaret's, tucked behind the Liberal backbenchers. It was rare she got a shot at Question Period. It happened maybe once a month.

The Opposition leader and prime minister in waiting, Claude McRory – known by all as Cloudy – was in his seat glaring at nothing in particular, a short morose man of pensionable age with a caustic manner and a deficient sense of humour.

The tribal rituals of the House were under way, Orders of the Day, bills introduced, the welcoming of constituents in the gallery. Today's lot included a championship Saguenay bowling team, a young woman from Southern Ontario who'd rescued twelve cows from a burning barn, and the winner of the Prince Edward Island Monster Potato Contest.

Here came Margaret, bending the ear of . . . yes, that must be the *separatiste* Chambleau, young and dapper, a ring in his ear. Arthur could remember when that used to mean gay, but these days it was anybody's guess. A Green sympathizer, *très vert*.

Question Period opened with Opposition Leader McRory rising to a standing ovation from his members: a form of silliness that both sides of the House engaged in for the TV cameras. Arthur was constantly amazed at the puerility on display here; it reinforced his disdain for politics.

McRory seemed unable to frame a question, contenting himself with a blustery speech about "an exponential rise" in home foreclosures. Clara Gracey had numbers at her fingertips and taunted the Liberal chief for relying on an aberrant statistic – in fact, foreclosures had held steady in the last quarter and were projected to fall. Tory backbenchers rose like marionettes in furious applause.

She and Lafayette were the bright lights of a lustreless cabinet, a patchwork group chosen more for regional interest than keen intellect. Arthur found the Liberal Opposition no more impressive, while the smaller parties of the moderate left, the New Democrats and the Bloc Québécois, were relegated to the role of irritants. The country was in a sorry state.

A question from the NDP leader about a stalled bill to control gasoline prices was quickly parried by Prime Minister Finnerty. "I recognize that the honourable member has a serious problem with gas . . ." The rest was drowned out by laughter, shouts of derision, applause, table pounding.

Awaiting her call, Margaret looked serene and confident in a smart tailored suit. Arthur was finding it hard to bring back a picture of her in muddy jeans pitching hay at Blunder Bay. Constant in her vows, committed to her ideals, quick as a whip – how unlike his first wife, Annabelle, from whose perfidy he'd found escape in a bottle.

"Recognize the member for Cowichan and the Islands."

"Thank you, Mr. Speaker. Will the Honourable Minister of Foreign Affairs inform the House why he is proposing an exchange of ambassadors with the so-called Democratic Republic of Bhashyistan, a tyrannical regime whose jails are bursting with dissidents, people of faith, and homosexuals, and which makes virtual slaves of half its remaining population – those unfortunate enough not to have been born with penises?"

Gerard Lafayette, who had been conferring with the prime minister, looked up, seemingly startled at the bold mention of the male reproductive organ. There was a stirring in the House, some gasps – was this beyond the pale, unparliamentary? – but also some laughter.

Lafayette quickly regained composure. "I hope it will not offend the honourable member if I frame my response in more delicate language. While it may be true that Bhashyistan has suffered some growing pains, we on this side conceive it as our democratic duty,

indeed an international imperative, to help bring this young republic from isolation into the world of free nations. To that end, we
propose not merely to give their visiting delegation a big-hearted
Canadian welcome but also to demonstrate the blessings of democracy and the rule of law."

Well spun. Though Lafayette had a good mind, Arthur felt he
put it to suspect use. He was a darling of the conservative think
tanks for his attacks on "the fuzzy-brained liberalism" that in his
view had too long prevailed as the Canadian ethic. "Make the *Right*
choice" had been his slogan at the leadership convention.

Margaret stood again for her supplementary question. "Does the
minister deny that the prospect of a multi-billion-dollar concession
to an Alberta oil company is the real reason for this big-hearted
showering of affection?"

Lafayette spoke sharply. "The answer is no, and I would advise
the honourable member that such rhetoric may compromise delicate foreign negotiations." Boos from the Opposition. Applause
from the other side, shouts, catcalls, heckling – a rowdiness that
seemed more befitting of a high school mock parliament.

Arthur sat through Routine Proceedings awhile, but when
Margaret left the chamber he made his way out too, down to the
foyer. She was already behind a screen of microphones, a couple of
Opposition critics looking on, glum, jilted at the dance.

"What do you know about this oil deal, Ms. Blake?"

"That's a question you should ask M. Lafayette. Ask him if he's
going to open the books on this deal. Let's find out just how far
into bed they've crawled with Alta International."

She went on like that, tying the Conservatives to Alberta oil,
expanding her thesis, accusing them of encouraging a fossil fuel
economy while most of the modern world was turning green. "Oil
slicks," she called Finnerty and his cronies.

She ducked away, took Arthur's arm. "Let's grab a sandwich."

As usual, grabbing a sandwich meant returning to her office,
where there was usually a platter of them. Somehow she'd wangled

a thousand square feet in the Confederation Building, not quite on the Hill, but in the Precinct, on the river side of Wellington. Most rookie backbenchers were barracked in commercial spaces across the street, but Margaret, as parliamentary leader of an emerging party, had won her case for special treatment.

Stepping out into the grounds, she closed her eyes and raised her face to the warm afternoon sun. "Grade me."

"Eight and a half in the scrum and a full ten in the chamber."

"I got Lafayette going. Did you see his face turn red?"

"I was too busy admiring you."

The compliment went nowhere. She was still in Bhashyistan. "This thing really stinks. We have to move fast before the Libs steal it – they're desperate for an issue. We're getting some quiet help from the Bloc."

"Julien Chambleau. The word is all around the Hill."

"Really? Well, he's an activist, a brother. Sierra Club, Rainforest Coalition."

"Attractive young man, looks quite bright. But a separatist. Makes for odd bedfellows." An unfortunate expression, and he made it worse by trying to recover. "Not in the literal sense of course."

"His bedfellow is a guy." She gave him a hard look, accusatory, making him feel like a closet bigot. "Separatist or not, we have common ground."

The blocky Confederation Building loomed, another neo-Gothic structure whose spires and fortresslike walls spoke of God and the British Empire. Beyond was the brooding, portentous Supreme Court of Canada, an art deco monster glowering over the Ottawa River.

"Standing Committee on Global Warming Initiatives tonight. I have to be there." Apologetic. "We'll go somewhere for dinner first."

Another late night alone.

~~~

Unlike the official parties, the Greens had limited funds and minimal full-time staff. But they didn't lack for young, clever volunteers, and today, as usual, the outer offices were abuzz, bodies in motion, loud chatter, phones ringing, printers humming, a radio on, C-SPAN, piles of newspapers and magazines, the walls swathed in charts and maps.

All hail the queen as Margaret swept into their midst. Applause for her jabs at Lafayette – they'd seen it on the internal TV feed from the Commons. "Okay, folks," she said, "I think this thing has legs." A young woman hiked up her skirt and got laughs.

Arthur was feeling, as he often did these days, like a useless artefact, a rickety piece of furniture. The youthful energy in this room rattled him. The cheery, bright-eyed idealism. Here was Margaret peaking in early middle age, leaving him in her dust. Arthur had peaked decades ago, had felt in steady decline ever since. *Eheu fugaces labuntur anni.* Alas, sighed Horace, the fleeting years slip by.

There was no role for him here, that was the trouble. Maybe he should rethink his proclaimed intention to retire, and do what he did best. A good old-fashioned murder case. He wasn't vying with Margaret for notice, not at all, it was his situation he found demeaning, the male escort, attendant to the star, a ceremonial figure. In a major role reversal he had become the little woman.

"We've got a jump on everyone, we're the unofficial opposition on this one. Let's get everything we can on Alta International. Who's doing freedom of information?"

A hand rose from behind a laptop computer. "I'm on it."

"Alta beat out the competition with the bigger bribe," Margaret said. "That's why we're grovelling to a despot. Anything more on Bhashyistan?"

The slight, nubile lass who'd shown off her legs handed Margaret a binder. Pierètte Litvak, her parliamentary assistant. A sharp-witted wag, but serious now. "Unemployment sixty per cent. Soviet-style bureaucracy, shitloads of red tape. Active underground economy. Transparency International has them fighting for top spot on the corruption scale. North Korea is the only country lower on the press freedom index, but on overall individual liberty rankings, the Bhashies are at the bottom, one point eight out of a hundred."

Arthur worked his way listlessly through a multigrain tomato-and-lettuce sandwich, feeling as square and dumb as a block of cement as Pierètte recited this off the top of her head. She was young enough to be his granddaughter. Hers was the vigorous new generation, humankind's last chance. His was the dying one that had buggered everything up.

"Population seven million. The capital and largest city is Igorgrad. Three-quarters Muslim, but Mohammed plays second fiddle to Igor Muckhali Ivanovich, Mad Igor, who has named himself National Prophet and renamed the days of the week after himself and various favoured relatives, the months after dead sultans. His face is every-where, billboards, statues, currency. Total cult of personality."

Mad Igor had assumed the reins fifteen years ago after his father, the former ex-president for life, Boris Mukhamed Ivanovich, was fatally shot in Vancouver. A long-range rifle was found and a partisan of the Bhashyistani Democratic Revolutionary Front was arrested trying to slip across the U.S. border with a false passport. This much and more Arthur knew, for the winning defence counsel was his friend of many years, the scapegrace Brian Pomeroy. Who, if reports were to be believed, had got off booze and drugs and gone native in the Arctic.

Margaret went to her inner office to field some media calls. The others turned to the task of organizing a protest. "Let's do some-thing cool. Street theatre."

Arthur headed for the door, leaving word that he'd be enjoying the sun. He wandered to the riverbank, stared morosely at the cur-rents boiling from the Chaudière rapids. As if pulled by some Circean magnet, he found himself passing between the statues of Truth and Justice that guarded the steps of the Supreme Court building.

He stood for a while on the glistening Italian marble of the

Grand Entrance Hall, a fine example of fascist interior design with its flags, heads on pedestals, doors panelled with threatened species of hardwoods.

Then he was in the chamber of the court itself, empty now but for the usher and a lawyer packing up his briefs. He smiled at a memory of ill-tempered Justice Robichaud getting so balled up he stomped from court. That duel with Liebowitz, C.J., on the Charter of Rights, that was a high point. Fuelled by a four-martini lunch at the Rideau Club, he'd won him over, the swing vote, five to four.

Tragger, Inglis, his old office, had been phoning incessantly. Maybe he should return the calls, maybe they had a juicy murder . . . Forget it. He was happily retired.

~~~

Out of principle, Margaret preferred to walk or take public transit, but used a leased Prius on occasions like this evening's, one of their rare dinners together. The restaurant they were looking for was in downtown Hull – they'd dined well there once – but they couldn't remember its name. Portuguese, informal, intimate.

They found a parkade and walked around, finally spotting the restaurant halfway down the block. "Pause for a moment, Arthur." Margaret pretended interest in the offerings of a dress shop window. "I think we're being followed. Don't look."

But Arthur did, without thinking, stepping around her and almost bumping into a tall man in a long black coat. Light brown hair, dark glasses. Spectral, sharp featured, gawky. "*Pardonnez-moi,*" Arthur said.

The stranger continued on in silence, then started shuffling across the street and was nearly hit by a swerving, shouting cyclist. "*Watche-toué!*" That persuaded him to remove his dark glasses before continuing to the opposite curb.

"He was behind me in a blue compact. He drove into the parkade just as we walked from it. I don't know if he's drunk or what."

Arthur had picked up tobacco breath, but no alcohol. As they reached their restaurant, the man stopped at a well-lit brasserie directly across the street and studied the posted menu.

"Just one of those odd coincidences. He was going to that restaurant."

Margaret didn't seem so sure. "Works for the Alberta oil lobby. His assignment – get the dirt on Margaret Blake. I'm with my husband, you creepy idiot."

The supposed spy took an outdoor table, lit a cigarette, donned wire-rim spectacles, looked quickly at them, then hid behind a menu.

Margaret asked the head waiter for a table by the window.

"With pleasure, Madame Blake, we are honoured." He held her chair. "Madame will accept a complimentary champagne?" Arthur was Mr. Invisible.

~~~

To anyone but Arthur, a two-bedroom apartment with a sunset view over parkland and lake would be anything but a prison, but that's how he'd come to see it. Before he'd made the great leap forward to Garibaldi, he'd been a city dweller, but on a capacious lot, with garden, lawn, and trees.

Now he was relegated to four pots of frostbitten gardenias on a balcony ten storeys above what soon would be a frozen wasteland. The half-century-old blocky building, befitting the suburbs of Moscow, was near Carleton University and full of noisy students. Apartment 10B was on loan to Margaret from a fervent Green, now a visiting professor at Oregon State.

"We can afford better," he'd argued.

"We can't disappoint him," Margaret insisted.

Muffled rock and roll from the flat below, disjunctively married to an obscure Handel opera from 10C – one of a pair of grad students there was working on a thesis about the prolific composer.

On weekends, the squeaking-gate atonalities of her preadolescent violin students had Arthur rushing for earplugs.

Arthur watched the sun die over the Rideau Canal and the lake it fed, a wash of purple and pink. This was the day's highlight.

He went in, slumped onto a hard sofa, fiddled with a book. He wasn't used to reading the classics without a roaring fire of alder and fir. Instead, apartment 10B featured that most abhorrent of modern fixtures, an ersatz fireplace, flames flickering around imitation logs. He missed his old club chair that over the years had ungrudgingly accommodated itself to his former rangy shape. The joyous chores of bringing bounty from the land had burned the calories, and when he'd donned his robes for the occasional trial he'd been as fit as Spartacus, ready to take on the Roman legions.

Perhaps, he thought wishfully, some crisis had newly occurred at Blunder Bay that would demand his return. For instance, Stoney and McCoy jailed for packing Purple Passion into the Berlin-bound sculpture.

He was hesitant to call Zack and Savannah during evenings, he always seemed to be interrupting something: dinner, a quarrel, a meeting. They were forever holding meetings. Savannah picked up.

"I hope this isn't a bad time."

"Not at all," she said, good natured, used to his fussy intrusions. "A few friends are over from Vancouver. Coastal Forest Coalition."

He could hear loud conversation, sounding of more than a few friends. "Nothing to report, I take it?"

"No, everything's going wonderfully. How's Margaret?"

A little paranoid, he wanted to say. The klutz in the black coat had finished a wine, then wandered away without another look at them. "Splendid. Tireless in the struggle. Animals are well? The garden?"

"We're eating from it. Everything is lovely, Arthur, we're so glad to be here."

Arthur found himself more depressed than ever. From the flat next door, a stagy roar: "I will never retire! I will never give way!"

Ibsen, Arthur suspected. The male partner of the Handel scholar was studying theatre, and could often be heard emoting through the thin walls.

~~~

Dear Hank, Mom, Katie, Cassie, Jessie,

Well, I finally got a chance to put my feet up. Those dogs are tired! We just got back from touring the old market of Samarkand. Some people in our group dropped out, went back to the bus. All terribly ancient, the Silk Route, it goes back to the second century BC, silk, perfumes, spices and incense and gems. Pretty bleak here, though, in Uzbekistan. Tomorrow Tashkent. Almaty in Kazakhstan after that. (Don't worry, Exotic Asia Tours doesn't stop in Afghanistan!) I hope you girls are doing your homework and not keeping your grandma from her nap with your screaming guitars. Love you, Dr. Hank. Love you, kids. You'd do really well here, Mom, your Russian is so good, here it's like everyone's second language. Maxine and I get by. Back in a week.

Love, Jill XOXO

4

———

Clara Gracey told her driver to pump up the heat. Winter had come in late November with a frigid blast from somewhere north of Baffin Bay. But her prayer for a traffic-snarling snowfall hadn't been answered, so she lacked a credible excuse for skipping tonight's bash for the Bhashies.

The visitors, eight large, ruddy-faced males, had arrived yesterday on an old Ilyushin 62, trooping off in identical bear coats and bear hats. They were ready for the weather, unlike Clara, who hadn't brought a sweater or jacket, just this flimsy coat. In the political life, fashion rules, style over comfort and warmth.

"I am on bended knees *begging* you to come, Clara," Finnerty had said, smiling, avuncular. "This is their big farewell reception. You're my first minister, they'll take it as an insult. And what'll it look like to the press?"

"There won't be press. This is invitation only."

"They'll be outside, counting heads."

Cabinet solidarity must prevail. It was Lafayette's show anyway – he would carry the can if this disgusting love-in with these Mongol invaders went haywire. The red carpet he'd unfurled for them was a national humiliation. A colour guard! The governor general dragged from the sickbed to witness the signing of protocols. They'd been wined and dined, a stretch limo provided, a tour guide, interpreters, gifts of Inuit art and sterling silver embossed with maple leaves. Bhashyistan's gift, a yak from the personal herd of the Ultimate Leader, had also been in the Ilyushin, in the aft cargo area. That delightful interlude, the ceremonial unloading of the shitting yak, had been on all the newscasts. It was trucked off to an animal farm in Chibougamau.

Foreign Affairs had also arranged for an entire wing of suites in the Westin Hotel. Treasury wasn't paying for these, thank God, or for the several street women who'd ended up there last night, according to RCMP watchers.

Clara cracked open a window and lit a cigarette. Her driver tut-tutted, but he was used to it. Ice on the canal, a frozen slick. Bringing to mind Ms. Blake's well-reported sound bite about oil slicks. And their champion, the slick foreign minister.

So much for Lafayette's concept of educating these characters in the benefits of democracy. Only four showed up for the tour of Parliament yesterday. They'd sat in the Speaker's Gallery for forty minutes, bored to numbness, then went shopping at the Rideau Centre. The Ilyushin was later observed being loaded with barbecues, dishwashers, and home theatres.

At least the sovereign state of Canada had not demeaned itself by apologizing for permitting twelve of its peons to acquit the alleged assassin of the Great Father, Boris Mukhamed Ivanovich. His son, Mad Igor, had named a planet after him. Mars was now known, in Bhashyistan, as Boris. Venus had been named after Boris's second wife, Igor's Revered Mother. It was now called Nanotchka.

A ceremony honouring the Great Father seemed to satisfy the Bhashies: expressions of deep regret, the laying of a wreath at the National War Memorial, another honour guard. Shameless. A *huge* demonstration outside the Centre Block today by a coalition of green NGOs abetted by the usual peaceniks and Amnesty Internationalists. One of nine such rallies across the country, a sizable crowd even in Calgary, outside the Alta International Tower.

This government was in peril. The thought of jumping ship,

returning to academia, continued to tempt Clara, but would be painful, a rebellion against five generations of party faithful. Her great-great-grandfather had served under Sir John A.

Clara summoned strength as they arrived at 99 Bush Street. The fifteenth-floor Rideau Club was a venerable institution restored from premises devoured by fire some decades ago. A lavish affair was promised, allegedly bankrolled by the Friends of Bhashyistan, an organization previously unheard of, likely slapped together for the occasion. Presumably Canada *had* some friends of Bhashyistan, even immigrants from there, but Clara had never met one.

There weren't many on the Hill who doubted this was Alta International's treat.

~~~

Somehow, Gerard Lafayette hadn't expected the Bhashies to have a minister of culture, but here he was, in the Rideau Club's dining salon, raising a glass. "To Canada, like patriotic song saying, glorious and free." A throaty voice from a barrel chest. This was the tenth toast of the evening; these eight beefy, genial visitors were taking turns, some twice. Most had a smattering of English, with strong Russian accents.

Prominent among them was the minister of police, Mad Igor's brother-in-law, a boisterous fellow with flashing gold teeth. Of possibly higher rank was the Ultimate Leader's nephew, a big, shambling ruffian without a word of English, already half pickled, a clump of caviar in his beard. The defence minister, General Buhkyov, who'd been like a leech on Lafayette, was in a uniform dripping with medals and braid.

"Oh, say can you see, we stand on guard for north strong and free," the culture minister intoned from his trove of memorized anthems. "Is still part of British Empire, no?"

"Is no longer called Empire, is Commonwealth," said the education minister. "But is still great contry."

Standing corrected, the culture minister carried on: "Is good news that Canada break free from British rule – like Bhashyistan, free of Kremlin. We are brothers, together we sharing national dream. To freedom!"

He slugged back his vodka and gave the prime minister a hearty bear hug – there'd been an incalculable number of these. Lafayette had got his share over the last two days, and was staying on the move so as not to get trapped. Finnerty, though, was keeping up with the Bhashies, drink for drink. The old Fundy fisher was showing them what Canucks are made of – he'd still be standing when they were all on the floor.

Next up, the Bhashyistan defence minister. "But Canada still honours English queen. Is figurehead, nice lady, like grandmother. To royal queen, God willing forever may she reign."

Lafayette had begun to wilt under the pressure of their interminable toasts, presumably a national art form. To glorious new friends and brothers of great democratic republic of Canada. To all people of Canada, including French and Indians. To national tree with red leaf.

They'd been bundled off to see the sights of Montreal that day, so were spared the sight of the demonstrators outside Parliament with their placards. "What's Alta Paying You?" "Send the Bhums Bhack to Bhashyistan." "No Deal with Fascistan." Every tree-hugger and anarchist in the Capital Region had turned out.

Here was Clara Gracey, the minority of one, conscripted into service. Elegant in a long dress of low cut, more than a hint of bodice, denying her years with foundation and blush. One would think, given her aspirations, she would show more solidarity with this Bhashyistan initiative, get on board, try to place herself for the next race, after the stopgap P.M. founders.

The Bhashie minister of penal corrections did the closing piece, a recitation of a few stanzas of "The Cremation of Sam McGee," first in English – the queerest thing Lafayette ever did see – then in the consonant-laden Turkic tongue of the republic, a variant officially known as Igor. Lafayette took Finnerty's cold glare as a signal: you, Lafayette, you have brought this on, you will reply.

He vaulted up to a small stage, comfortably above everyone, then reached down and, with modest panache, cleanly plucked a Chablis from a passing tray.

He thanked the visiting dignitaries – he dared call them that – for their offer of an exchange visit, and claimed to be champing at the bit to sample the renowned hospitality of their country. Otherwise, he kept to generalizations: good health, prosperous future relations, may we absorb each other's culture and gain from that. When it seemed he had little else to say, some Bhashies looked distressed, so he threw in something vaguely laudatory about the Ultimate Leader

General Buhkyov was approaching the stage, voracious grin, arms splayed. He'd been lobbying to place his sons in college here; Lafayette was expected to put in the fix. Dismounting from the platform, he slipped behind an alcove, pretending he had an important phone call. Buhkyov veered away toward the bar. Others of his troupe had headed off to the billiards room.

At the door, flashing her invitation, an unexpected presence – the media sweetheart, Margaret Blake. All the socialists in the House, among whom Lafayette counted half the Liberals, had boycotted this event, so it was doubly surprising to see her here. Especially given that her office had been the operations centre for a ten-city multiplex of demonstrations.

Just a touch of makeup for this handsome woman, a natural tan, piercing grey eyes, spindle-waisted, best pair of legs in the House, and a constant, annoying burr in Lafayette's side. A goat-keeping agronomist from a West Coast backwater, slow to learn the rules, the decorum, the way things are done. An idealist. They never lasted long here.

Still, she seemed to be enjoying her blip in political history. It might be amusing to relate to her. She was chatting with some of his ministry staff, who, after he joined their circle, politely dispersed.

The leader of *le Parti Vert* seemed a little stiff in his presence, so he sought an opening that might relax her.

"I don't know whether I should feel complimented that you have targeted me, Ms. Blake, but I am bandaged head to toe from the wounds of your unerring darts."

This elegant paean didn't even buy him a smile, just a cool, silvery stare. But of course she must pretend to be unflattered by the attentions of Gerard Laurier Lafayette. "Nothing personal, Minister."

"Where is your husband, the eminent barrister?" A.R. Beauchamp, former leading counsel, now an artefact. His biography was being written, invariably an indication one's career is over.

"He was afraid he'd find himself gushing in the radiant company of your guests. He's such an admirer of megalomaniac dictators. I hear Mad Igor has even named a slave labour camp after himself."

"All of which begs the question of why *you* are here." He was miffed, he'd expected deference.

"To keep an eye on you guys. I'm counting the bear hugs."

"If you'd like one, I'm sure that can be arranged."

The acerbic tone didn't deter her. "I heard the cabinet was divided over this."

He flicked a look at Gracey. "We stand as one. It is trade, madam, free trade, the opening up of barriers, that brings a struggling nation out of darkness."

"And makes a bundle for Alta International."

"Canadian businesses ought to be permitted to compete in the international market. If exchanging ambassadors opens the door for opportunities, why should they not take advantage?"

He could see from her startled eyes that his nimble rejoinder had struck home. But then he saw that those eyes were fixed on General Buhkyov, advancing like the Light Brigade. "Tovarich!"

She slipped away just before he swooped.

This lusty assault occurred as Huck Finnerty was strolling by to confer with the attorney general. He paused to watch, with relish, as Lafayette got his ribs squeezed and back slapped with meat-tenderizing blows.

"It must be love." A woman's voice, behind him. Turning, he brushed her shoulder, nearly causing him to spill his rye and soda. Margaret Blake, the Green sharpshooter, who had also been watching this wrestling event. No damage done, but Finnerty apologized profusely.

"There are strange things done in the midnight sun," she said.

He laughed. He liked this plucky woman, despite knowing that if she had her way the family trawling business would be kaput. He wanted to linger with her, enjoy a conspiratorial chuckle at Lafayette's plight – backed against a table, with a stiff, gaping grin – but he'd had a skinful, he had to get out of here.

He was planning an escape route when Guy DuWallup urgently beckoned him, a bad-news look on his unlovely mug. They met in a quiet corner.

"Problem with Abzal."

"Abzal? Help me."

DuWallup sighed. It was always "help me" with the P.M. He was an old pal, though, and was carrying the party through some of its toughest times. "Abzal Erzhan. The sniper who immortalized the Great Father. He has disappeared."

Finnerty was too swizzled for those last three words to settle in right away. Erzhan. Vancouver. Fifteen years ago. Right. He'd got refugee status or something. "He disappeared?"

DuWallup heard "dishappeared." He took the P.M.'s rye whiskey and set it down. "Let's go for a walk, Huck."

"Leaving anyway. Give me the bad, let's hear it."

"Erzhan didn't show up at work this morning. He's been eight steady years as a high school teacher in Chambly, just east of Montreal. He was last seen leaving his home to walk to his school."

DuWallup steered him toward the coat check. Huck seemed to be walking okay; he might get past the press unscathed. "I'll get your driver." He dialed his cell.

"Juss a minute, the RCMP was supposed to be watching this guy."

"He slipped past them, it was very quick. There's an indication a friend picked him up in a car."

Finnerty fussed and grumbled as they headed down in the elevator. What was he supposed to do about this? Very bad time for a Bhashyistani assassin to be on the loose.

He waited by the front entrance while DuWallup peeked out, summoned the liveried driver. "Not too many reporters out there, Huck."

"They know anything about this?"

"It's under wraps. Do we warn our Bhashie friends?"

"No bloody way." Finnerty didn't want anything to delay their morning departure. They had behaved like the Mafia, had half a dozen women up at the Westin.

"The other option is doubling security," DuWallup said.

"Yeah, right, let's stick to the timetable, get these jokers out of here. We tell nobody."

Huck's driver joined them, and the three walked together from the building, Finnerty held in place between them. "A fine evening," he called out, too loud, to the converging press. Keep the smile steady. There's the car. A smelly pall of cigar smoke from a clutch of Bhashies by the sidewalk. Clara Gracey out here too, with a cigarette, waiting for her car, looking cold.

He made it into the back seat, a persistent microphone at his shoulder. "Sixty M.P.s signed a pledge to boycott this event, sir. What do you say about that?"

"They weren't missed."

Reporters laughed. So did Clara, who envied Finnerty's easy rapport with the media. Drunk again, but somehow he always kept his balance. It must be all those years on the high seas.

The Bhashie culture minister had been eyeing her and now was approaching with the family pictures he'd been showing around. Where was her car?

"You like seeing my people in traditional costume?" A fistful of glossy prints. "This my wife." A woman in a burka and a gorgeous patterned robe. "This my wife too." A sombre young woman in an imposing headdress.

"How many wives do you have?"

"Only four now. You are also some man's wife here?"

"Not exactly." Be pleasant. In ten hours they head home with their goodies and their trade treaty.

"You like I show you fine jewellery my country."

"You have it with you?"

He produced a gold locket, dangled it. "Is more in hotel room."

Here came rescue, her driver.

5

———

Arthur is in an old folks' home, staring out at a pastoral scene, maybe Blunder Bay. He strives to go there, but his wheelchair can move only backwards, nurses and attendants skipping out of the way, laughing, patting him on the head. They're all on cellphones and Blackberrys, planning something cool, street theatre.

His bedside radio, programmed to drag him out of bed at eight-fifteen, rescued him with a sonata. He regretted having to turn it down. Schumann was a salve after that dismal dream. Rolling backwards, that's what he's been doing. Backwards into senescence.

Sleeping soundly beside him was his stay-up-late wife, who'd slid into bed after midnight, waking him briefly from fitful sleep. He'd thought it unwise, but she'd gone to an event for the Bhashyistanis. "Farewell Reception," the embossed card read, an oxymoronic keepsake. Presumably, she went out with her gang afterwards, to regale them.

He didn't approve of such late nights, was fearful for her safety ever since the spectral man in the black coat had proved to be a follower indeed. Several nights ago, after leaving a committee meeting on the Hill, Margaret had turned to see him in distant, shuffling pursuit, wearing either a black toque or a wig. And at least twice she'd seen him in her rear-view mirror in his small car, a Mitsubishi, this time with a moustache that seemed pasted there. A detective hired by Alta International, that was their best guess. He seemed unlikely to be a government hireling – if exposed, that would ignite a scandal. Margaret had morbidly taken to calling him her personal death angel. She no longer went out at night without a swarm of friends attending her.

Arthur quietly slipped from under the covers, and she rolled over but slept on, dreaming her own vivid dream. A low laugh, the kind sleep disguises as a pleasant guttural rumbling. Arthur envied her dreams, which seemed abnormally congenial, unstirred by the repressed pain that energized his own harrowing nighttime travels.

An old, lined face, buttered with foam, stared at him as he scraped it with a dull razor. He'd been considered handsome once, despite the elephant's trunk, but age had begun to expose the codger within. He resented having to shave every day, having to wear a tie, but Ottawa had imposed its will. Anyway, it's how he always dressed for the city, suit and tie, even on his walks. It was something neurotic, the fuddy-duddy syndrome.

As he performed his morning routines, he was plagued by a sense that his marriage had begun to show gaps, ever widening, a gulf between two islands. His slowly sinking beneath the sea, hers high above the tide line, full of bustle and battle. The thought of losing her had been causing palpitations, panic attacks.

Friday, November 26. Why did the day feel so oppressive? He had to shake this mood. A sprightly pre-breakfast walk along the canal ought to help, though it looked bone-chilling cold out there. Global warming had yet to target the nation's capital.

A morning spat from next door, quickly drowned by a baroque concerto. The neighbours had arisen.

The phone rang as he pulled on his pants, and he nearly stumbled in them as he raced to arrest a second ring. "Good morning."

"Good . . . well, it's actually not a good morning, Arthur." Savannah Buckett, in Blunder Bay. It was five-thirty out there.

"What happened?" Was this, finally, the prayed-for crisis that would wing him to the western shores?

"I didn't want to bother you last night, but they're not letting him out."

"Who?"

"Zack. They've got Zack. The cops. They say he's going to have to do the rest of his term, five months."

He'd been at the rally in Vancouver, outside the bank tower housing Alta International's B.C. office. Arthur was shocked to learn he was accused of violating parole by joining a public demonstration. "Do I understand a term of parole prohibits Zack from attending public protests?"

"Yeah, both of us. That's why I didn't go."

"Read me the language."

"We are barred from organizing, participating in, or attending any public demonstration relating to political or environmental issues. Zack says that's against the Charter of Rights."

"Fundamentally so. There was no court order enjoining this protest?"

"No. The police didn't intervene at all except to keep order and grab Zack."

"Savannah, you are to call Tragger, Inglis in Vancouver and ask for my secretary, Gertrude Isbister, and give her what she needs for an affidavit for a judicial review. Regrettably it can't be heard until after the weekend, but I'll be there."

"You're a lovely man, Arthur."

He felt a tingle of relief, anticipation. Perversely, Zack's arrest offered an antidote to his felt uselessness.

Still no stirring from the bedroom. He left a note: "Gone for a nippy walk."

And nippy it was. But the sun was out, and a fast walk warms, and there was comfort in knowing he'd be in Vancouver by the weekend enjoying the dying autumn's softness. Back in the saddle. Doing what he did best.

He walked south on Bronson Avenue, a busy artery feeding the Airport Parkway. His usual route would take him to Dow's Lake, the pathway along it, past the skaters' changing huts – unused as yet, but as this freeze continued the lake and canal would soon be thronged with hardy commuters skating to work, an Ottawa rite of winter.

Approaching from the north came a vehicle with its flashers on – an RCMP cruiser, moving with a funereal lack of speed. Behind it came a troop of Mounties on motorcycles, followed by a second cruiser and, some distance away, a stretch limousine, which seemed deliberately to have slowed the procession's pace. From its open windows, swarthy men were waving to pedestrians. "Maple leaf forever!" one shouted. "On marge of Lake Labarge!" called another. They were passing a bottle.

Clearly, this was the infamous band of Bhashies, who had profoundly failed to charm staid Ottawa. Heading for their Ilyushin and a polar flight home. An RCMP van was impatiently pressing them from the rear. A police helicopter roared overhead. The Crown must have called out the reserves to get rid of its guests.

As he reached the bridge between the canal and Dow's Lake, Arthur momentarily lost sight of the procession in the backed-up traffic. But as he gained the apex of the bridge, he recoiled with a gasp on seeing a brilliant flash below, accompanied by a whump so loud it seemed to reverberate drumlike within his chest cavity. Pedestrians froze, cars braked. A puff of grey smoke, swallowed by darker clouds, billowed skyward. The lick of flames reflected red from the frozen surface of the lake.

People were pouring out of cars and stalled buses. Arthur, craning over the bridge railing, could see the twisted remnants of the stretch Lincoln on Colonel By Drive, by the lakeside. A skaters' change hut was aflame, as was an adjoining Beavertail hut.

As Arthur picked up his pace, others overtook him, running, and by the time he found his way down to the disaster scene, police and emergency vehicles were arriving, brakes screeching, uniformed men and women bounding from them.

Soon, extinguishers were dousing flames around the sprawled, blackened bodies in the limousine. Collateral damage had been

43

done to the RCMP cruiser behind it, whose two dazed occupants were sitting on the sidewalk, receiving first aid.

Arthur felt faint, grasped a lamppost, took several deep breaths. He'd seen dead bodies before – his career had hardened him, but not enough; never had he witnessed such carnage. A missile or a roadside bomb. A direct hit. Clean, expert, unerring, ghastly.

Police were throwing up a cordon, ordering the crowds back with the frantic bawling of the severely rattled. A woman next to Arthur was vomiting. He felt his stomach roiling too.

~~~

An improvised explosive device, that was the verdict of the experts who testified before the news cameras. A remote-controlled IED, the odious weapon of choice for the fanatics of the modern age of terrorism, tested and refined in the battlefields of Iraq and Afghanistan. Likely triggered by a cellphone, the experts said. Ten dead, the entire Bhashyistan delegation plus the chauffeur and their ambassador, who'd been seeing them off to the airport.

Here was a day-old clip of that ambassador, his face lit by a smile as he cut a ribbon outside a brick duplex being renovated for an embassy. Here were clips of the Bhashie delegation being welcomed, feted, inspecting the honour guard. The sole Canadian victim, the chauffeur, was a retired naval warrant officer, whose children were shown grieving.

Arthur was still shaking. Margaret was still in her robe. They'd been staring raptly at the screen for the last hour, as the networks scrambled to interview witnesses, mobilize pundits, piece together the story, fill in with backgrounders. The IED had apparently been hidden high up in the changing hut. Some pedestrians were rushed to emergency with shrapnel cuts, none severe. For some reason, Ottawa International had been shut down, planes were being diverted. The city had come to a halt, the parliamentary sitting cancelled.

No arrests. No indication any were imminent. Three Bhashies remained in town: their embassy staff, quartered in a small hotel on Sparks Street, hiding there, unavailable to the press.

Still no response from cabinet, just footage of them heading to a briefing room, fleeing pursuing cameras, getting jammed up at the doorway in their haste. There'd been no reaction from Bhashyistan either, calls from newsrooms not answered, the country's entire phone system down. The silence seemed ominous. Arthur couldn't imagine what Mad Igor was thinking right now. Fifteen years ago, his father murdered on Canadian soil. Now his top ministers. One would not have to be wildly delusional to see Canada as complicit.

Arthur got up to the intercom to buzz in Pierètte Litvak, Margaret's assistant, who announced from the lobby: "Sorry I took so long, I had to change, I actually peed my pants." This was information Arthur didn't care to know. A minute later she came sweeping in, throwing her ski jacket on a chair, giving him a peck, then rushing to Margaret and hugging her. "Wow, you all right?"

"I'm in shock. Who wouldn't be?"

"The BDRF, the Bhashyistani Democratic Revolutionary Front." Pierètte smiled a thanks to Arthur for the coffee he extended. "Catch me up. Why is the airport shut down?"

It was a mystery, the press didn't know; there was a news embargo. But now Arthur's travel plans were in disarray. He'd told Margaret about Zack's arrest, and they'd agreed he should fly out the next day if possible. A travel agent was working at it. Meanwhile, he'd left a message with his secretary instructing her to file the appeal within the day.

Pierètte squatted on the carpet, lotus position, got her Blackberry and laptop going. Arthur had been surprised to learn this political junkie was almost thirty. She looked eighteen. A Quebecer, bilingual, political science degree.

"That guy who assassinated the Great Father, isn't he supposed to be around here somewhere? Quebec?"

"The RCMP won't confirm," Margaret said. Old footage had been shown of Abzal Erzhan being arrested, being freed, an extensive backgrounder. A wiry, intense-looking fellow. An unbelieving pinch-me look as he walked free from the Vancouver Law Courts. A clip of Brian Pomeroy, his counsel, in his barrister's robes, bantering with reporters at a post-victory scrum.

"Are we making a statement?" Pierètte asked.

"We need to confer about that. I haven't been answering the phone."

"You could thank the bomber for scuttling Alta's oil deal. Joke. Condolences, it's a black day, that sort of thing. You can't make political hay with it. Yet. My advice is wait, respond to the government when they get their shit together. If."

Talk stopped. A news bulletin. "CBC has just learned that an airliner took off without clearance this morning from Ottawa International Airport. Just a minute . . ." The announcer flattened a headset against his ear. "We have breaking news from Canadian Forces Air Command. CF-18 interceptors from 3 Wing in Bagotville are in pursuit of that aircraft, an Ilyushin 62 believed en route to Bhashyistan."

"Wow, this is some freaky shit," Pierètte said.

For the next several minutes, not much new. They learned that Ilyushin 62s, four-engine jetliners, once the mainstay of Aeroflot, had gone out of production in the 1970s. Only a couple of dozen still in service. Regarded as a jinxed aircraft, a history of disasters. This one had a cockpit crew of captain, first officer, flight engineer, navigator. Three cabin crew and one for the yak. The fore quarters had been modified into a gilded, sumptuous lounge. It was the Ultimate Leader's personal plane.

Pierètte, who was flipping through media sites, looked up from her laptop. "Turn to CTV."

A solemn newscaster. "We take you live to Pamela Burns in Chambly."

A camera panned a pleasant, tree-lined street, brick tenements, spiralling cast iron staircases. "These are the typical residences of Rue Talon, a typical street in a typical Quebec town." A teenaged boy made a face, then ducked under the moving camera, which settled on Pamela Burns, shivering, shrugging into a jacket.

"And this, 740 Rue Talon, is the home of Abzal Erzhan, who, fifteen years ago in Vancouver, was acquitted of murdering the visiting ruler of Bhashyistan." The camera was looking at the upstairs flat of a duplex, its door guarded by three uniformed police. More were on the sidewalk, keeping the curious at bay. "We're not being allowed to talk to anyone inside, but no one has been arrested, no one is coming or going from that house but RCMP officers." As if on cue, a bristle-haired man in a suit exited, conferred with the guards. "We're looking at Inspector Luc Poirier, senior officer on duty here." Zoom on him, a deep frown, tight lips. A face at a window, a woman in a hijab, apprehensive.

Inspector Poirier descended to the street. Reporters converged. "Inspector, can you confirm that Abzal Erzhan has disappeared?"

"*Pas de commentaires.*" He shouldered gruffly past them, into his car, hunched over the police radio.

"*C'est de la grosse foque,*" Pierètte said. A total fuckup. "Means an election, can't see them surviving." Fingers dancing over the keyboard. "Radio-Canada, give me something. Whoa, here we are. Looks like our interceptors have made contact with the Ilyushin. Oh, baby, I'd donate a kidney to be a fly on the wall in the cabinet room."

6

———

R adio static crackled from a transmitter-receiver they'd lugged into the cabinet room, onto its long oval table. Tense male voices. Positions, bearings, Aircom jargon, gobbledygook to most of the cabinet, including Clara Gracey. Six fully armed CF-18 Hornets were somewhere near Ungava Bay, zeroing in on their quarry.

"Squad Boss, Squad Boss, this is Alpha One."

"Roger, this is Squad Boss, over."

"Do you have a visual?"

"We're right on him, about angels twenty, just above the goo. We're looking at some weather down there."

"You're looking at a fast-moving Arctic front. That flying junkpile could fall apart. How's your juice?"

"Ten minutes to bingo. Out."

Clara could barely endure the stench emanating from the male armpits in the room, sweat born of fear, confusion, desperation, with an acrid overlay of resentment. She'd been the lone dissenter, and now no one could look at her, not even Finnerty, and *especially* not Lafayette. The tattletale, spreading word she'd broken cabinet secrecy. All the more hurtful for being true.

The feed was courtesy of General Buster Buchanan, Canadian Forces chief of staff, who'd been joined by a few other brass plus a radio technician. Plus the national security adviser and the RCMP commissioner. Throw in several PMO staff and three dozen cabinet members, and it was a full house. Huck looked shaky. A bad day to have a hangover.

"Alpha One, this is Squad Boss."

"What have you got?"

"We're practically touching wings, but the driver's pretending he can't see us."

"Weapons safe. Stay with the drill."

"Roger wilco."

"Let's try to avoid Plan B."

"Roger that for sure. Wait one." More static, then: "Hey, BH-zero-niner-niner, you see me now?"

A heavy accent. "Have trobble with radio."

"I think you hear me real good. Can you *see* me? . . . Right, that's me, playing left wing for *les canadiens*. You know hockey, captain?"

"Is national game. Have many hockey heroes."

"Here's your chance to be one. You get to be goalie. We're the forwards. You know what forwards do?"

"They shoot puck."

"That's right. How many parachutes have you got?"

"Two, but not working."

"Okay, so think of your wives and families, and throttle down to a nice, easy three zero zero knots, and I'm going to give you a set of coordinates, and we're all going to glide back down to a friendly little air force base."

"I talk to fellow workers." After a moment, the pilot returned to the radio. "We ask your contry giving us what you call refugee state. Not send back ever to Bhashyistan. If no deal, okay, shoot puck."

Buster Buchanan looked at Finnerty, who glanced around – at everybody but Clara. A woman, she wasn't expected to hold useful views on military strategies.

"They're going to screw us around. Blast 'em out of the air." This hard line, from Dexter McPhee, the defence minister, earned an embarrassed silence. Clara knew it was just bluster, but the P.M.'s aides looked shocked.

"This isn't a time to joke," Lafayette said. "They face execution if deported. Their terms should be accepted."

Finnerty agreed. Buster Buchanan went on air personally to tell Bagotville it was a done deal. A few seconds later, the squadron leader came on, sounding relieved. "Alpha One, this is Squad Boss, we're taking this bird in."

"Bravo Zulu, Squad Boss."

Sighs of relief. Finnerty rose unsteadily to stretch and refill his coffee. Clara felt sorry for him. Events had propelled him well beyond his normal range of competence. Commissioner Luc Lessard, normally so thoughtful and phlegmatic, was looking unusually distressed after the RCMP's botched security job. Probably wondering how far his head was going to roll.

At the far end of the table, near the non-functioning fireplace, sat Gerry Lafayette, a headset on, a secure line to his ministry. While others seemed befuddled by events, he was intent on showing stern, decisive coolness. He bore no responsibility for this mess. The buck stopped at Finnerty, and one did not have to be a diviner of souls to see the resignation in his face. He had been at this job only a year, would be remembered only for this catastrophe. However tragic was this terrorist act, it accelerated Lafayette's resolve to lead *les bleus* from the wilderness.

He looked around at the strained, expectant faces and slipped off his headset. "Staff has been trying to message them every conceivable way, through the Brits, through the Yanks. *Rien que silence.* I suspect we must issue a statement soon. The fourth estate is anxious. The Ultimate Leader may especially be eager to hear our carefully worded regrets." The PMO's director of communications took this as a directive, went off with the press secretary to hammer something out. "I wonder, Prime Minister, now that the cabinet is briefed, if we could dwindle to a slightly more manageable size."

The bulk of the ministers got the message and began filing out, probably feeling relieved and perhaps guilty that Gerard Laurier Lafayette was showing the leadership their party had denied him. He took the chair next to Finnerty, at mid-centre of the long table, and spoke low: "Information has not been kept close to our chests, Huck. Or our breasts, if you take my meaning."

Clara didn't hear that but saw them glance at her. She didn't need the equation written in chalk on a blackboard. That silky Iago was making a move on the operationally challenged old trawler-man, who was so hungover, so out of his depth, he was delegating power to his adversary.

Invited to stay were three Finnerty cronies, Dexter McPhee of Defence, Attorney General DuWallup, Charley Thiessen of Public Safety. Plus the P.M.'s chief of staff, executive assistant, communications director, national security adviser, and the RCMP commissioner.

The finance minister, however, was getting the bum's rush. "Nice job, Gerry," she said, on her way out.

"You're very kind."

"No, I mean it."

"I hadn't thought otherwise, Clara."

Clara needed a smoke badly, she was stinging from the insult of being excluded. She was deputy prime minister! But she maintained outward composure as fellow evictee Buster Buchanan held the door for her. McPhee called after him: "General, let us know when our boys get back home safe."

In the anteroom, Clara joined the other exiles in retrieving cellphones and Blackberrys from the bank of safety deposit boxes – wireless transmitters were banned at cabinet sessions. She took Buchanan aside to pass on her thanks to the heroes of Bagotville. "That Cool Hand Luke up there deserves a medal, General."

"Ma'am, he'll get one."

Ma'am – she loathed that, it made her feel eighty years old. From the restricted zone known as the Horseshoe, outside the PMO complex, she could see down to the foyer and the press thronging there, an impatient, hungry wolf pack. How she would love to toss them some meat.

Instead, she charged up to her office and stomped inside, her angry vibrations scattering the huddle at the TV set, sending them silently to their desks. She slammed into her private office and screamed: "That rat's asshole!"

Panting, shaking a little, she searched her bag, found her Number Sevens, lit up. Percival Galbraith-Smythe, her fussy, starchy executive assistant, knew exactly what she was up to and walked briskly in, opened a window, situated Clara close to it, and brought the ashtray out from behind the shelf of Hansards. "Lafayette, I suppose."

"It's a putsch. I have been effectively purged from government. He's got the Huckster under his thumb, he's schmoozing with DuWallup and Thiessen and McPhee, getting their blessings. I want it all over town that I opposed this Bhashyistan initiative from the get-go."

"Already done, precious. Informed sources will hint that this day would never have happened had it been up to you."

~~~

Finnerty tilted his flask while he took a whiz. The hot burn of aged rye gave him a hit of courage; he might yet make it through this day. "What do you think the Bhashies will do, Charley?" They were alone in a washroom, he and Thiessen, at adjoining urinals.

"Well, they sure aren't going to be recalling their ambassador. Don't see any solution but we send over eight of our ministers for them to kill. Maybe they'll settle for Gerry. You may want to reel him in a bit, Huck. He's stealing the show."

Clara Gracey would have been a counterweight; Finnerty felt a little crappy about excluding her from the loop, a slap in the face. But let it be a lesson. She'd been leaking like Molly's rowboat.

"Be glad the cops have to carry the can, buddy." Thiessen left Finnerty to finish his piss, an anxiety-constricted stop-and-starter, requiring exertion. What had been his orders to DuWallup last night? Increase security, stick to the timetable, tell nobody a Bhashyistani assassin was on the loose. How was he going to get out of this?

Though it was only noon, this was already close to being the worst day of his life – worse than when his engine conked during Hurricane Zelda, maybe worse than when he stumbled onto his wife giving head to her yoga instructor. The only good news was the Ilyushin was safely on the tarmac at Bagotville.

The Canadian government's official outpouring of remorse, though quickly seconded by many other countries, had been met with continued loud silence by Bhashyistan. He tried hard but couldn't conjure an image of the Ultimate Leader on his throne, or wherever he sat, reacting to the slaughter of his cabinet, the arrest of his personal jetliner. No one seemed to have a handle on Igor Muckhali Ivanovich, except that he was some kind of psychopathic blowhard.

The cabinet room had been set up as a crisis centre, several plasma screens, images dancing on them, but volumes down. A server followed Finnerty with trays of sandwiches, and he joined the chow line, everyone hungry but Lafayette, who was what you'd call a dainty eater, and the RCMP commissioner, who wasn't showing much of an appetite.

An aide thrust a note at Finnerty. The CEO of Alta International, urgent, please call. Quilter was probably going berserk. "I'll get back to him."

Finnerty tried for a meaningful look at DuWallup, but saw he was listening to Commissioner Lessard, who had just got off a secure line with his explosives people.

"Semtex, they think. One of those super-IEDs that are showing up in the Middle East, explosive penetrators, copper-jacketed, directional, effective to fifty metres."

"Pretty sophisticated," DuWallup said.

"We're not dealing with amateurs. These are trained terrorists."

"Run it by us again, Commissioner, how Mr. Erzhan vanished on us." Lafayette, sitting back, examining his fingernails.

Lessard summarized a written report: "Thursday, yesterday, at eight-fifteen hours, Abzal Erzhan left home with a bag lunch in a satchel, as he has done every school day for the last eight years. He's a teacher in a local secondary school – mathematics, science, and physical education. Earned his certificate teaching leadership skills at an immigration centre. Industrious man."

"Age?" Finnerty asked.

"Thirty-five. Wife, two children. It's a twenty-five-minute walk to his school, but he didn't show up. We have two confusing accounts that suggest a car stopped for him. We've instructed his wife not to talk to the press, or to anyone, as it could compromise the investigation. There's no basis for holding her, no sign of bomb making in the house or its attached garage, no traces of Semtex. So far."

"Yes, but to get back to Abzal." Lafayette saw it his duty to take on the role of cross-examiner – Finnerty clearly lacked the energy to resume the reins. "You had surveillance on him yesterday?"

"Eighty per cent coverage. We couldn't follow him on foot everywhere."

"Of course. You were trying not to be too obvious. So he slipped away during the twenty per cent non-surveillance?"

"I suppose so."

"And knowing that, knowing the standard scenic route to speed dignitaries to the airport was along Bronson and Colonel By, you didn't alter it for the Bhashie cavalcade, didn't check it, sweep it . . . I hope you don't mind these questions."

"I'm not sure what you're implying, sir." Lessard was getting testy.

"I don't understand why you didn't warn us immediately that Abzal Erzhan had slipped surveillance."

"But I did. After we made every effort to track him, I alerted Justice Minister DuWallup."

"Pretty late in the day, though." DuWallup, a pathetic attempt to smile.

"Well, sir, I believe you called back that evening and instructed us not to depart from the security program, except to double the escort."

Everyone was staring at red-faced DuWallup. He didn't once look at Finnerty, who was sliding down in his seat, ready to crawl under the table. But Lafayette, smooth as chewed sealskin, said, "Obviously one of those misunderstandings that occur after a long, taxing day."

Commissioner Lessard didn't buy that. "I assumed he'd conferred with the prime minister."

Finnerty felt his chest tightening through a long moment of silence.

"No, I didn't discuss it with the P.M." DuWallup was taking one for the Gipper, he wasn't going to weasel out the prime minister of Canada. "He was exhausted. I took it on myself to deal with the situation." He was looking appropriately hangdog.

Lafayette retreated from that prickly topic by asking if Erzhan had entertained any visitors of interest while under surveillance. That information was being collated, Lessard said, as were telephonic records.

Lafayette led the commissioner to the door, effusive in his thanks: the RCMP was correct in everything it did, the government could be counted on to stand behind its fabled federal police.

Finnerty caught DuWallup's eye, nodded. He would owe big time for this. An appeal court appointment. High commissioner to New Zealand.

The door secured, Lafayette said, "Awkward matter. The press are going to wonder why the public – and our important guests – weren't warned."

"Who's to say they weren't?" The PMO's chief, gnomelike E.K. Boyes. "Given there were no survivors." Finnerty's brain they called him.

Finnerty recoiled a little from the gnome's cold, deadpan logic, but after a moment's hesitation told his staff: "See what you can come up with." His publicity wonk took that to mean, rightly, that he was to get something on the drawing board fast, so he got up and left.

"Let's get an update." Finnerty, with teeth-gritting effort, was taking back the gavel. "Tell me, Gerry, is there anyone at risk in Bhashyistan if things go sour? Any Canadians there?"

"My people are looking into that."

"Tell them to stop looking." Thiessen indicated one of the TV screens. A press conference. In the background, the Alta International logo, in the foreground, its boss, A.J. Quilter, who, as the volume was raised, was sounding irritated, raw. "Vice-president for foreign development, two from our legal team, a geologist, and an accountant, a total complement of five men. I am not suggesting they're in harm's way. Our worry is that we haven't been able to make contact since early this morning."

A reporter: "How would you normally make contact?"

"Satellite phone."

Another reporter: "Can you tell us how long they've been there, what they're doing?"

"They've been there nearly a week. It's not news that we've been in delicate negotiations with the Bhashyistan government."

"Sir, have you enlisted the aid of the federal government?"

"I'm still waiting for the prime minister to return my call."

7

———

Margaret and Pierètte were donning their coats to leave for the Hill, but Arthur was slow to join them — it wasn't easy to pull away from the set. He wondered at the presumption of this fellow Quilter — he was waiting for the P.M. to call. Prairie tan and jutting chin, the fearless look of the self-assured.

Arthur doubted if satellite phones could be jammed. Maybe the batteries had run down. Maybe these unfortunates – already dubbed by the press the Calgary Five – had been ordered to surrender their phones. They'd been staying at the Igorgrad Grand, the city's one prestige hotel.

The news outlets didn't have much recent footage from Bhashyistan. One of the networks had found a still of that hotel, a drab, square, fifteen-storey box on a riverbank. Some clips from a ten-year-old National Geographic travelogue of the mountains-markets-and-mules variety. Mad Igor presiding at a viewing stand: broad, bemedalled chest and flat, pocked, crabbed face.

Pierètte was holding his coat. "You coming, Counsellor?"

Arthur followed them to the elevator, shrugging into his coat, straightening his tie. A headache was creeping up on him, born of the strain of suppressing recent memory, the carnage, the horror, those ten blackened bodies – a scene that was bound to surface in dreams.

Pierètte pedalled off on her bicycle, blowing Margaret a kiss, calling to Arthur: "See you later, litigator."

The weather was still crisp but kinder, and they decided to walk, they needed the air, the peace of this suddenly quiet city. As they strolled through the leaf-littered, church-thick streets below Wellington, Arthur brought out his new cellphone, with its alarming array of gimmickry. He dialed his travel agent one-handed, with his thumb (he had practised this), and put the phone to his ear, imagining himself as cool, modern, online.

"Sunday at noon is the best you can do? Well, fine, then, thank you, my good man." To Margaret: "They're reopening the airport. I'll be staying at my club in Vancouver until I resolve this imbroglio over Zack. Probably drop in on Garibaldi for a couple of days."

"Take a bunch, Arthur. December's coming. I know how you suffer here."

Did she seem almost eager to see him go? As they crossed a street she gripped his arm tight, leaned her head on his shoulder. "Arthur," she whispered.

"Yes, my darling?" Expecting a soothing endearment.

"I have this weird sense he's behind us."

They were near St. Patrick's Basilica, a grand, stone-walled cathedral set behind a fenced lawn. From within, choristers could be heard rehearsing. Arthur knelt to retie a shoelace, flicking a glance behind. The death angel in a leather jacket, brown hair tucked under a black toque, about fifty paces astern. "Let us take a walk around the church."

They entered its parking lot, where the choir sounded louder, sweet hymnal harmony in defiance of the day's barbarity. Near the rear of the church, they followed a long cement ramp leading to a gift shop and grotto hall, the entrance wedged open by the foot of a rotund priest sneaking a smoke.

"Aha, Father," Arthur said, "caught sinning."

A finger to his lips. "Don't tell the Almighty." He extended a hand to Margaret. "Though we don't agree on all things, Ms. Blake,

I'm delighted to meet you." Proving once again to Arthur that Ottawans knew their politicians as teenagers knew rock stars. Margaret graciously introduced him as her "life partner," the ancient word *husband* apparently out of fashion.

As they chatted about the day's dire events, Arthur studied his phone, trying to remember from the manual how to work the camera. When the follower came into view, furtively walking by, Arthur called, "Good afternoon," and the man turned, startled.

The camera flashed. The stalker froze in his tracks. He looked at each in turn, Arthur, Margaret, the puzzled priest, then proceeded on, with his odd shuffle, and seemed about to bolt into the parking lot. But he came to a tottering halt, turned slowly around. A long thin face, sans moustache today, sans sunglasses, the eyes green and haunted. After a few seconds, he came down the ramp. "Father, I'd like to do confession," he said softly.

"Of course, my son." The priest, obviously eager to hear his story, held the door for him.

The sad-eyed man paused by Arthur and Margaret, and whispered, "I shall need absolution from you as well, Ms. Blake." And with that enigmatic declaration he followed the priest inside.

~~~

Margaret's office was bustling as usual, but the energy had altered: a thick layer of tension where there'd been gaiety. The room's focal point was a flat TV, high on a shelf, like an idol, its worshippers gathered below. The prime minister had been on, speaking of his government's "measureless remorse" and issuing a plea to the Ultimate Leader to ring him at his office to discuss, among other things, the well-being of his five guests from Calgary.

A printout of Arthur's photo of the confession-seeking ghoul was beside Pierette's computer screen. "I think I know who this guy is," she said, furiously working at a keyboard. "Come on, come on, Google me, baby, beam me up."

On the television, an attractive dark-eyed woman in a hijab was leaving the Erzhan duplex in Chambly, carrying a shopping bag, heading to a corner *dépanneur*. Vana was her name, Abzal's wife. Their two children, eleven and seven, stared solemnly out a window, an older woman with them, presumably their grandmother. A woman officer bulldozed a path for Vana through the media swarm.

"I'm sorry, I have nothing to say." To a thrusting microphone, a sad but not unmusical voice, accentless English – she'd emigrated from Afghanistan as a child. As reporters relentlessly followed her down the street she kept apologizing. "I'm sorry, *je regrette, pardon*."

Arthur was perplexed at how badly the feds had bungled the Erzhan surveillance. Sirens should have wailed as soon as he vanished from the streets of Chambly. That had happened only twenty-six hours before the bombing, according to what the press pieced together. The government was silent, other than to say the matter was being looked into.

Pierètte called Margaret to join her, exultant. "He *is* a spook."

Arthur looked over their shoulders at a photo accompanying a four-year-old story in the *Toronto Star*. The gawky spectre himself, his hair more blond than brown, looking despondent. Ray DiPalma, then thirty-nine, an agent of the Canadian Security Intelligence Service. He'd been suspended for losing a laptop to a thief after leaving his car unlocked at a suburban Toronto mall. There'd been quite a foofaraw, Arthur recalled now, questions asked in Parliament, an inquiry urged. CSIS had had to change some of its codes.

The incomparable Ms. Litvak printed this out, along with follow-up articles and commentary. The computer had been recovered after three days – by means unknown, though a columnist speculated that Toronto police had warned known receivers of stolen goods that heads would be broken. CSIS claimed the hard drive hadn't been accessed, and there were no state secrets in it anyway. The furor quickly died, and eventually DiPalma's suspension was lifted.

Arthur wondered if it was for penance that this agent had been assigned the profitless job of tracking such an unlikely subversive as Margaret Blake. *I shall need absolution from you as well, Ms. Blake.* What an odd comment to make to one being spied on. What was his game?

"Formal protest?" Pierètte asked. "Press conference?"

"What do you think, Arthur?" Margaret asked.

Had he heard correctly? Was his advice being sought? "I have a feeling you'll find more profit in waiting. This fellow may be seeking to reach out to you."

Pierètte looked at him wide-eyed, as if surprised he had anything useful to say on the matter. "Maybe Arthur's right. Let's keep this to our ménage à trois for now."

He was pleased to be included. He was emerging from oblivion.

~ ~ ~

As of late afternoon, as Arthur and Margaret were readying to go home, there'd been no breaking developments, but it had been a pundits' field day, with endless speculation about what was going on in Bhashyistan. All tourists had been bussed to the nearest border crossings, now sealed. All airports had been closed too, Air Bhashyistan's fleet of twelve wheezing craft fetched home from Tashkent, Ulan Bator, and Lahore. Phone lines down. Power down through much of Igorgrad, according to Western embassies contacted by satellite phone. They weren't saying much else other than that the city was calm.

They paused outside the monolithic front portal of the Confederation Building to find Wellington Street thronged with rush-hour traffic in the darkening twilight. They took a few steps and heard a softly voiced, "Good afternoon." Ray DiPalma, lurking in the gloom beside the recessed entranceway.

Margaret hesitated, but Arthur was less wary. *Audentes fortuna juvat* – fortune favours the bold. From what he'd learned, this fellow was more sad sack than death angel.

DiPalma drew Arthur deeper into the shadows, looking about as if to ensure he himself were not being spied on. "Please meet me tonight at parking lot eight, Carleton University, outside the Loeb Building. I'll be there at precisely eight. Trust me, I beg you." He put his sunglasses on, almost tripped at the sidewalk's edge, and disappeared among the press of home-going public servants.

At home, worried that their phones were bugged, maybe their entire apartment, they turned the radio up, spoke low and close to each other, debating the wisdom of appearing at the appointed time and place, speculating whether this was a set-up, wondering whether to bring reinforcements. They hadn't been able to reach Pierètte; she was at her yoga class, her cell switched off.

Ray DiPalma's approach to them, his apparent reaching-out, was so odd that Arthur feared he might be emotionally unstable, though he didn't seem to pose a physical threat. He assumed DiPalma had chosen the Carleton campus because it was close to their apartment building, though it was also, ominously, only a kilometre from the site of the terrorist bombing. On the way home, they'd scouted the proposed rendezvous, a short-term parking lot, and found it safe enough, well lit and busy.

To Arthur, the prospect of a cloak-and-dagger tête-à-tête was too intriguing to let pass. "If you're nervous about this, your devoted life partner will attend alone."

"I suspect it's me he wants to talk to, Arthur. We'll both go."

Both jumped as a door slammed. It was only the neighbour in 10C returning home, the theatre arts major, currently in rehearsal for a student production – "Marital Bonds," a comedy. Arthur could use some comedy.

~~~

On the dot of eight o'clock, Margaret pulled into the parking lot and turned the engine off, and they waited in silence. Soon after,

DiPalma rapped at a side window, startling them. Arthur unlocked the back door, and he slipped in and slouched low in the seat.

"Admirable car, a Prius." A low, melancholy voice, a well-mannered way of speaking. "I ought to have bought a hybrid myself. I feel I'm part of the problem." As if unsure they grasped his meaning, he added, "Carbon emissions are out of control." He smelled faintly of tobacco and alcohol, well-aged rye whiskey, likely – Arthur had a trained nose for spirits. "Ray DiPalma. I work for CSIS."

"We know," Margaret said. She and Arthur were turned halfway in their seats, studying him. Arthur had advised her to say little, to let this character do the talking, the explaining.

DiPalma stared for a while at car headlights reflecting on the Rideau River. "That's why you took my photo, of course, to ID me. I hope I didn't give you cause to be alarmed. I'm a threat to no one but myself. Does anyone else know we're meeting? Ms. Litvak, I presume." This was neither affirmed nor denied, so he carried on. "I expect she can be counted on to be discreet. We have to be extraordinarily careful."

He gestured toward the campus buildings. "I got my master's here, modern history. Fresh out of college, third in my class, I became the wonder boy of CSIS, one of their best field men. I worked the Balkan desk in the nineties; heck, I ran it. I was barely thirty years old. I got commendations. Then they dumped on me."

"We read about it," Margaret said. Arthur cautioned her with a look.

DiPalma began chewing on something, candy or gum, maybe a breath mint. "I have no idea why I left the car unlocked, other than . . . well, there'd been some marital issues, I was anxious, distracted. There was nothing on the computer, no analysis, no secrets. A few awkward sites I'd bookmarked. Personal stuff . . . No need to get into that."

The continued silence from the front seat seemed to unsettle DiPalma, who apparently had trouble getting to the point. Arthur couldn't guess what that might be: some manner of discreet advice or friendly warning? Maybe something more significant, a political bombshell.

"Let me do the talking, that's the idea, isn't it? Often the best technique in dealing with a subject who so obviously needs to unload. Where does one begin? I suppose by saying I regard you, both of you, as incredibly fine people. There's no one classier in the courtroom than you, Mr. Beauchamp, that's what your biographer says. I saw an interview with him on TV. And no one has shown more political integrity than you, Mrs. Blake . . . Ms. Blake."

"Margaret." This offering of her given name seemed to come from habit, a politician's habit.

"I'm sympathetic to your goals. I'm more than sympathetic, I am firmly in your camp. I follow organic practices. I recycle, I avoid the trap of consumerism. I have my lapses, but we all err. Was it politically wise of you to hire Zack Flett and Savannah Buckett? Probably not, but it was generous, it's the way you are, doing what feels right, not cynically calculating the main chance."

"Have you been tapping my phone?" she asked, calm but assertive.

"Absolutely not, it's illegal. That's so, isn't it, Mr. Beauchamp?"

Arthur felt forced to speak finally. "Yes, absent judicial consent."

"Do I understand you were assigned to follow me?" Margaret asked.

"Do you think I *asked* to take on this stinking file?" A sudden burst of temper. "You're harbouring terrorists, that's their concept, not mine, it's as if you're a danger to the nation." A deep breath, and his voice softened. "My instructions were simply to execute follows – that's spy jargon, sorry – to shadow you, Margaret, to see who you're in contact with, collect names, create target profiles." He was still low in the back seat, shaking from the cold – or from something else, Arthur wasn't sure. A need, nicotine, alcohol.

"Do you mind if we take a little drive, Ray?" Arthur asked.

"No, let's go."

Margaret wheeled onto University Drive, then south on Colonel By, away from the crime-scene roadblocks still slowing traffic at the bombing site.

"Who instructed you to do this, Ray?" Arthur asked. "To target my wife."

His response was circumspect. "Have either of you met Anthony Crumwell?"

"We know who he is," Margaret said.

"Old school. Commies under beds. Enemies of the state lurking behind lampposts." DiPalma drew close to Arthur, who got a whiff of spearmint over stale tobacco breath. "Is this conversation safe, Mr. Beauchamp? Is it covered by solicitor-client privilege? Otherwise, they'll throw the book at me. Treason. Sedition. I need to talk to someone I can trust."

"Has it to do with what happened this morning?" Arthur asked. "The bombing?"

"Can we go somewhere comfortable and private? Is your apartment free?"

"You would risk being seen with us," Arthur said.

"Let me out a block away, and I'll join you in five minutes. If this does get back to CSIS, I'll explain I was infiltrating you." A rare smile from this sombre man.

For all Arthur knew, DiPalma *was* infiltrating them. But he sensed that was neither likely nor a concern, given that he couldn't conceive they had anything to hide.

They stopped on Bronson, not far from where police were still combing through rubble under searchlights. DiPalma got out clumsily, dug hungrily into a pack of cigarettes.

As Margaret pulled away, she said, "How unbalanced do you think this guy is? Or is he conniving at something? 'Carbon emissions are out of control.' Thanks for telling us, Ray, we had no idea. I think the klutzy thing might be an act. I don't trust him."

"Let's hear him out. The priest may not have given him the hearing he'd hoped for in the confessional, and I have a sense of a dam about to give way. He shows all the indications of a man falling apart." During his several decades as a trial lawyer, Arthur had learned to make quick and accurate appraisals of witnesses, their body language, speech inflections, eye movements. He was willing to gamble – cautiously – on his reading of this fellow.

"Well, it's obviously your ear he wants, with all your solicitor-client privileges, so you entertain him."

Arthur was distressed that she seemed aggrieved by that. But they shouldn't risk compromising her – M.P.s and even priests were compellable witnesses, and Arthur had a sense that DiPalma's secrets could ultimately be tested in a courtroom. An interesting character, and whether real or a fraud or a nut, he represented a chance, finally, for Arthur to elevate his role from that of loyal side-kick to his life partner.

~~~

Dear sweethearts,

We got split up from the group again, because of some mix-up, and, boy, they happen a lot here. We got to departures late, Ivy was throwing up, something she ate, and there were only two seats left on the direct flight from Tashkent to Almaty so the three of us were put on this grungy prop plane to someplace called Igorgrad so we can make connections. I swear, we'll NEVER do business with Exotic Tours ever again. The old man next to me said, "Why you go Bashtan?" I said, "What's Bashtan? We go Almaty." He says, "Good luck."

So that started us worrying and we checked with the flight attendant and he didn't speak any English, but he did have some Russian and all we could figure out is there's some kind of trouble and the connecting flight will be delayed or something. Well, it's another adventure, I guess.

Hank, I hope you got Ruffy to the vet so he could be fixed. (Don't try to do it yourself, I don't care if you are a surgeon. Have the girls got their flu shots?) I'll try to slip this into an envelope and mail it from Bashtan, but the way things work around these parts I'll probably be back home before it arrives. If it arrives.

I hope I can find something lovely in Bashtan for Katie for her thirteenth.

Weather's been great, but we seem to be heading north, so I'm glad we brought our parkas. Maxine says hi. A year after Wally's funeral, and she's only now climbing out of it. Ivy is hopeless, still pining for that loser of a boyfriend, Maxine is sure he's into drugs. Her idea was that a few weeks away would cure all her hopeless moping, but I don't know. When I think we'll be dealing with three teenagers in a few years, I go, "Yikes!"

Love you and miss you. Love you all. I'm going to come back with stories.

Jill XOXO

8

———

eturning from his third trip to the can, feeling a little rosy, Huck Finnerty nodded in passing to Anthony Crumwell, operations head of CSIS, who was going over his reports, waiting for his turn in the war room, as the cabinet room had been dubbed. The P.M. always got a chill just looking at this cold fish, Canada's sphincter-eyed head spy, with his maimed right hand – he'd lost three fingers to a letter bomb. An import, a Brit, former head of MI5's anti-terrorist wing.

Before the break, Lafayette had heaped about fifteen minutes of praise on DuWallup before taking him off at the knees. *Only your resignation will save this government, mon ami.* Poor DuWallup. They'd spent all afternoon doctoring something up for the media, but an outright lie (such as: the Bhashyistanis had known full well Erzhan had split, but insisted on taking their chances) was not going to fool even the *Ottawa Sun*. It struck Finnerty as odd that Abzal's name had never been mentioned by the visiting Bhashies, or his whereabouts queried. But maybe they were forbidden to talk about him.

As a gesture of loyalty, he made a point of settling in beside DuWallup before reopening discussion. "Anything new?"

"There have been stirrings," said Boyes, the PMO chief. "Bhashyistan national TV interrupted its programming – patriotic songs all day – for an announcement there's to be an announcement.

Presumably by the Ultimate Leader. Meanwhile, we've shown clips worldwide that the Ilyushin crew are all safe and in good health."

"Okay," Finnerty said, "while we all wait with bated breath, let's hear from our head spook. He's been shining his pants out there." Someone went to fetch him. Finnerty was willing to put more trust in CSIS than the RCMP, especially after the way Commissioner Lessard dropped the dime on DuWallup.

So Lessard was out, Crumwell in, and Clara Gracey back. Finnerty had been so riled at Lafayette's pushiness he'd insisted on her counsel. He also needed her for balance.

"Thank you, gentlemen – and lady, of course – for making time for me," Crumwell said. "Much of this you may have heard from my esteemed colleague Commissioner Lessard. However, we've made additional inquiries." The spymaster spoke in clipped phrases, with a superior old school inflection that Finnerty found irritating. He tried not to be distracted by the sight of his two-fingered hand – only the thumb and middle finger had survived.

"Erzhan. Abzal Erzhan. Do not be surprised if you hear positive testimonials from fellow teachers and neighbours. Many knew of his history, but most shrugged it off. None remember him talking much about his homeland, or his army service there, or about politics. Popular with students, good family man, loves his children, that sort of thing. Seemingly proud to have become a Canadian citizen."

Charley Thiessen: "Somehow it doesn't compute for me that after fifteen years in Canada this teacher, this solid citizen is . . . what do you call it, a sleeper terrorist?"

"A very smooth and patient one, Minister. There was absolutely nothing in his house, or his school, that might incriminate him. His passport was found – one holiday trip to Cuba two years ago, so he may have connections there. No suspicious long-distance calls. No hits on Bhashyistan showed up on the family computer. Which seems so unlikely as to be suspicious in itself."

"Isn't that a reach, Mr. Crumwell?" Clara Gracey asked. Out of pride, she had balked at returning to this all-boys circle jerk, but wilted under Finnerty's entreaty. *We need your unique perspective.* She understood her role: help trim Lafayette's sails, keep the wannabe usurper in line. "You're saying the absence of evidence is in fact proof against Erzhan."

"A subtle but appropriate inference when one is dealing with the sly and devious. In our field we often find value in what is *not* done or said."

Talking down to Clara and her fellow morons. She'd distrusted this guy ever since he started pushing for a national DNA registry. Not just of felons. Everyone. Still fighting the Cold War, seeking out subversives. "You don't find it odd that he left his passport behind?" she asked.

"Not at all. These people have no difficulty obtaining false ones." Crumwell flipped open a page on a dossier. "Mr. Erzhan is highly motivated to seek revenge against his country of birth. After he was acquitted, his mother and father were executed and his three adolescent siblings tortured and jailed."

A hush. Clara was revolted all the more that her government, her country, had sought to play footsie with these beasts. Still, she knew she had to swallow any sympathy she might have for Erzhan – but only if he were indeed a mass murderer, which seemed assumed though not proven.

"Presumably, Abzal learned he was being watched – I offer no comment on the effectiveness of RCMP surveillance – and planned his vanishing act accordingly. We have two reports of a car with an unknown number of occupants pulling up for him on a quiet residential street, a block from the Erzhan residence. One lady saw, from her porch, a man with a satchel accepting a ride in a black sedan. But this woman, who is of a certain age, had on her reading glasses and was a hundred metres away."

"What is a certain age?" Clara asked.

"About eighty."

"Thank you."

"The other report is even vaguer, and comes from Vana Erzhan, who claimed her landlord saw her husband being drawn into a car. But that person, when questioned, declined to cooperate, and seemed hostile. One wonders why. This landlord, gentlemen – and lady – may be a person of interest. Iqbal Zandoo, lives below the Erzhans, in the lower unit. Born in Pakistan, emigrated twenty-three years ago, now aged sixty-four. Did well developing properties, owns several duplexes. We believe he has an al-Qaeda connection."

He paused for dramatic effect. Clara wondered if he was waiting for them to clap.

"Our partners in the war on terror have been superbly forth-coming. Needless to say, the CIA has left no stone unturned in its efforts to connect the dots between known enemies, and in tracing the Zandoo family tree has learned he is blood-related to a known terrorist."

"Please spare us the suspense, Anthony," Lafayette said. "And the metaphors." Immediately he regretted that sarcastic aside. Crumwell was an ally. A vital ally. "Excellent work, by the way, excellent work."

"Thank you, Gerry. The known terrorist, Iqbal Zandoo's cousin, one Mohammed Aziz, aged twenty, is being held in an American detention centre in Kabul. He spied for the Taliban, fought for them. He confessed to having attended an al-Qaeda training camp."

"And what have been Mr. Zandoo's recent dealings with this terrorist?"

"We're looking into that."

Lafayette felt the air seeping from this balloon. "Visits, phone calls, correspondence – what do you have along those lines?"

"Nothing yet. Our American friends are, uh, working on their guest."

Finnerty too had been expecting more. "A cousin, you say."

"His mother's uncle's grandson. Technically, I suppose, a second or third cousin." A disappointed silence. "Family ties are unusually deep, of course, over there."

Dexter McPhee, a diversion: "What about the religious factor here? Taliban, al-Qaeda – are we dealing with Muslim fanatics? Don't get me wrong, I have many friends in the Muslim community. My riding treasurer is one of them."

"Spent a lot of time myself among followers of the Prophet," Crumwell said. "I daresay I've gained some experience in how to handle these people. They're not that different from you and me. Their philosophical constructs are simpler, a little more stringent."

Clara assumed he was a misogynist too. Most bigots were.

"This landlord, Zandoo," Guy DuWallup said. "Is he also an ideologue?" Not that he was particularly interested, but he couldn't sit around like a cipher just because his days here were numbered. He wasn't interested in being a judge or ambassador; he preferred the Senate – he was ready to retire anyway.

Crumwell was studying his dossier. "Local cricket club, Neighbourhood Watch . . . Ah, here, Zandoo subscribes to the *Guardian Weekly*."

"Okay, and Erzhan," DuWallup said. "Is he another of your Muslim fanatics?"

"He may be covering up, because he presents a rather secular front. His wife is observant, though. Takes a bus to Montreal weekly to attend a mosque, does volunteer work there."

"Would that be one of those places that preaches hatred?" The defence minister.

"Not in so many words. But when one carefully parses the phrases used by their imam one can detect a certain unpatriotic subtext."

Gerard Lafayette scanned the screens on the wall. No developments, just endless analyses. He wondered if the Ultimate Leader enjoyed keeping them in suspense. He was likely calculating what he could demand in compensation. Hundreds of millions, maybe, which he would personally pocket. "What's the latest on Erzhan, Anthony? Where do you think he is?"

"I'd wager he's in Montreal. One assumes his terrorist cell keeps a safe house there. We're working on this, but we don't have a lot of manpower, gentlemen. And lady. There is one man he may seek to connect to. A Vancouver barrister, Brian Pomeroy. Defended him on the assassination charge. A framed photograph of him, in his robes, is hanging on a wall of Erzhan's living room."

"You have eyes on this Pomeroy?"

"He too has disappeared. An agent sought an appointment with him today, on the pretense of seeking advice on a hit-and-run accident, and learned that Mr. Pomeroy is on some kind of ramble in the Barrens of the Arctic. We have people trying to locate him, but . . . as I say, we're likely to go over budget on this one."

"That will be looked after," Finnerty said impatiently.

"In fact," said Lafayette, "this may be a time to consider loosening not just the purse but the legal restraints. Forgive me if I remind everyone this is the very kind of crisis that my amendments to the security bill were intended for."

"They got shot down, Gerry," Clara said. "Mr. Crumwell, I want to make sure we're not turning a blind eye to suspects other than Abzal Erzhan and his confederates. You constantly hear of authorities getting so hooked on a theory they get tunnel vision . . ."

Crumwell interrupted, not kindly. "Minister, we are *not* putting all our eggs in Mr. Erzhan's basket. There are other distinct possibilities, and I was about to get to them." A raised hand commanded attention. "Anarchists. Eco-terrorists. Seeking to spoil the deal with Alta International."

"That's exactly what I was thinking." Defence Minister McPhee. "Where you've got fossil fuel issues, you've got the environmentalists. The violent ones, the fringe elements, it doesn't take much to stir them up. I'm not talking about the Sierra Club or the Green Party." Murmurs of assent. "But you get people who dynamite dams and bridges, attack refineries. That lot."

"In that regard," Crumwell said, "you may be interested to know that two such individuals – members of the Quatsino Five, who infamously caused millions in losses to one of our major logging firms – are currently employed by the member for Cowichan and the Islands."

A nervous shuffling. Clara recalled there'd been some noise around that last year, especially on the call-in shows. Two young people on parole, hired to caretake Margaret Blake's farm on the Gulf Islands. Unwise of her, but she'd stoutly defended the hiring.

"In fact, we have someone who's been, ah, monitoring that situation," Crumwell said. "One of our most resourceful men."

E.K. Boyes turned up the sound on a monitor, a live satellite relay from Igorgrad.

A desk, the Bhashyistan flag in background, a symbolized hand holding three jagged lightning bolts. A technician was setting up a microphone on the desk, laying out some pages. Music, the national anthem. The technician scurried away. A few moments later, the Ultimate Leader himself entered and sat, picked up the text, frowned over it, then spoke in a deep rasping voice, muted as a translator spoke over it:

"Weep, oh my comrades. Yes, all Bhashyistan weeps on this, the blackest day in our proud history since the traitorous and bloody assassination of our country's beloved Great Father. Today I announce the barbarous murder in Canada . . . by the henchmen of imperialist dogs clinging to power of sixteen . . . no, seventeen great patriots of our nation."

The interpreter was having trouble keeping up, getting it right. Someone gasped: "*Seventeen?*"

"Shut up."

". . . loyal and dedicated advisers in an unarmed vehicle ambushed by the terrorist Abzal Erzhan, who has been welcomed in Canada despite . . . murdering the Great Father of our country . . . and also eight crew members of our glorious nation's presidential plane, which was brought down, though unarmed, by Canadian fighter planes . . ."

"*What?*"

"Shut up!"

"Our proud people . . . my countrymen, do not cower like slaves. We resist! We fight to the last drop of patriotic blood! To that end, as leader of glorious Republic of Bhashyistan, I declare against Canada we are in state of war! God save Bhashyistan!"

9

_____

Settled on a sofa by the faux fireplace, Ray DiPalma took another sip of brandy before continuing his rambling discourse. "I had the best ears in Belgrade back then, played a major role in busting Krajzinski, the Balkan wolf – you remember him?"

Arthur nodded. "One of those Serbian ethnic cleansers."

"He earned forty years from the War Crimes Tribunal, and I earned a promotion to run the entire South Danube bureau. Then they suddenly pulled me out, God knows why, and one rotten stolen computer and I'm shelved, stuck in a corner cubicle."

Arthur nodded sympathetically. Margaret had excused herself a while ago, was in her office, on the phone or her laptop. An hour earlier, after ushering DiPalma into their flat, she'd asked if he cared for tea, coffee, juice, or something stronger. His disarming politeness in choosing the latter was, to Arthur, a typical mannerism of one who regularly sought escape in drink. As an AA veteran of nearly twenty years, Arthur recognized him as a brother of the bottle, a perception reinforced as DiPalma worked his way through half a litre of wine plus a substantial share of the five-star brandy kept for guests.

It was as if he needed drink to keep his vocal cords from drying out. He seemed unable to stop talking, mostly about his own sad life, and Arthur wondered if he had crumbled under the pressure of work, the pressure of keeping secrets for a living. An alternative theory was open, that he was performing – "conniving," as Margaret put it – but if so, DiPalma had missed a distinguished career on stage, one finer than would ever be enjoyed by the theatre major in apartment 10C. But if this was all a clever act, what purpose would it serve?

"When CSIS got the laptop back they found I'd logged onto a wife-swapping site. It was just an idle thing, I was surfing, but they made an issue of it, showed it to Janice, my wife. That's when the marriage headed south. And, yes, there were some photos of Janice and me at a nudist camp on Lake Massawippi. She went ballistic when Crumwell asked her about them. It was stupid of me to leave them on the computer. Now they're monitoring my Internet use, at least at the office – I heard them laughing over a couple of lonely-hearts sites I'd accessed during lunch."

So far, DiPalma had not divulged any state secrets, or offered an inside scoop about anything, including this morning's multiple assassination. Occasionally, he stepped out to the balcony for a smoke, taking his glass with him. But otherwise he sat by the roaring phony fire blathering away about his fall from grace, as unlike a trained spy as one could imagine. Arthur had known many who'd suffered breakdowns; this man matched the type. The heart-break type. Brian Pomeroy was the worst case he'd known: alcohol, cocaine, he'd gone delusional, spent time in a care facility.

"This is her picture." Janice, in a wallet photo folder, blond, winsomely appealing. "She went off with a lobbyist for the mine industry, a rattlesnake, no human values, he's all about money and power. I phoned her a few times, maybe I got too loud. All I wanted was to talk with her, so I went to her house one afternoon, and of course she complained I was stalking her."

DiPalma jumped at the angry shout from next door. "I am not *seeing* another woman! I am *fucking* her!" Arthur explained to DiPalma that the aspiring young actor was rehearsing for a comedy about the travails of matrimony.

DiPalma took a moment to recover. "That sent shivers, a little too close to home." He fumbled for his pack of Rothmans, then had to retrieve a couple of cigarettes that spilled to the carpet. When he slid open the balcony door, Arthur could hear the anxious noises of the city, plaintive howls of sirens, giving way to his neighbour crying, "Come on, it's just a game! Just don't tie me too tight . . ."

He got up to a ringing phone. Wentworth Chance, said the caller ID, the nagging biographer. Arthur let it ring. Wentworth had been his junior counsel on a notorious case, the murder of a judge. In a weak moment, Arthur had agreed to a series of interviews, and this lanky young apostle, who regarded him with an awe befitting the gods, was constantly on the phone, assailing him with questions.

"I'm a mess, but they don't know it in the service," DiPalma said as he came back indoors. "I'm a fairly good actor, I play it cool, straight. I don't have anyone to talk to any more since Janice took off, that's the problem. I used to tell her all my woes until she became one of them. I lost my mother when I was six, to cancer. My father, forget it, I didn't exist for him." DiPalma drained his glass, looked woefully at the brandy bottle, now empty.

Arthur directed him away from what he feared would be a maudlin history of childhood trauma. "There's something you wanted to tell me, Ray. If you want legal advice, I'm prepared to give it. We're now solicitor and client. I may not, without your permission, divulge what you say."

The moment was punctuated by screaming guitars from the flat below. That was met by a banging on the floor next door, which persuaded the rock fan to turn the volume down.

Suddenly, Margaret raced from her office. "Oh my God, Bhashyistan has declared war on Canada." She turned on the console TV. "The Calgary Five have been arrested on some trumped-up charge."

On the screen, a reporter in the lobby of the Foreign Affairs Building: "They are accused of insulting the Revered Mother, apparently a crime in Bhashyistan. The state police are seeking, quote, the usual fifteen years' imprisonment. Back to you, Mark."

"We'll continue to stay on top of this dramatic story." Mark, looking wan and weary, was sharing the camera with a bearded political analyst. "Dr. Jethrop, what's your reaction to that?"

"Well, I'm sure it will take them all of five minutes to convict these innocent Canadians, who are obviously intended as pawns in a scheme of criminal extortion. Insulting the president's mother, that is utterly farcical. Bhashyistan's institutions of justice are an insult. The entire country is an insult."

"The cabinet has remained behind closed doors ever since Bhashyistan's declaration of war," Mark said. "What do you think their reaction should be?"

The expert hesitated, stumped. "I shall leave that up to wiser heads than me."

Cut to the Alberta premier, urging swift and decisive action. Cut to the Liberal Opposition leader, describing Bhashyistan as a terrorist nation. The U.S. secretary of state: her government will always stand beside its allies and neighbours. The British prime minister. The French president.

Reaction from people on a Toronto street. "I guess we have to put our trust in the government." Others were less typically Canadian: "Let's show them who they're dealing with." "Go in there and take them out." DiPalma watched all this with a quizzical frown, then jumped as the phone sounded, Pierète's ring. Margaret took it in her office.

"Okay, Ray, what did you want to tell me?"

He played with another cigarette, then looked up. "Abzal Erzhan didn't just disappear. He was *disappeared*." He slurred that slightly: dish-appeared.

"How do you know?"

"You ought to talk to Vana Erzhan. She wanted to see a lawyer, but the cops encouraged her not to. You should also talk to their landlord, Mr. Zandoo."

"How could this be arranged?"

"Julien Chambleau." Margaret's friend, the Bloc Québécois member for Iberville-Chambly. "They live in his riding."

Arthur nodded. "So it would be appropriate if he visited." He was tantalized by this intrigue. His planned getaway to the West Coast might have to be made brief.

"Who do you think might have disappeared him, Ray?"

"I'm trying to get something on that."

Margaret breezed back, woke up Arthur's desktop computer. "Pierètte says to check out YouTube."

All Arthur knew about YouTube was that people posted all sorts of twaddle there, video clips of kids playing dress-up and puppies being bathed. Margaret typed in the link she'd written down, and in a moment the Bhashyistan flag appeared, words superimposed: *A Production of Third Son of Ultimate Leader Films.*

DiPalma put on a pair of wire-rim spectacles. "Third son of six. Mukhamet Khan Ivanovich. Computer sciences degree from the University of Dusseldorf." The CSIS agent might be a wreck, but he was a well-informed one.

The Ultimate Leader's webwise progeny was narrator of this film, a fat young fellow with thick glasses and a multicoloured skullcap. "Here we have rooftop terrace of Igorgrad Grand Hotel, and here you seeing tables and umbrellas for tourists for gazing on beautiful city below and mountains. Over there, in Park of the Revered Mother, is her famous statue." A fifty-foot pyramid topped with a gold-plated Amazonian figure wielding an axe and carrying a swaddled baby, a load of firewood strapped to her back.

"Close up, here are busts of great heroes of Bhashyistan." An array of them on the low wall surrounding the terrace. "And here is rooftop swimming pool for use only in summer, and here is bar." A wooden structure with stools. "Here is hidden video camera in case of spies or enemies of the state." Its lens was one of a pair of glass eyes in a bust of the Great Father. "And here is pickup for sound." Mukhamet bent, pointed to a small microphone under a table. "Surprise, we are not so backward here in Bhashyistan."

DiPalma seemed impressed, a little puckered whistle. Then Mukhamed's cherubic smile filled the screen. "And day before yesterday, here is rock-solid proof how our ungrateful guests insulted Revered Mother."

A dimmer, dusky light, the Calgarians relaxing with drinks, five men enjoying a sunset.

"Eight point five."

"Nah, doesn't beat a Prairie sunset."

"What's that weird shit on the pyramid over there? Mad Igor in a dress?"

"Looks like an ape carrying an axe."

"That's the Great Mother. It's in one of their brochures, some bullshit fairy tale about how she went out to the forest to gather kindling and lay down in a field of flowers and gave birth to the Ultimate Leader." Laughter.

"He wants another half a billion on closing."

"Has to be untraceable, that's going to be a bitch."

"Hey, keep your voices down."

"Paranoid, Clyde?"

"You bet I'm paranoid." A glance toward the bar. "Five days in this shithole. Don't dare talk in the rooms."

Clyde and two others rose, moved off, out of sight, presumably to confer about Igor's extortion fee.

Back to Mukhamed. "So you seeing why are being tried Canadian running dogs for unbearable insult to great lady of People's Republic of Bhashyistan. Also notice scheme for bribing our glorious president. Stay tuned for more breaking news, this is Mukhamet Khan Ivanovich, reporting from Igorgrad."

~~~

Arthur was spinning when he finally got to bed, after midnight, after DiPalma practically had to be carted out to a taxi. Sleep was slow in coming, stalled by excitement and by a long bedtime colloquy – mostly about DiPalma, of whom Margaret was highly distrustful.

"He's just too damn eager to betray CSIS and the oath he swore on joining it. It could be a diabolical scheme. That stolen computer could have been set up to make it seem plausible that's he's embittered against his employer. His stage director probably thought up the klutziness, the heavy drinking, the nervous breakdown. It's all too clever."

A fan of spy thrillers, she'd read John LeCarré's entire oeuvre. DiPalma was a spy who would someday come in from the cold, she insisted, like his fictional counterpart, who'd played the turncoat.

Arthur was entranced by the intrigue, didn't want to buy into her doubts, preferred to buy what DiPalma was selling. He was encouraged to believe the fellow could unveil dark, thrilling secrets, high-level scandals. He begged Margaret to believe he was an excellent judge of character, a faculty that had rarely failed him. Like a mantra, he repeated, "What have we got to lose?"

10

———

It was nine-thirty, the weary back end of a day of unrelenting hell. For the first time in his political career Huck Finnerty regretted the ambition and circumstances that had propelled him to his country's highest office. He felt stymied, freighted with self-doubt, by a sense he wasn't the man for this job. He badly needed a drink, a steadier, but if he slipped out to the john one more time they'd be wondering if he needed a bladder operation.

The martyr DuWallup, accepting he was out of it, had wished them well and gone to bed. But a few more advisers were here, E.K. Boyes's crew. Others kept popping in, dispatches, questions, consultations. Breaks were becoming more frequent, people pacing, conferring in corners, weary laments, an occasional desperate laugh.

Finnerty had got angry on the phone to A.J. Quilter. "You're goddamned right I'm concerned! You don't have a monopoly on concern! We're busting our ass working on this!" Finnerty had turned him over to Crumwell of CSIS, who was calmer, got Quilter to book overnight flights to Ottawa for a couple of his people who'd done stints in Bhashyistan.

The P.M. had brusquely vetoed a proposal to bring in the official opposition to make common front. He couldn't believe Cloudy McRory wanted to be anywhere near this stinkpile, nor did he want McRory sitting around telling him what to do; Lafayette was bad enough. Mr. Cool, unflustered, no sweat patches on his shirt, and with a smile no less mocking than that of the sculpted Great Father on the terrace of the Igorgrad Grand. Even Hitler in his bunker showed more despair.

The video by Third Son of Ultimate Leader Films had been transposed to one of the big screens, everyone groaning as they watched, slapping their foreheads. Those smart alecks from Alta International with their careless talk about a cash bribe – that wasn't going to rally world support. Nor was calling Igor's mother an ape with an axe.

Clara Gracey, equally distressed at the way this shmozzle was playing out, was cursing her bad judgment in allowing herself to be pressed back into service. Now she must share the burden of blame and shame – the Privy Council was in utter paralysis, without focus, strategies, energy. All but Lafayette, with his espousal of an unlikely benefit to this ugly contretemps: "This is Canada's chance to dominate the world stage." He didn't address the logistics of how that might be done.

The tireless hawk Dexter McPhee once again was railing on about the need for extreme action. "I say we send our boys in and pummel these Mafia mobsters. We can't just *not* declare war back at them. What's it going to look like to the world if we sissy out?"

Charley Thiessen: "Never mind the world. The folks I represent in Grey County. Some of us want to get re-elected."

E.K. Boyes: "If I may be so bold, Ministers McPhee and Thiessen have a point. We can't allow some rogue state to run roughshod over the rules of international law. All the Western democracies are watching us, as are Japan, India, Russia. We can't be seen as soft."

Clara was impatient with this hard-and-soft stuff. "Good God, rise above it, toss it over to the UN."

To McPhee, that seemed an unworthy solution. "We're in a state of war whether we like it or not. What are we supposed to do, grovel, surrender?"

Lafayette had in mind a more cerebral stratagem: "I suggest we ignore their declaration of hostilities for the time being. We remain stern, unbowed, express appropriate outrage, call for all Canadians to unite behind the government, and so on. No desperate pleas for international support – that makes us look like beggars. Though we don't issue our own plea to the UN, we'll not stand aside if a friendly nation calls for an emergency session of the Security Council. That can be arranged."

After more debate, Lafayette got his way, and someone went off to draft a communiqué with the appropriate outrage. Clara had to hand it to him, the way he manoeuvred through the muddle to come up with these calculated compromises.

Discussion ensued as to how to address the Canadian public. A press release was not enough. E.K. Boyes urged they go live tomorrow in front of the networks, a full and fearless statement of the government's position. Schedule it for mid-morning, after everyone had a good night's sleep, allowing time to brief the caucus. Lafayette suggested a full-scale press conference ought to follow, but with only the prime minister on the dais – the nation needed reassurance its leader was in calm control.

Clara thought it odd the foreign minister would so gracefully decline the spotlight, then realized he was positioning himself to dodge the flack. A staffer sped off to announce to the score of media still massed in the foyer that at eleven a.m., Eastern Time, Finnerty would speak to the nation.

Then another break, people shifting about restlessly, as if waiting for the crisis somehow to resolve itself. Lafayette looked at them sadly – didn't they understand this was Canada's moment in history? They'd fallen prey to that great Canadian illness, vacillation.

One of his staff called on the secure line: a fax had arrived from Moscow. "Don't bother to translate it," he said curtly into his headset. "Just send a runner."

The two pages that ultimately arrived were in Cyrillic script, from the Russian embassy in Bhashyistan via the Canadian embassy in Moscow. Everyone waited as Lafayette quietly read through it. Finally, he looked up.

"Presumably this has been sent with Kremlin clearance. It summarizes a conversation between the Russian ambassador to Bhashyistan and a senior aide to President Ivanovich. The Russians, by the way, are loathed as former colonizers, but they're a fact of life, biggest trading partner, largest embassy in Igorgrad, and they're listened to, however resentfully." He paused for a suspenseful moment. "The Bhashies want Abzal Erzhan. We are accused of harbouring this murderer, and they want us to turn him over."

He turned to Crumwell. "It might help to put this communiqué in context, Anthony, if you summarize the psychological profiling your people did on Mad Igor."

"Cutting it to the bone, Minister, the Ultimate Leader has never properly dealt with his father's death, is still grieving, obsessed with thoughts of requital, vengeance – presumably in the form of Erzhan's beheading. In other words, he seeks closure."

Thiessen scoffed. "Closure? Give us a break."

Lafayette quoted the Russian communiqué: "'Bhashyistan may be willing to cease formal hostilities with Canada if Erzhan is surrendered to their authorities.'" Everyone seemed suitably impressed by his competence in the tongue of Tolstoy and Lenin. "The Bhashyistanis apparently don't believe Abzal has flown the coop."

"Maybe we can send someone who looks like him." Thiessen again, chuckling.

"Why don't you volunteer, Charley?" Clara asked.

They were getting testy; Lafayette must remain steady at the helm. "Our Russian friends also indicate that Bhashyistan will amend its claim we shot down their aircraft. Their latest version is that it was forced down, with all crew members under arrest in harsh conditions. This revision will soon be going out on their national radio. In the meantime, the Ultimate Leader has used the crisis as an excuse to round up hundreds more suspected dissidents." He turned to Crumwell. "What's the latest on the local front, Anthony?"

"Our best estimate from immigration and census records is we have about three hundred Bhashies resident in Canada, mostly exiles who came over during perestroika, a window when borders were opened. The largest grouping is in Montreal, about sixty or seventy, many belonging to a seemingly informal society. It meets regularly, but those we contacted seemed evasive. None, of course, admit to knowing Erzhan more than casually, and all claim not to know where he is."

"Can you get someone in there?" Thiessen asked.

"I'd prefer, gentlemen – and lady – not to speak of specific investigative techniques. All I can say is we are working up some approaches with the RCMP, but we feel hamstrung . . ."

"You'll get the funding," Finnerty growled.

"I meant, Prime Minister, hamstrung by the laws." Crumwell's maimed hand held high a copy of the Anti-Terrorist Act.

"As I read that act," Boyes said, "it empowers you to arrest and hold without warrant, and to question witnesses in secret."

"But only with a court order. We were wondering, Prime Minister, if a declaration of international emergency is contemplated."

Crumwell was addressing Finnerty, but looking at Lafayette, who was pleased that the foxy old Brit was alive to the Emergencies Act and its powers to search and seize from anyone, anywhere, anytime. Its advantages were clear: extraordinary powers to enact laws without delay, stilling the carping voices that invariably rose in knee-jerk response to national crises. A politically touchy issue, however – this aborted child of the War Measures Act was deeply reviled in his own province.

Boyes said, "The FLQ crisis was a little before your time here, Anthony, so you may not be aware of the political ramifications . . ."

Lafayette quietly broke in. "E.K., we have an international emergency here. We should commit to nothing that will tie our hands. Invoking emergency measures, yes, that might be difficult, but at all costs we must avoid timid thinking, we must be bold, prepared to do whatever it takes."

McPhee: "Hear, hear."

"Like what?" said Clara. "Mimic the Ultimate Leader? Arrest all the dissidents?"

Lafayette looked coolly at her. "We shouldn't assume, Clara, that lawful Canadian authorities would abuse such privileges as have been granted by Parliament."

The patronizing ponce. Showing her his haughty snoot, a look often captured by the political cartoonists. Clara was sure he had some scheme to create turmoil for the P.M., force him to resign.

"Let's put that on tomorrow's agenda," Finnerty said, coming alive. "Where are we on this eco-terrorist angle?"

Crumwell flipped through his notes. "We have a list of every known organization that advocates or may be sympathetic to violent environmental protest. We'd propose to visit them unannounced, as it were, should this government grant us emergency powers . . ."

"Well, we haven't, so far. Go on."

"We are also reviewing, during what spare time we can afford, every available video of people attending the several street protests of Thursday. One such individual – I may have mentioned him, Zachary Flett, Ms. Blake's caretaker – is in jail in Vancouver as a result of joining such a protest. You're aware he has a record for terrorism."

"That's a little broad, isn't it, Anthony?" said Clara Gracey. "A lot of timber floated out to sea. No lives were threatened."

Crumwell offered her the weary look he reserved for those he regarded as soft on terror.

11

———

Nestled into his favourite lounge chair in Vancouver's Confederation Club, Arthur fuelled up with coffee, juice, and a guilt-inducing buttery croissant while wading through the Monday morning papers. Accounts of the prime minister's press conference, which he'd watched live on Saturday, portrayed Finnerty as confused and inept, having eschewed the folksy style, the self-deprecating humour, in favour of a ponderous, cliché-ridden call for courage and clear-headedness, qualities he seemed to lack. Some observers ventured that the P.M. had been hung out to dry by frightened privy councillors.

His responses to reporters' questions had been guarded. The five captives: "Anything I say might put them at further risk." Why was Canada not responding to the declaration of war? "We're acting on the assumption those words were spoken without diplomatic care." As to the grossly uninformative DuWallup, an encomium, then: "We will, of course, be discussing his future role in the government."

Regarding efforts to track the bombing culprits: "First we must identify who they are. Clearly our prime suspect, Mr. Erzhan, didn't act alone. I have instructed the RCMP and CSIS to leave no stone unturned in apprehending these evildoers." If Erzhan had been abducted, as Ray DiPalma claimed, the prime minister was either in the dark or being cagey.

Buried in the inner pages was this quote from the P.M.: "There has been a certain amount of passion around the effort to open relations with Bhashyistan, as evidenced by the many undisciplined demonstrations on our streets. People have a right to their views, but Canada is home to several groups which make no bones about advocating violence."

That set Arthur worrying that the government, in its desperation, might be about to cast a wild and reckless net, targeting activists like Zachary Flett, whose case he would be indignantly arguing this morning.

"Alta International. Dump it." Irwin Godswill, the legendary tycoon who played the markets like a Vegas craps table and rarely lost, was on his phone, talking to his broker, his back to Arthur, no one else within earshot. "After we know what they want for ransom, we may go back in."

Such pessimism about Alta's prospects seemed justified. Bhashyistan law seemed unlikely to be tempered by notions of fundamental rights, and the Calgarians would be hard to dislodge from jail without hefty penalty. Reparations for the murders in Ottawa would be extreme too. Arthur felt it foolish to underestimate the Bhashyistan leadership, whose war declaration seemed a ploy, to be withdrawn in negotiations.

Godswill, still oblivious to Arthur, said something about Anglo-Atlantic Energy, then raised his voice, impatient. "I *have* read the earnings report. Something's going on, they're taking off. Just do it."

Irwin Godswill was in his aching, complaining eighties, still fattening his accounts, living proof that money can't buy happiness. Normal people retire from the chase. Or try to.

~~~

Among the forest of concrete giants sprouting from Vancouver's downtown peninsula was the BMO tower, four floors occupied by Tragger, Inglis, Bullingham. The forty-third was the lair of the senior partners, where Arthur ran the gauntlet of secretaries and staff – no easy task on his increasingly rare visits to his old firm. "Lovely to see you, sir." "You're looking exceedingly well, Mr. Beauchamp." "When is the book coming out?"

"Never, I hope, my dear." That damned biography. *A Thirst for Justice* was the cruel title, trumpeting his years as a dipsomaniac, revelling in his drunken courtroom excesses. He'll be the laughingstock of Ottawa and, worse, Garibaldi.

More greetings from various senior partners, eager to talk about Canada's international crisis. In contrast to the tension elsewhere in the nation, in these mahogany halls there was a sense of guilty joy at the perils facing the government. The firm had lost tens of millions in fees after the Liberals' defeat six years ago.

Gertrude Isbister gave him a businesslike hug and handed him a file with multicoloured tabs, precedents for a twelve-page brief of habeas corpus law. "He whipped this up on the weekend."

Old Riley, she meant, the geriatric mole from the fortieth floor, many times Arthur's saviour. He almost lived in the library, had rarely been seen outside it.

"I sent him the usual." Chocolate truffles. "I had to come in Sunday myself, but no big deal."

A blatant hint. Flowers to her doorstep.

"Beware of Mr. Bullingham. He wants you to do a murder."

Too late. Alerted to Arthur's arrival, here he came, last of the founding partners, ninety-one and still on his horse. Another ancient who couldn't stop working. People should read more poetry.

"Ah, Beauchamp, a rare honour. Visiting the troops, are we? Looking for an entertaining diversion, perhaps?" He drew Arthur toward his anteroom.

"I shall be quickly in and out, Bully." A nickname that only the upper-tier partners dared use. "A vital issue of civil liberties this morning, a couple of days repose at my island sanctuary, then I must scurry back to our lovely capital."

"And miss a treat? If I know Arthur Beauchamp, he will not be able to resist it. The Cameron murder. Gravelstein is handling it, but he'd be more than eager to serve you as junior."

"The Cameron murder? I forget."

"The highways minister, surely you remember. Found dead in an Abbotsford bordello twelve years ago?"

It came back. Headlines about orgies, love drugs, hot-tubbing hostesses. Cameron in a closet, impaled through the heart by a spear. DeCameron, they called it.

"His widow was arrested last week. A sting, or whatever you call it – they had a woman officer pose as a psychotherapist, and she inveigled Mrs. Cameron into some incriminating statements. Some issues there to slack the old thirst for justice, eh?" Ribbing him about the biography, a friendly punch on the arm.

"Far too pedestrian. I do only cases of international import now."

Bully, taken aback, turned sardonic. "Let me guess. You've been retained by Alta International to represent their five ignoramuses. Off to Igorgrad, are we, to raise constitutional issues in the people's democratic court?"

"For your ears only, Bully, I'm looking into the possibility of representing the family of Abzal Erzhan." A case to truly slake the thirst for justice, the defence of the disappeared, the inexplicably disappeared. "An informed source tells me Erzhan may have been shanghaied, perhaps murdered. It would be interesting to learn if agents of the federal government were involved."

"Do say." Bully seemed intrigued, if only because Arthur might turn up more dirt against the reviled Conservative government. If Erzhan had been kidnapped, mysteries abounded as to who did it. DiPalma had insisted Erzhan's wife and landlord could shed light on the matter – maybe enough light to affirm the alcoholic spook's good intentions. Margaret was working through friendly channels to set up a meeting with them, and Arthur must remain ready to jump on a plane.

"There may be expenses. I don't imagine the Erzhan family has vast resources."

Bully frowned. He was famously stingy, but Arthur's high-profile cases brought in substantial business. "Spend prudently."

"Bully, I also want to enlist the help of our Ottawa branch plant. I'd like to make some quiet inquiries about a CSIS agent named Ray DiPalma."

"Antoine Salzarro is your man, recently joined us from the government side, was number three in Public Security. I'll get on to him about this DiPalma fellow. He's your informed source? Never mind – I've always held to the tenet that if you can't keep a secret, don't expect anyone else to keep it for you."

~~~

Arthur didn't have time to visit Zachary in the cells, so he wheedled the sheriffs into bringing him into court before the sitting. On entering, Zack raised two defiant handcuffed fists in salute to his many supporters, young environmentalists who stood up to honour their martyr.

Brittle-tempered Zack was less angry than Arthur had expected, his attitude one of cynical bemusement, as if his arrest were the sort of thing one should expect from the guardians of a dying order.

"They came by twice this weekend, high-level bulls. Because I freed some captive timber from a log boom, I'm a prime suspect for blowing up nine Bhashyistanis, right? Problem is, I was in custody on this bogus charge when it happened. So these *fascisti* implied I was the instigator, Mr. Big pulling strings from Cellblock A of the Burnaby Correctional Centre. Alternatively, I'm accused of stirring up hatred, spurring the rabble to acts of murder. They finally gave up on that line and went to Plan C, promising to do right by me if I rolled over on my Eastern contacts. A financial reward, plus witness protection. The government's in a stinking pile of shit over this, man, they're looking to bust *anyone*, your aunt Albertina and her three-legged cocker spaniel."

Zack had declined to talk on the phone from jail, thus this outpouring, and it didn't cease as the clerk called the court to order. He clutched Arthur's sleeve, whispered: "Give my love to Savannah if I don't get out. Give it if I do, because I'm going to need a couple of days to warn friends about the heat. Can't do it by telephone, obviously. And you got to believe they're reading all our emails."

Paranoia. Another growing aspect of the Canadian condition. "Keep out of trouble," Arthur said. Zack had earned a fearsome reputation as a hothead.

"Mr. Beauchamp, are we ready?"

Arthur looked up: Mr. Justice Gundar Singelar, whom Arthur remembered as a young, aggressive prosecutor. Suddenly he was a judge. Arthur had worked against him a few times. These ex-Crowns often tended to nurse long-term wounds from their losses.

"Ready, milord." Arthur retreated to counsel table, Zack to the prisoners' box. Arthur prayed the young man would not again show the bad taste of urging a judge to go to hell. Mind you, Arthur had been known to say similar himself, in more eloquent ways.

"I've read your brief, Mr. Beauchamp, and that of the justice minister." Represented here by a Ms. Kwon, a new face, pink-cheeked with inexperience. "Excellent both. I have a busy list here today, so I wonder if either of you wish to emphasize any points."

Shorthand for: keep it brief, I'm on overload. Arthur spoke for only five minutes, ex tempore, a rumbling salvo about the freedoms of speech and assembly, about how the right to make vigorous, peaceful protest was the hallmark of democracy and the bane of totalitarian regimes.

Singelar frowned at the rippling of applause from the gallery, pursed his lips with the air of someone in doubt. Arthur decided that was play-acting because the judge immediately lit into Kwon. "Mr. Flett was arrested at a demonstration that you concede was lawful."

"That's right, milord. But my position is that the parole board, not the court, has the duty of determining whether the petitioner broke a condition –"

"But Mr. Beauchamp is saying that condition is unconstitutional, it flies in the face of the Charter. If so, what's left for the parole board to determine?"

"Well, ah, they have an overriding discretion in parole matters, and given that Mr. Flett has shown no indication of repentance –"

"Just a minute – they have an *overriding* discretion? You mean they override me?"

It went on like that for a few minutes. Singelar had obviously made up his mind early, but he had a good house to play to, and as a former prosecutor he probably saw a chance to establish credentials for being even handed. Arthur tended to get such breaks these days, after kicking around the courts for several decades. Respect came more with age than talent.

An ancient and lovely remedy, the habeas corpus, and it freed the corpus of Zachary Flett, who walked proudly from the room and gave Arthur a hug. "If I'm away three or four days, Savannah will understand. We have much work to do."

Arthur took that as the royal we. He watched as Zack was hoisted briefly by his disciples and borne to the escalator. He disappeared amid the throng waiting for him at the courthouse door.

~~~

The ferry to Garibaldi would not leave for several hours, so Arthur enjoyed a stroll to the old Gastown area, nexus between tidy, shiny uptown and the tourist no-go zone, the pocket of skid road known as the Downtown Eastside. In the eighties, he'd defected from his firm for several dismal years to run a practice for the poor here, defending losers and lushes while a loser and a lush himself. A time remembered patchily, scenes dimly returning of rowdy commotions in bars and restaurants, even courtrooms, the rest hidden behind an impenetrable fog of gin fumes and day-long hangovers.

Ah, but soon to be celebrated, those years of despair and cuck-oldom, in *A Thirst for Justice*. He recoiled from thoughts of being stripped bare by his biographer with his probing, unanswerable questions. "But I want to hear about *you*, your feelings." Unlovely images of his nakedness had been erupting in his dreams.

Gastown had been pimped up for the tourists several decades ago and hurriedly gentrified for the Winter Olympics, but retained a flavour of the past: cobbled streets and lanes, Blood Alley, Gaolers Mews, and that favourite of the pigeons, Gassy Jack's statue, hon-ouring the patron saint of West Coast drunks. Overlooking that statue was Arthur's destination: a nineteenth-century brick build-ing whose ground floor had till recently housed the Leap of Faith Prayer Centre, closed since its charismatic evangelist was arrested for bilking parishioners.

"Opening Soon," said a sign posted on the door: "The War Room." A martial arts training centre, a list of options ranging from karate and kick-boxing to "Commando Techniques" and "Disabling your Opponent." Several husky men and women were inside studying floor plans. Mats piled against walls, materials for a ring, ropes, corner posts.

An anti-Bhashyistan poster was stuck to the window: "Bring 'Em On!" Arthur couldn't tell if it was serious or a lampoon. Probably serious.

Entrance to the foyer and elevator was by a separate door bearing a shiny bronze plaque: "Macarthur, Brovak, Sage and Chance." The feisty little criminal law firm had apparently disappeared its ex-senior partner, Brian Pomeroy, and added the biographer Wentworth Chance. Arthur was anxious to locate the former and avoid the latter.

In this preserved low-density neighbourhood, the firm's third-floor offices claimed views of Maple Tree Square and Vancouver's hustling deep-water port on Burrard Inlet. Beyond, the North Shore Mountains were already coned with snow.

The receptionist gave him a cheery welcome – Arthur was known here, had privileges; its lawyers had all worked with him. Max Macarthur III was in court, John Brovak with clients, Chance in the library, but Augustina Sage was in the coffee lounge staring morosely out the window. Still attractive in her forties, a cloudburst of curly black hair.

"Why so blue?"

She looked up, smiled. "You don't have time to hear it, Arthur."

Another love affair must have bottomed out. She went through men like a mower through weeds, a failed lifetime search for the sensitive male.

She bussed him. "All men are assholes. All but you."

"You might benefit from a few rounds in the War Room, my dear."

"That joint gives me goosebumps. A gym where psychopaths learn ways to kill. Just what we need in the neighbourhood."

Some requisite chit-chat followed about the Bhashyistan crisis, the conspiracy theories, the government's stunned, slow reaction.

"And that," Arthur said, "brings me to Brian Pomeroy, hero of the Bhashyistani Democratic Revolutionary Front. Has he been ousted from the firm?"

"He ousted himself. That's another depressing subject. Just up and quit the practice. He went bonkers last year, you know. Became a cocainiac when his marriage went kaput."

Arthur knew all about it. Knew too much. He'd helped pick up the pieces, had to salvage a murder trial when Pomeroy fell apart in court and signed himself into a drug treatment centre.

"God only knows where he is. A cabin somewhere in the tundra of the Northwest Territories. He's gone Indian. That's not racist." Not from her. She was Cree on her mother's side. "He has a mail drop somewhere up there. I'll try to find it."

Arthur slipped behind the door as it opened. A high-pitched, excited voice. "Front desk says Mr. Beauchamp dropped by. Where did he get to?"

Augustina shrugged. "Search me."

Wentworth scowled. "Damn, he promised to spend a few days with me."

Arthur held his breath until the door closed again.

12

——

balmy ten Celsius on the last day of November on Garibaldi Island (ten below in Ottawa), the fields draped in mist, a splendid day for a jaunt to the General Store – a cherished routine: get the mail, buy groceries, catch up on island gossip, while away an hour of lazy afternoon.

From Blunder Bay to Potters Road to Centre Road, up the Breadloaf Hill hairpin, past the driveway to the handsome new community hall, and as one descends toward the flats a cinemascopic view of scores of four-wheeled relics rusting in Stoney's two acres. There was Arthur's beloved 1969 Fargo, waiting in line outside the garage, waiting for the master mechanic to install the rebuilt transmission promised two months ago. From within that garage, the revving of an engine, an ugly spew of exhaust from a broken window. His helpmate, a stubby fellow known only as Dog, scrambled out, coughing.

Stoney claimed to be selling his crop for top dollar, and there was evidence of that in the yard, a boat trailer with a shiny twenty-foot cabin cruiser. As well, it was rumoured that he had bought a hot-air balloon from a mainland hobbyist. Arthur shuddered, almost uncontrollably, at the thought of going up in one of those things. With Stoney.

Next door, the Shewfelts, as usual, were rushing the season: Christmas elves had appeared on their lawn. They'd be garishly lit at dusk, a frightening sight to any tourists wandering by. Soon, Santa, Rudolph, Donner, Blitzen, and the rest of the herd would make their annual appearance upon their flat roof.

Arthur had pulled into Garibaldi late yesterday, in good cheer after his rescue of Zack Flett, looking forward to some repose at Blunder Bay. A few days, maybe, while a powwow was set up with Erzhan's wife and landlord. He must engage with Brian Pomeroy too, who maintained a mail drop in Fort Malchance, a village in the Subarctic vastness, off the telephonic grid. Augustina Sage was trying to locate someone up there with a satellite phone, the mayor or chief or whoever was in charge.

Savannah Buckett, predictably, had been hosting a meeting when Arthur pulled in, lending her expertise to islanders opposing Starkers Cove, a condo development at the bottom of Norbert Road. That curling country byway was to be widened to highways standards, a waterfront acreage to be deforested. "When on Garibaldi, act locally," she said. "Save Lower Mount Norbert Road," said their stencilled signs.

Savannah had rewarded Arthur with a bone-crushing hug for freeing Zack, who'd called from Vancouver, where he was conferring with radical soldiers of protest in the inner city. He was off to the Kootenays next, taking on a larger role, organizing, speaking at rallies, seeking coalescence among eco-activists. Savannah seemed not to be pining for her mate – maybe she needed a break from their squabbles.

That night, while reading in bed, Arthur had been startled to see her enter his bedroom, in her pyjamas, looking confused. A sleepwalking episode. She'd confessed to bunking in his room after some chilly set-tos with Zack, so Arthur presumed she'd acted out of unconscious habit. After dazed hesitation, she'd reversed herself, descended to the main-floor bedroom.

He took a turn past the Bulbaconi vineyard, another failed enterprise by another hobby-farming dilettante, this year's crop green and small and hard as pebbles. Another curve, and Hopeless Bay opened up, and he could see carpenters hoisting roof beams for Abraham Makepeace's new tavern. The dour, skeletal postmaster-bootlegger was finally going legitimate.

Wildly out of character with the venerable old store, the addition was of radical design, cantilevered over the saltchuck, offering opportunities for the drunk and depressed to contemplate a watery end. In the meantime, it was business as usual in the enclosed porch, which for years had provided liquid relief to islanders. Practically every local had signed the petition in support of the lounge licence, all attesting to the owner's fault-free history.

The five poker players at the far end of the porch seemed weary and worn, faces stubbled with old growth – all but Emily LeMay's – and reeking of booze and sweaty effort.

"They been at it for four days and four nights." Makepeace rang up Arthur's few purchases, staples for the kitchen. "Some drop out, others join. Herman Schloss hasn't slept for two nights running, only stops to piss and shit." Schloss, a music impresario from Los Angeles – either retired or on the run – had recently bought twenty-three acres up by Sunrise Cove. He brushed long tangled hair from his glazed eyes, peeked at a down card, folded.

Makepeace brought out a grab bag of mail, uncollected for several days. "Your *Geographic* and *Lawyer* magazines, postcard from your grandson in Australia, he's looking to graduate from high school with top honours, so you may want to wire him a little reward. This here fancy letter is from Simon Fraser University, they want to give you an honorary degree next year."

Arthur picked it up. The flap was sealed, didn't seem tampered with. "Abraham, I'm not making complaint about your reading my mail, that seems part of the local folkways, but please tell me how you know what's inside this envelope."

"You hold it up like this." Toward the fluorescent lamp. "Half the stuff coming in here is junk mail, which, if you recall, you asked me to intercept." He sounded peeved. "It's a lot of extra work."

"Well done. You're absolutely right."

"Overdue notice from the phone company. Maybe them two renegades up at your place aren't taking care of business." He reached under the counter. "Here's a roll of posters they ordered. Bundle of mail for your good lady. Mostly friendly, a couple neutral, one hate letter."

Arthur stuffed everything into his backpack with the groceries, but didn't shoulder it yet, took a moment in the lounge with the several kibitzing locals. Oddly, they seemed more interested in watching the poker game than yakking about Bhashyistan's war declaration. Maybe because it was beyond contemplation. How far Garibaldi Island seemed from the wearying world.

Arthur felt privileged to be in on the making of a rumour about Starkers Cove, so-called because of its summer use by local skinny-dippers. "It's gonna be a nudist colony." "Where'd you hear that?" "Look how they adopted its historic name. I saw them people at the bylaw meeting, they looked tanned all over." Other vital news of the day: the Sproules's ram sneaked into Mabel Grundy's pen and seduced her heirloom ewes.

He shared a coffee with Al Noggins, Reverend Al, as everyone called him, the local Anglican priest, who was ruefully contemplating the poker players. "I'm here on assignment from Schloss's wife. If I don't get him out of that game, she's going to shoot him. I can't budge him, so she's going to have to do that."

The undercapitalized Hollywood impresario, it turned out, had lost four cords of winter wood to Ernie Priposki, his DVD collection to Emily LeMay, his twenty-foot cabin cruiser to Stoney, and two of his twenty-three acres to Cud Brown.

"Duck. Here she comes."

Mookie was her name, minor fame as a 1980s B-movie starlet, still attractive but red-faced now with anger. Ignoring Reverend Al, striding directly up to Schloss, pulling him by his pigtail. "Goddamnit, Herm, you're coming home right *now.*"

"Last hand, baby."

"You said that at eleven o'clock last night."

"Killer hand, babe."

If it was a bluff, it didn't work. Local cultural icon Cud Brown, a scrofulous poet who subsisted on grants and readings and part-time jobs, raised him back the two acres of land he'd won. Everyone else threw in their hands, stared solemnly at Schloss, who frantically scribbled something on a slip of paper.

"I thought we agreed, man," said Cud. "No more IOUs."

Reverend Al bent to Arthur's ear. "Cud wants his Land Rover. Herman dotes on that car."

Mookie jerked his pigtail again. "Let's fucking get out of here while you've got your skin."

"Two nights with her," Schloss blurted.

"With who?" Cud asked.

"Mookie. A weekend."

Arthur couldn't read anything in her face, not even astonishment. Lost in the State of Catatonia.

"Don't blame me if she decides to stay for a week." Cud laid down his hand. "Full house, aces on top."

Schloss laid down four nines and a joker. "We did it, baby!"

Mookie toppled him backwards over his chair, and he somehow managed to get stuck in the rungs. As he flailed she kicked him in the ribs while howling curses. Reverend Al finally pulled her away, while others scrambled to pick up cards, chips, and IOUs that had spilled to the floor.

After several minutes, peace was restored, and after a long debate about apportioning the spoils the game resumed, the players despondent over losing the mark. Herman Schloss was last seen fleeing by foot from his presumptive life partner.

Arthur's appetite for local colour satisfied – Margaret would delight in his dramatic retelling – he was about to hoist his backpack when he heard a voice behind him, chillingly recognizable. "I heard there was a game."

He turned to look upon smiling Ray DiPalma – the crisp new jeans and Stetson defined him as a tenderfoot from the city. Arthur edged away, unsettled, confused. Should this man be in a ward for the emotionally disturbed? Why was he leeching onto Arthur?

But DiPalma paid him no heed. He was answering a come-hither call from the poker players, another city slicker to be skinned.

~~~

Two hours later, in the shank of the warm and misty afternoon, still grumbling about DiPalma's intrusion on his sanctuary, Arthur was tossing bales into his hay wagon, the last of the fall crop from the northeast pasture. Too damp for animal feed after recent rains, but fine for mulching the garden.

A white compact slowed on Potters Road and disappeared behind a dense thicket of blackberries that served as a natural fence. Seconds later, as Arthur was about to mount his tractor, he heard the frantic squeal of spinning tires, and he sighed and clomped off to help. He could make out the white car, glimpses of it, through the thick tangle of leaves and thorny vines.

Even the sorriest fool wouldn't park among blackberries, but somehow the incident made sense when it was confirmed for him, unsurprisingly, that the driver was Ray DiPalma – who was now struggling through the heavy growth, catching his new country clothes on the barbed vines, gingerly prying them apart, ducking, crawling.

Arthur ducked too, so he could see him, five feet away, his wire-rims hanging from his nose, a bloody scratch on his cheek, a lesser one on his forehead, others on his unprotected hands.

"Arthur, just the man I want to see. You alone?"

"Yes. Stay there, I'll cut you out." The preferred alternative being to attach a chain to his leg and pull him out with the tractor. He retrieved long-handled clippers from the toolkit behind the tractor seat, and on returning found DiPalma squatting, lighting a cigarette.

"Saw you pitching hay, needed a place to park where I wouldn't be seen. What a tinpot car, no traction, I kind of slid in there. You look peeved, Arthur, I don't blame you, but I had to see you about Zachary Flett – they have him down as some kind of ringleader."

"We've figured that out, Ray." Arthur was close enough now to take in the smell not of nicotine but of cannabis, with an underlying base of Makepeace's cheap rum.

"There was a crew working him over all weekend – he's tough. So the deal is this: I was assigned to nose around here on Garibaldi. I told Crumwell, my handler, that I'd been in your apartment, that I'm infiltrating you guys – I had to, in case it got out. He congratulated me, he thinks I'm doing a masterful job. I'm back onside with him."

Arthur gave him a hand, pulled him to freedom. "Am I to understand that this Crumwell fellow has sent you here to spy?" Arthur's relationship with DiPalma was threatening to become a comedy of errors. Or no comedy at all, something dangerous. It was hard to believe DiPalma's superiors were so dull as not to know he was in a state of near collapse. If indeed he was, if it was not a pretense.

Arthur led him to the tractor, where he kept a first-aid kit, and brought out ointment and Band-Aids. "Crumwell thinks you think I'm on your side. Which is true. The last part, I mean. I *am* on your side, but he doesn't know I'm actually a double agent. In other words, he thinks you think I'm embittered because of the way I was treated over that lost computer . . . It's a little complicated." Lost in these spiralling convolutions, he settled onto a hay bale, began wiping his glasses.

"This is my home, Ray, my sanctuary. It is not a place where I make a habit of entertaining spies. Please reserve the next flight back to Ottawa."

"Whoa, Arthur, you're my lawyer, trust me the same way I trust you. I mean, you're like a . . . like a mentor, a father figure."

That was something Arthur dreaded hearing. He unhitched the hay wagon. "I had better pull your car out of there."

"Arthur, please listen, this is our chance to feed the dogs of war at CSIS. Throw them a few bones, send them off on a wild goose chase. To make this work I've got to be seen as cozying up to Savannah and Zachary. The more confidence Crumwell has in me, the more he'll share with me, and the more likely I'll get inside access about who did what to Abzal Erzhan. That make sense?"

Arthur had to still a deep unease. Was DiPalma working from a brilliantly conceived script? For now he would stick by his earlier diagnosis: a nervous breakdown, complicated by resentment toward his superiors and by his new, greener *Weltanschauung*. And by excessive intake of ill-advised substances.

"So they've created a legend for me, as we call it, a fake biography. I'm one of those anti-American Americans who come up here to escape from the evils of capitalism. I'm an environmentalist, I'm looking for land, and I stumble onto Zack's group and let them know I'm a friendly. You saw the way I can meld into the community, hang around, play a little poker with the boys, share some hooch and a toke or two. I met a pal of yours named Stonewell, by the way, he gave me a sampler." He gestured with the joint, then pinched it out.

"I will not introduce you as an anti-American American land buyer."

"I implore you, Arthur. As we speak, Zack Flett is on a train heading for Revelstoke. An agent is sitting behind him. Others will follow the VW van that's going to pick him up. With me in deep cover, they'll pull these agents out – as I told you, they're stretched."

"I fail to grasp how this double-agent business can work if you don't confess your role to Zack and Savannah."

"But then it could get out on the street."

"It will be on the street as soon as they look you up on the Web. You were outed by the *Toronto Star*."

"Sure, but that was a few years ago. You didn't recognize me right away . . . Okay, you have a point, there could be blowback. Maybe I have to be more up front." He stood, paced. "By the way, where's the nearest bank machine?"

"Garibaldi Island isn't blessed with bank machines, I'm pleased to say."

"I had a bad run at that game, I think I got hustled. Any chance I could borrow a stake to get by for a day or two?"

"I can advance enough to put you on a ferry."

"Darn it, I can get some dynamite stuff if we do this right. Rumours are flying around at Ogilvie Road that Erzhan was abducted."

"Ogilvie Road?"

"CSIS. Nobody talks details, or maybe they don't know any. You've got to friendly up with that landlord, Zandoo, he knows something." He looked about, as if suspecting listeners were behind every bush. "Do you know them well enough, Zack and Savannah? Would they backstop me on this?"

Arthur would not play falsely with Savannah and Zack – their militancy often made him uncomfortable, but they were friends. At the same time he didn't want to discourage DiPalma – if reliable, his information could ignite a political firestorm.

"Okay, let me reassemble the pieces here. If you were to carefully explain the situation to Savannah –" DiPalma broke off, quickly slipping behind the tractor as Constable Pound's van came down the road, slowing as it reached the blackberries.

The engine cut and a door slammed. "Is that you, Arthur?" Pound was barely visible on the other side of the tangle.

"Yes, Ernst, I'm bringing in the late hay."

"Well, this here has the look of an infraction. Driving without due care and attention."

"The gentleman was parking, Ernst. He slid into the bushes."

"He a friend of yours?"

Arthur sighed. "Yes."

~~~

Dear Hank, Katie, Cassie, Jessie, Mom,

I don't know where to start. All I know is we're half a world away from Saskatchewan, and we're hiding out at a farm, a Bhashyistan version of a B & B that seems to be held together by staples. They call it a yurt. (It's COLD in here. And the smells! It's lined with sheep fat!)

I can't imagine Exotic Asia Tours Inc. hasn't got word out that we have disappeared from the face of the earth, and what I don't want you to do is worry, if you even get this letter, because we're being looked after. This craziness can't last forever. The story we get, from the local radio as translated by our hosts who thank God speak Russian, the husband at least, is Canada is being blamed for shooting down a Bhashyistan plane with a whole load of its politicians on board, though I'm not sure if we've got it all straight, especially the business about a declaration of war.

But here's what happened. I won't go into detail about how we got here because that's in an earlier note I mailed from the Igorgrad airport (and God, was that a task!). Anyway, there was no connecting flight to Almaty because all the Air Bhashyistan planes were grounded and the airport closed.

Maxine, Ivy, and I were taken into this office at the airport, where the head of immigration said we'd have to go to jail for not having visas, and we were just petrified, and then he said instead of jail we could pay him "the regular fine," he called it, of two hundred dollars each, and fortunately we had enough in rubles but not much more, and of course try to find a bank machine in this place. The official seemed insulted when we asked for a receipt, but he let us go, and we got our bags and headed outside.

That's where we met Mr. and Mrs. Babichov, they were holding up a sign offering lodging, in English, German, and Russian, a kind of farm stay, which given Maxine and I were born on a farm looked like a better deal than some of the hotels which also had people out there jostling for our business. Plus they seemed like kind folk, which they have proved to be. Abrakam and Flaxseed (I call her that, I can't pronounce her full name). He comes from Omsk in Siberia, she's more local. They're in their seventies, their children have all flown the nest.

Anyway, we jumped into this decrepit old Lada and headed off away from the city about thirty clicks out, rolling hills, pine forests, meadows, sheep, sheep, sheep, and we get to this paint-peeling frame farmhouse, which isn't much, sort of like Bob Slotznyk's dump down by the Yorkton highway, in a permanent state of falling down.

Back of it, next to their barn, is their rental quarters, our yurt, our home for the last four days. (Yurts get rented out around here so tourists can get a taste of local colour.) Two beds in a makeshift loft, where it isn't so stinky as below plus you get more heat from the barrel stove but also more smoke. So Ivy because of her asthma sleeps on the cot below.

But mostly we stay in the main house, where I am now, writing this. Abrakam and Flaxseed seem to be more than happy with the little we can pay them, and their home is our home, sort of thing. They're not letting on to anyone we're here except for a few trusted neighbours of their faith, which is Baha'i, not Muslim like most around here, and they're really not supposed to practise their religion. We explained we're from a religious minority ourselves, Doukhobors, even though we're not all that observant.

As we get to know our hosts better, they're opening up, giving us clues that they're not very sympathetic to the national government, which is a dictatorship. We've taken to helping them with the chores, but when they see anyone coming up the driveway (you can spot them easily, three miles down the hill) we have to hide. Abrakam says we could be in great danger, being Canadian. We're so relieved our saviours are so protective, so wise to the ways of this strange land.

Well, we've finally got used to the fatty mutton and sheep's milk and some weird kind of curd as part of our daily diet, and we have our cribbage board which I play with Abrakam in the evenings, and there's some old Russian novels — you wouldn't believe how the language is coming back. It's actually quite pretty around here, the valleys and the far snowy mountains, but it's getting really wintry, the snow sticking, and the little river down in the valley is into freeze-up.

No phone here, and I wouldn't trust it anyway. Abrakam says he'll try to find a safe way to mail this letter, but I told him not to take any chances. We heard some Canadians are in jail in Igorgrad, big wheels, oil company executives, and with their clout, if they're in trouble, we'll stay right here, thank you.

Meanwhile, I hope nobody in Ottawa does anything stupid to make matters worse. We're about five hundred miles from the Russian border, Siberia actually, and it's way the hell over the mountains, so we're sticking it out until peace has been declared.

Take care. Don't worry. Be strong.

Gobs of love,

Jill XOXOXO

13

———

inally, at sundown, Savannah's visitors left — a boisterous bunch from Vancouver Island this time, foes of fish farms — and it wasn't until they were prepping dinner (unfarmed salmon, local) that Arthur told Savannah about DiPalma. She took it as a joke, naturally, when he asked if she'd mind being infiltrated, and continued merrily cutting up lemons. "Hey, invite him for dinner."

"I'll summon him from his B & B." The Lovenest, Emily LeMay, prop., specializing in season in honeymooners, anyone who dares during the rest of the year.

Finally convinced he was serious, she demanded a trustworthy witness, not just Arthur, before she would consort with "a fucking CSIS agent." Reverend Al Noggins was their choice, three times winner of the Garibaldi Upstanding Citizen Award, and he arrived almost simultaneously with DiPalma, bringing several bottles of his prize-winning fall fair wine, misunderstanding this as a social event.

For three hours, over barbecued salmon, then apple pie, they listened with incredulity to DiPalma, his words flowing out as copiously as the prize wine flowed in. He seemed unconcerned about confiding in Reverend Al — the priest might be Protestant but he was a man of the cloth, and that was enough for this God-fearing secret agent.

Savannah decided to play along with "whatever's going on," as she put it. But after the guests left, she expressed doubts about DiPalma that echoed those of the local member of Parliament. "I'm going to watch and wait and see."

"I have some people checking him out. Nothing to lose."

"I wonder."

Though it was nearly midnight in Ottawa, Arthur chanced a call to Margaret, whose line had been tied up earlier, and got her out of bed. "He's here." Breathless, low, he wasn't sure who might be listening.

"Who?"

"You know."

"Not *him*."

"Yes, on Garibaldi."

"Arthur, you have to back *off* from him. This isn't good. Damn, don't do anything bizarre. I have an early interview. I'll call when I can."

Arthur felt like a resentful child, unfairly spanked. He retreated to the non-judgmental solace of his old club chair, opened a book recommended to him, *Empires of the Steppes*.

He was three hours into its eight hundred pages, halfway through the history of Bhashyistan, when he nodded off, and soon he was playing lead actor in the theatre of the subconscious. This time, not a sweaty nightmare of the carnage on Colonel By Drive, starring instead Ray DiPalma, sneaking up on him, or jumping from behind a door or tree, morphing from clown to evil genius to mad Hamlet, frightening Arthur with his intimate disclosures. "I love you like a father." Weeping, clutching him.

He woke at an hour uncertain with a painful thud: *Empires of the Steppes* had fallen on his foot. He massaged a sore toe, then a creaky neck, then switched off the lamp and manoeuvred toward the stairs, finding his way in darkness relieved only by a glow from the kitchen.

He looked in – the fridge door was open, and Savannah, in a

frozen state of unconscious indecision, in pyjama top and bikini bottoms, was staring blankly at the leftover macaroni. She'd been dieting, but the unaware self had not paid heed. Averting his eyes from her bent-over bottom, he sought to gently wake her, speaking her name. She was unresponsive.

When he sought to pry her hand from the fridge door, she jumped, looked wildly about, stepped quickly back, the fridge door swinging shut, darkness enshrouding them.

"Who are you?" she cried. "What are you doing?"

"It's just me, Savannah."

"Who? Arthur? Where are we?" She took some time to orient herself, even after Arthur found the light switch. She blinked, looked about, breathing heavily. "I should be in bed, I'm sorry."

Arthur followed her there, settled her in, made hasty retreat upstairs.

~~~

"Breakfast!" Savannah hollered from downstairs. Coffee's seductive aroma, the sizzle of bacon. No vegan she, unlike her stringy, over-healthy partner.

"Coming!" He padded off to his bathroom. Normally, he shared kitchen duties, but somehow he'd over-adjusted his inner clock to West Coast time, slept in till almost nine on this first day of December.

Wet-haired and gleaming from his shower, he found Savannah cheerily breaking eggs into a pan, listening to the CBC, no residual damage from last night. Rarely did she discuss her sleepwalking, shrugging it off as a minor life nuisance, and she didn't mention it this morning. She greeted him with a bold hug, however, a full body press that threatened to arouse (he was ashamed to admit) an inappropriate physiological response. But she drew away in time.

"What's on the news?" he asked.

"Bhashyistan. This thing looks like it's subsided into a phony war, world leaders huddling, Security Council in no hurry to meet, NATO sitting on the sidelines. Nobody seems to be taking this seriously but you, me, and the Ultimate Leader. And maybe that freaky geek you saddled me with."

~~~

Arthur got tied up in the early afternoon because Papillon, the adventurous nanny, got stuck in a fence attempting one of her miraculous escapes. When he returned to the house, a dozen locals were already in session debating strategies against the developers of Starkers Cove.

Among them was Ray DiPalma, who had penetrated the Committee to Save Lower Mount Norbert Road. He was squatting on the floor, polite, unobtrusive, a newcomer though well enough regarded, especially by those who had a little acreage to sell to an anti-American American. Savannah was guiding the debate, a facilitator more than agitator. One begins by politicizing people locally, she'd instructed Arthur, with issues that affect them just down the road, issues they can grasp.

Scraps of conversation, overheard as Arthur washed up and puttered about the kitchen: "We had a lovely view of that beach, and now this." "So what if they go around buck naked – somebody tell me what's the big deal." "Well, we're appalled, aren't we, Desmond, at the prospect of seeing . . . well, *everything*." "Yes, dear, if you say so." "Some folks got a bug about nudity, not me. The body is the temple of the . . . whatever."

Savannah: "I thought we were fighting a road widening and a clear-cut."

This was politics in the raw, as it were – a livelier debate, however, than any Arthur had witnessed in Ottawa.

During a refreshment break (Maud Miller's muffins, Zoë Noggins's biscuits, Blunder Bay's goat cheese), Ray shuffled up to

Arthur, who was outside plotting his escape. "This is working, Mr. B., I'm getting in with the locals. What great people. Straight shooters. I could really dig living here."

Arthur didn't encourage him. "I feel quite uncomfortable about this, Ray. I almost feel I'm betraying my friends."

"I'm on their side on this Norbert Road campaign. Keep Garibaldi green. Save the trees, save the planet. The nudity issue, personally I don't care. But I do have some experience in that area, Janet and I having frequented a naturist club in Quebec, though just out of curiosity."

"Janet? I thought she was Janice."

"Why did I say Janet? Anyway, I'm thinking of doing a little fact-finding mission, check out this Starkers bunch. Maybe pretend I'm interested in investing."

"And what do you suppose your boss is going to say when he finds out you're investigating a supposed nudist group?"

"All in the line of duty. Speaking of getting naked, what's the lowdown on this Emily LeMay and her Lovenest B & B? I don't know how many times she's asked me to jump in the hot tub with her, and there's a no-clothes policy. She comes on a little strong."

"Ah, yes, the local sex goddess. That's her modus operandi, the hot tub. Soon she'll have you hog-tied to her four-poster."

"Oh my God, then what?"

The fellow seemed to lack a sense of humour. Arthur still couldn't quite get a handle on him. Naive at times, but glib too, and with a disarming frankness. Some of his pro-green rhetoric seemed studied. Calling his wife Janet was a highly unusual slip. Arthur was expecting a kind of security check on him from Antoine Salzarro, who had been with Public Security and had met DiPalma several times.

"It's Margaret, Arthur." Savannah came out, passed him a cellphone, a borrowed one – DiPalma seemed sure their line wasn't being intercepted, but Savannah was less confident. She hustled Ray back inside. "Do you want to help with the letter-writing campaign or do picket duty?"

Margaret spoke briskly. "Ten-thirty on Saturday in Montreal, at a mosque on Sherbrooke Street. Vana Erzhan will be there, and the landlord. Also the local imam, Dr. Mossalen. You'll have to book a flight to Dorval for Friday. I'll pick you up there and arrange a place to stay." Rapid-fire, businesslike, a woman on the march, things to do. Politics and city living had sped her up.

"The tension around here is nearly intolerable, Arthur. Nothing *seems* to be happening, but you sense underlying currents. We don't know what cabinet's doing, thinking, planning. The Tory majority is down to five with DuWallup shunted off to the Senate. Finnerty's favourite footman, Charley Thiessen, has his portfolio for the time being. The P.M. hasn't been around for Question Period, and his ministers are being totally obtuse. We're worried they're about to spring the Emergencies Act on us. Bug all the phone lines, demand DNA from half the population, seize all the computers."

"Slow down, dear. You're running a little hot."

"I *am* hot. What's going on with you know who?"

"He's currently helping organize a campaign to save Norbert Road from a threatened invasion of nudists."

"Spare me the details. He's such a wild card, Arthur. I really feel it's a mistake to have got so tight with him."

"I'll give you a complete report on Saturday, my dear."

At least she didn't lambaste him this time. But Savannah had already talked to her, persuaded her to let the show run a few more days.

Arthur returned to the living room, grabbed a muffin, and slipped out for his daily hike just as Ray was saying, "I have an idea."

~~~

The next day, Thursday, was brittle bright, the thermometer climbing to new global warming heights, perfect for a pound-pruning jaunt to Gwendolyn Valley Park. Before setting off, Arthur listened to his messages – three from Wentworth Chance and one from Antoine Salzarro. Arthur used the borrowed cellphone to call him back.

"His only major blot involved the infamous stolen computer," Salzarro said. "Otherwise, an outstanding agent, with a splendid record from his several years working out of Belgrade. Came to the service right out of Carleton, master's degree, honours. Quite the athlete there, I understand."

"*Athlete?*"

"Played right wing with the Ravens. Rowing. Water polo."

"I see." Though Arthur didn't. "Family history? Parents? Spouse?"

"As I recall, there was something about his mother . . . yes, it comes to me she died very young of cancer. I'll do what I can to find out more."

"But there was a mini-scandal, Antoine, was there not, about some sites found on his computer?"

"That does come back. Something to do with . . . partner-swapping? A nudist club? I remember we all had a great laugh over that."

"And was he relegated to some lowly form of deskwork?"

"Not for long. He was considered too valuable to waste."

"Wife problems?"

"I believe he had difficulty letting her go."

"Do you recall her name?"

"Afraid not."

"Bad habits? Smoking, drinking?"

"Aware of none. Quite the health nut, it seems to me. I'll see what more I can find out."

Arthur promised to pop in to see him on his return to the capital. He felt dissatisfied, suspicious, even angry – at DiPalma, for not quite being as advertised. Yet almost everything added up – the drinking may have started after his marriage began to dissolve. But athletic? This fellow stumbled around on two left legs. But maybe the drinking accounted for that too.

Arthur stayed on the phone, booked a ten a.m. flight the next day from the Victoria airport. That meant he'd have to catch the seven-fifteen ferry. And that meant, since Savannah didn't drive . . . Bob Stonewell.

"Garibaldi Taxi Service and Hot Air Holidays," said the answering machine. "How may we help you?"

Garibaldi's sole taxi operator engaged in the dubious business practice of rarely being by his phone, but was usually in his garage or his charnel yard of skeletonized vehicles. No major detour required, he'd hike up by Centre Road.

Puffing from the hairpin climb, Arthur saw Stoney and his support group gathered in his front yard – missing was Hamish McCoy, reportedly still living high in Berlin, being coddled by the arts community.

Stretched out on the ground was a giant polyester sheet, pancake shaped, striped like a barber pole – the hot-air balloon. The group was in head-scratching discussion, studying a manual, presumably instructions on how to assemble this inflatable flying machine.

Seeing Arthur enter by the rickety gate, Stoney ambled toward him, pausing to pat the bow of the twenty-foot cabin cruiser he'd won from Herman Schloss.

"A beauty, eh? But what I want to direct your attention to is this baby here." The balloon. "We're not quite prepared for liftoff – there are some safety rules we got to adhere to. Like you don't want to go up until that propane tank is full and what they call the blast valve is working. As soon as we figure everything out, the world's our oyster."

"Surely you need a licence of some sort to go ballooning."

"Yeah, like for pilots, but this is Garibaldi Island, the last frontier, ordinary rules don't apply. Soon as we figure out how to get this sucker aloft, we're going into business, island hopping. That there gondola can carry six normal-sized tourists." A commodious wicker basket.

Arthur saw this as a pipe dream – surely on sober reappraisal Stoney would put this project aside, as he had many other of his airy-fairy ideas. The middle of January. High over the Salish Sea, at the mercy of every gusting wind.

Stoney patted Dog on the head. "When we get the kinks worked out, Dog here has volunteered for the honour of being test pilot. Right, Dog?"

The squat little fellow puffed himself up as if to indicate he was indeed the man for the job, but his strained smile hinted he wasn't quite so sure.

Arthur asked Stoney about the Fargo.

"Next in line. Give me two more days."

"You said that two months ago."

"This time I mean it. Anything else I can do, sire, I'm always at your service."

"I need a pickup at six-thirty tomorrow."

"No problem."

"In the morning."

"The *morning?*"

"If it's not too much to ask."

"Well, six-thirty tends to be outside my normal working hours – I'm usually in bed by then. But in your case, as a valued customer, there'll be only a small surcharge. Unpossible ain't in my dictionary."

Arthur began wishing he'd arranged for a backup, an early rising neighbour, but he hated to impose.

Stoney returned to the task at hand. "Okay, boys, let's figure out how to get this baby airborne. We ain't got all week."

~~~

That evening, over garden greens and leftover macaroni and cheese, there was again no mention of Arthur's rude interruption of Savannah's automatonlike foray into the fridge. He wondered if she remembered any of it.

As he settled into his club chair with his book and a mug of tea, Savannah took a call from Zachary, a guarded conversation. "I think you should include Garibaldi Island in your next itinerary, Zack. Lots to do here. Lots to talk about . . . No, damn it, Sunday *wouldn't* be too early. Get your ass down here."

A severe tone of urgency that went beyond their usual bickering. Arthur could only speculate as to what might be his reaction to Ray DiPalma and his counterspying.

Savannah disconnected, went to the computer. "He wants us to look at YouTube."

Arthur peered over her shoulder as she expertly manoeuvred through the offerings on the screen. Here it was, another production of Third Son of Ultimate Leader Films. Again the chubby face of Mukhamet Khan Ivanovich, chief geek of Bhashyistan.

"Always first with the news that counts, today we presenting footage of national holiday for most terrible day in history, when Great Father was shot in Canada by cowardly scum. Here we see display of armed might."

A uniformed battalion goose-stepping past the presidential palace, the Ultimate Leader on a reviewing stand, his hand over his breast, advisers behind him, almost a parody of May Day marches from the salad days of Stalin and Brezhnev. The troops seemed ragtag, some in helmets, others in turbans or other traditional headgear, rifles pointed haphazardly in the air. Rockets trundled by, then a score of tanks and other armoured vehicles.

"Here we showing world we are ready for coming conflict with Canadians who have no stomach for fight with patriotic army and air force." The latter consisted of a couple of MiGs zooming overhead. The display seemed reasonably threatening, if not to high international standards. Less fearsome was a troop of dancing maidens – they stopped before the reviewing stand and put on a commendable hula-hoop demonstration of synchronized twirling.

A fadeout, then a closer view of Mad Igor, still on the stand, speaking from notes in his Turkic tongue. Mukhamet translated: "If spineless Canadians not responding to war declaration, he is saying, our country very soon declares victory, mission accomplished. He is saying reparations of ten billion dollars is price of peace. Not taking less, is firm offer. And here is reminder to Canadians watching."

An exterior view of a forbidding fortress: narrow barred windows, wooden shutters. "Here is impenetrable state prison in Igorgrad, and here on ground floor is section for prisoners of war." Cut to a cell occupied by the five languishing Alberta oilmen, staring sullenly at the camera. The national flag then filled the screen, with its three lightning bolts, and the video concluded with the stirring but fading notes of the Bhashyistan anthem.

"Wow," Savannah said. "Here we show shitload of bluster."

"How do you think our government should react?"

"Ignore 'em."

"And the so-called prisoners of war?"

"Let them do penance."

"That seems hard. They're merely employees."

"Okay, but schemers, a veep, two lawyers, fat cats. I mean maybe some are innocent, the accountant, the geologist, but if the Alta board of directors had any guts they'd offer themselves in exchange. This is all about oil, Arthur, and bribery and greed and extortion. Sure, these Bhashies are a joke, but the world doesn't need their oil, it's planetary poison. Maybe this is a wakeup call."

Arthur was troubled by her stern, unyielding view. His softer heart went out to those five unfortunates in a cold, foreign jail. But he was just as troubled by the truth she spoke. Margaret had often said as much: Canada – the world – needs shock therapy to recover from the self-destructive sins of the last several profligate decades.

~~~

Dreams returned that night of charred bodies in a burning limousine. But they were succeeded by images less awful, more complex. He was in court, speaking a language he didn't understand, to jurors laughing at him. Then he was running across the steppes, but with sludgelike speed, he wasn't going to make the seven-fifteen ferry. He found himself lying on the moss, felt a shifting, a turbulence, something soft falling across his chest – gently, like a caress, a woman's caress.

"Hey, Arthur, man, you wanna make that ferry or not?"

This familiar voice from the realm of the conscious brought him half-awake. Stoney was standing at the open doorway to his bedroom, gaping, as astonished as if he'd just witnessed a landing of Martians. Nestled beside Arthur, on her side, her arm draped loosely over his chest, a warm breast at his ribs, was Savannah Buckett, in a deep and sonorous sleep.

Hoping this was a continuation of the dream, knowing it was not, Arthur gently lifted her arm off, aghast, barely able to speak. "Forgot to set the alarm. I'll be down in a moment."

"Right," Stoney said. "I'll, uh, be in the car."

Rattled, Arthur donned some clothes, fled the room, grabbed a small, pre-packed suitcase, and raced out into the morning darkness to join Stoney in his taxi, an aging Buick. It was just before seven – he would make it to the boat on time.

Stoney concentrated on his driving – difficult enough, given one headlight was burnt out. For a few minutes he said nothing, grinning occasionally at Arthur in a conspiratorial way. Finally: "Didn't know you had it in you, Arthur."

"She must have sleepwalked right into my bed."

A guffaw. "Nice try, but that ain't gonna wash. You gotta come up with something a little more conceivable. When the cat's away, eh? Who could blame you, she's a pinup, man. I got new respect."

"You whisper one word and I'll strangle you with my bare hands."

"Well, that puts a new light on our long relationship, don't it? I wanna cry when I hear you speak with such distrust. I'd cut out my tongue before I'd betray my friends. I got a code of honour. See no evil, speak no evil, that's my golden rule."

As they pulled into the ferry dock, he added: "Anyway, man, no one's gonna believe it."

14

———

Huck Finnerty stared at his sad and haggard reflection in the washroom mirror. He would have to change his shirt; his sweat glands were working like bilge pumps. Deodorant. A couple of Tylenols. A nip of rye. He was having trouble breathing. It occurred to him he'd better cut down on the booze and burgers or he wouldn't last the session.

Question Period had done all this damage. He felt he'd been pepper-sprayed by each opposition leader in turn. That loudmouth Liberal, Cloudy McRory, screaming and sputtering as he tabled his non-confidence motion.

Patience, he'd urged. Crises are made only graver by ill-thought-out reactions. The government was *not* dithering. It was not in freefall but rising to the occasion. It was working quietly behind the scenes in the time-honoured Canadian way.

With 156 members to the opposition's 151, the government would hobble off with a vote of confidence, but some backbenchers were restless – he'd picked up faltering, disaffection, Lafayette's people whispering, conspiring, even as they listlessly thumped their desks. His whip had been working the caucus relentlessly, intimating that dissidents would be hanged from the beams of the Peace Tower.

All he needed was some breathing room. A few more days until Operation Eager Beaver was launched. A medal of dishonour for whoever came up with that corny name.

E.K. Boyes was waiting impatiently by Finnerty's desk, organizing the clutter, lining up memos to be read. "Admirable, Huck, truly admirable. Calm in the midst of the storm. Mind you, referring to the socialist leader as 'the honourable windbag from Winnipeg North' might have crossed the line." A snicker. Whenever the chief of staff smiled – not often – he had the look of a contented gargoyle.

Finnerty lowered his aching bulk into his high-backed swiveller – it was like a wheelchair, he could do loops around the room, he never really had to get up. "Where are we meeting?"

"Right here. You'll want to say this was hatched in your office. Assuming matters don't go awry."

"They won't," he said overconfidently. That *would* be the end of his government. Thumps from above – the Opposition leader's office was directly above him, McRory a heavy walker. Occasionally you could hear him bellow.

"The issue of whether to invoke war – uh, emergency measures is still to be resolved, Huck. Lafayette won't say so publicly, but he believes we can justify it."

"That's real brave of him." Finnerty wasn't ready to touch that one and risk losing their eleven francophone seats. "You notice he wasn't there to take any of the flack? He didn't ask me if he could take the day off."

"You need him onside for now. If Eager Beaver works, he'll either be your obedient puppy or you can cast him adrift." The gnome, for all his shrivelled morality, was comfortable to have around calling the shots.

Finnerty rolled over to a sideboard, surveyed its offerings of hard-boiled eggs, sliced salami, salted thins, pickles. No. He opened a Diet Pepsi instead.

E.K. leafed through the dispatches. "One of the Bhashyistan embassy staff has joined the ranks of those seeking refugee status. We have something to gain from that. He's familiar with the Igorgrad prison."

"Former head torturer, I suppose."

"Nikolai Globbo. He was assistant deputy director of political corrections."

"Say no more."

~~~

Globbo looked up nervously from the maps, charts, and diagrams spread across the table, trying not to stare at the maimed hand of this frightening man beside him – he was like a mangai, the monster of the Altay Mountains remembered from childhood myths. He wondered what was this mangai's crime, why they had cut off his fingers, and why he was back in power. A regime change maybe.

With the mangai were three men in uniform, a general, two colonels, and two others in civilian clothes, and also a Russian interpreter. Globbo had a sickly smile, and was sweating, scared that if he didn't tell them what they wanted they would take his hand too.

He wondered how they had come by these detailed aerial photographs – satellites, drone aircraft? He could make out buses, fruit vendor stalls, even donkey carts on the streets of Igorgrad.

But this is what they wanted to know about, the central prison, the three-storey rebuilt Mongol fortress on the banks of the Five-Year-Plan River. The overfed third son, on a computer site called YouTube, had shown the Canadians sulking in one of the big cells on the main floor.

Globbo was surprised they weren't being kept with the agitators and subversives crowded into the dungeons below. The ordinary criminals, thieves and homosexuals and other scum, were crammed into the second floor. The prostitutes and loose women who'd survived abortions were on the top floor, guarded by prison matrons. "Conditions are not too bad up there," he said, "because they are only women."

Globbo was having trouble keeping up with the questions. How many guards outside? How many in? How were they armed?

How well trained? Where stationed? Where is the nearest army base? Show us on the map. Describe the prison, cell blocks, stairs, doors, corridors, exterior accesses.

Globbo continued to sweat as the mangai's surviving fingers impatiently tapped the table. He thought of his wives and mistresses; he would miss them. But not as much as his occasional official visits to the delights that had awaited him on the third floor of the state prison.

~~~

Gathered around Finnerty's desk were the few and select who made up the Eager Beaver team, men he could count on, plus Lafayette and his pal Crumwell. The others were E.K. Boyes, Charley Thiessen, Dexter McPhee of Defence, forces chief Buster Buchanan, and a general from Air Command. Uncomfortably present also, in spirit only, Sir John A. Macdonald in a gilt frame on the carved oak wall, looking bemused at these lesser mortals, suppressing a smile.

"Before we get into the gritty substance's of today's meeting . . ." Lafayette paused. "You two gentlemen from the services might wish to absent yourselves for the moment." The two generals rose. "No offence, a slight detour into the arcane world of politics."

"No problem," Buchanan said, and led his compatriot out to the waiting area in the Horseshoe.

Finnerty wondered why Crumwell was not excused too. He wasn't supposed to be political. "What's this detour, Gerry?"

"Huck, I have decided there are sound reasons why you ought to consider invoking the Emergencies Act. Let us remember that it was steamrollered through by a Liberal government, post–nine-eleven, so they'd be hard pressed to oppose. We might lose a few Quebec members – indeed, I might face a difficult situation in my own riding were my position known – but we could gain substantially elsewhere."

"Whoa, just pause there, pardner," Charley Thiessen broke in. "You want Huck to take the rap for proclaiming emergency laws, and you're going to say you were opposed?"

"Of course not, Charley. Cabinet secrecy prevents me from saying anything."

"The civil libertarians will be screaming blue murder. I'm head honcho at Justice, the guy they'll be nailing to the cross. Sorry, Gerry, no disrespect, but it's too risky."

"Let's hear him out," Finnerty said. "Try to convince me, Gerry."

"Very well. The electorate, however fickle during tough economic times, rises as one to support a nation in peril. Declare an emergency, justify it, and what prudent voter would want a change of guard in the heat of a crisis? Call a snap election, and patriotism becomes the unbeatable theme."

"That come with a parts-and-labour warranty?" Thiessen said, back in good humour. "Sorry, Gerry."

Lafayette smiled right back at him, mending fences. "Charley, ask yourself: what honest, law-abiding Canadian would object to such reasonable measures as tapping terrorists' phone lines and foraging through their computers?" His audience was attentive now. "The trick, however, is to find a target substantially more threatening to Canadians than a handful of Bhashyistan dissidents. We must up the ante on the eco-terrorist file with a warning about a cabal of violence-prone environmental hotheads. We'll be perfectly justified in doing so. They're out there, and we know who they are. *D'accord,* Anthony?"

"We have names and résumés and last-known addresses," Crumwell said.

"I like it," said McPhee. "Maybe this Erzhan fellow was in concert with them."

The defence minister was not among the best and brightest, but Finnerty didn't weigh loyalty in terms of brainpower. Still, Lafayette's approach had merit. Blame it on the crazies, the publicity-seeking idiot fringe in their Zodiacs, harassing the hard-working boys on the trawlers.

"I buy it as an election strategy," he said. "But I don't know why we have to fiddle around with war measures. Too extreme." Clara Gracey and her little troop of red Tories would have a fit.

"The statute requires something like an insurrection," E.K. said. "Rather difficult to manufacture. I'm not suggesting a snap election is a bad idea if we can show a plausible terrorist threat."

Crumwell said, "I might be able to deliver."

Finnerty would have liked some elaboration, but Crumwell's hooded eyes discouraged inquiries, and meanwhile the two generals were being fetched by Lafayette. "Very well, gentlemen," he said, "Operation Eager Beaver. Where are we with that?"

"An elite unit is ready to roll, sir," Buchanan said. "Aching for action. Anyone see that crap on YouTube, that goose-stepping parade of armed Bhashyistani might? What a joke."

"Our boys will be in and out faster than grease through a goose." Dexter McPhee. He'd never risen above sergeant-major in the army, now owned a fleet of trucks, but Finnerty had needed a defence minister from Quebec, the land of peaceniks, even if he was *un anglais.*

The Americans, with a timidity out of character, had to be coaxed but were finally on board – a costly payoff involving access to the Northwest Passage – so the starting point, Buchanan explained, would be their base in Kyrgyzstan, 480 kilometres to Igorgrad – just within turnaround range for Sikorsky Cyclones with accessory fuel tanks.

There would be support from Air Command, a squad of CF-18s, a Hercules troop carrier. The state prison was at the western end of the city, the army base thirty kilometres to the south, beyond the airport. According to the defector Globbo, six men with Kalashnikovs regularly patrolled outside the prison when they weren't lounging by the little tea room across the road.

The two-pronged operation would take place in the dead of night. As a diversion, paratroopers would land near the airport and hold their ground while commandos descended from helicopters to the flat concrete roof above the prison's third floor, others to the ground outside, "to disable any security elements," as Buchanan put it.

Photos from a surveillance drone were shown: the prison grounds surrounded by a razor-wire fence, the roof, its steel-barred entrance to a staircase and the cells. That door would be blown open. No guards were stationed on the roof, and since the upper floor was a women's unit, little resistance was expected. The Calgary Five would be led from the ground floor to the roof and helicoptered out. Twenty minutes.

"And are these soldiers as eager as beavers?" Finnerty asked.

"They're our finest, sir. Hardcore."

"We'll show the world what Canucks can do." Dexter McPhee beginning a rant. "Look at those *canadiens*, people will say. They'll be remembering how the Americans botched their rescue of the Iranian hostages. Yes, sir, our boys have got the big testicles, just like that ace who brought in their Ilyushin."

"Okay, Dexter, calm down." But McPhee's enthusiasm was contagious, and Finnerty felt a welling of hope. The military seemed confident. It could work. The election writ would be on the governor general's desk within the hour. Forget the Emergencies Act, forget creating an eco-terrorist bogeyman. "Is this show good to go?"

"Three days from now," Buchanan said. "Monday. Fifteen hours EDT. We just need a green light, sir."

The stakes were high, but Finnerty was a gambling man. Coming up sevens meant four more years as prime minister, maybe with a plump majority. Boxcars meant it was back to beachcombing on the Bay of Fundy.

"Good luck. God bless."

~~~

Lafayette emerged from the meeting smarting from the lukewarm reception for emergency measures. He carried on down to the second floor, paused under a portrait of Mackenzie King, the spirit-rapping P.M. who took Canada gloriously into the Second World War, pushing through every emergency measure one could imagine. No offer of guidance from his pursed, stern lips.

Crumwell joined him, then Thiessen, ebullient, optimistic. "If this works, it wins us a quick winter election, and we won't have to screw around with emergency laws."

Lafayette was weary with such quailing approaches to high matters of state. Trudeau had proclaimed war measures, and he remained, unaccountably, a great Canadian hero.

"Let us hope," said Crumwell, "that the armed forces prove more competent than the RCMP, which seems uniquely incapable of sniffing out known terrorists like Erzhan."

"Yes, I'm afraid our internationally renowned force is letting us down again." Lafayette understood Crumwell's vanity, his need to be seen as running the more competent show. "Anthony, you'd mentioned an informal group in Montreal, Bhashie refugees. Uncommunicative, you said."

Crumwell looked for permission to Thiessen, under whose aegis CSIS functioned.

"Fill him in, pal," Thiessen said.

"Language has proved a problem in getting inside. However, one of our people – she's working under the standard cover, as a journalist – expects to find someone willing to accept an informant's fee. Not unheard of in their culture."

"Who's she supposedly working for?" Lafayette asked.

"Online magazine. We crafted a backup website, CanadianFact Sheet.org."

"You'd better tell him about DiPalma," said Thiessen.

"Ray DiPalma, bright fellow, ran our Danube desk, was doing jolly well before a bit of a lapse with a lost computer – you might remember that – but he's back at the top of his game. He's in B.C.

right now, playing a brilliant undercover role, cozying up to leaders of a known eco-terrorist group."

"Whom a member of Parliament is harbouring." Thiessen was beaming. He shared the general view that Margaret Blake had been grossly naive in hiring and befriending two ex-jailbirds.

"Utterly fascinating," Lafayette said. "No chance your agent could be exposed?"

A smile on Crumwell's monkey face. "Oddly enough, he has been. Or to put it more accurately, he exposed himself."

"Hope he didn't do it in public," Thiessen said. "You can get busted for that."

Lafayette forced a laugh, pretending he found that funny. "Go on, Anthony."

"Agent DiPalma has convinced everyone he's seen the light, the green light, as it were. Essentially, he's posing as a quisling to the service that employs him. Quite a good actor, that fellow. Has some amateur theatre credits, actually."

"Sounds like quite the master spy." Lafayette had to still his discomfort when he found himself grasping the two-fingered hand. "Good show."

He took his leave, remembering he had one more ticklish matter on the day's agenda, those Saskatchewan women who'd vanished on their Central Asian tour. It hadn't made the news yet, but the member for Yorkton–Duck Lake was dealing with some distressed constituents.

Ralph Babchuk, a raspy-voiced cattle auctioneer, pounced on Lafayette as soon as he opened his office door, a grasping of flesh, a big arm around his shoulder, glad-handing him all the way into the inner office. Lafayette wanted to shrug free of this sweaty supplicant, but he wasn't going to offend a man who'd delivered half of Saskatchewan at last year's convention.

"Gerry, I know you got the weight of the world on you, but this situation ain't good." The door was closed but Babchuk was still holding on to Lafayette, by the elbow. "I got a doctor in Canora waiting for my return call. He's real insistent. When I explained, like you told me to, there may be security issues, he started shouting at me. We don't come up with something, he's gonna go to the press."

Lafayette broke free, picked up a report from his desk, did some speed-reading. "Okay, it seems they failed to reunite with their travel group in Kazakhstan. Unfortunately, their tour company – Exotic Asia, a Central Asian specialist, main branch in Moscow – stalled for several days before alerting our embassy in Almaty. It appears these three women didn't get on the plane with the rest of the group and may still be in Tashkent. Not the first time they'd taken detours from the itinerary."

"Well, that's what them Russians told Dr. Svetlikoff too, but he says those ladies aren't idiots, they'd have contacted Exotic, or phoned home, made contact somehow instead of just wandering around lost. He's worried they somehow ended up in Bhashyistan, which was a kind of optional add-on to the tour."

"Our information argues against that, Ralph, given they lacked visas and the border has been closed to tourist traffic. But give me the good doctor's number."

Lafayette had his front desk dial the medical office of Miller, Svetlikoff, physicians and surgeons, in the doubtless homely town of Canora, Sask. He could imagine it, dust storms and wilting wheat fields and tradition-bound babas making perogies.

When the doctors' receptionist tried to put him off, he said, "I'll be pleased to wait until he's done with his patient, but you might tell him this is Foreign Affairs Minister Gerard Lafayette."

That, not surprisingly, brought him quickly to the phone from his obstetric examination, or whatever the task. Lafayette started off with an uplifting assurance that the federal government was doing its utmost to guarantee the safety of his wife, widowed sister-in-law, and niece. A foreign affairs officer was, as they spoke, winging his way to Tashkent to coordinate efforts to locate the women. It could work against everybody's interests, given the current complex situation, if theories were noised about that they'd found their way to Bhashyistan.

"Mr. Lafayette, that rings of typical bureaucratic bullshit. I want answers, I want action, and I'm not going to be sluffed off. You have one day to come up with some results or this becomes tomorrow's headline."

"All I can pray for is patience, Mr. . . ." *Sacre bleu*, he couldn't remember that impenetrable surname.

"Svetlikoff," Babchuk said.

"Mr. Svetlikoff. *Dr.* Svetlikoff. I can assure you we have the deepest concern for your wife and loved ones."

"I want to believe that, Mr. Lafayette. If you had any wife or loved ones, you'd believe it too. Twenty-four hours, then I go public." With that, he hung up.

Lafayette found himself shaking as he placed the phone in the cradle. "Is this doctor, uh, generally onside, Ralph?"

"The Svetlikoffs? New Democrats mostly. But I got to look after everybody, right?"

"Of course." Lafayette picked up the phone again. "Tell our embassy in Kazakhstan I want someone in Tashkent by sundown. No excuses. And get somebody face to face with a mulish doctor in Saskatchewan. Beg him, stall him, at least until late Monday, or heads will roll."

15

—

Arthur was in agony, desperately seeking the right moment to brief Margaret on the Episode, as he preferred to label it, the bed-sharing that morning with Savannah Buckett. It hadn't seemed decent to mention it right off the bat when she picked him up at Dorval, or during the drive into Old Montreal, and somehow it felt highly improper to do so while treating her to a fine dinner in a stylish restaurant.

Anyway, there was too much on her agenda.

She fumed over salad and entree over a leaked government poll, a testing of the waters about the Emergencies Act. "A police state, that's what they want. This country's losing its democratic soul, we're engulfed in paranoia, we'll soon be a First World version of North Korea." She was practically the only M.P. complaining about the jingoistic talk in the House, much of it from the official opposition, too quick to swing in line behind the Tories over Bhashyistan.

As to DiPalma, she was aghast that he'd appeared on Arthur's doorstep. He was either a faker or a fool, and either way he could cause disaster. Arthur said he'd received a reassuring report about him – but didn't mention his athletic prowess; that would only get her going again. He insisted DiPalma could be a valuable asset, and if not could easily be unmasked and the government shamed for spying on an M.P. What did they have to lose?

"How is Blunder Bay surviving?" With this, Margaret finally gave him an opening. Which he didn't take.

"Splendidly. Not much to report. Oh, the poker game." That took up ten minutes of avoidance time, and Stoney and his hot-air balloon another ten.

"No gossip? No monkeyshines, nasty rumours?"

He nibbled his poached trout, finding refuge in Talleyrand's sardonic aphorism: speech is a faculty given to man to conceal his thoughts.

"You haven't mentioned Savannah. How is she?"

Words continued to fail him. He had to clear his throat to unblock them. "Fine. Constantly on the go." He felt a flush of embarrassment, hoped it didn't show across the candlelit table. He ought to have phoned Savannah, begged her to give witness to his innocence. But she'd not remember, she'd slept through the Episode, and something, maybe a warped sense of propriety, continued to hold him hostage to inaction and silence.

~~~

"Wipe that grumpy look off your face." Margaret glared at Arthur across a table set for four. He was looking morosely at the concoction in his cereal bowl. It resembled birdseed.

Their hostess, Jo Rosenstein, swept in from the kitchen with another jug of a beverage with carrots and something else, maybe beets – it had the colour and consistency of blood. "Fill up, you two. What do you think of the granola muffins?"

"Unique," Arthur said. That was too accurate. "Very tasty." His stomach screamed for bacon and eggs, but it might cost his marriage to offend these over-obliging folk, stoutly Green – Sam Rosenstein had run for the party federally.

This had to be one of the curses of political life, being captives of the kindness of others, B & B operators like the Rosensteins. Why would they want this lovely nineteenth-century home to suffer the intrusions of strangers? What was the custom when the owners refused payment? Does one leave a handsome tip?

He could only assume that this genial couple suffered a disorder characterized by feelings of acute loneliness when not surrounded by others of their species. Last evening, they'd fluttered about, giving them nuts, sliced apples, asking questions, nattering, ensuring no conversational void would go unfilled. As a consequence of that, Arthur was too exhausted on retiring to mention the Episode. It would have been hugely inappropriate to do that, anyway, in bed.

"We keep butter for guests," said Jo Rosenstein, seated now beside him. Arthur begged her not to get up, claimed to be savouring this healthy breakfast. Sam was at the table now too, carrying on about supermarkets selling New Zealand apples when you can get better quality in your back yard.

Margaret made motions to rise from the table, tugging discreetly at Arthur's sleeve. "Arthur and I have an appointment, I'm afraid."

"Before you head out, you should try the chicory coffee," Jo said.

~~~

Gaia House was on Avenue des Pins, not far from the mosque on Sherbrooke, and since the sidewalks had been cleared of the night's snow, Arthur and Margaret decided to enjoy a suddenly sunny day. Another chance to confess. But to what? Confession was for miscreants, and he'd done nothing blameworthy. But would she believe that?

The problem was not so much in the telling but in the manner of it. Should he make a joke of it? Ho, ho, ho, there she was half draped over him as Stoney barged in. Maybe he should come on affronted. How dare she! The brazen woman, thoughtless even in her sleepwalking state.

How to counter Margaret's questions? *Isn't she staying in the bedroom below? Why on earth would she have sleepwalked upstairs?*

Stoney saw her snuggled up to you? What explanation did you give him? And he believed you?

Stoney hadn't, and neither would Margaret. She'd go off like a moon rocket, forever distrust him for having betrayed her at a most critical juncture of her life and career. After she cooled, guilt would assail her – she'd been too immersed in politics to focus on his needs for companionship. His husbandly needs. But how had he demonstrated those last night? With flaccidity, fibbing excuses, alleged fatigue, complaints of feeling like an intruder in this strange house.

Yet if he didn't tell her, what if she found out, what then? *Why was I the last to know?* Arthur would be in a hopeless situation, backed against the wall by his unworthy silence.

"Such a lovely day," Margaret said, taking his arm.

~~~

The Mosque of the Holy Prophet was a converted greystone mansion, with little but its sign to designate it as a religious centre. By the door was a corkboard advertising a coming debate: "When Belief and Doctrine Collide," two Christian clergy, a rabbi, and the mosque's religious leader, Dr. Mossalen. Workers were washing a red swastika from the wall.

They slipped off their shoes, Margaret tied a silk scarf on her head, and a young woman led them past the sparsely attended prayer hall to the imam's office. Dr. Mossalen rose to greet them, a furrowed, white-bearded face. His doctorate was in religious studies from Cairo University. Arthur had been told he was not one of the fire-and-brimstone mullahs the media preferred to focus on.

"Welcome, welcome to our little holy institution. Not one of the grand mosques of our Asian and African heartlands, but more peaceful than some. I content myself with the knowledge that God does not discriminate against homely houses of worship." Efforts at introductions were waved aside. "Your names are well known in these precincts. Mr. Beauchamp, the eminent barrister, and his industrious political spouse. Mrs. Blake, yours is a sane voice amid the howls of consternation over this Bhashyistan business."

He placed them on a settee, poured them coffee. "I hope it's not too strong for your taste."

"As long as it's real coffee," Arthur said, the bitterness of the chicory lingering.

"Keeps one awake. Otherwise I tend to sleepwalk through my mornings." Arthur almost choked on his coffee. "Vana and Iqbal Zandoo are without; she's showing him through the mosque. I know her well and can attest to her probity. I haven't met Iqbal, who I suspect is not much of a believer."

Margaret asked him how he felt about the Bhashyistan mess.

"Much as you do, I imagine. Distress. Confusion. Some fear of the consequences of overreaction. Of interest, we play host peri-odically to a group of that nation's emigrants. Maybe they'll talk to you, I don't know – they're a close-mouthed lot who harbour much hostility against their despotic home government. In their lan-guage, Erzhan means soul of a hero, and these people believe him to be one, whether he be guilty or innocent. "

"Have the police questioned any of them?" Arthur asked.

"Not to much effect. A journalist has been working them over too, rather insistently, in fact."

"A police agent?"

"That's what they suspect. Allegedly works for an online journal. I saw its website, and it looked hurriedly cobbled together. At any rate, our Bhashyistanis are right to be cautious in expressing their feelings toward Erzhan, though I suspect none can truthfully say where he is. There are suspicions. But I am stealing your valuable time. Vana and Iqbal are at the door."

Vana entered shyly, followed by Zandoo, late sixties, bearded and balding, with a scowl that could curdle milk. His handshake was restrained, perfunctory. Mossalen attempted to put them at ease, offering greetings in Pashto and Urdu, then seemed embarrassed at his show of linguistic prowess. "One picks up various tongues along the way in the racket of giving spiritual guidance. This is very much a polyglot mosque."

"I grew up speaking English," Zandoo said, surly. "Maybe not as fancy as you."

"And you speak it very well, as does Vana. I told her, Mr. Beauchamp, that she can fully trust you. A brave woman, these are trying times for her."

Zandoo sat back, arms folded, declining an offering of tea or coffee. But Vana took the former, offered a tentative smile. "I don't know what to think about all this." She looked prettier than on TV, but sadder. Dark, solemn eyes.

Arthur began his questioning by asking after her children. They hadn't been sleeping well but were back in school, where there had been taunting; it was difficult for them. Further gentle probing revealed nothing unusual or amiss about this unexceptional Canadian family – Erzhan may have had a rebellious past, but had apparently integrated into the new world with remarkable ease, a respected teacher.

He loathed the Ultimate Leader and his loyal, clinging minions. No sensate being would reprove him for that – after his acquittal in the Canadian courts, his parents had been beheaded, his two brothers arrested, beaten, tortured, his teenaged sister serially raped by her jailers. But Vana insisted he wasn't involved in an anti-Bhashyistan cabal. Any political involvement was local – Neighbourhood Watch, park and playground cleanup campaigns – or athletic – high school hockey and soccer. He was a hockey player himself, in an amateur senior league.

He had rarely discussed his youthful years – which had included a stint in the army and his desertion from it – or the fate of his family or his alleged role in the assassination of Great Father Boris Ivanovich. He'd told his son and daughter of his arrest and trial, however, and proudly spoken of his great protector, Brian Pomeroy, a photograph of whom hung in a place of honour.

Vana's account of the morning of November 26 had not been made public, though repeated many times to investigators. It had begun as a very ordinary day. Abzal had read the newspaper over breakfast, as he regularly did, commenting on items, reading passages aloud, often bewailing the state of the world. An observant and dutiful citizen, Arthur assumed, rightly cynical about the murky realm of politics.

"I packed his lunch, and he left for work, and that's all I can say. The police asked me if he was nervous or worried, and I told them, no, he was normal, like every day."

"And did they seem satisfied with that?"

"I don't think so."

"The cops kept bugging her," Zandoo said. "Me too, like we were criminals. To me, these guys were racists."

"No, Iqbal, they were doing their work." Vana said this reprovingly. "Everybody is a racist but you." To Dr. Mossalen: "Iqbal has a good heart, but . . . he finds his own path."

Mossalen smiled. "And it does not often lead to the mosque."

"In this place, I will not say what I think." Zandoo refused to meet the imam's eye. "But I respect."

Throughout this, Margaret sat smiling, taking the safe route of silence. Her implicit message: you take on this curmudgeon, Arthur. Dr. Mossalen excused himself – he had other visitors, duties to attend to.

Arthur took on Zandoo carefully, searching for openings, asking about his family (none, never married) and finally finding a shared interest in flower gardening. They talked tulips and begonias and asters, then dogs: Arthur's own rambunctious Homer, Zandoo's basset hound, Gaston.

"Twice a day he takes me to the municipal park, summer and winter. He knows every bush, every tree, and honours them all in the traditional way." Smiling now, opening up.

And it was in the morning of the ill-famed November 26, as Zandoo and Gaston made their way through the leaf-strewn streets of Chambly toward the park, that he spied, about a hundred yards away, a black car pull up beside Abzal Erzhan.

"A big car, not a van, I couldn't say the make. Quebec plates. To me, it looked like they were asking directions, one man leaning out the front passenger window, two others inside. A rear door opened, like they were inviting him in, and when he didn't accept, two of them got out – not the driver, I never saw him."

"Or her?"

"It could be a her. The other two seemed to be insisting. I didn't see a gun but maybe they had one. They bundled him into the back seat. Abzal didn't cry out, and he looked limp, and I'm thinking maybe they injected him with something."

Arthur was astounded. "And did you not tell this to the police?"

"Me, I don't have anything to do with police. Never have. They are always protecting the racists. Once I broke up a fight, a Somalian girl being pushed around by three white girls, and when the police came, they arrested me for assault. Three hours in jail before they let me go. With a warning. Pigs."

"How well did you see these two men?"

"I couldn't identify. One wearing a jacket, another a sweater, also a toque. But they were not Asian."

"White?"

"Yes, and not too young, maybe in their forties, one tall and tough looking, one very thin."

"How remarkable." Also remarkable was that although Vana had relayed Zandoo's account to the police, they had not worked him over harder. He'd made things awkward, however, by not being frank with the police. But who was Arthur to be righteous about being frank? An anxious glance at Margaret, an unnerving recall of the Episode.

"Vana, I would like to act for you and your husband." Rarely did such invitations come from Arthur, whose clients often waited in line. But he was itching to take this on. Margaret smiled approvingly.

Vana hesitated. "You are a very important lawyer, I understand that."

"It will cost you nothing."

"I would get it in writing," Zandoo mumbled, a little apologetically.

"Without question."

"Oh, yes, thank you," Vana said, "thank you, Mr. Beauchamp. We have been so alone, I didn't know where to go."

"All I ask is that you keep your silence, Vana. Speak to no one without my consent. Refer them to me if necessary. And you, my friend Iqbal, would you be interested in my representing you on similar terms?"

"I am an innocent man, sir. Lawyers are for the guilty."

"It's the innocent who most need their aid, Iqbal. You must tell your story to the Canadian public. And do so soon – delay breeds scepticism. I'll be at your side when reporters ask questions. For your friend Vana, for Abzal, for justice, I am asking you to do this. If you're willing, I'll spend the hours needed to prepare you."

"I am not afraid." A brave thrust of chin. But then he mused, as if trying to quell his inbred lack of trust. "If I may ask, sir, what's in it for you?"

"My thirst for justice, Iqbal. My thirst for justice."

16

―――

From his angle on his couch, Finnerty saw Sir John A.'s smile as sympathetic, sharing, but it hardly lessened an all-day hangover inflamed by heartburn – he'd hoovered a stack of flapjacks this morning, a double patty and fries at lunch. It was the tension that caused these excesses, the tension of waiting for three o'clock, Operation Eager Beaver.

He'd survived the weekend by hiding out – from friends, advisers, the press, for whom he'd run out of jests and bons mots. Hiding within the uncounted drafty rooms of 24 Sussex, taking cover from his sternly teetotal wife in search of bottles squirrelled away and forgotten.

E.K. was getting impatient, raising his eyes occasionally from his dispatches. "It's almost time. They're gathering in the war room. I suggest you get it together."

It was a quarter to three. Finnerty had fled Question Period early, avoided the scrums in the foyer. Earlier, he'd briefed the full cabinet, a gruelling task, questions flying, alarmist comments from some, hurrahs from others that the nation was finally taking action. Afterwards, he'd drawn Clara Gracey aside. He'd seen her expression: resentment that the deputy leader had again been exiled from the insiders' club, that she'd had to hear about the rescue plan at the eleventh hour.

"What am I, an untouchable? Am I to be sent to the girls' room every time the men plot their war games?"

He'd insisted the circle had to be kept as tight as humanly possible.

"Fine. I don't want back in. Let Lafayette be the goat if things screw up."

He'd let it go at that. She'd already leaked her opposition to military intervention, obviously didn't want to go down with all hands if things indeed screwed up. But they weren't going to. He imagined himself smiling tonight from every TV screen in the country. *Please share in my immense pride in our heroic men and women in uniform . . .*

"It's time, Huck. Up, up, and away."

~~~

As Question Period petered out, Lafayette rose leisurely from his front-bench seat, pondering whether to indulge the clamouring gang in the foyer with the gentlest hint they were about to enjoy a watershed moment in history. But he stilled the urge, confusing them by walking off with a smile. The camera-toting press clung to him like pilot fish until he escaped into the no-go zone.

He paused at a window: opposing factions on the steps, the anti-poverty idealists and the hard-boiled patriots. "The Real War is at Home – Jobs Not Guns." A banner with an alternative view: "Make War Not Peace."

Happily, the truculent Saskatchewan doctor had been put on ice awhile, persuaded to wait until day's end before yelping to the press. But the news from Tashkent had been less than helpful – the three women, if confusing accounts from Exotic Tours were true, had indeed boarded a flight to Igorgrad, where they'd disappeared into the gloom.

Here was Anthony Crumwell waiting in the Horseshoe, seeking a colloquy. "Charley Thiessen suggested I pass on an unusual tidbit about a suspect alliance among the wife of our slippery friend Abzal Erzhan, their landlord, Zandoo, and . . ." A moment of contrived suspense as they planted themselves on a couch. "The honourable member for Cowichan and the Islands."

"Do tell, Anthony." A smile to disguise his impatience.

Crumwell described a surreptitious tête-à-tête at a Montreal mosque two days previous, also involving Margaret Blake's spouse, the noted barrister. They'd conferred for fifty-three minutes, apparently in the office of the local imam. Yesterday, Sunday, Zandoo had been fetched to the law offices of Tragger, Inglis in Ottawa, where he met again with them and with Julien Chambleau, M.P. for Iberville-Chambly.

"And what do you make of all that?"

"I pick up a whiff of conspiracy. An effort to protect the itinerant assassin, hide him, cover his tracks? A delicious development if that can be proved, do you not think?"

"No, I do not." Lafayette decided he was dealing with a low-level neurotic, a conspiracy theorist. "Beauchamp et al. can't be so naive as not to know Zandoo is under constant surveillance. They may be conspiring, but only to embarrass the government." Crumwell looked chastened. "Have you or your minister spoken of this to anyone else?"

"Negative."

"The prime minister?"

Crumwell hesitated. "If you think I should . . ."

"Maybe not for the time being."

It was just after three when Lafayette led Crumwell into the war room. He'd half expected the group of seven to have become eight, but Finnerty had wisely abided by his counsel to keep Clara Gracey out of the mix.

The P.M. looked notably more blotched and pasty than usual, like an uncured fatty ham with a pink protrusion representing a nose. Lafayette sat well away from him so as not to endure his boozy scent.

"Nail-biting time," said Thiessen beside him. A distasteful image. Lafayette's own nails were tastefully manicured.

"T minus six minutes," said Dexter McPhee, looking at the clock. All were seated on one side of the room's massive circular table, watching the screens.

General Buchanan removed his headphones. "Gentlemen, CF-18 Hornets are descending on Igorgrad. From now to zero hour, we have radio blackout."

"Let us pray," said McPhee, bowing his head. Lafayette watched as several others dutifully followed this execrable example.

Several of the plasma screens were tuned to the major networks. At the hub of attention was the English service of Al Jazeera – the only network to have bribed its way into Bhashyistan. Other broadcasters were focused on the Security Council's deliberations, finally under way.

Al Jazeera, with voice-over from an announcer with a Scottish burr, was showing daytime scenes of the placid streets of Igorgrad, a vegetable market, lineups for buses, the people sullen, restrained, uncomfortable under the gaze of cameras. Depicted also: the overblown statuary, the Revered Mother with axe, firewood, and swaddled infant. The state prison, from several angles. The crew had been forbidden access to the jailed Canadians, and it was impossible to know if theirs were among the hands waving from several barred, unshuttered windows.

These transmissions ended abruptly. Back to the Al Jazeera studio, a bulletin. The announcer, McKay, a long-faced Scot with implacable British cool, announced to the world that foreign forces were landing in Igorgrad.

Cheers went up. Buchanan rose and pumped his fist. "Go get 'em, boys!" Even Lafayette was having trouble maintaining his unflappable air, and found himself jostling for a position by the screen.

The only calm voice in the room belonged to the phlegmatic Scot. "It is the dead of night in Bhashyistan, and sirens are sounding throughout its capital city. Fighter jets are reported swooping over Igorgrad, their country of origin unknown, and parachutes have been seen south of the airport. As I speak, one of Al Jazeera's mobile units is speeding to the scene of the action . . . One moment. It has now been learned that helicopters are approaching the western edge of the city, near the state prison. Please stay tuned, we will update these events as they unfold."

The air in the room was electric as the announcer stalled with backgrounders and clips. The carnage on Colonel By Drive. Mad Igor's declaration of war. Then Finnerty saw, through the fog of hangover and tension, an uncomfortably familiar face – his own damned face, straining to convince his countrymen he was not dithering. His flask weighed heavily in his suit pocket.

"We have just received word that explosions have been heard from the vicinity of the Igorgrad airport. The city has been blacked out, and . . . there . . . we can see it, flashes of light to the south, that must be the airport area. One second. Yes, we are now transmitting live from a mobile van racing through ominously deserted streets toward the state prison."

Flickering images of darkened buildings swishing by, helicopter searchlights beaming from above, the clatter of their blades, excited words in Arabic from the camera crew. McKay: "Can we have some voice, please."

"Ben Ahmed Husseini here. We are five minutes from Igorgrad prison . . . Yei-la-Hai!"

Finnerty gasped as the cameras swung in the direction of a tank barrelling toward the TV crew from a side road. "Almighty God," said McKay, finally flustered. The Al Jazeera van swerved around a bend, courageously pressing on.

Suddenly the van was bathed in light from above, and there came a helicopter's roar, swooping from on high. A flash, screams from the camera crew, and Finnerty was climbing from his skin expecting a horrendous international incident. But the target had been the pursuing tank – it veered from its path into a crevasse created by the copter's missile, its occupants fleeing like ants.

Thiessen leaped, high-fiving with an air force general. The Al Jazeera van skidded around a corner into safety. People were on the streets now, running helter-skelter.

"We are still live on air," said McKay. "And hopefully all are still alive. Are you there, Ben? Come in, Ben."

"I'm . . . we . . . mother, holy shit. Sorry, are we transmitting?"

"You are on air, Ben. Is everyone okay?"

"I'm checking. All here." Some words in Arabic to his crew, then: "We're proceeding by foot."

"Be safe."

"Keep it down!" Buchanan shouted, silencing the gabble in the room.

"A seminal moment in history," Lafayette announced.

The sound of helicopters lifting off. The crew's camera peered around a concrete wall, at an opening blasted through the razor-wire fence, the darkened prison beyond. A tea house, two armed guards hiding behind it, three others sprawled nearby, still clutching automatic rifles. Prisoners were fleeing en masse through the front door, which had been blown open. No one tried to stop them.

All the ground troops had made it up to the roof now. A last helicopter was inching upwards from it, a woman being helped aboard. Then it grunted into the air. A woman? Finnerty thought that most odd, and found himself laughing as he eased himself into his chair.

Dexter McPhee began singing the national anthem, dreadfully off key.

~~~

It was nearly an hour later that Air Command began transmitting from the U.S. base in Kyrgyzstan. By then, the Al Jazeera unit had retreated from the prison, fleeing down back streets to avoid the rumbling tanks and troop carriers hurrying to the scene. The news crew's efforts to interview Bhashyistani officials had been curtly rebuffed.

Other networks had finally caught up, but with only patchy details, and though it was assumed Canada had launched a successful rescue mission, nobody was saying so officially – including those closeted in the war room. All were smiling but enervated, gabbing restlessly, awaiting confirmation.

Buchanan said Colonel Thorne was coming on line – the commanding officer of Operation Beaver. "General Buchanan here. Do you read?"

"Sir? Is this a secure line?"

"Encrypted, decrypted. Let's have the news, Colonel. We're on tenterhooks here. What took you so long?"

"Well, uh, we had to so some intensive debriefing, sir. But it seems . . ."

"Seems what, Colonel?" A chill engulfed the room. Finnerty felt a sharp pain and bent over, tried to catch his breath. Gas – he'd downed that Reuben sandwich like a starving dogfish.

Colonel Thorne was having trouble finding words. "The, uh, good news: all military personnel safe and accounted for. Minimal enemy losses. We took aboard some of their political prisoners. However . . ."

"Yes? Yes? Spit it out."

"The target wasn't met. They weren't there. The hostages."

"Weren't *there?*"

"Sir, we blasted through that joint, every sealed and locked door, all three floors and the dungeon below, and . . . well, the dissidents we took on board said no Canadians were ever in that lockup."

Gasps. Dexter McPhee went down on his seat with a thud. Thiessen hurried off to the washroom, looking green. E.K. Boyes emitted only a mouselike squeak of despair. Finnerty turned as white as alabaster, and as cold. The room seemed to be closing in on him.

Only Lafayette remained still and voiceless, staring at Crumwell with venom, Crumwell, the brilliant international spy chief who'd interviewed the defector Globbo and got bullshit, corrupted information.

Lafayette paid no heed to the P.M. until, as Finnerty slowly bent toward the table, his nose finally met it with a thump. Then his bulk slid sideways off his chair and he fell like a bagged rhino onto the floor, glassy eyed, no longer of this world.

~~~

Dear Journal,

That sounds silly, addressing a notebook, but I'm keeping it as a record in case . . . well, in case something happens. That sounds bleak, but at least my words will live. I hope I don't have to eat these pages if we hit a roadblock — I can't put people in danger. They're so brave, so full of hope for freedom from their oppression. So kind.

I'm confused about what went on the night before last, but I gather a jail in Igorgrad was stormed by Canadian soldiers and all the prisoners freed. So that's been a matter of rejoicing by the insurgents helping us and putting us up along the way. Hundreds of Bhashyistan freedom fighters escaped, and everybody we've met is singing Canada's praises.

The official version is different. The government claimed to have repelled a massive invasion, and the radio is full of patriotic songs and guff about Canada licking its wounds. But we got the true story from one of the escapees, Atun Gumbazi, a strapping young man with a long beard and a fantastic smile. (Hunky, says Ivy.)

He's sitting in the cab of the truck, a four-wheel king cab, with a Kalashnikov on his lap, one that he grabbed off a dead guard. We're all hiding under sheepskin jackets in the bed of the truck, Maxine, Ivy and me, and three shy men and a woman, freedom fighters, they proudly call themselves, members of the BDRF, the

Bhashyistani Democratic Revolutionary Front. We're waiting in the woods for night to fall so we can be on our way again.

Reading this, even I'm confused. Let me back up. Yesterday, the morning after the raid, Abrakam and Flaxseed woke us up because a car with soldiers was coming down the road. We gathered everything and hid in the bushes by the river, scared out of our tree, scared for our hosts. But they received the soldiers, gave them tea, showed them around, the yurt, everything, told them they hadn't heard anything about any Canadians, and they didn't get beat up or anything. Elders are pretty well respected around here.

And when we crept back into the yurt, there was Maxine's travel kit, with all the tickets and maps and brochures hanging from a peg, fortunately behind a framed photo of the country's president for life, which I guess they didn't dare touch.

So later in the day, one of their grandsons came by with a horse-drawn sled full of these same stinky sheepskins, which thank God for because it was snowing hard, and he got us out to the main road where there was no other traffic because of the conditions. At one point he had to shoo off a bunch of kids who tried to climb onto the backboard. Boy, were we sweating.

We pulled into some kind of town where you could hear speakers blaring from a minaret, and onto a side street. It was getting dark by now, they have these short December days just like home, I guess we're at the same latitude. And we were bundled into a concrete building, a block of flats, and that's where we met Ruslan and a few of his band.

Ruslan Kolkov is like the local leader of the BDRF, and he's a story, and he had lots of them to tell, he must have thousands. About fifty years old, I'd say, looks like Redbeard the pirate, with the scars and the black eye patch to prove it — he'd been tortured, escaped, spent years on the run. Russian-born, from the steppes. Right now he's our driver, up in the cab with hunky Atun, who arrived during the evening to cheers and kisses and back-slapping.

They broke out the vodka and made toasts to us, to our heroic Canadian soldiers, to all Canadians, to peace and freedom and also to some guy named Abzal Erzhan, who is their great national hero, like Tommy Douglas is to us, I guess, and it turns out he'd been living in Canada, a suspected assassin or bomber. Very confusing. Ruslan did a Russian folk dance (boy, can he do the prisyatki).

It was after midnight when we sneaked out of town, slipping and sliding, heading down into a valley, travelling for eight hours. At dawn, we veered off into this forest glen, where the snow is less dense. Cold potato pies and yogurt, more stories from Ruslan Kolkov. (Do I believe he wrestled a ravenous bear, felling it with a blow between the eyes?) Tonight we'll continue toward the Altay Mountains, beyond which the rivers flow north, to Russia.

It has become dark, and we are moving.

17

——

rthur leaned over the railing of his apartment balcony, bundled up against the chill wind, his pipe blowing sparks. There was an eerie, almost spooky, feeling about the city spread below him on this Wednesday, December 8. The streets were almost deserted of traffic, as if Ottawans had been too depressed to leave their homes. Few skaters on the canal. From somewhere, a sullen wail of siren. Adding to the sombreness: a dirgelike oratorio from apartment 10C.

It was two days after the abortive raid on the Igorgrad jail and the sudden death of the country's P.M. Acting Prime Minister Clara Gracey had immediately declared a day of mourning, and the entire nation was still in a torpor, numb with disbelief and shame.

But life somehow goes on. Arthur would soon be off to Parliament Hill, where Question Period started at two-fifteen, with opposition members lining up like a firing squad waiting to let loose their volleys. Margaret wasn't on the Speaker's list, but her friend Julien Chambleau had earned a turn.

Returning inside, he was drawn to the computer, still open to the video on YouTube. He couldn't help himself – he clicked on it again, number one on the most-watched list.

"Hello, especially to unhappy viewers in Canada. This is Mukhamet Khan Ivanovich, and the breaking story we are working on today is how Bhashyistan sent your invaders to glorious defeat."

Arthur was mesmerized by the taunting third son and his cherubic, confident smile. This was the third time he'd watched this clip, a form of self-abasing penance.

"Correcting lies of international news like CNN, we showing graves where many Canadian soldiers paid ultimate price after repulsed by glorious national army." Mounds of earth in a barren field. "Yes, Canadians, I trick you by showing state prison, making you think oil company spies are in there with common criminals, but surprise – we have other, secret jails."

The Calgary Five were shown, unshaven, in prison clothes of loose orange fabric. They didn't look ill fed, and had managed to secure playing cards and board games.

"Today we celebrate while you Canadians mourn leader, who was brought down by mighty strike from invisible hands directed by National Prophet." Finnerty had been felled by a coronary, but the allusion seemed symbolically correct.

"Here we showing victory parade." Another procession of soldiers and tanks. A shot of Mad Igor on the dais pinning medals on army officers. "In other news, December sixth is now proclaimed Illustrious Victory Over Canada Day. And coming soon, we hoping all viewers tune in for unveiling plan to make Canada pay for failed insult to national pride. Operation Beaver – hah! Is big rat with flat tail for slapping water when scared. No recession here, Canada! No unemployed! From secret location in Igorgrad, this is Mukhamet Khan Ivanovich signing off."

Arthur stomped off to the elevator, where he encountered a few nodding acquaintances who avoided eye contact, as if embarrassed for their country. Yes, Canada had replaced Bhashyistan as the world's laughingstock, the joke all the more hilarious because of the helicopter rescue of several prostitutes. They were freedom fighters, they'd claimed, jailed for their views, not their ancient practices.

Adding to the national discomfort: a U.S. army photographer at the Kyrgyzstan base had wired photographs of buxom young women partying with Canadian commandos, the men loose and mindless with strong drink. One young lady was shown on the lap of a hardened fighter, offering solace with roving hands. *The Daily Show* and *The Colbert Report* had a heyday with winking references to Operation Eager Beaver.

But the humour had died with the suddenness of a hammer blow after a televised plea by a Saskatchewan doctor for the rescue of family members who'd disappeared into the heart of darkness. Three women lost in Bhashyistan – imprisoned, violated, dead, no one knew. Dr. Svetlikoff had accused the government of plunging ahead with Operation Beaver while ignoring their welfare.

Arthur plodded north, up Bronson, usually a busy artery, but the streets were ghostly, the city in mourning for the unrescued and the missing, for the loss of national pride.

Against these events, the death of a prime minister paled in gravity, but he'd been given due remembrance. The day before, the Commons was recessed after appropriate tributes from all party leaders. Margaret's contribution had been pro forma but kindly enough. She'd not disliked Finnerty personally, a man blind to the environmental ills befouling the planet but with a basic human kindness.

Ille dolet vere, qui sine teste dolet, Martialis wrote. He mourns honestly who mourns without witnesses. But the mourning from sources in Foreign Affairs was public and loud, crocodile tears disguising a rush to blame the dead: the scheme had been hatched by Finnerty – it was his brainchild, his gamble.

Most columnists, however, suspected Gerard Lafayette was the architect of Black Monday, a view bolstered when Acting Prime Minister Gracey, in a solemn address to the nation, let it be known that the perpetrators of Black Monday had got incomplete advice from security and foreign office staffs, had failed to heed alternative views. The government had committed errors, she said, pleading for all Canadians to unite. A cabinet shakeup was in the offing. Gracey was wielding a new broom.

Arthur wondered how long her tenure might last – the no-confidence vote was scheduled for the next week, and some government backbenchers were reportedly reluctant to be whipped into line.

~~~

The prime minister's heart attack had so jolted Arthur that he'd vowed to redouble his efforts to keep in trim, so he walked the nearly six kilometres to the Hill, where flags were listlessly flapping at half-mast. Even today's assortment of demonstrators seemed lethargic: a score of listless patriots singing "O Canada" on the frozen lawns of Parliament.

Arthur took a deep breath before heading up to the Members' Gallery. Margaret would be looking for him there, seeking his strength and comfort, oblivious to his ostensibly wanton behaviour of five days ago. The Episode.

Fretting and sweating, he'd reached Stoney the day before after several tries. "Just checking on the home scene," he'd said with false jocularity.

"Hey, man, if it's about you balling Savannah, my silence is golden." Shouting so loud that anyone within fifty yards might have heard. Sadly, Stoney had found himself cash short as a result of the recession and was seeking new opportunities. Might this be the right time for Arthur to get his decaying dock rebuilt to standard? Arthur promptly accepted his bid, the price of golden silence.

~~~

The chamber was packed, backbenchers glued to their armchairs as Cloudy McRory rose. Dyspeptic, humourless, his brows knit together like an upside-down smile, he called on the acting prime minister to apologize to this House and to the world for the fiasco that was Operation Eager Beaver.

"Who has come home?" he thundered. "Who did our country free? Prostitutes! This failed adventure has become the fiasco of the ages! This House demands a credible explanation."

The Liberals rose in unison, a full-throated cheering, jeering tsunami. Margaret might have been the lone member to the Speaker's left who didn't join in. She'd been appalled by the official opposition's warlike trumpeted efforts to prove they were tougher than the government.

Arthur searched for her, found her among the Bloc benches, whispering to Chambleau. She looked up, wiggled a wave that he answered with a weak smile. He was desperate to believe in Stoney's promise of discretion. Were they not the truest of friends? Almost family.

Clara Gracey stood. "Mr. Speaker, there is less shame in trying and failing than in acting the snivelling coward. It is not this government that should apologize, but the honourable leader of the Opposition, who should be on bended knee to the proud men and women in uniform who bravely risked their lives. No fault lies with them. Their duties were brilliantly executed."

"Hear, hear," called government members, rather weakly.

"Those who designed this operation acted with the best intentions upon information at hand. Inquiries are being made as to why such information may have been incomplete. In the meantime, we shall continue efforts on every front to bring our citizens home with honour and in peace."

In an emergency caucus on late Monday, Conservative M.P.s had quickly acted to confirm Gracey as interim leader, lining up behind her as their one luminary untarnished by the debacle. Lafayette had supported her, but, insiders said, only because he couldn't muster enough support for himself.

Finnerty's empty chair sat between Gracey and Lafayette, a gulf as wide and cold as the Labrador Sea. The foreign minister seemed sapped of former ambition, sombre, moody, awaiting her verdict, expected the next day, as to who would sit on the front row.

The New Democrat leader, Marsh Jenkins, a Winnipeg labour lawyer, dug into his trove of sound bites, throwing out "scandalous costly boondoggle" and "boneheaded bumbling" in framing a question as to whether Monday's raid was just a smokescreen to hide the government's plans to declare war against its own citizenry by invoking emergency measures.

Thiessen handled that one, denouncing Jenkins for relying on baseless rumours. The government had no such plans, was fully committed to freedom under the rule of law, in proud contrast to Bhashyistan's oppressive Stalinist regime. Clara Gracey stood, led the applause.

Jenkins stood again, eyeing the Press Gallery, which was on overflow, eager for blood. "Maybe the minister of foreign affairs, who I see is somehow still clinging to his job, can help us with this one. Unless it has escaped his notice, he will be aware that a family physician from Saskatchewan has expressed alarm to the national media that his wife, niece, and sister-in-law were detoured into Bhashyistan while on holiday, and are facing the gravest of perils. My question: why did the government proceed with Operation Eager Beaver knowing these women were at risk, and what, if anything, is the government doing about them?"

Arthur still felt a trembling when those clips of Dr. Svetlikoff's entreaties came back to him. A straight-talking but emotional man, grey templed and trim, who hadn't been able to continue what he began, breaking down, choking and sobbing. Arthur had felt the whip of his pain, found himself daubing his eyes with a napkin.

Lafayette heaved himself up. "Mr. Speaker, I can assure the honourable gentleman that this government is deeply aware of Dr. Svetlikoff's concerns, and just as deeply committed to doing everything in its power to guarantee his family's safe return." Arthur wondered how anyone could be satisfied with that half answer.

"Shame! Resign! Resign!"

The Speaker squelched the shouts and catcalls with a demand for order. "The member for Iberville-Chambly."

Julien Chambleau rose. "Question for the minister of public security. Is the government aware that Mr. Abzal Erzhan was forcibly abducted into a car two hours prior to the bombing of November 26?"

Thiessen took a moment as the words were translated from French, then removed his headset. "Au contraire," he said before retreating to English, "we have reason to believe Mr. Erzhan voluntarily entered a vehicle occupied by his collaborators. If the honourable member has other information, we would be pleased if he would share it."

"With pleasure. I formally invite the minister to attend a press conference in the National Press Theatre at ten o'clock tomorrow morning. In fact, I dare him." Thiessen appeared taken aback.

Arthur worried how the obdurate Iqbal Zandoo would handle a siege by the press. But the telling of his account could not be put off. Arthur had spent hours with him in Tragger, Inglis's Ottawa office, and again the previous evening in a nearby hotel where Zandoo was sequestered. He'd even rehearsed him in front of a video camera, one of Pierètte Litvak's many toys.

Proceedings grew tiresome as government members rose with planted questions aimed at bandaging their leaders' wounds. Reporters scurried out to file their bulletins. Arthur casually scanned the Public Gallery behind them, blinked, rubbed his eyes, focused. The ubiquitous Ray DiPalma. Looking solemnly back at him through his wire-rims. A nod. A hand held tightly at his chest, fingers splayed. The gesture repeated. Ten fingers, ten minutes? Both hands meeting as if in prayer, then forming a steeple. St. Patrick's Basilica.

Me and my shadow . . . Yesterday, Arthur had conferred at the Tragger, Inglis office with Antoine Salzarro, who'd retained a private investigator to profile DiPalma through friends and acquaintances, from his college days to the present. The detective, a woman, was hoping to get close to his former wife. Janice. Or Janet.

DiPalma rose, shrugged into a parka as he shuffled past the

security officer and out the Public Gallery door. Arthur waited a minute, musing, half listening to the tedious refrains from below excoriating the Opposition for, of all things, playing politics.

~~~

From the entrance to the basilica's ersatz grotto, DiPalma watched Arthur descend the ramp, then butted a cigarette and walked in. Arthur waited until an elderly woman exited in a motorized scooter, then entered a spacious hall with a bookstore-cum-souvenir shop and a chapel, where a scattered few sat in prayer. Few others were about. DiPalma was on a bench by a wall, reading the morning paper.

"Crumwell's got constipation," he said. "He hasn't gone to the toilet for forty-eight hours. He's so icy, when it comes out it'll be frozen. He claims he didn't really buy that dodge from the third son, insists he relied on info from Russian sources. Ogilvie Road is in turmoil."

Impressed by these confidences, Arthur again quelled his doubts about DiPalma. "Let's hope that at least the campaign to save Lower Mount Norbert Road remains afloat."

"Turns out the Starkers crowd *are* nudists."

No liquor breath on him today, so maybe he was in recovery from the trauma of his marriage breakdown. Arthur wanted to probe him about his student days as a Carleton jock, but didn't want him to sense any distrust.

"Savannah sends her love." A meaningful look at Arthur.

"What?"

"I think you know what I mean." A severe, almost condemnatory expression. "I have to warn you that most of the island is on Margaret's side. Maybe not the loafers who hang about the store – they're either jealous or in awe. Emily LeMay – who's finally given up on me, by the way – insists it's been going on since last year, but you know how she exaggerates."

Arthur sat there with his mouth open, too numb to stanch the torrent of bad news. He grasped at a fleeting hope: DiPalma was kidding him cruelly. But that would suggest he had a sense of humour, however macabre.

"I wasn't sure if Margaret had chucked you out of the apartment with your clothes and toothbrush, so I asked some of the intel officers at Ogilvie Road this morning and they hadn't heard anything. I hope this entanglement doesn't complicate things for us, and that you two can make up, because I'm on the verge of a breakthrough."

"Forgive me for interrupting, Ray, but I have been convicted without trial." There was nothing for it but to divulge the entire innocent version, and that he did. DiPalma appeared to be struggling against scepticism.

"How come no one seems to know Savannah had this sleep-walking problem?"

"I know! Margaret knows!"

"Down, down, people are staring."

Arthur fought for control. "Tell me, Ray, does the entire island also believe you succumbed to Emily LeMay?"

"Not any more, because I finally told her I was gay, and she put the word out. Now *I'm* the centre of gossip." He thought about it. "Okay, point taken. What did Margaret say when you told her?"

"I haven't," Arthur croaked.

"Well, she's going to hear."

Arthur eyed the chapel, where a young priest was lighting candles. No, there was but one person to confess to. He must sit down with his life partner post-haste, take his bitter medicine, plead with more might than he'd ever summoned for the most sceptical jury. He was so engulfed in grief that he was slow to realize DiPalma was going on about something else.

"Usually these days it's Romania. Poland's going out of the business. Malta's a possibility, but mostly a switching station. Egypt? Too unreliable. Albania is a growth industry, it's the only country in the world that has loved America through thick and thin. My guess is the Yanks provided one of their facilities, as well as expertise in rendition."

"Rendition? Whom are we talking about? Erzhan?"

"I see you have your mind elsewhere. Yes – the scuttlebutt is he was rendered out of the country. One of my workmates heard that, she was troubled by it, needed someone to talk to. Enter Ray DiPalma. Aretha-May is her handle, a knockout, by the way – she's on the idiot fringe desk, neo-Nazis, white supremacists, and she'd been seeing a married guy in the next cubicle, a communications traffic analyst. The affair bottomed out, she felt used, and the two of us have started seeing each other. Nothing intimate, we're just sharing our wounds – I told her all about Janice, of course. We had a little cry together. Anyway, where was I?"

"Erzhan. Rendition." Arthur's own marital woes had been put on hold. "From whom did Aretha-May hear this? The traffic analyst?"

"Right. And he heard it from an intel officer I usually avoid, name of Sully Clugg, a thoroughgoing jerk but I'll buy him a whiskey and get his version. Just a minute." He answered his cell. "I'm on him now. Downstairs, St. Patrick's Basilica. He's spotted me, he's waving me over. Got to go, sir." He disconnected. "Crumwell himself is handling me. He wants me to weed out what I can on this Zandoo guy. Can you feed me anything?"

Arthur felt a tremor. Not fear but outrage at his loss of privacy. "You obviously know where he is."

"Suffolk Hotel, room 18."

"Fine. Tell them you coaxed that out of me. And that he's going to say Abzal was abducted."

"Touché, tell them the obvious. Don't worry, no one's going to grab Zandoo. They thought about it, but it's politically dicey. I told them you've probably got him on videotape."

"As indeed we have. Let's get back to Abzal. Who kidnapped him? CSIS agents?"

"Unless they're renegades it doesn't add up. What would be their motive?"

"What would be anyone's motive?"

"Somebody who didn't want the Alta International deal to go ahead."

~~~

Arthur had got too distressed in that grotto, so he headed home to shower and change. As he stepped from the taxi, his stomach was roiling with the ugly sense of being watched. They were outside his building now, probably in that cream sedan looking for a parking space. Or was it that minivan just pulling into the lot? Darkened windows, that would be their style.

So it was now confirmed Crumwell was targeting both Margaret and him, to the point of phoning DiPalma for updates. The voluble spy had shown such candour that Arthur now regretted sicking a private eye on him.

Before going up, he called from a lobby payphone, not trusting his cell, though he was only making dining reservations. His next call, to Margaret's private line, was answered by Pierètte.

Over-jocular: "Is her ladyship anywhere about the palace grounds?"

"I suspect she's still in the House, Arthur."

"Well, uh, if you speak to her, tell her I . . . I love her."

"She doesn't know that?"

He cleared his throat. "And that I've made reservations for the Cézanne at seven-thirty."

"Some kind of anniversary?"

"No, I don't have any particular excuse. Reason, I mean."

"Just that you love her. That's sweet."

"One thing more, Pierètte. Alta International was vying with several other players to develop Bhashyistan's oil and gas. Who were they? After Alta, who had the best inside chance?"

"On it already."

In the elevator, he mused: Erzhan had seen his captors – the two that had exited the car were Caucasian, according to Zandoo – so why would they not have silenced him permanently to avoid being exposed? Why render him to a secret foreign facility? To torture a false confession from him?

He wondered if even a multinational oil company, despite its vast riches, could engineer what was known in the trade as an extraordinary rendition, torture by proxy. Surely some government agency had to be involved. Only one superpower had proven expertise, though others might easily have learned by example.

From 10C, "Water Music": a composition he disliked for its easy familiarity, Handel's fawning curtsey to the first King George. Through the vents, a cry: "Damn it, Sally, you tied the knots too tight!"

He checked his phone messages. Wentworth Chance again. He'd been interviewing Arthur's old cronies, digging up discreditable episodes from a past that would have made even Bacchus blush. Now he wanted to spend a few days prying around Garibaldi, that cesspool of gossip. That had Arthur quaking, wondering how to dissuade him.

He stepped into the shower, turned the water on hot and full, looked down to see his feet in his now-soggy slippers.

~~~

Candlelight and soft harmonics from a jazz trio. Cézanne and Pissarro prints on the walls. An attentive waiter who had the courtesy not to announce his name. For Margaret, a vintage Bordeaux; for Arthur, Perrier and cranberry juice. The buttered clams were probably delicious, but he couldn't taste them.

"How romantic, darling," she'd said as he escorted her in. "I love surprises."

He shuddered, buried her untimely utterance beneath inquiries about her take on fast-moving events. Half an hour later, she was still holding forth, fretting that the government's climate change measures, skimpy as they were, had been forgotten in the midst of crisis.

"They're planning an early Christmas break so they can run and hide from everyone. That's if they're still in power after Thursday. I need to get back to the riding – I've been neglecting it, I have an endless list of people to see. I'll be running around like a hyperactive squirrel."

And maybe never set foot on Garibaldi? No, Beauchamp, don't even think it, screw up your courage, man. But still he stalled, playing a game with Margaret: who among the diners was the spy from CSIS? The bald gentleman eating alone. The sad-looking woman at the bar. The impatient boor claiming he had a reservation.

A deep breath. "Margaret, I have a small event to relate. A ridiculous event. I've been having trouble putting it in words. For that, only that, I haven't been fair to you."

"Do tell." Her smile, poorly suppressed, confused him.

He took a long swallow to force open his gullet. "Matters were not what they seemed, and may God smite me on the spot if I'm not entirely frank about that." The unswerving gaze of her electric silver eyes. "While we've been in Ottawa, Savannah has, uh, often retreated to the bed upstairs when matters between her and Zack . . . you know how they squabble. And, of course, she has sleep-walking difficulties."

In an attempt to spread his hands in a helpless, shrugging motion, he knocked his glass over, spilling its residue. An ice cube skittered off the tablecloth. The waiter was on the spot with a cloth. "May I replenish that, sir?"

"Ah, no, not right now. Thank you, no."

Margaret reached out to press his shaking hand, and he was so jittery that he almost pulled it away. "I'm sorry, I shouldn't let you go on like this, Arthur, it's cruel. Savannah phoned me on Friday to tell me." A chiding expression, as from a tutor to a truant child.

Arthur was nonplussed, speechless. Friday? Five days ago?

"You woke her up. As you got out of bed and left with Stoney."

It took a while to digest this. He sagged finally, weakened by the tension. "He's . . . well, Stoney . . ."

"Yes, he's probably outdone himself, he must be hoarse by now. Come on, Arthur, people may want to believe the worst, but surely no one does. I mean, be serious. Virtuous Arthur, a faithless lecher? Making a move on a woman half his age? *You*, Arthur?"

She smiled, but Arthur felt the bite of sarcasm, of mockery, her way of punishing him for his tardy guilty plea. Sneaking its way into his mix of emotions was a smidgen of resentment. Virtuous? Stuffily incapable of dishonour, was that her implication? But he managed a weak smile, and in truth felt much relieved – even as Margaret stifled laughter.

18

———

A t eight o'clock, bright and early, Charley Thiessen strolled through the parliamentary corridors to the dining room. He was in pretty good spirits despite everything, despite the Bhashyistan shambles, despite the sudden death of his leader and mentor, despite the pall that had settled over everyone.

That was because Clara Gracey had phoned him the night before. She'd congratulated him for the smooth way he'd handled himself in Question Period, especially in putting the Emergencies Act to rest. Then she apologized for "needing" him, practically *begging* him to stay in cabinet and keep his two portfolios, Justice and Security. He'd told her she could always count on Charley Thiessen. Loyalty breeds loyalty, that's his first principle.

Charley Thiessen, attorney general, minister of justice, minister of public security – he'd come a long way from family law, fore-closures, and fender benders in Flesherton, Ontario. Who would have thought? His mom, maybe, who'd never stopped believing.

He was a big, broad-backed, hearty guy, and let's face it, hand-some – his mother said he looked just like John Wayne, he had the same confident way of moseying, the same easy manners. A man of the people, that's why Charley had risen above the others, the corporate lawyers in their Bay Street suites, the slick Q.C.s wearing silk and driving Porsches. Snobs who lacked the common touch, who'd never taken the temperature of the times in a local bar, barbershop, or bingo hall.

That's why he'd bonded with Huck – they were made of the same stuff, they'd risen the hard and honest way, up from Main Street, slapping backs, getting out to all the weddings, christenings, funerals even if sick or hungover. He felt a pang remembering Huck, the many nights they'd spent drinking and laughing and scheming. He'd spent half of Tuesday with Huck's family, and wept with them.

As he strolled into the Parliamentary Dining Room, it was, "Morning, Charley, you're looking exceedingly well." This from the manager. He was always Charley, never Mr. Thiessen, he'd insisted on it. More greetings from M.P.s and senators, Charley, Charley, he gives you no blarney. One of his campaign slogans.

Here, hunching over a tablecloth with rolls and coffee, was E.K. Boyes. Thiessen would normally steer away from him – the PMO head honcho wasn't the liveliest of company – but Guy DuWallup was with him, Canada's new senator, who'd taken a hero's bullet for the boss.

"Morning, Charley," they chimed.

"You boys look clapped out – you'd think there was a crisis going on." He chuckled to let them know he was joking, and sat, signalled the waiter for a coffee.

"We are awaiting our call to duty," E.K. said.

Waiting for the high priestess to get out of bed, Thiessen assumed – Clara had been up late. She would go through the motions of asking their advice before announcing the big shuffle. DuWallup was in her inner circle, a key player even in disgrace. E.K.'s job would be to tell her what skeletons were hiding in what closets.

"I understand you've already had a little talk with the prime minister." E.K. spoke low because of the bright acoustics in the room.

"Woke me out of bed at a quarter to midnight. Don't know where she gets the staying power, she's an Amazon."

"Yes," E.K. said, "the interim P.M. is a woman of impressive fortitude."

Thiessen heard a slight emphasis on the word *interim*. The gnome had a way of coding his messages.

As Thiessen's coffee arrived, E.K. rose. "Must be off to prepare some notes of fulsome thanks and deep regret."

"That's got to be one of the toughest jobs." Letters to the poor bastards being sent to the back of the bus. Thiessen wanted to ask if Gerry Lafayette would be among them, but decided that might not be cool.

When DuWallup began to rise, E.K. motioned him to stay. "Why don't you gentlemen have a little chat?"

Thiessen watched the little man leave, puzzled. "Chat? What about?"

DuWallup looked him over like a tailor sizing him up for a new suit. "Actually, about you."

Thiessen snared a roll, fiddled with it, suddenly lacking appetite. "Yeah, really?" What had he done now?

"You know what I admire about you, Charley? You got where you are by playing fair. Never stuck a knife between anyone's shoulder blades."

"Yeah, make friends not enemies, I find that works pretty good in this business."

"Lord knows that's held you in good stead. Forty-nine years old, raised in the heartland, lovely young wife, three great kids, party member since you were in jumpers, two pluralities in two elections. And the camera loves you. You've got the manner, you've got the look. Housewives swoon."

"Don't forget the winning tackle in the Vanier Cup."

DuWallup rose, urged Thiessen into one of the alcoves, where they huddled. "A lot of people think you should put your name up."

Thiessen got a little ego surge when he realized that's what DuWallup and E.K. had been bouncing around. Gracey faced a confirmation vote as party leader, at a convention to be called soon. Thiessen had expected her to slide through, Lafayette being pretty well out of the picture. This wasn't something he'd really thought about, except in rambling daydreams. Or when his mom used to embarrass him with her "My Charley's going to be prime minister one day."

He was astonished that Gracey's own chief of staff would plot against her. Maybe it was personal, maybe political – E.K. was hard-core Tory blue, almost to extremes, scared of a leftward drift under Gracey. Also a kind of closet misogynist.

"Yes, your name keeps coming up. Jack Bodnarchuk, just yesterday, he sees you as Huck's heir apparent. He could bring in Alberta, eighty per cent of their delegates. Most of our western power base, in fact – they're very uneasy about an ex-economics professor from Toronto running things. That shift away from the oil economy we've been playing up, she actually believes in it. And let's face it, under her watch we've seen all the major indexes continue to fall, we're running a massive deficit. Frankly nobody thinks she's going to last, even if we win next week's vote."

With Huck and DuWallup gone from the House, the non-confidence motion would hang on four votes, maybe only three if a suspected maverick hiding in the wilds of Newfoundland failed to show. He'd shot a few toes off while moose hunting, maybe on purpose. Meanwhile, the Opposition would be bringing in the troops on wheelchairs and stretchers.

"And of course you'd have most of Huck's gang. New Brunswick, half of Nova Scotia. Your own stomping grounds, rural Ontario, even if Clara has TO and the 905 sewn up."

Thiessen was intrigued but uncomfortable. Just last night, he'd told Gracey she could always count on him. But as DuWallup continued to muse about where Clara might take the country (snarled relations with the U.S., letting the automakers go under, abortion clinics in every mall), he began to ask himself if maybe his first allegiance was to the party, to conservatism. In that sense, he could hardly be accused of disloyalty.

~~~

Thiessen paused under Brian Mulroney's portrait as he adjusted his tie, shrugged into his coat. There was a similarity: the noble chin, the barrel chest, the hearty booming voice. A standout leader, an inspiration, a model. Yeah, he could be the guy to get the country back on its economic feet.

He pictured himself as an international figure, photo ops with presidents and prime ministers, popes and potentates. Kind of beats being named Grey County Citizen of the Year 1996. Yeah, that smarmy Divisional judge who told him he couldn't argue his way out of a paper bag would be shitting purple. To hear DuWallup, it was a walk. Did he have the balls for it? The smarts? The tools? That he even asked these questions said he lacked confidence. He'd call his mother that night.

He slipped out a side door, past the smokers, determined to avoid the rabble on the steps, that ever-growing mass of pimpled peaceniks and welfare-addicted anarchists with their placards and clown suits and rubber masks. But he couldn't resist a look back while waiting for the light at Wellington. They had a Laurel and Hardy act going, complete with pratfalls. Women dressed as prostitutes posing seductively for the reporters waiting for that insufferable *indépendiste* Chambleau to set up his own ridiculous show in the Press Building.

Thiessen wasn't going to play chicken and lose face, not Charley boy, the new white hope of the party of Sir John A. and Diefenbaker and Mulroney. Chambleau had publicly dared him to turn up, and he would damn well do that, take the shine off the performance, wisecrack with the press, be ready with some quips if the show fizzled. His sense of humour, that was an asset DuWallup failed to mention. He had his cabinet colleagues in tears sometimes.

He pursued a backpedalling cameraman into the National Press Theatre, plowing through a scrum – there were scores of reporters. He didn't miss a beat. "Thought I'd just wander through the bazaar and see what they're selling."

Near a table at the back, loaded with croissants and jugs of juice, Julien Chambleau was also being scrummed, mostly by the French press. At the podium table were two old grizzled guys, Zandoo the magician and his mouthpiece A.R. Beauchamp, the Paki looking tense, the lawyer leaning back, thumbs behind suspenders, like a cattle boss from some old Western flick.

Party records showed that Beauchamp had been a member as a young man, back in the Progressive Conservative days – he'd followed Diefenbaker in, the great Prairie orator and lawyer, but let his membership lapse. Now he was consorting with eco-terrorists, Flett and Buckett. They were on his payroll.

The guy's spouse wasn't here, out somewhere hugging trees. But maybe he shouldn't be so dismissive of her views, her push for stiff environmental laws. He was confused by global warming, all those theories about the coming big melt, the calamities to follow. His kids, especially his older daughter, were on him constantly about it.

Julien Chambleau paused from working the press to approach him. "So you accepted the challenge, Minister."

"Hey, I'm just plain old Charley."

"In any event, we're delighted to have you among us."

"Couldn't resist, heard you were serving baloney sandwiches." That drew a blank with Chambleau – maybe it was lost in translation or he was just humourless. Thiessen declined the offer of a seat close up, preferring to sit in the raised area at the back with a friendly pundit from the Fraser Institute.

After correcting a few sound problems, Chambleau said a few words about how the people of Quebec were shoulder-to-shoulder with all of Canada in these difficult times – a typical separatist spiel: we are with you but not of you. He introduced Zandoo, a constituent, proud Quebecer, naturalized citizen, community activist, and so on, then turned the mike over to Beauchamp, counsel for the Erzhan family and Zandoo. Pro bono, but Thiessen knew he was doing it for the publicity.

More problems with the mike, but Beauchamp started off fine without it, he had a voice you could hear a block away in heavy traffic. "Okay, while that contraption is being looked at, give me your ears, folks."

"You come to bury the government, not to praise it," someone said to laughter.

"'I come not, friends, to steal away your hearts. I am no orator, as Brutus is.'" More laughs.

Thiessen was reminded of Finnerty, his rapport with the media. Funeral this weekend, he'd be sharing top billing with Gracey and the Opposition leader. He'd probably cry, it wouldn't be an act – they'd been like brothers. The heir apparent, that was starting to sound right. Huck had somehow become more popular in death than life, so that could be a boost. If Thiessen decided to go for it.

They were laughing again at something Beauchamp said. In French, no less. French, or the lack of it, that was one of Thiessen's drawbacks. Never needed it in Grey County. A history of lacklustre report cards was another problem – he'd had to repeat third-year law.

Now Beauchamp turned serious. "To those among you who may wonder why we bring this matter not before the private scrutiny of officialdom but before the press, I paraphrase Edmund Burke: a power far more important than that of kings and parliaments resides in the fourth estate. And that power used wisely and boldly is democracy's lifeblood."

A touch of honey for the media flies. This guy was a natural. Why wasn't he in politics?

"Mr. Zandoo has a statement to read. I'm confident you'll listen to and question him respectfully."

The microphone, working now, was passed to Zandoo, who

must have been nervous, but hid it with a gruff manner as Beauchamp drew from him some personal history: born where, immigrated when, made a living how. The podium backdrop, an array of loosely hanging maple leaf flags, had the unfortunate effect of giving the guy a kind of patriotic credibility.

Thiessen tried to hang in there, but too much was on his mind. He'd need a campaign committee, endorsements from respected names. He'd need money. Maybe a few French lessons, but, hey, Dief the Chief hardly spoke it, and he amassed the biggest majority in Canadian history. Hardest of all, he'd need to find some way to square it all with Clara Gracey. He'd tell her he couldn't fight the pressure, they were coming at him from all sides. Also, a fair and tough debate about goals and principles would be healthy for the party.

The national executive was planning a February convention. Maybe by then Gracey would have put this Bhashyistan thing behind them, with honour. If not, let's face it, the party, the entire country, would be looking for new leadership. Where would Lafayette's votes go? Maybe Thiessen should soap him up a little. Even if he ended up today as minister of interprovincial livestock standards, he could still be a broker.

Back to Zandoo, carrying on in his gravelly voice about this so-called abduction, a black car pulling up for Erzhan, two white guys getting out, urging him to get in, then pulling him in, pushing his head down like the cops do on the TV shows, but without resistance, his legs buckling. Zandoo just happens to be there to see this? How convenient. Then he doesn't tell the police because he was leery of them over some racist incident? Come on.

It bugged Thiessen a little, though, that Zandoo had told this story to Erzhan's wife immediately afterwards. She'd confirmed that, it was on record with the cops. Why hadn't they given him the third degree when they had the chance, Crumwell too? Maybe that's why the sullen bugger was having a little problem with the bowels.

He was fighting a dry throat, so he went to the refreshment table for a glass of tomato juice, smiling and waving at the lenses that followed him there and back.

When Zandoo started fielding questions, Thiessen's reaction was: where are the attack dogs? Beauchamp must have played a little hockey in his time, or maybe refereed, the way he calmly skated around and kept reporters from getting their bodychecks.

But here, finally, was the Fraser Institute maestro – Thiessen had passed him a note – asking Zandoo about his jailed cousin, the al-Qaeda terrorist.

Zandoo looked confused. His questioner prompted him with a name, Mohammed Aziz. "Means nothing," Zandoo said. "Why would I know a terrorist? If he's some kind of religious fanatic, I have no dealings with such people, they disgust me."

The pundit glanced at Thiessen, frowned over his note. "Your, uh, mother's uncle's grandson. Twenty years old, fought for the Taliban. He's in an American prison in Kabul. Does that ring a bell, sir?"

"No bells are ringing. I have lived in Canada twenty-three years, never returned. How would I meet some crazy young man not born when I came to this country?"

This line of questioning was going over like a lead balloon, Beauchamp sitting there with a big fat grin, offering his two bits worth. "If the justice minister has other equally compelling information he hopes might tar my client, maybe he can offer it directly rather than through an intermediary."

From somewhere, poorly stifled laughter. As Thiessen stood he slopped tomato juice on his shirt and tie.

"Someone get the minister a straw," Beauchamp said. Uproarious laughter.

Thiessen's face went as red as his shirt, and he stammered, his knack for the sharp comeback deserting him. It seemed like half a day as he stood there with his mouth open. Finally, he could only grit his teeth, sit back down, and accept his licks. He'd pulled a boner coming here. He'll nail that smug bugger. Someday, somehow.

~~~

As Clara Gracey led Dexter McPhee to the door of the P.M.'s office, she opted for a handshake – a hug seemed inappropriate. "We're polling at almost sixty per cent of retired troops, so don't let anyone tell you Veterans Affairs isn't an absolutely key portfolio. No one can work the Legion Halls like you, Dexter; I've seen you in action too many times to doubt that. I'm so proud to have you aboard."

McPhee walked out stiffly, mumbling, "Proud to be serving, Clara. Good luck." The insincerity was palpable.

Clara mopped her brow, lit a cigarette, leaned on her desk for support. That was a tough one, but McPhee had been too closely tied to Eager Beaver. "Give me strength," she prayed, hoping someone up there was listening.

Percival Galbraith-Smythe slipped in, frowning, turning on the desk fan to blow away the smoke. She'd brought him over from Finance as executive assistant, much to the discomfort of E.K. Boyes – the chief of staff suffered more than a mild homophobic disorder.

"M. Lafayette is outside on the phone to our UN ambassador, pretending it's business as usual. Please put that out, it will make him think you're rattled."

One last draw, then she butted out, slid the ashtray into a drawer. "Did you reach Sonja?"

"She's delighted."

Sonja Dubjek, a former diplomat, the new face of Foreign Affairs. The gender gap tightens. "How did Chambleau's press conference go?"

"Thiessen waltzed in there and made a complete bloody fool of himself. I know he's cute, darling, but otherwise what *do* you see in him?"

"I like him, he lacks ambition. What did he do?"

"Later. The prince of darkness awaits."

Clara popped a breath mint. "Send him in."

Percival gave way to Gerry Lafayette, hiding behind a smile as he pocketed his phone. "Good news, Clara, the UN is sending a high-ranking emissary to Igorgrad. Assistant secretary-general, no less. Plans to warn them that if they don't see reason they'll be internationally condemned as a pariah state. Sanctions, embargos, the whole package."

An initiative that should have been sought in the first place. But Clara didn't say that. "Excellent. No movement from Security Council?"

"Our allies are awaiting the result of this initiative."

"And the Russians?"

"I think they want things settled down. They're hoping to get their grubby hands on the Bhashyistan oil fields, of course. Privately, they still see our Mr. Erzhan as the key. Find him, render him to Bhashyistan justice, and all will go swimmingly."

"Easy for them to say. The abduction business – anything to it?"

"A clever ploy to set up an alibi. Arthur Beauchamp shouldn't be underestimated." He peered out the window. "Snow's melting. They say we're in for some relief, a warm spell." Turning to her. "By the way, Clara, you're looking exceedingly well. Your new role becomes you, and you embellish it as much as I'm sure you relish it."

That was pathetic. Clara fiddled with some papers, embarrassed for him.

"Gerry, I'm afraid this whole foofaraw over Bhashyistan has stirred up separatist sentiment across the river. Rhetoric about how *les québécois* are ashamed to be part of Canada, that sort of nonsense. Remarks from the Alberta premier aren't helping either, and the provinces are squabbling. We're going to need someone to help keep this country together in tough times. A powerful, respected Quebec federalist. No one fits that bill like you."

Lafayette showed little expression, though his facial muscles tightened.

"I want to move you to Interprovincial Affairs. I'm going to make it a front-bench job, and you'll be chief Quebec spokesperson as well. I'll be in your debt if you take this on."

"Interprovincial Affairs," he repeated softly, then turned for the door. "Have a nice day, Prime Minister."

Half an hour later, one of Clara's aides reported that Lafayette had resigned from the cabinet and the Conservative Party.

19

———

An interminable two-stop flight to Vancouver followed by a fitful night had Arthur in a sour mood as he huddled over his poached eggs in the Confederation Club dining room. He listened dully to the voices behind him, aging executives resigned to the predictable precipitous fall of the Tory government.

"Proud to say I backed Lafayette for his run last year. The right choice, but the party made the wrong one."

"Liberal in sheep's clothing, that's what he called Gracey. Can't say I disagree."

"Smart chap, Lafayette, good fundamentals. Has he got a name for his party?"

"Progressive Reform."

It was Tuesday, December 14, eight days after Illustrious Victory Over Canada Day, five since Lafayette bolted from the Tories, taking two disciples with him, determined to bring down a government that Lafayette had excoriated as having tilted dangerously to the left. Even with full attendance, the Conservatives could count on only 152 votes for Thursday's confidence motion. A united opposition had two more.

An election was at the bottom of Arthur's wish list. Working the main streets as the toy boy of the leader of the Parti Vert du Canada. Listening politely to foul-breathed supplicants. The sweaty backrooms, the speeches, the sniping, the attacks on probity, private lives bared.

It was hard to conceive of an election going ahead while the standoff with Bhashyistan continued. The UN emissary had been thwarted by the stubbornness of Mad Igor, his fiefdom now isolated, in deepening penury, trade routes closed, only smugglers thriving.

Arthur's thoughts went to the women who'd landed in Igorgrad by happenstance. Jill Svetlikoff, mother of three young girls; her sister Maxine, single mom of twenty-year-old Ivy, a recently laid off lab technician. It seemed odd that during all his bombastic effluvia the third son hadn't mentioned the capture of three more Canadians, given their value as bargaining chips. That might mean they were alive and hiding. Or dead and buried.

From behind him: "Gracey's bright enough, not hard to look at, but too soft. I'm not sexist, no one can accuse me of that – equal but different, I say. The little lady runs the kitchen staff and I pay the bills. But you don't make them fleet commander."

"The Iron Lady won the Falklands War."

"Different. She had manly qualities."

When Arthur saw Bullingham enter he tried to hide behind a back section of the *Sun,* but the old boy was on him like a bird of prey, his spindly fingers peeling down a corner of the paper.

"Reading the want ads, are we, Beauchamp?" He grunted into a chair beside him. "There's plenty of work to be had at Tragger, Inglis. Forty million missing from the provincial public works budget. Minister's aide one of the suspects. Wants you, no one else."

"I'm up to my eyeballs, Bully."

"Yes, representing an indigent terror suspect."

Arthur lowered his voice. "Bully, if I have a hand in bringing the government down, Tragger, Inglis could be back doing federal business. The deputy minister is small change."

A voice from behind: "I can live with McRory. Business background, not one of their tax-and-spenders."

"Full of blather."

Bully grimaced. "Can't see how you expect to defeat the Tories by sitting around in this nest of thieves. But I will say you did a nice job on that nincompoop Thiessen." Bully was an anomaly in this house of conservatism, a prominent Liberal bagman without liberal ideals – and therefore respected by all. "What brings you back?"

"I'm not entirely sure. A possible break in the case." A phone call from Augustina Sage had brought him west post-haste.

"And your Mr. DiPalma – has he been vetted to your satisfaction?"

"Not quite." Early returns from the PI's inquiries had ranged from equivocal to worrisome. He had an apartment in the Glebe, an upscale district, not far from a friendly neighbourhood pub, but no one there knew him. Acquaintances willing to talk didn't view him as a heavy drinker – or particularly religious, certainly not a churchgoer. More unsettling: he'd been a fair hand at Ottawa amateur theatrics. *I'm a fairly good actor, I play it cool, straight.*

DiPalma's ex – Janice was indeed her name – was currently on a Caribbean holiday, but her best friend insisted DiPalma was the blameworthy party, accusing him of extramarital flings. The most torrid of which was, no surprise, with a woman named Janet. A neighbour believed Ray and Janice were equally adulterous – she'd often had male visitors while he was stationed overseas.

A confusing marital history. In any event, Arthur would henceforth be more cautious in his dealings with this chameleon. Zack and Savannah must be warned away from him.

"I know better than to pry," Bully said. "Keep those expenses down." He drifted off to join some lawyer cronies.

Arthur had been pursued in his dreams by black, slick, oil-dripping colossi. Oil company giants? He'd been reading the material Pierètte Litvak had culled from the Web – business journals, oil industry newsletters, analysts' websites – about the many suitors competing for Bhashyistan's petrol riches.

Gazprom, the muscular Russian monopoly, seemed to have an inside track until old national resentments surfaced. Others included China Petrochemical, Royal Dutch Shell, Exxon-Mobil,

Anglo-Atlantic Energy, and a clutch of smaller players, alone or in consortiums, with Alta International slipping through the middle of the pack.

Alta had a stake in Kuwait, but few other international interests. Some lucrative oil and gas fields in Alberta, B.C., and the Grand Banks, a refinery, an interest in a chain of gas stations, but it was a middling operation, and experts were shocked by its successful bid. The word *bribery* rarely surfaced in the reports, but euphemisms abounded: "ex gratia payments," "unanticipated extras," "development bonuses."

It was unclear who was runner-up, but Arthur had reason to suspect it was Anglo-Atlantic. An umbrella corporation, sheltering several midsize hopefuls from the U.K., Texas, and Alaska, with backing from unnamed Saudi sources. Big names on its board, a former U.S. vice-president, a British chancellor of the exchequer who'd left office under a cloud.

The clue had come by happenstance, from Irwin Godswill, overheard in this very club two weeks earlier telling his broker to pull out of Alta and into Anglo-Atlantic. Sly Irwin, whose insider knowledge and uncanny instincts for the market were legendary. Arthur looked about, saw no sign of the old crapshooter.

As he signed his chit for the maître d' he asked, "Mr. Godswill – seen him about lately?"

"I believe he's in his Palm Springs residence this week, sir."

"Ah, well, next time."

~~~

An hour later he was in Gastown, outside the War Room, where a sign read, "Support Canada's war effort." He paused to watch a kick-boxer being helped off the mat, his nose bleeding, as the winner leaned nonchalantly on the ropes. Arthur shuddered, took the elevator up to Macarthur, Brovak, Sage and Chance, where the receptionist told him Augustina was finishing with a client.

"And is Wentworth lurking about?"

"I'll ring his office."

"No!" More softly: "Please don't disturb him."

"But he asked me to let him know when you showed up."

"Let's keep that a secret between you and me for now."

Just the day before, the author of A Thirst for Justice had slipped through caller ID by using a payphone, demanding more details for Part Two: "The Wet Years." An hour taken up with a struggle to bring back misty memories best left buried.

Augustina came out after a few minutes, leading a grieving young woman to the door. Arthur couldn't imagine having the emotional strength for the family law she practised; cold-hearted murderers tended not to tug at the heartstrings.

She embraced him, led him to her office, produced a ziplock bag enclosing a thin, unopened envelope.

"I intercepted it before front desk could forward it to his mail drop. Haven't touched it."

The addressee's name was in pen, capital letters written in a hand unused to English, an awkward slant, misspellings: "BRIN POMOROY, LAYER." The address was barely sufficient: no postal code but the right street number. No return address. An Albanian stamp.

Arthur unsealed the plastic, lifted the envelope free by the corner, examining it but finding no smudges that might yield prints. "Any luck locating Brian?"

"The woman who runs the trading post in Fort Malchance – that's his mail drop – says he took off on a snowmobile over the Mackenzie Mountains to a ramshackle tourist lodge that's closed all winter, i.e., nine months of the year, and he must have hid out there for a few weeks. Searchers went out in a ski plane, but no Pomeroy. He'd been there, though. A forgotten shaving kit. A few .30–30 cartridges on the porch. He'd been subsisting on ptarmigans and snowshoe rabbits."

"He has a rifle."

"So has everyone else up there. But I know, that's not good."

Suicide was a real concern. Five hours of sunlight, if that, at this cruel time of year in the Subarctic. One didn't need a gun to die there.

"He'd left some scribbled notes that made no sense – something about a lost gold mine. That rang a bell. He recently beat some charges against a couple of hardrock miners over a stolen claim. I couldn't find the file – he may have taken it with him. According to our ledger, those guys never paid a retainer. What does that suggest to you?"

"That he's not as mad as we think." A gold mine could be a lucrative fee.

Arthur held the envelope up to the light, but he lacked Abraham Makepeace's gift of X-ray vision. He could make out a few lines written on a torn scrap of lined paper.

He slit the envelope with a letter opener, pulled the note out. Fractured English. The name "Brin Pomoroy" again appeared, and the line below read: "Abzal Erzhan, he say pliss help." Arthur swallowed hard. A name: "Hanife Bejko." An address in a town called Gjirokaster. "No telfon here. Pliss you cum here."

Augustina went to her computer, searched for Gjirokaster, which a website proclaimed to be a UNESCO World Heritage Site, a historic Ottoman town built on five steep hills in southern Albania, not far from the Greek border. Birthplace of Enver Hoxha, Albania's long-time Stalinist dictator who'd learned from the same manual as Boris Ivanovich.

She went off to make several copies of the letter and to store the original in the office safe. Arthur sank into an armchair, tingling with the impact of this confirmation of an uncertain theory, and with relief that Erzhan was still alive, though God knew in what health. Especially if he'd been subjected to that monstrous euphemism for torture, enhanced interrogation techniques.

Hanife Bejko – someone who'd shared a prison cell with him? Scared, presumably, and ultra-cautious. Albania had been newly born as a democracy after decades of Communist rule. Friendly to the West, but still unsteady on its feet.

In his turmoil, Arthur hadn't thought to close the door, and there was Wentworth Chance in the corridor, frowning at him. "I hope you can set the day aside, I have a million things to ask you."

"I meant to pop in, Wentworth. Today will be rather busy. I have a flight to Garibaldi at noon."

"I'll go with you. There are lots of people I have to talk to for 'The Garibaldi Years' section. There's so much going on in your life right now, I don't know how to end the book."

"Maybe if I got driven over by a cement truck, that would solve the problem." Wentworth looked shocked. "Sorry, that was dungeon humour. I do have private business on the island, Wentworth. Let's set a date and meet elsewhere."

"I have a first-draft deadline in three *weeks*. I'm also kind of limited on the early years. Your press coverage was skimpier back then, a lot of transcripts are missing. Grant me an hour now, a simple, measly hour, *please*."

Arthur must pay for the hurt he caused. He followed Wentworth to his office, a poorly soundproofed space looking over a fire escape. Through the floorboards could be heard thumps and yells and curses.

He looked balefully at the overflowing boxes of transcripts, letters, clippings, photos. Arthur's many triumphs were stored here, some bitter losses, but there was nothing to reveal the insecurity, the constant sense of impending failure that horse-whipped him to excel. Nothing to tell of the price the law demanded, or why he'd struggled in vain to escape into retirement. Unable to win a divorce from the law, that soul-destroying bitch, he was now representing the most wanted man in Canada, in Bhashyistan, and maybe the world.

~~~

Syd-Air ran an erratic and perilous service from Vancouver's Coal Harbour to the Gulf Islands with its one ill-maintained seaplane, but despite Syd's unwitting propensity for scooping up crab traps with his floats, his trips took only twenty minutes. Arthur always felt guilty about these eco-unfriendly flights, but he was in no mood to spend half a day on the ferry.

As the aircraft dipped below a sodden mass of cloud toward Blunder Bay, he saw that his dock was in total disarray. Planks missing, bumper floats missing, tools all over, beer cans, the *Blunderer* at anchor nearby, too close for comfort. As Syd made a flypast, Stoney and Dog scrambled to shore as if fearing an aerial attack.

Arthur took what comfort he could from the fact that they were already working and it was only half past twelve. He might have waded to shore, but he was in a suit, carrying his briefcase with a copy of the letter from Hanife Bejko. "Hopeless Bay, then," he told Syd. He could get a ride from the General Store. As they gained altitude, he saw Zack setting fence posts – and being aided, inevitably somehow, inescapably – by Ray DiPalma.

He was in a dilemma whether to show Hanife Bejko's note to him, to seek his advice – who would better know the ins and outs of Albania than the man who'd run the Balkan desk for CSIS? But if DiPalma were to leak the note to Crumwell – and through him to Abzal Erzhan's renderers – not only would Abzal be in deeper danger but Bejko's life might also be at risk. And Arthur would bear the burden of that.

As the plane settled in near the Hopeless wharf with a spume of spray, it barely missed Gomer Goulet's crab boat, just pulling in. Safely ashore, Arthur deflected Gomer's ire by buying a few Dungeness for dinner, enough to finance the old crabber's habit of a bottle of rum a day, and they walked together to the store.

Gomer nudged him slyly. "You came back for a little more, eh?"

"I beg your pardon?"

"The babe with the high-beam headlights. Your caretaker. She been taking pretty good care of you, eh?"

Fama volat. The rumour has wings. "I'll not dignify that crude suggestion with a single word in response." Instead, he'd used about a dozen.

Gomer nodded, unfazed. "Don't worry about Gomer Goulet. He knows when to keep his mouth shut. In fact I been telling people it ain't true."

No one will believe it, Margaret had said. She'd been away from Garibaldi too long, lost touch.

On the porch, several locals were taking an extended noon break, with junk food, cigarettes, and the house special, well-fortified coffees that had a couple of the boys already tipsy. The poker game had finally petered out, but a checkerboard was in play.

All eyes were on Arthur as he walked in, greeting everyone by name. "Ain't he looking all la-di-da in his city duds." Baldy Johansson, the electrician – oddly spiteful, though Arthur couldn't remember injuring him in any way. Ernie Priposki, who had recently retired – though from what work no one knew – was glowering at him from the checkerboard, but, oddly, the women were almost unctuous in their welcome.

"I think he looks *gorgeous* in that suit," said Tabatha Jones, bussing him on the cheek. "You bad boy," she whispered. Arthur went red.

Voracious Emily LeMay leaped up to fill his coffee mug. Peach brandy on her breath as she patted his rear. "You've lost weight, you sly old devil. Doing lots of push-ups?"

As he carried on to pick up his mail, the island seamstress, Thelma O'Dell, brushed by, so close he almost spilled his coffee. "Oh, sorry, Arthur."

"Not at all. You look lovely in that dress."

She lowered her eyes. "Oh, you."

He looked back at the sullen men, offering an apologetic smile. People could think what they want, he couldn't stop them. If those fellows wanted to believe he had hidden talents as a makeout artist, let them grind their teeth with envy. He'd not been unattractive in his younger years – tall, rangy, considered a bit of a catch, really – and the decades had added a patina of weathered, silver-haired robustness.

"Only thing in your box is this here flyer from Starkers Cove," Abraham Makepeace said. "Your, uh, your female associate was in already." With voice lowered: "Her boyfriend's back on the island. I thought I should warn you."

Arthur nodded, made a show of being absorbed in the Starkers leaflet, a response to islanders' concerns, rhetoric about how they respected their new neighbours, cherished this special island, and planned a development "in tune with nature," the obligatory mantra of the uncaring developer. Everyone was invited for a ground-breaking ceremony next month. Food, wine, games for kids, the Garibaldi Highlanders, the Fensom Family Fiddlers, and a touring off-island rock band.

"They're real nice folks." Makepeace nodded in the direction of a rosy-cheeked couple passing out T-shirts to his customers. The shirts featured a corporate logo and two stylized unclothed, well-endowed silhouettes. "Free yourself," said the embossed words.

"Everyone will be going," Makepeace said.

"What happened to the protest?"

"Well, that kind of fizzled out."

Arthur picked up a pack of pipe tobacco and strolled outside for a smoke just as Mookie Schloss alighted from her Land Rover. "He's *back!*" That seemed overly enthusiastic. Last seen, the ex-starlet was raging at her husband over his dishonourable poker bet. "I saw you on the tube, Arthur, you looked *so* commanding."

"And you look as radiant as ever, my dear." Not quite – some stress lines but still darkly attractive in her middle years.

"Need a ride?"

"You're an angel in a time of need, Mookie."

Arthur pulled out his pipe while she ran in for groceries; she was back in minutes, showing off her new T-shirt. "Nudists giving away clothes, that's original." As they headed off, she said, "Margaret must be in such a frazzle with everything that's going on. Was she able to make it back with you?"

"I'm afraid not."

"I guess it's really stressful, politics. It must be hard on you guys."

By now, Arthur was looking for double meanings in almost anything said to him. But surely Mookie was just being kind.

As she geared down for Breadloaf Hill, he checked Stoney's lot for his old Fargo. There it was, under canvas, on blocks, and beside it, *mirabile dictu,* the rebuilt transmission! He could soon be on wheels again, though carbon-negative Zack and Savannah mocked him for having a love affair with a pickup truck.

Next door on the Shewfelts' roof, Santa Claus sat Buddha-like, red-bulbed Rudolph leading the charge of the reindeer. The holiday season would see Margaret's return – she'd be furious to find the island rife with repugnant rumour.

Out of the blue: "Herman and I have split up. He's gone back to Los Angeles."

"I'm truly sorry."

"Oh, I'm getting by. I sometimes wish more friends would visit."

Arthur was flustered, unsure how to respond to this obvious invitation. He stammered something nonsensical about how charming women should never lack company.

"How sweet. You have *such* an awesome way with words, so easy to talk to. Hey, if you need to lighten the load about stuff that's bothering you, you'll find an attentive listener in a cozy cottage on Sunrise Cove."

What was going on here? Rampaging rumour had retooled the old duffer into the island heartthrob. He was seen as available, open to suitors' beds, his wobbly marriage manifestly doomed. Margaret was definitely in denial with her insistence that locals would laugh off the rumour, her refusal to recognize he still held appeal to the opposite sex.

Mookie let him off at his gate with a soft kiss on stiff lips that, with lack of use, seemed to have lost the art of puckering. The rich, womanly smell of her. Different from Margaret.

~~~

A light shower announced the arrival of a warm Pacific front with its gift of mild, sea-scented air, which Arthur sucked in greedily, relishing this reprieve from the East's lung-searing cold. His house seemed to spread its eaves in welcome, smoke spilling from the chimney, promising the cheering solace of a blazing fireplace. The grounds appeared well tended, the lawn lush, fences in repair. Savannah had been yeomanlike in shouldering the tasks of a working farm – without much help from Zack, who'd been long absent and seemed unlikely to stick around.

Arthur could make him out in the west pasture, with the tractor, digging postholes. The post-setter, DiPalma, seemed in pain, holding his back, a greenhorn in distress. Too many hours conniving at a desk or in airplane seats.

More convoluted were the labyrinthine rigours being expended on the dock. Stoney was leaning over the water, lowering a two-by-six while shouting instructions to Dog, who was splashing about, to no apparent purpose, in a wetsuit.

Savannah trotted from the house with an umbrella, closed on him with a hug and a kiss, the second such *beneficium* in ten minutes, this one met cleanly. She seemed thinner, more sinewy.

He hoped she might say something about the Episode, about having discussed it with Margaret. But she'd rarely been forthcoming about her disorder. The rumours could not have escaped her. Instead, as she toured him about, she chronicled her run-ins with local fauna: the Great Sheep Escape, the bum-butting ram, the deer that squeezed past the garden gate.

He praised her skills at farm management. She admitted to having been less adept at local politics: apathy and promises of food, drink, and music had subverted the Norbert Road campaign.

Two of those who'd turned out for her last meeting had been wearing Starkers Cove T-shirts.

But the developers had made concessions, narrowing the swath to be cleared along Lower Mount Norbert Road.

Finally she said, softly: "I'm sorry I embarrassed you. Stoney and his big mouth."

"Margaret thought it was funny."

"Well, it is a lark, isn't it?"

She laughed and took his arm, and they made their way to the house – despite his better judgment he was titillated, it was as if they were sharing an intimate conspiracy. On the veranda, as he kicked off his muddy brogans, he gestured toward Zack and Ray. "What's up with those two?"

"They're getting on like Batman and Robin. They're planning some kind of political hanky-panky."

"Like what, exactly?"

"Nothing serious, a diversion, misinformation, something to do with the tar sands. Ray's idea. He's pretty imaginative."

Arthur chose his words carefully in warning that DiPalma was being checked out and asking her to be circumspect in dealing with him. "He may not be what he appears to be."

"No kidding. He's convinced the locals he's queer, but that didn't stop him making a pass at me. He's the poor man's James Bond – he only has a licence to fuck. Maybe he swings both ways work-wise too. One day he's spying for them, the next day for us. I guess that's fair. He totally admires you – or so he says."

"I suspect he suffers some ill-defined neurosis relating to his father, but I think I'd prefer not to know the details."

"Hey, we're just playing him along, Zack and me. We keep testing him. He never quite gets the language of protest. With him, it's like, 'Down with the imperialist warmongers, power to the working class.' With Zack, it's a mind game, he's enjoying Ray, and if he can't convert him he's going to outsmart him. It's a kind of male thing, dogs sniffing at each other's balls."

Arthur decided to leave it at that – this wasn't the time to confront DiPalma.

While Savannah went off to collect eggs, Arthur tested his club chair, which lacked its old comfortable fit. He had indeed lost weight, in the bottom and shanks. Exercise and political stress had dampened his appetite.

He put his feet up, opened his briefcase, frowned over the letter from Hanife Bejko, seeking but not finding hidden meaning. He tried to picture the southern Balkans, a region unvisited during his occasional sallies to Europe. Maybe Albania was like Garibaldi, full of sheep and characters.

He saw Stoney through the window, jumping around, holding his thumb, a mis-hit with the hammer. Dog was flopping about on the beach like a spastic seal, struggling out of his underwater gear. The workday was coming to an end.

Savannah came in, humming off key. She swung by him toward the laundry room, stripping off her T-shirt, tossing it in the hamper, lowering her jeans. Nude bending over by Degas.

There came back, suppressed till now, the tingle he'd felt on awakening beside her, her breast plump as a pillow, her cradling arm, her warm breath in his ear . . .

~~~

As Zack and Savannah bickered in the kitchen, Arthur and DiPalma hunkered by the fireplace, Arthur sipping tea, DiPalma wincing as he pulled the tab on a can of beer. His second. He'd chugged the first.

"It isn't easy being green," he said, "but it's a darn sight harder being gay. That was not the most skilful of moves. Now I'm being courted by Kurt Zoller."

The accordion-playing island trustee. Arthur was astonished. He'd known him for eight years, hadn't assumed he preferred men – in fact hadn't presumed he had any sexual leanings whatsoever.

"He wants us to come out publicly. Otherwise, I'm an object of pity more than homophobia around this island. People detour when they see me coming, especially the machos."

"Amazing. Have you ever considered a career in theatre, Ray?"

"Played a creditable Stanley Kowalski in an Ottawa Free Theatre production. Ask your neighbour in 10C if the Alumni Theatre still remembers my 'Mourning Becomes Electra.'" He arched his back, grimacing. "I'm a government employee – I'm used to shovelling papers."

A secret sense of humour was unveiled. Arthur said, "I, on the other hand, am healthier now than I was in my youth. Never was much for organized sports." He wondered if he was playing that mind game himself, the sniffing of balls.

DiPalma didn't hesitate. "You're looking at the man who scored the winning point in the 1990 college intramural water polo championships. Chased some pucks for the Ravens. Those days are over, alas."

If it was indeed a mind game, DiPalma had just scored another winning point. The awkwardness he'd displayed on earlier encounters had to be related either to drink or the nervousness of one assigned to probe a prominent couple.

"Well, Ray, there's always old-timers' sports."

"Not for me. My medical examiner found some early symptoms of PD."

Parkinson's disease. Thus the impaired balance, the occasional slight tremor. Arthur found himself empathizing with DiPalma. Suddenly it was all making sense, the shuffling walk, the ill-advised comforts of cigarettes and booze, the reaching out to religion. Arthur's talent at judging character was not flawed after all; his first instincts had been right.

DiPalma had both a beer and a cigarette going now, the smoke rising up the flue. "Anyway, I've finished my stint on Garibaldi. I'm on the road, I'm Zack Flett's *consigliore* now. My boss is delighted. He put me in charge of the eco-terrorist section, with my own office."

From the kitchen: "Wash your hands before you even fucking *touch* that cinnamon roll."

"Wash your fucking mouth."

"Don't those guys ever stop?" DiPalma sat stiffly, words tumbling out between sips and puffs. "Okay, I talked to the agent I mentioned, Sullivan Clugg, Sully – he liaises with the limeys. He has good intel that an international security firm working out of London – mercenaries, basically, ex-MI5, KGB, Stasi – set up a ghost flight from Montreal last month. On contract for unknown employers. Destination, Albania."

DiPalma's information resonated with such credibility that Arthur wondered why he'd ever doubted him. He showed him Hanife Bejko's letter. DiPalma lit a fresh cigarette off the one he hadn't finished, fixed his glasses over his nose, and his mouth fell open as he read the note.

Finally he looked up. "Oh, baby. Gjirokaster – I've been in that town." He yelped, sucked a knuckle burned by the cigarette in his left hand. "I have to cut down." He read the note one more time, then looked up with a gleeful smile.

"Albania. Let's go."

20

—

Clara Gracey had moved into 24 Sussex and felt cowed, even bullied, by the thirty-four-room, energy-guzzling limestone mansion, the uncomfortable home of prime ministers since the 1940s. With its creaks and groans and hissing radiators, it was like living in the belly of a wheezy old whale.

She'd debated whether to move in – tenancy could be brief – but had felt guilty smoking in her chic apartment; here she could make the rules. And hold private council without intrusions.

Four acres and the Ottawa River and the cover of darkness would shelter Margaret Blake's arrival. A couple of the gals talking over a glass of wine – it was worth a try. The last hope, really. An expanded, loophole-free Species at Risk Act, half a billion for renewable energy, two more national parks – the cabinet wouldn't balk at those in exchange for a tie vote, with a compliant Speaker to break it.

Good riddance to that narcissistic traitor Lafayette – she wouldn't have to look over her shoulder any more. If an election were forced, he would get his reward, a deserved burial of the Progressive Reform Party.

So it was opposition 154, government 152, and to scramble for that, Clara had had to promise the seven-toed member for Twillingate that if he hobbled in on crutches he'd be in line for secretary of state for sport and tourism. The vote was set for the day after tomorrow.

Percival Galbraith-Smythe rang. "Ms. Blake is in the foyer. Shall I send her in?"

"Of course not. I'll come out to greet her."

She put on her most winning smile, butted her smoke, and headed out, turning the wrong way, finally getting directions from one of her staff.

Margaret was in the foyer by the grand staircase, looking aghast at its leopard spot carpet, a garish memento from the Mulroney years.

"Don't blame me," Clara said. "Every P.M. since St. Laurent has left his spoor." Finnerty's contribution: several hidden bottles of rye.

They settled in a parlour overlooking the river and the distant twinkling lights of Hull. Margaret chose a settee, crossed her legs, wary, a little tense. She had a good inkling of what this was about. "Stick to your guns," Pierètte had said. "Buyer beware."

She had respect for Clara: it took grit and intelligence to manoeuvre through the old boys' club to 24 Sussex. But she was an economist wedded to the old thinking, a pedigreed Tory playing the old games, out of touch with the realities facing this besieged planet.

"White or red?"

"The white, thank you."

"Mandarins, nuts, granola chews — sorry, I'm trying to lose weight. Look at you, you've never had that problem."

Margaret picked out a nut from the offered tray. Clara poured from a boutique B.C. Chardonnay, not hiding the label.

"Certified organic," Margaret said, acknowledging the gesture.

"They're always a little more expensive, aren't they?"

"Surprising, given the cost of herbicides, fungicides, and the other poisons most of them use."

Clara was having trouble with the concept of growing grapes with poison. She didn't care to mention that winemakers were big contributors.

Trying not to sound effusive, she dished out compliments on Margaret's performance on and off the floor, for representing so persuasively Canada's growing green electorate. "I'm so proud of you. Especially as a woman."

"One of those unfortunate accidents of birth, I guess."

Clara laughed. This is what she wanted, a little feminist bipartisanship. "Congratulations, by the way. The last Gallup had you at thirteen per cent."

"Thank you, but it's spread too thinly, isn't it?"

"That's our electoral system, sadly."

"If I recall right, Clara, a few years ago you were calling it a skewed system."

Clara kicked herself for opening the topic, but Margaret wasn't through. "It's a great curiosity, isn't it, that when in opposition the traditional parties forever talk about a reformed Senate and proportional representation, but it vanishes from the agenda when they're in power. Here you are at thirty-three per cent with almost half the seats; while our thirteen points translates to one, and I squeaked in."

Clara sipped her wine, wondering how to get back on track. "Christ knows you'll have little trouble holding on to it, Margaret." A gamble: "Just between friends, and if you repeat this, I'll deny, but I doubt we'll try very hard to win Cowichan back. We may just throw a nobody in there for laughs."

"Oh? I had understood you were targeting it."

"Strategies change." A deep breath. "Margaret, you're nobody's fool. You know why I wanted this little gab with you."

Little gab. Girl talk. The P.M. had slipped a rung in Margaret's esteem. "I'm open to hear you, Clara. I have to warn you – I've never learned how to play political prostitute."

If the insinuation was meant to draw blood, it worked. Clara sought to control herself, covered by tilting her glass and emptying it.

Margaret told herself to stop this sniping, it wasn't very mature. She searched for the source of it – maybe resentment of Clara, that she was to the manner born, thanks to a powerful, connected family, all the breaks and all the perks. "I'm sorry if that seemed sexist or personal. Political compromise is what I have a problem with. Some people think I suffer a stubbornness disability."

Clara laughed it off with "Save your shots for the floor of the House," but it took effort not to lecture this idealist. Compromise – her prostitution – was the lifeblood of the art of politics.

Down to business. "Okay, Margaret, I don't have to tell you these are difficult economic times, but here's what's on the table." Clara went down the list, renewable energy, species at risk, five hundred thousand hectares of national park. No reaction, just that impenetrable steel-grey gaze.

Clara wanted a refill but noticed Margaret's wine was nearly untouched. She splashed a little in her own glass anyway. She was starting to understand why Finnerty became a drunk on this job.

"Here's my counter-offer," Margaret said. "We're committed to a carbon tax, one that is neither token nor symbolic. Fifty dollars per metric ton of non-renewables, doubling in ten years. Plus an end to all subsidies to oil and coal producers. Full compliance with the Kyoto Protocol. Those are fundamental."

Clara had intended Kyoto as a sweetener anyway if things got desperate, so she topped up her bid with a ten-year plan to comply. But a carbon tax – fifty a ton or ten, it didn't matter – sent a chill down her spine. She'd crusaded against the concept as grossly unaffordable for a country struggling from recession. "Believe me, Margaret, a carbon tax won't get past the cabinet. You don't know what I'm dealing with."

"I know what you're dealing with. A bunch of non-renewables." It's not the economy, stupid, she wanted to say. It's planetary survival.

"Take it to your people." Clara couldn't believe they were all as bullheaded as their parliamentary leader.

Margaret was finding this ticklish. She didn't want to be tarred as the rotten apple in the Opposition barrel, the M.P. who saved an unpopular government, but a hamper of rations had been offered, and she could be spanked for not snatching it. This was not her call to make alone.

"Is anyone off limits? The press, I assume."

"I suppose they'll find out eventually. Later the better. For now, can we keep this among friends?"

"You'll take my counter-offer to your people?"

"Absolutely." Clara had zero hope.

Before escorting her guest to the front door, she showed her around a bit, talking about this and that: how Lafayette took a jump off the cliff, the Bhashyistan standoff, the alleged kidnapping of Abzal Erzhan, the clever job by Margaret's husband in using a press conference to set up an alibi defence. They even shared a laugh over Charley Thiessen's ham-handed performance at that event.

Margaret took one last look about as an attendant bowed and scraped at the open door. All the hoary old paintings and urns and vases and bric-a-brac. She'd heard it cost sixty thousand a year to heat the joint.

"Watch out," said Clara. "The day may come when you'll be sleeping in the main bedroom, having nightmares."

"Stranger things have happened," said Margaret, setting off for the waiting limo.

Clara felt a headache, the kind that came from banging your head against a wall.

~~~

Nine o'clock Wednesday morning. In half an hour Thiessen would be joining the rest of the cabinet to debate a dying effort to stave off defeat the next day and an election that could send the Tories tumbling to a grab bag of seats. His was safe, maybe the safest in the country outside the Bible belt. Clara Gracey's wasn't, the Toronto burbs.

He could live with the likely scenario, Clara slip-sliding back into academia, good old boy Charley Thiessen elected to succeed her, maybe by acclamation. A spell as Opposition leader, winning applause with his jabs and quips, galloping to an easy win in the next election. Prime Minister Thiessen. Call me Charley.

He sat back, his sock feet up on his desk with its old framed photo of his younger mom, smiling down at little Charley in his Cub uniform. Who'd have known?

He'd run that scenario past her last night. "That's my Charley," she'd told him. "You are the *man*." She hadn't said one mean word about how he'd wrong-footed himself in the National Press Theatre – though it had featured on the nightly newscasts, Charley in his juice-stained shirt, his mouth opening and closing like a fish freshly landed. Rick Mercer had done a prime-time skit on the CBC, in a dripping red shirt.

He picked up the phone. "Send him in." Crumwell, who'd called en route from Ogilvie Road with a promise of good news "that I'm sure you'll enjoy." Abzal Erzhan found hiding in the back room of a Montreal tenement? Arthur Beauchamp arrested smoking crack in a bordello? The consensus at CSIS was that Beauchamp's kidnap scenario stank. Cooked up for a murder defence. That gasbag and his smirking put-down.

Crumwell slipped in like a thief, quietly closed the door.

"How's that problem with your, uh, works, Anthony?"

"Much better. You wanted something on Arthur Beauchamp."

"All you got."

"I hope this isn't too rich for your blood." A rare, puckish smile. "He's having an affair with a convicted felon."

Thiessen almost slipped off his chair as he sat upright. "Are you putting me on?"

"Savannah Buckett, his farmhand. One presumes she's progressed from raids on timber booms to a more intimate form of radical action."

"You got proof? Photos? Tapes?"

"Nothing quite so graphic, but you can take it to the bank. God knows why our man on Garibaldi was so slow in forthcoming – Agent DiPalma is a bit reserved about such matters, a goody two-shoes – but it's all over that island."

Thiessen didn't know exactly where Garibaldi was. He tried to picture it, barren, windswept, the mail packet pulling in twice a week, tobacco-chewing fishermen in their Wellingtons, slatternly housewives at their clotheslines gossiping with neighbours.

"Ms. Buckett is known to be publicly quarrelling with her partner, who is rarely seen on the island any more. But here's the clincher: there's an eyewitness to one of Beauchamp's coital diversions with this young woman. One Robert Stonewell, a local businessman, caught them in bed." An impish grin.

Thiessen couldn't suppress a whoop of triumph. Revenge was his, sweet, sweet revenge. That sneering bugger had been caught with his pants down – and not just with some run-of-the-mill tramp, but an eco-terrorist. The old wolf didn't exactly look like a hotshot with the ladies. Maybe he used his smooth tongue to slick his way into her panties. A task eased by her being on his payroll – that added a scurrilous element.

"Does his wife know?"

"I'm given to understand there are no secrets on Garibaldi Island."

The possibilities were rich, an explosive scandal, a messy divorce in the middle of an election campaign. "How do we nail this down? Tell me about this Stonewell."

"An exemplar, an esteemed community leader. Owns multiple businesses, building trades, taxi service, full-service garage, car lot. A tourist venture too, a hot-air balloon concession, so he obviously has a commercial pilot's licence. Agent DiPalma says he's quite a go-getter, highly regarded by his peers."

"My kind of guy. Would he sign an affidavit?"

"Can't say. DiPalma isn't sure how close he is to Beauchamp.

But he believes Stonewell may be open to, shall we say, magnanimous gestures. Not out-and-out bribery, of course, that's out of the picture."

"Oh, yeah, definitely. Politics?"

"Well, he hardly sounds like a wild-eyed radical, does he?"

Thiessen turned to the window, another demonstration out there, against animal testing. Someone in a monkey costume, another a dog, a big furry head with a jovial smile. It brought back Beauchamp grinning at Thiessen, asking for someone to bring a straw. Maybe a little human animal testing was in order.

"Anthony, let's say we were to bring Mr. Stonewell here on some pretext, a good citizenship award, something like that, show him a good time, get one of your guys to loosen him up over a few tots . . ."

"With a hidden microphone, just in case."

"Brilliant. And we invite his wife too, or his lover or companion, whatever he has, fly them first class, put them up in the Château. I could meet him myself, buy him lunch or dinner, impress the hell out of him."

Crumwell smiled his squinty smile. "You don't think that would be pushing it?"

"Naw, I've got a knack dealing with small-town, average-Joe businessmen." He rehearsed, a jocular voice. "Robert, I guess you must know Arthur Beauchamp. Lovable old sod, but I hear he's quite a scamp."

Crumwell nodded with approval. "There are rumours, Charley, that you may take a fling at the leadership."

Thiessen tried to look pained. "Yeah, there's pressure, they're coming at me from all sides. I'm resisting. We can't look divided, we have to throw all our weight behind Clara."

"Of course." Looking at him with his cold, pebbly pupils, seeing right through him.

"Not that Clara has to know about Operation Stonewell."

"You understand, Charley, that this is, let's say, a titch beyond our mandate."

"I'll cover you." Thiessen grabbed his jacket, he had to run. "This conversation never happened, okay?"

"I'll see what we can do. As a favour, Charley."

~~~

Thiessen got to the cabinet room a little late. Clara was reading out a shopping list from the Green leader that was being met with frowns and groans.

He found a seat beside Jack Bodnarchuk, whose arms were folded in tight defiance. He grumbled to Thiessen: "This goes through, Alberta's out of the confederation."

The resources minister was a key player in delegate-rich Alberta. "This goes through over my dead body," Thiessen said. In truth, though, he worried that his party could be on the wrong track on energy issues. He'd been helping his oldest son, fifteen, on a climate change project – the schools pump kids full of that stuff these days. He'd had to sit through that depressing Al Gore documentary, had been forced to read a lot of alarming stuff from scientists. His daughter Joy was even worse, had practically joined the green camp. He'd told her to find balance, seek out opposing views. "From who?" she'd scornfully demanded. "Oil company apologists?"

Anyway, the P.M. definitely wasn't touting any deal with the Greens. She was going on about how she gave it her best shot, how Margaret Blake had blown her chance, how it would rebound against her party. Calls would now go out for a star candidate to bring home Cowichan and the Islands. Applause.

Thiessen drifted away, half listening to the debate, which was one-sided anyway. A star candidate. Maybe that's the pitch to give Mr. Stonewell. *Robert, there's another reason we've brought you and your good lady here. Our party is looking for a respected, business-oriented candidate . . .*

~~~

Margaret was hunched over her desk with Pierètte, in near fury as she read the PMO's noon press release: the government had flatly rejected the Green Party's costly, recession-deepening ultimatums. Its leader had spurned the government's own generous bundle of initiatives for a healthier environment.

"That fraudulent hypocrite!" Mocking Gracey's sugary tone: "'Can we keep this among friends?'"

"Cool down," Pierètte said. "The corrections we're sending out are angry enough."

"Goddamnit, she *begged* me to sit down with her."

"Exactly what we're telling the media. What did you do, critique her hairdo?"

"I did *not* let my temper carry me away."

"Temper? You have a temper? Hey, you did great, you didn't buy her girlie guff so she showed her claws. I'm proud of you." She zipped up her jacket.

"Where are you going?"

"To McRory. I'm going to tell him you're still straddling the fence and may grab Gracey's offer as something that's better than nothing. He's hungry, he can taste it. Let's see if he can swallow the fifty-buck carbon tax."

Alone, Margaret tried some yoga breathing. Still your anger, find peace . . .

A staffer crept in, nervously dropped off a draft of Pierètte's press release. Margaret scanned it. "Fine. Fax it around."

She turned up her TV – there it was, top of the news, her recession-aggravating, gun-to-the-head ultimatum. Just the tail end of that, then A.J. Quilter from Calgary, proposing to sue Ottawa for his lost profits from Bhashyistan. A mere two billion dollars.

The third son, a clip from his latest infuriating YouTube dispatch. "From where Canada gets this dead leaf as symbol?" Displaying a ragged Canadian flag. "Turns red, falls from tree, decomposes. What else they have – loon, goose, old sailboat. We have snow leopard, Siberian tiger." A shot of him standing under snarling head trophies. "Still some live in zoo. This is Mukhamet Khan Ivanovich, your unvarnished source of fast-breaking news. Tune in very soon for Operation Storming Ram."

Still no mention of those poor women from Saskatchewan. Margaret listened awhile to a pundits' guessing game about Storming Ram, then clicked the set off. Question Period coming up. She might miss most of it while in the foyer with the press. She will control her temper. She will.

Think love and peace.

~~~

For the first time since his rise to stardom in this House, Gerard Lafayette found himself on the far back bench to the right of the Speaker. And for the first time in his life, he'd allowed pride – ignoble pride, his one damnable weakness – to provoke him into an act of measureless stupidity.

Stunned by his demotion to the bowels of the Conservative cabinet, he'd reacted unthinkingly, in the heat of the moment, and was now in the throes of regret. He was being tainted as resentful and impetuous. The most savage swipe, from the NDP leader: he had deserted the sinking ship "not like a rat but a spoiled brat."

A major setback to his ambitions. A miscalculation. He'd expected at least a dozen core supporters to join him, but had commandeered only two, and with an election looming, he had no time to build a base. He could lose his own riding of Montréal Nord.

He sat back, masking his pain, his self-inflicted wounds, as members lauded today's lot of heroes: three Restigouche campgirls who saved a drowning friend, the winner of an oyster-eating contest, an armless Afghanistan veteran. Lafayette rose wearily to join in the applause.

Claude McRory hurried in late, half shaved, his furred eyebrows screaming for manicure scissors, a bull-faced expression. He beckoned his shadow cabinet to huddle. Lafayette had a sense of what this was about – the parliamentary aide to the Green leader had been observed courting audience with McRory, presumably to barter Margaret Blake's vote in exchange for an extortionate carbon tax.

He could see heads nodding. The message was clear: Blake's blackmail had succeeded, she had bound the Liberals to a recession-worsening tax as the price of bringing the government down. The huddle quickly dispersed as Gracey came waltzing in for Question Period.

McRory scrambled to his chair ready to fire one of his wild salvos, but Gracey got the Speaker's nod.

"Mr. Speaker, I have the pleasure of informing this House that I have just met with the governor general, who has proclaimed that this Parliament is to be dissolved forthwith and a general election to be held on Monday, January twenty-fourth. On that date, the people of Canada will decide whether they want their nation to be run by those who seek to represent them truly and honourably or by the tax-and-spenders who in their thirst for power would leave our economy in ruins. Season's greetings to all. Enjoy the holiday."

McRory began spouting, but couldn't be heard over the brave shouts and loud shuffling of government members as their benches emptied. Lafayette saw Margaret Blake enter, looking con-fused, unaware this Parliament was at an end – probably her polit-ical career too, now that she'd failed to enforce her dictates. *Le Parti Vert est en ruine.*

~~~

If I hadn't found a calendar page in the back of this journal I wouldn't have even thought of Christmas. A week away. It's a jolt, and it sent me spinning back to Canora, to home, to merry Christmases past. Being with my husband, my darlings. I'm in trouble . . .

Get it together.

Okay, just a little crying jag, I'll start this again, a fresh, dry page.

I lost track of the days because I've been on Igor Time. Officially, this is called Death to Soviet Empire month, and today, if I've got it right, is Izbar, named after Igor's eldest son.

Nobody around here takes all that stuff seriously, the renaming of all the days, and stars and rivers. They make jokes about the Ultimate Leader. They name toilet paper after him, and horse droppings. "Don't step on the Ivanovich," someone will say.

They call the dictator the Cockroach for Life. "God be praised, it will be a short one," Aisulu said. She only just found her way here, one of the dissidents who escaped from jail when our soldiers freed everyone. I love her, she is so brave. She had a chance to jump on one of the helicopters but chose to stay and fight. She'd been beaten and raped many times in there, and she can still laugh at Ruslan's tall stories. She has that tough old bullshitter wrapped around her finger. Redbeard the pirate, we all call him.

Where we are is in the Altay Mountains, which look huge for a girl from Saskatchewan, maybe not as high as the Rockies but close. We're in a well-guarded valley, with outlooks and snipers up on the rocky ledges, and there are no roads, we had to hike in because the horses were too laden. However, this is as close to paradise as winter permits. It's one of Igor's private reserves and no one is allowed in but his park maintenance crew, three guys stationed in a yurt at the end of the road. It had the biggest "No Trespassing" you've ever seen, a billboard.

The three of them awoke at dawn and found themselves staring at Atun's Kalashnikov. After a long talk over a samovar they decided to join us, but maybe out of fear, I don't know. So we (the rebels, I mean) now have two snowmobiles, three more rifles, extra food. Skis, snowshoes. We'd have had a working satellite phone if the battery hadn't run out. One of our guys took off with it yesterday, and he's going to try to buy a battery from a smuggler.

So now we're squatting the Ultimate Cockroach's lodge, which he only uses in summer. Massive wooden beams, ten rooms (a den full of animal heads, ibex, bear, lynx, deer, snow leopard), three baths, and hot water. This is because of the hotsprings just a three-minute walk up stone steps to where a bathing pool has been blasted into the rock. The overflow keeps the lodge warm, though it's dark in here. Ruslan doesn't want to start up the diesel generator, it makes too much noise. Maxine, Ivy, and I have candles, which I'm using now to write. Maxine is asleep and I suspect Ivy is downstairs with Atun. Doing whatever they do in the darkness. Maxine is resigned to it, sort of, preferring a gun-toting revolutionary to a dope-dealing dropout.

There must be close to seventy people here now, more coming every day, bedraggled and cold, diving into the borscht that Maxine and I keep going on the propane stove. She's volunteered as head chef, and is dazzling everyone.

Someone got a Canadian flag from a smuggler, and it's hanging outside, just above a rough sign that says, translated, National Headquarters, BDRF. Little Hasran, who is only fourteen, has a dream of becoming a Canadian pilot someday. One time they chorused us with "O Canada," it sounded hilarious. I was truly shocked to hear a partisan recite a dozen stanzas of "The Shooting of Dan McGrew."

And they're always carrying on about Abzal Erzhan, the great things he did, sending the Great Father the way of Dan McGrew, blowing up "those nine sons of whores who sucked on Igor's tit and stuck their heads up his Ivanovich," as bowlegged old Ilyich crudely put it. (Ilyich has no fingernails, but he wasn't born that way.)

They meet a lot, Redbeard the Pirate in the chair, trying to keep things on keel, but they shout and argue. A lot of them can't speak Russian, which is the second language here, but I could still pick up they're talking guerrilla warfare; incursions into the countryside to give hope to the people there and bring more fighters into the fold. Sort of like Castro in the Sierra Maestra.

Plans to smuggle us across the border are on hold. "When the time is ripe," Ruslan says. "Not taking chances with our beautiful

Canadian ladies." Sometimes I writhe with worry. Sometimes I'm at peace and full of hope, not just for ourselves, but for this defiant ragtag band of warriors.

Christmas, I'm having trouble visualizing it. The tree, the turkey, the hanging stockings. Old Tom Witherspoon in his creepy Santa suit, snockered on rum punch. Mabel Zytishin and her jinglebell necklace and out-of-key carolling. The girls dragging us out of bed at half past six. I have to stop now.

21

———

Arthur stared into the half-emptied closet, wondering what to pack for Christmas in Albania. Three suits would be too many; he'd surely find a dry cleaner somewhere. A warm sweater or two, an umbrella for the rainy winter climate. No point in taking his cellphone. Its reach did not extend beyond North America.

All Margaret's clothing was gone but a pair of briefs that had somehow got mixed in with his underwear. He pocketed a stray earring, one of a pearl set he'd bought her for a Christmas past. Christmas present would be spent in Albania, where a Christmas present must be bought for her. Surely that struggling little republic would have something distinctive on offer, some handicraft or colourful fabrics.

Before heading off to her riding to set up her campaign, she'd given his trip her tentative blessing, warning him not to let DiPalma lead him into trouble – despite Arthur's latest efforts to champion him, she was sticking to her view that he was capricious and unstable. At the slightest hint of mischance, she would hand a copy of Hanife Bejko's letter to the deputy foreign minister. Until then, no one in government would know about this mission – certainly not Crumwell, whom Arthur heartily distrusted.

Margaret had called from Garibaldi, to inform him, with frost in her voice, that a klatch of women had come by to buck her up with cookies and sympathy, welcoming her to the cheated wives' club. "Christ, this island is hopeless. Arthur, you didn't . . ."

"Damn it," he'd moaned. "If it will shut them up, I'll pay for a full-page denial in the *Bleat*."

"Please don't."

Piling his arms with clothes, Arthur listened dully to the scales on a violin, repeated monotonously – it was Sunday, when 10C's musicologist gave lessons to neighbourhood youngsters. When he returned to the living room and his yawning suitcases, the scritching of strings was succeeded by the bawling of the male lead of "Marital Bonds," who'd been exiled to the balcony. "Jules and Patsy? You *what?* Invited them *over?* Tell them I'm tied up!"

"Give him a gag too," someone called from below.

Arthur turned the radio up for the news, catching the back end of the lead item: " . . . not only hacked into, but all hard drives on their networks rendered inoperative. Here's a further report from Angela Brinker in Toronto."

"Clyde, members of the RCMP electronics crimes division said the virus has clogged computers of several big-box chains with some kind of screensaver that is multiplying exponentially like amoebas gone wild. It's in the form of a high-resolution banner that reads in translation: 'Death to the Assassin Erzhan.'"

Operation Storming Ram. Arthur got it: Random-Access Memory. Either the third son or one of his helpmates was a genius. Cyber warfare had struck at the true heart of Western democracy, not government but consumerism, the prime engine of commerce, mega-mall shopping outlets. Just before Christmas.

"While the virus seems to have originated in Bhashyistan," Ms. Brinker said, "it has been traced to a proxy Internet provider in Russia. Experts say it will be days before all computers can be cleaned. Losses are expected to be in the tens of millions. Back to you, Clyde."

Arthur listened without much heart to condemnation from government, politicians, industry spokespersons. International figures too, but Canada's powerful Western allies seemed unwilling to move off the sidelines, as if expecting Bhashyistan to implode on its own and the problem to disappear.

Arthur could only guess what awaited him overseas; he harboured little faith that his quest would end well. He'd followed the horror stories from Guantánamo and Abu Ghraib, terrorist suspects crippled for life or driven to madness by waterboarding, sleep deprivation, acts of unbearable humiliation. Or killed.

Who had engineered this extraordinary act of extraordinary rendition of a Canadian citizen named Abzal Erzhan? Russia seemed well in the picture, given reports from Sully Clugg that ex-KGB agents may have been involved. Billions in oil revenues were at stake for Gazprom if the Alta deal could be scuttled. As well, the computer virus had been traced to a server in Russia, where cyber crime flourished and the rule of law was idly enforced.

But Arthur preferred the signs that pointed to Anglo-Atlantic Energy, with its wealthy backers and powerful British and American ex-politicians – who, presumably, had easy access to the former spies mentioned by Agent Clugg, international mercenaries operating under the cover of a London security company.

Given the ease with which Abzal had been plucked from the streets of Chambly, might CSIS operatives also be involved in this shadow world of espionage agents? What about Clugg himself, whom DiPalma called a "thoroughgoing jerk"? Was Anthony Crumwell complicit? His background, after all, was as former head of MI5's anti-terrorist wing. Arthur had never met him, but heard he was embittered at the world after a letter bomb shredded his hand.

Arthur returned his attention to the radio: the first poll figures of the campaign were out. Liberals forty-nine per cent, Conservatives eighteen and on the verge of a near-historic collapse, the NDP, Bloc, and Greens in low double digits. Progressive Reform was sniffing at the leavings while busily nominating candidates – a few respected names but many malcontents, fringe elements. Lafayette had been busy, scouring the country in an effort to patch together a credible team.

Arthur was not looking forward to this tedious, crowded global warming flight, but to kill time he'd picked up a Lonely Planet tour guide and an Albanian phrasebook. As he zipped up his bag, there came strained laughter from the neighbour's balcony. "Don't get the wrong idea, Jules – the straps are to keep me in bed. I have a sleepwalking disorder."

Arthur sighed, wondering if he would forever be haunted by the Episode.

~~~

Tragger, Inglis's Ottawa branch was small in numbers but big in rarefied specialties: trademarks, patents, private international law. Arthur's first stop there was the office of Antoine Salzarro, the former Public Security mandarin who'd liaised with CSIS for many years.

Arthur had already apologized to this portly, pleasant gentleman for having put him to so much trouble over DiPalma before instructing him to pull out the hired investigator. And now he apologized further for seeking to tap into his knowledge of Sullivan Clugg.

"Ah, yes, Sully. Interfaces with MI5, MI6, quite a character. I believe he has a black belt in something or other – a hard man, as the term is used in the service. Did a stint in Iraq with Blackwater before coming on board, bit of a dark past there, I've heard."

Arthur found this brief CV intriguing and asked Salzarro if he might be able to fill it out. "Nothing classified, of course."

"Of course."

"But it might help my client's case if I found out the names of his closest work companions."

"Mr. Bullingham has put me entirely at your service. Indeed, he has asked if I might determine if any CSIS personnel may be susceptible to, uh, certain temptations."

And whose misdoings might aid in the downfall of the party in power. Good old Bully.

The firm's senior Ottawa solicitor, Sidney P. Biggles, was an unctuous former parliamentarian who'd gone down with the Liberal ship in the last election. He pounced as Arthur returned to the waiting room, rubbing his hands with glee over the poll results while regretting he wouldn't be on the hustings this time.

"No, my duty lies with Tragger, Inglis, Bullingham – and even more proudly with their illustrious senior counsel. In the humble expectation you might squeeze out a few moments to sign them for staff, two dozen copies of *A Thirst for Justice* are already on order."

"They might prefer to wait for the movie."

"Marvellous. Have they engaged a leading actor? Someone with sufficient panache, I hope."

Arthur considered spinning the joke out, but instead apologized for his feeble sense of humour. "Could you spare me an office, Sidney? I have matters to discuss with a colleague . . . and here he is now."

Ray DiPalma, freshly groomed and in the requisite uniform of Ottawa grandees, a dark pin-stripe, shiny shoes, black valise, horn rims today. "Honoured to meet you, sir," Biggles said, escorting them down a windowed hallway to a spacious, plushly furnished office.

"This is my own humble workplace." Biggles raised a hand to deflect protests not made. "No, no, I shall insist, you must have it. Just shove those papers aside. Phone, fax, two computers, tape recorder should you care to dictate memos to our senior secretary. She will bring you coffee and something tasty to go with it. She's yours for as long as you wish, do with her what you will and she'll merely ask for more." Rattling on like that, proving himself DiPalma's match in logorrhoea, he sidled out the door.

"We should've insisted on champagne and exotic dancers," DiPalma said. "I couldn't get first class on the plane, though – heavy Christmas bookings. How much cash are you bringing?"

"Twenty thousand, mostly in traveller's cheques."

"May not be enough to buy the favours we'll need."

From the way DiPalma rubbed his fingers together, Arthur gathered payouts would be exorbitant. "I have credit cards."

"You'll be lucky to find a functioning ATM in Albania."

"I can wire for more." But he dreaded having to face the ire of the skinflint Bullingham.

DiPalma closed the room's venetian blinds, brandished a cellphone. "Global roaming privileges." He opened the valise and spread its papers out. "Overnight to Athens, a feeder to Corfu, hydrofoil to Albania. No maps needed – I know that country backwards. Serbia, Kosovo, Macedonia, Albania, I did them all when I was tracking Krajzinski. I have files on who's who, who pulls the strings, whose palms to grease."

DiPalma seemed phenomenally alert today, efficient. His tour of duty in the Balkans had been his time of glory, and he was excited to be returning. A last hurrah, Arthur assumed, for one coping with the gradual debilitating effect of Parkinson's. Only lately had Arthur picked up on DiPalma's tremors, a slight shaking of the hand. He was young for the disease's onset, but famous other sufferers had achieved renown: Eugene O'Neill, John Paul II, Pierre Trudeau.

"I'm Ray DiPalma the developer. I specialize in vacation resorts. That's why the new threads. Apex International Getaways Corp., properties in the Caribbean, South Pacific, Florida, Mexico. Albania is developing a tourism infrastructure, they'll be drooling to get their hands on my money. I was up all night cobbling window dressing – letterheads, financial statements, brochures. I'm looking for beach property, you're my mouthpiece."

"I presumed I was going in as Abzal Erzhan's lawyer."

"Right, and you'll be on the next plane back. Trust me."

Arthur had brought documents too: a letter to Abzal from his wife, also signed by their children, along with photos of them. Those would introduce him, as would a recent front-page story, complete with smiling pictures of Arthur standing shoulder-to-shoulder with Zandoo at their press conference.

"You're absolutely sure CSIS knows nothing of this?"

"I told Crumwell I'll be incommunicado for a week or so while I'm worming my way into the Environmental Revolutionary Front. Which doesn't exist, except on paper – Zack and I phonied up some cryptic emails and some maps and diagrams of tar sands facilities in Fort McMurray. We're scheming to plant some bombs – that's what they're supposed to think, but it's just a form of paper monkeywrenching."

This sounded more serious than the "diversion" Savannah mentioned. *Ray's idea. He's pretty imaginative.* "I would suggest you put that on ice."

"Too late. Come on, Arthur, every cop in Alberta and half the CSIS staff will be freezing their butts off in the northern boreal forest while we enjoy our Adriatic holiday. It was Zack's idea, the guy is brilliant."

"It sounds of criminal mischief."

"The stuff I handed over is too vague. No mention of explosives. I let them draw that conclusion. I've got a get-out-of-jail card with the greymail I've got on CSIS – that's trade talk, means soft blackmail. Trust me."

Hopefully, DiPalma would find safety behind the shield of Canada's whistleblower laws, which Arthur had taken pains to review. But he'd gone beyond his role as double agent. Whether or not this was DiPalma's idea – and he seemed unwilling to take credit for it – he'd become an agent provocateur, practically a subversive.

"I assume that when you fellows came up with this novelty you were on some potent Amazonian hallucinogen."

"I'm off intoxicants. Cigarettes too, in case you hadn't noticed. I'm on the patch. Cleaning out the system."

Maybe that accounted for his being so alert and organized. Arthur suspected he'd never seen DiPalma entirely sober before.

"Now I want you to sit down, Arthur, I want you to relax."

Arthur subsided onto the couch, fearing the worst.

"I had to tell Crumwell about you and Savannah Buckett, because it's all over your island. I also had to mention Stoney as the source, because the old man gave me the third degree and I didn't want him to think I was hiding something." Arthur went numb as DiPalma prattled on. "Crumwell wanted me to get some kind of statement from Stoney, but I explained that would compromise me. So he just let it drop, and I don't know if they're going to pursue it."

He took Arthur's hand, clutched it hard. "No way, I mean absolutely no way, am I going to let them smear you. It would be like . . . like standing by while they go after my own family. I'll go public, I'll swear on a stack of Bibles about how CSIS's top spy tried to engineer a vicious slander campaign. He won't get a job picking up dog droppings in the park. So let's put it out of mind while we're hot on the trail of the biggest screw-up since Maher Arar."

Arthur remained silent as he once again reassessed his presumptive fellow traveller. Unreliable and unstable, according to Margaret. DiPalma fidgeted, patted his pockets out of habit, looking distressed – the patch may have lost some potency.

"We are solicitor and client, Ray, a relationship we entered into some time ago at your request. So I may not repeat what you have just divulged unless you release me from my obligation of silence. Otherwise, our communications remain privileged to the end of time, even should you suddenly, right now, drop dead in front of me."

As if recognizing this as black humour, DiPalma attempted a stiff smile, then had to still a tremor of his hand.

"So this is what we're going to do, Ray. You are going to free me from my legal restraint – conditionally. You are going to recite on tape your role, as mandated by Crumwell, to spy on Margaret and me, and you will detail this last conversation with him. I'm going to seal the tape in an envelope, which will be signed and dated by

Biggles and at least two other lawyers. It will be placed in the safe here with instructions it not be opened unless you and I somehow fail to return from Albania."

"Bet your life we're coming back."

"Do it, or forget Albania."

DiPalma hesitated only a moment. "No problem." He sat at Biggles's desk, and began talking to the tape machine.

~~~

Within the first ninety minutes of their crowded Olympic Airways flight, DiPalma had already broken his pledge not to drink, and was two vodkas to the bad – "Just enough to take the edge off" – but he was antsy, scattered in his conversation, an endless flow. Arthur's concentration on his Albanian phrasebook was regularly spoiled by pokes and nudges.

He learned things he didn't care to know: Sully Clugg, the ex-Blackwater bruiser, was suspended for three days after grabbing a secretary's crotch at the office Christmas party. DiPalma had become so soused that he'd blown his chance with Aretha-May, passing out on her sofa. He was feeling sexually frustrated. He wished he'd been a better husband to Janice.

Arthur closed his eyes, tried to sleep, but DiPalma, keyed up, wired on the want of nicotine, lurched into a ramble about Albania. "Money will have to be the big mediating factor. Everything and everyone is for sale over there, politicians, government officials, but you have to break through the layers of the old Commie bureaucracy."

Then came a primer on rendition practices: the Lear 35 the vehicle of choice, the victim encased head-to-toe in a black jump-suit, diapers, sleeping drugs. Torture by proxy. Electrodes to the genitals, mutilations, mouths without teeth, fingers without nails.

Not for the first time, Arthur reconsidered the wisdom of this mission, this leap into the unknown. But he would heed the Bard:

Our doubts are traitors, and make us lose the good we oft might win by fearing to attempt.

Many hours later Arthur awoke to DiPalma's snores and the sun streaming through his portside window, land below, Germany maybe, or Poland. It took a while for him to shake off a chilling dream of lying shackled on a cold concrete floor, Anthony Crumwell snipping off his fingers, leaving bloody stubs.

Crumwell had earned this role as the black hat of Arthur's nightmares through the fear and revulsion he'd provoked by prying into Arthur's every intimate doing. If the gods are just, revenge will be delicious.

22

Slimed with mucky oil, slipperier than the greased porker he'd outclassed at last year's Garibaldi Summer Games, Stoney crawled from under the Fargo and washed up at his outdoor sink. Job done, he was free at last, free of Arthur Beauchamp's constant, heartless grousing. It took a while, but so did the Sistine Chapel.

He'd tie a ribbon around this baby, park it in Arthur's driveway for when he returned for the holidays, a reminder it was Christmas bonus time. Heartbreaking to lose the old girl, she'd been in the yard so long she was like family. No sense letting her sit idle. A master mechanic must always break in any rebuilt trannie, and there was excess herbage to be ferried to friends at undisclosed border crossings.

Now he could go back to getting his latest business venture off the ground. Hot Air Holidays. His main task: sticking a broom up Dog's puckered ass – his test driver insisted on tethering the balloon to the ground. Made it only six feet up last time.

The phone was complaining again from the house. Probably that grasping witch from the collection agency – she'd been hanging on his heinie like a Rottweiler for the last three weeks. Herman Schloss, the world's worst poker player, had committed the highly unethical lapse of not disclosing the lien on his cabin cruiser.

An energy transfusion was needed. He fumbled through his eight-pack for a Lucky. The tab released with a comforting *phsst*, and he cranked it back, wiped his lips with the back of his hand.

The phone again. He went inside, waited as his machine reeled off his powerful new greeting: "Garibaldi Taxi, Loco-Motion Rent-a-Car, and Hot Air Holidays, offering twenty-four-hour-a-day prompt and efficient service. All our lines are tied up, so please leave a message."

A male voice, whiney and pleading. "Mr. Stonewell, please pick up, this is my third call this afternoon."

Which didn't make sense, it wasn't even noon. "Customer service," he said, disguising his voice in case it was some other leech from the collection agency. "I'm sorry, our establishment has been experiencing heavy traffic today. Whom may I inquire is calling?"

"Is this Mr. Stonewell? Robert Stonewell?"

"Mr. Stonewell is busy with other customers at the present moment. May I be appraised as to the nature of your inquiry?"

"I am calling from Ottawa, sir, with some news he'll be delighted to hear. I'd like to speak with him personally."

Stoney suspected a trick, but he called, "Mr. Stonewell on seven!" then switched the phone to the other hand, returned to his normal voice, but gruff. "Stonewell here. Sorry, I'm up to my neck, can you make it short?"

"Mr. Stonewell, my name is Burton, from the federal Department of Small Business. Your name has been chosen from a list of a dozen outstanding entrepreneurs who have made unique contributions in the start-up of –"

"Hey, man, I don't take junk calls, eh, so stick it where the sun don't shine."

"Wait! This is totally legitimate! I'm calling on behalf of a program to honour a select group of achievers. You will represent the West Coast. We're inviting you and your wife to spend two nights in Ottawa, all expenses paid."

"Come on, man, who is this? Honker, is that you?"

"Bear with me, please. We're offering gratis two tickets first class, a luxury suite in our finest hotel, and a thousand dollars to cover expenses."

Stoney sipped his Lucky, jiggled his cigarette pack, picked one out with his teeth, lit it. The guy sounded sincere enough, and Stoney *was* in fact an outstanding entrepreneur. How did they get his name? "This isn't a gag?"

"No, sir, this is the real thing – a courier package with the tickets and vouchers has been requisitioned and you may expect delivery within the day. It's a rush, but the election call has upset our timetables, so we'd truly appreciate it if you can fly out tomorrow – I hope that's not an imposition. You'll be back two days before Christmas. Arrival Ottawa International at six p.m., but take a later flight if that suits you. All we ask is that you and your spouse keep our program absolutely confidential until we make a formal announcement."

"I don't have an actual spouse right now . . ."

"Your girlfriend, partner, companion, whomever you wish to share this opportunity with."

For a moment, Stoney thought he was hallucinating, maybe the brewmeister at the Lucky Lager refinery had been dropping tabs of acid in the canned goods. He studied the phone, but it wasn't melting in his hand or anything.

"As an essential part of the program, we want to hear your views on how we, the government, can help small businesses work better for the country."

"You want an earful, you got the right man." Stoney stubbed his cigarette, he was buoyant, a believer now. "Number one, your environmental regs are killing business, you got to pull back on your emissions limits, and while you're at it take a look at all them restrictions on hot-air balloon travel." An emphatic knocking at the door. "Just a sec, I got a customer."

"Allow me one second more."

Stoney called: "Coming! Just a sec!"

"Can we count on you?" Burton said.

"I've got a dozen clients to service tomorrow, I hate to let them down . . ."

"Perhaps the following day . . ."

"But I can't let my country down neither. Okay, I'll cut ass outta here tomorrow."

"I can't emphasize this enough, please keep it between us."

"You bet, you can count on Bob Stonewell." He disconnected fast. He'd just seen an unwelcome sight out the window. Maybe he was the butt of a good news–bad news joke, because the bad was standing on the welcome mat: Constable Ernst Pound. No time to hide the five K's of product sitting on the kitchen counter. He'd have to brazen it out.

He slipped outside, backed Pound away from the door. He was holding a sealed envelope, probably with another summons over some cheesy hassle or other. "Yo, Ernst, you caught me at a bad time, I been on the phone with the big boys in Ottawa, they want me to hop a plane there. I been chosen as an outstanding example of entreperennial spirit."

"In what? Growing dope?"

"I find that hurtful. I got a reputation. I been nationally recognized as an achiever. That's my new project over there." Indicating his big striped balloon, neatly folded, on a tarp

"I hope you've got a licence to operate that there thing."

"Yeah, it's in the mail. You got a Christmas present for me there, Ernst? I feel real awkward, I didn't get you nothing."

"This came by dispatch, personal for you. They got me running around like I was a delivery boy."

Stoney ripped the envelope open: a letterhead from Ottawa, the Department of Small Business, signed by this same guy, Burton. He was pleased to nominate one Robert Stonewell as small-business entrepreneur of the year representing British Columbia.

Two first-class return tickets, hotel vouchers, ten hundred-dollar bills so crisp you could pick your teeth with them.

Pound's eyes went huge. "Holy Jesus, I thought you were shitting me."

Stoney was goggle-eyed too. "Mom lied, there is a Santa. Hey, I'm gonna tell my Ottawa connections about the splendid work our local constable has been doing here. About time we considered a promotion." Before closing the door, he added, "Oh, and keep all this under your hat, eh, until we're ready to go public."

"Yes, sir."

~~~

By ten the next morning, Stoney was in Ottawa, critically examining the Château Laurier as it loomed beyond the taxi window. All peaks and turrets, a grand, sprawling structure equal to the standards he expected. "I hope you have change for a hundred, my good man. I usually don't carry nothing smaller."

The taxi driver made the change, from which Stoney, feeling brotherhood with a fellow cabbie, tipped him fat. The doorman was already at the trunk, hauling out the suitcases Stoney had borrowed from Honk Gilmore because his own was mildewed. A porter was wrestling with Dog for possession of his ratty, patched duffle bag, but Dog won, and they entered an elaborate, bustling lobby, some kind of Christmas brunch starting, three-piece suits and designer dresses – these had to be the heavy-pocketed civil servants Stoney was supporting with his tax money.

He stationed Dog by a pillar to guard the luggage from thieves, then joined a lineup of people checking out. He didn't complain about not being rushed to the front – it was his own fault, he hadn't let his sponsors know he was making his grand entry earlier than expected. A quick call to Air Canada had got him first-class seats on the overnight flight, so why waste a day in the service of Her Majesty?

When Dog had finally showed up yesterday to do his test flight, wearing an old army flak jacket and carrying about fifty metres of tether rope, he hardly reacted, except with relief, to Stoney's announcement of a change in plans.

After a pit stop to pick up the suitcases – and regale Honker on what was going down – they'd packed up, got the late ferry, high-tailed it to the airport, parked the Fargo in the short-term lot, and boarded in time for the first serving of champagne.

It was the first time Dog had been on a plane, and he'd sat there like a frog on a log, bulb-eyed, clutching the armrests as they took to the air. Stoney had done his best to explain what this trip was all about, but Dog still didn't seem to grasp it, just nodding, no questions. Dog never asked questions. Stoney couldn't remember when he'd last strung three words together.

The stewardess had thought they were rock stars, and Stoney almost didn't have the heart to correct her. Her expression said she didn't buy his being a select achiever; she obviously pegged him as a major international drug dealer, which he kind of slyly confirmed. She was hip, they got on pretty good.

The day's excitement had taken a toll, Stoney falling asleep on the plane before he could finish his last after-dinner liqueur. But as a fortunate result he wasn't too hammered this morning. Neither was Dog, who'd been too shy to ask the stewardess to keep the beer flowing.

Stoney finally gained the front desk and the services of a snotty-looking stiff with a carnation in his lapel and a name badge, "Fortesque."

"Ah, yes, Mr. Stonewell." Studying what looked like a government fax. "A little early for us, I'm afraid. We can have a suite ready for you and your wife in about two hours. One of the porters will be pleased to store any luggage . . ."

"I got my own porter." Stoney beckoned to Dog to come forward with the bags. "This gentleman here ain't exactly my wife. He's my companion."

Dog got flustered under the clerk's frigid gaze, and took off his ball cap, twisting it in his hands. Fortesque studied the fax. "Companion, yes, of course. My instructions may be incomplete . . . I see we are to charge a government account. Room, meals, refreshments . . ."

"The whole assload, yeah. We're on government business."

Fortesque looked at him sternly. "You *are* Mr. Robert Stonewell?"

"Well, I ain't Mother Goose."

The clerk's neat little moustache twitched when he tried to smile. "One moment, please." He disappeared into an office, people in the lineup sighing and grumbling. Fortesque then hurried back with a letter-size envelope, suddenly all apologetic. "I'm sorry, this should have been, uh, presented to you immediately on registration."

It was embossed with the name Charley Thiessen, Office of the Attorney General. Stoney ripped it open and shook out two tickets to the National Ballet, the next night. The handwritten note he pulled out was from this Thiessen guy, wanting to meet tomorrow at half past ten for brunch. Probably some lawyer with contracts to sign so Stoney could collect the honours being bestowed on him. He showed the note to the snot behind the desk and got instant reaction.

"My deepest apology for any confusion. Corner suite on the sixth floor, it's almost ready, the maid is doing final touches. If you will please sign here, for yourself and your companion . . ."

"Yo, Dog, what's your last name?"

A massive throat clearing. "Zbrinjkowitz."

"Yeah, I can never remember. That's why we call him Dog. It's got two beds, eh? Dog's feet get kind of cheesy."

~~~

The suite was skookum, stuffed chairs everywhere, bureau, wardrobe, fancy lamps, a bed that could sleep half a dozen without trying, an extra bedroom with its own TV and private bath with a tub, shitter, and a weird urinal for pissing while you squat. A view out over a snowy park and a frozen river. And to top it off, a little fridge full of the necessities of life.

Dog was like a frozen statue, looking like he was afraid to touch anything or the dream would end. "Wake up and smell the good life, Dog. The queen slept here, along with Mick Jagger and Madonna and the biggest names in Hollywood."

"Arnold?"

"Yep." Schwarzenegger, his hero. Stoney tossed him a Heinie, twisted the cap off a miniature V.O. rye. "Kick off them boots and relax. They got a pool here, you remember to bring your bathing suit?"

"Bathing suit?"

"Wear your gonches, no one's gonna mind. Hey, man, we got a shitload of time, so let's finish unpacking and then go see if we can sell some of this dope."

~~~

The Honker was ten years retired, but he'd worked Ottawa and still had good contacts. Like the older couple Stoney invited to the room that afternoon, quality buyers, purveyors to the top class of civil servants.

He popped some bud into a hookah his customers brought along as a Christmas gift, got a good burn going. "This is radically mellow, a hybrid of Garibaldi Gold and my own specialty, Purple Passion. Normally it sells around five centuries a pound, but for the favoured few, *aficionados* of the finest, I got a special on at three-fifty, comes with a guarantee you'll be walking home in a winter wonderland. Goes good with some early Led Zep. Dog, get the lady a glass of champagne."

"Blithe," the guy said after his sample toke. "Truly blithe."

A big sale resulted, a merry Christmas for all, these old pros would be quadrupling their money. Stoney was wishing he'd brought more than thirty pounds.

Another guest who called up from the lobby was the hip flight attendant. Stoney almost forgot he'd invited her. She did a taster, bought two lids, one for her boyfriend, a pilot.

By midnight, his luggage was twenty pounds lighter and his entire suite smelled like a cannabis fart, but he was in hog heaven, a good day even by the standards of an outstanding achiever.

Dog was lying on the bed, stoned beyond normal human capacity, watching a TV movie, a tearjerker, you could hear him snuffle. "Come on, Dog, the night is young. Let's hit the bars. This town's full of needy, lonely women."

It was time to party.

23

———

Charley Thiessen paced about his office, waiting for Crumwell – he was unsettled, he hadn't been sleeping well. Big speech next day in Windsor to kick off the area candidates, but he hadn't read it yet, couldn't get past the first page. Then Sarnia, London, Kitchener. Charley, as one of the all-stars, had to blanket Ontario.

Headquarters had issued a directive: no media blitzes, no blatant in-your-face door-to-door stuff until after the holidays – the voters would be resentful. So the Tories had settled for a series of kick-off rallies, then Thiessen would spend Christmas week shaking paws on the main streets of Grey County and recording TV and radio spots in a Toronto studio.

This morning he had other business, vital in its own way, a duty that had to be discharged so he could get his campaign in gear. Operation Beauchamp, the bringing down of the put-down artist, his descent into ignominy.

Thiessen had pulled into Ottawa late the night before, after learning that Robert Stonewell had checked in at the Château. Easygoing, joke-telling Charley must be at his beguiling best. Brunch at ten-thirty, in forty-five minutes, over caviar and eggs Benedict in Stonewell's suite, away from the gaze of the public and the omnivorous press.

Reception buzzed to say Crumwell had finally shown up, hopefully with his promised backgrounder on this character. "Send him in."

"You're aware, sir, that Privy Council is meeting in the cabinet room at noon."

"Yeah, yeah, I have it on the calendar. Don't put anyone through for the next half-hour." There'd be no notes taken, no record of this tête-à-tête with the spymaster.

Crumwell slipped like a ghost into the room, looking unhealthy, pallid. The Bhashyistan business had got to him big time, the continuing cyber attacks: some big hotels had been hit, a grocery chain. Everybody was exasperated at Canada's show of impotence. Which is why the Privy Council would be meeting, to chew over another scheme the PMO had come up with, something called Operation Blow Job – that couldn't be it. *Snow Job.*

"Sorry I'm late. Still on the mend, and I've been a bit fagged with work."

"No problem. Let's get right to it."

"We're still a little skimpy on this Stonewell fellow. The case agent on this file – he's using the name Burton – wasn't able to spend more than ten minutes on the phone with him. Busy chap, on the go, but he bit hard, apparently took an overnight flight – so that suggests he may be eager to cooperate."

"Age?"

"Somewhere in his thirties."

"Educational background?"

"That, uh, remains a bit of a blank."

"Physical description."

"That too is a bit hazy. One assumes he's fit. Most workaholics are."

Thiessen was getting annoyed. "Bad habits?"

"None we're aware of. He doesn't mind doing a little flutter at the poker table, according to our man on Garibaldi."

"Soft spots. Where do I probe?"

"On that, we do have something helpful. A firm indication he's gay. Can't say it didn't come as a shocker, but he checked into the hotel with a male partner."

Always expect the unexpected, Thiessen's mom had drilled that into him. "That helps. Maybe I should come on to him." When Crumwell scrunched up his face in horror, he added, "Joke."

Crumwell washed down a couple of painkillers, grimaced. "I had best explain why we don't have a more complete book on the chap. It is, of course, a bit dodgy, non-priority, and, uh . . ."

"Hey, you've gone beyond the bounds of duty, I'm not complaining."

"Our best profiling source, Agent DiPalma, seems to have gone off-line. Can't fault him. Deep cover on the eco-terrorism file. Doing a majestic job. In case your deputy hasn't briefed you, DiPalma has uncovered a scheme to take out a tar sands facility in Fort McMurray. We've been quite distracted with that, pouring all our energy and manpower into Alberta. The plan is to catch them with their knickers down."

"You pull that off and maybe we don't get buried next month. We're fighting it out for scraps with the Marijuana Party. Let's get back to Stonewell – has anyone seen him since he got here?"

"We are undermanned, Minister."

"Charley. Okay, I get your point. Your case agent – what does he call himself?"

"Burton. That's all you need to know, Charley. We do have to, uh, cover our tracks on this thing."

"What else did Burton say about our top achiever?"

"That he has a few rough edges – not unusual for some of these backwoods entrepreneurs. He has a well-trained staff, and they're inordinately busy. This may help: he's not one of your greenies. Has quite a bone to pick with the environmental laws."

That was the sort of thing Thiessen wanted to hear. Stonewell couldn't be very palsy-walsy with Blake or her mate.

"Is anyone else but you, me, and Burton privy to this, um, exercise?" Thiessen almost said "caper."

"There's no courier service to Garibaldi, so a local Mountie delivered the envelope to Stonewell – but he doesn't have any idea what's in it. Burton is very discreet, and he'll be meeting you at the hotel to smooth your way. You'll recognize him by his blond hair and trim beard and moustache."

All phony, Thiessen assumed. The cost of this was going through CSIS, so he hoped there'd be no fallout from that. Fortunately, their books weren't inhibited by the Freedom of Information Act. "Get on the blower, tell Burton I'm on the way."

~~~

Thiessen was delayed in the lobby by some hand-shaking of staff and guests – unavoidable but it was the political life, the price of recognition. He was finally pulled away by a crisply dressed blond fellow with a neat goatee, who whispered, "I'm Burton, your, er, political aide for the morning, sir."

"Call me Charley." They found privacy behind one of the lobby's massive colonnades, where Burton slipped him a miniature digital recorder, round-topped so it would fit neatly in the palm of the hand. "Nicad battery is charged, suction cup holds it in place under a table, press this red button to record."

Thiessen pocketed it. "Great. So we're all set up?"

"Except for a minor glitch. Mr. Stonewell must have forgotten he instructed the operator to hold his calls."

"When was that?"

"Seven o'clock."

"Probably needed a good night's sleep."

"Seven o'clock this morning, sir."

"Well, I suppose he's just being prudent. He obviously knows I'm coming. Room service has been alerted?"

"I believe they're standing by."

"Then let's go."

In the elevator, Thiessen gave battle instructions to Burton. He would do the introductions. Stonewell would be told that the small business minister was off campaigning and had sent regrets, so Thiessen would act in his stead. Palms would meet, then Burton would quietly slip away.

No homo jokes, Charley reminded himself. He'd have to do some bantering with the guy's lover too. These gay boys loved their malicious gossip.

A room-service waitress was already at the door with her cart. Thérèse, said her tag. "Bonjour, mademoiselle," Thiessen said in his clumsy French, extending his hand while rapping on the door with the other.

No response. It was ten-forty. They hadn't hung up the "Do Not Disturb" sign, but the *Globe* was there, unwrapped, untouched. Maybe they'd forgotten to reset their watches, gone out for a walk.

Burton took a turn knocking. Not a sound from within.

"Okay, miss," said Thiessen, "you've got the house key?" She shook her head, but summoned a housekeeper from down the hall, a stout Haitian woman. Burton had good French and managed to cajole her to unlock the room.

"*Mon Dieu,*" Thérèse said as she pushed the cart in.

Thiessen's view was obstructed by her for a moment. Then a scene of profligacy opened up that had him gaping with dread.

A skimpily dressed young woman was stretched out on cushions on the floor, sleeping or passed out, a two-foot-tall hookah pipe beside her. On the bed, two more human forms, or at least two lumps under a sheet, covers bunched up at their feet with their clothes. Empty mini-bottles strewn everywhere, the fridge wide open, empty but for some chocolate bar wrappers. Two flower vases chock full of cigarette butts. The thermostat had been set to a stultifying high, and the room reeked of tobacco and marijuana.

Thiessen stood in the doorway transfixed as the housekeeper raced in, scuttled about, picking up frantically. The woman on the floor, aroused by this, raised up, stared right at Thiessen, who with a sudden shock of recognition recalled her as an exotic dancer from a Lower Town club he'd been dragged into by a visiting Nigerian judge. "It's the fucking heat!" she yelled, scrambling around for her outerwear and shoes.

Thiessen started backing out, bumping into Burton. "Let's get out of here."

Too late. A gaunt young man, glistening with sweat, a cannabis leaf tattoo on his upper arm, lurched from the bedroom, shirtless, pulling on a pair of jeans. "Wha . . . What day is it?"

The stripper bolted past them, pulling a sweater over her head. But Burton, mindlessly sticking to the script, took Thiessen's arm and pulled him in. "Mr. Stonewell? Burton, Small Business." Stonewell took his hand, but not much awareness showed in his red-rimmed eyes as Burton continued his spiel.

Thiessen had backpedalled into the corridor and was about to bolt when Burton pointed to him with a frozen grin. "Mr. Thiessen here is pleased to act in his stead." Charley gritted his teeth: this agent was an idiot, an automaton programmed to obey.

"Thiessen? Oh, yeah, *Thiessen*. Got your note somewhere here."

"Charley." Stepping inside, feeling suicidal. "Call me Charley."

Stonewell still seemed slow to come to, looking hazily about, at Thérèse; at the flustered, busy maid; at the cart with its steaming covered trays. At the bed, where the two bodies were stirring. "Yo, Dog, we got guests, take your friend to the bedroom, the maid can do that later." The two forms, still draped in the sheet, scuttled off like crabs.

The skinny stoner grabbed Thiessen's arm, yanking him toward the table where Thérèse had laid out the brunch. "We'll leave you to it, then," said Burton, making like a coward for the door, Thérèse following him out, the maid still flying about like a whirlwind.

"Make yourself at home, Charley, grab some of them eggs. Guess we forgot to move our watches ahead, but I'll be ready to roll soon as I shower up." Stonewell slathered a cracker with caviar and disappeared into the washroom.

The maid had drawn the curtains by now, opened some windows, and was making the bed. "Psst, miss, please get rid of that thing." The hookah. She seemed unsure what to do with it, then finally shoved it in the wardrobe. While she was diverted, Thiessen turned the recorder on, stuck it under the food table, pressing it to make sure the suction cup held.

He had no appetite. Feeling faint, he subsided onto a padded chair, then raised up to remove an empty wine bottle from under the cushion. A disaster was enfolding. His ire at Beauchamp had blinded him to the unexpected.

If the press got hold of this . . . Thankfully, he hadn't seen any reporters in the lobby. What option did he have except to follow an abbreviated script, play it out and get out?

The maid had gone by the time Stonewell emerged, hair dripping, a wedge of shaving cream on his chin. The vaguely pornographic T-shirt he pulled on read, "Starkers Cove, Free Yourself."

"Well, you, um . . . What do I call you, Robert, Bob?"

"Call me grateful, Charley." Stonewell slugged back a glass of orange juice, scooped more caviar. "Yeah, the folks back home are gonna bust with pride when this goes public."

Thiessen cleared his throat. "Now, I should warn you that the announcement may be months away. So far, it's just among you and me and the selection committee. You haven't, of course, mentioned this to anyone."

"Didn't have time. Just Ernst."

"Ernst?"

"The local law, Constable Pound. Don't worry about him, he's so dumb he's already forgot. Now let me get this straight – you're like one of the head legal beagles here, eh?"

Thiessen emitted a strained chuckle, assuming Stonewell was jesting. "I guess you could call me that. The big beagle. But, hey, titles don't impress me either, I'm a no-bullshit country boy just like you. Charley gives you no blarney, that's my motto."

"That's great, man. To be honest, I was expecting some pompous prick."

Thiessen laughed again, his voice cracking slightly. Strained chitchat followed, mostly about Garibaldi Island, Thiessen not getting a very clear picture of it, his powers of concentration dulled. This was broken off as Stonewell opened the door to a houseboy wheeling in a tray of mini-bottles to restock the fridge.

"You're a mind reader, pal."

The young man grinned broadly, knowingly. Word about the debauchery had spread like a virus through the hotel. Thiessen watched as Stonewell peeled a twenty from a thick wad in his pocket, slipped it to the departing waiter, then cracked open a beer. "You look like you could use a straightener too, Charley. Fuel up, eh, be my guest."

Thiessen had a rule, no drinks before noon, but this was an extreme situation. His hands shook as he poured himself a whiskey neat, tilted it to his lips, felt a searing rush of warmth, of courage, however false.

"So, Robert, you must know Arthur Beauchamp and his famous wife. Your island's most prominent couple, I would imagine."

"Known them for yonks, man. In fact, I just finished retooling the old shyster's heirloom Fargo."

The old shyster. Thiessen liked the sound of that. Encouraged, he said, "Bit of a ladies' man, I hear."

Stonewell patted his pockets, pulled out a bent cigarette, lit it with a groan of satisfaction, blew out a stream of smoke. "Man, I feel I'm regressing to normal. So you got something there for me to sign, Charley, like a non-disclosure agreement? I mean, what's the deal here, because everything's been pretty vague. Like am I supposed to sit down with a panel of experts and advise about business solutions? I jotted down a few ideas here." Pulling a sheaf of notes from his pocket.

"No hurry, Robert. This is just a . . . get-acquainted interview. We wanted to fill in some of the gaps . . . uh, your various businesses, daily routines. And friends, of course, like Arthur Beauchamp. I met him, I was really impressed, he's a legend, bigger than life. A bon vivant with an eye for the chicks, they say, but hey, man, nothing wrong with that, more power to him. Boy, I'll bet you must know some stories about the old shyster."

Stonewell slugged back the rest of his Tuborg, then belched, stuffed his butt into the empty bottle, tapped another from a pack, lit it, squinted at Thiessen through the smoke. "Hey, Charley, you wanna burn one?"

"I'm trying to quit."

Thiessen couldn't figure out why Stonewell laughed. Then he blanched as he realized this hoodlum wasn't talking about tobacco, was pulling some loose marijuana from his pocket. He rolled a joint so expertly he could've been Vladimir Horowitz playing a Chopin mazurka. The neatly packaged rollie suddenly landed on Thiessen's lap.

He picked it up gingerly by the tip, pocketed it. "Thanks, buddy, I'll save it for after. Normally I don't toke up until after dinner. But, hey, man, another one of those Johnny Blacks would go down good."

"You bet, Charley." Refilling him, smiling at him with hooded eyes. "Here's the deal, Charley. I got Arthur Beauchamp on my payroll as house counsel, so we got this, like, solicitor-client privilege that prevents me from revealing anything going between us."

"Of course, sure, that's out of bounds. I was just thinking of the . . . fun stuff."

"Plus he's a bud, man, like family, and he's got his own private life, and I got to respect that – the word unfaithnessless ain't in my dictionary."

~~~

It had been a three-whiskey morning, so Thiessen was fairly muzzy as he slumped into his seat in the cabinet room. He prayed he wouldn't be called upon to contribute to debate; he could barely rub two brain cells together. His head was swimming with images from that suite in the Château, and maybe with the second-hand fumes of the pot.

Thiessen had walked into the aftermath of a classic orgy. *It's the fucking heat!* The stripper's cry still echoed somewhere in Thiessen's auditory canals. No way she recognized him. Bad enough that the hotel staff did. Thank God Stonewell's pal and his bedmate never emerged.

Adding to his problems, a headache, and when Gracey banged her gavel it felt like a spike piercing his skull. He looked around: only four ministers here, everyone else out on the stump, but there was a slew of advisers led by E.K. Boyes and Gracey's fey toady, Galbraith-Smythe. Buster Buchanan, two other generals, three colonels. They were setting up to do a show-and-tell.

"Operation Snow Job," Clara said. "Named in honour of that smarmy snow job artist, Mukhamet Khan Ivanovich. We're going to shut his yap." She pointed an imaginary gun at Thiessen, who jumped when she mimicked pressing the trigger. "Joke, Charley." She'd been ribbing him mercilessly since the tomato juice debacle.

He play-acted dead, which, in his condition, wasn't hard. Everyone laughed at this, almost too much. But maybe they were laughing with relief – Canada was finally coming out of its corner. He found the strength to join the huzzahs that greeted Gracey's announcement that two days hence airborne missiles would be reducing Bhashyistan's Information Ministry to rubble.

But he subsided again into anguish. That insufferably laidback stoner, with his pious claims to tact and nobility, his obviously insincere defence of Beauchamp. Thiessen had disguised his mission well enough – how had the rube clued in?

Charley had felt he was being tested, that's why he'd twisted open a second whiskey – letting Stonewell know he was hip to the scene, a party-hardy guy himself. "Got to split for the sweatshop, man," he'd said, bolting to the elevator. He'd flushed the joint in the nearest john, and, to still his tremors, downed a third Scotch at the lobby bar.

Damn Anthony Crumwell – he'd carry the can if this charade backfired, he never had the right goods, and neither did his so-called genius in the field, Agent Ray DiPalma, the computer-losing screw-up. Thiessen would give Crumwell a one-way ticket to the mother country, cheerio, you wanker.

The military guys were clicking through a PowerPoint on the big screen at the back of the room: maps, charts, photos, a slideshow as meaningless as Jackson Pollock's drip paintings. Phrases buzzed by, CF-18s, wheezy Russian interceptors, air-to-ground missiles, a surgical strike on Mukhamet's cyber centre.

He wondered why Clara was frowning at him, wondered if his fly was open. She gavelled for silence. "Charley, can I ask you a question? That bulge in your breast pocket wouldn't be a cellphone?"

"Oh, crap." He drew out a Blackberry, scrambled to his feet. "It's not on, honest."

"It's still a capital offence."

He hurried out to lock it away, resumed his seat with a stiff, sheepish grin, trying to make a joke of it, repeating Clara's gesture of miming a gun, at his forehead. "Bang." No one laughed.

Something else was nagging at him – something about his muddled morning was struggling to rise from the grave of suppressed memory. Determinedly, he shoved it aside, tuned in to a debate over whether Christmas Eve was appropriate for Operation Snow Job. Buster Buchanan's regretful response: "War doesn't pause to celebrate Christmas. Surprise tactics are central to the art of war, and we intend to strike when the enemy least expects it."

E.K.: "Expand on how we seek to limit civilian casualties."

"A first wave will take out their air defence – with, hopefully, minimal enemy losses – then a leaflet drop will alert those in the Information Ministry to the impending strike. The third son will probably be the first to scram out of there, but we found some interesting photos on his website – he drives a yellow Hummer. Our eye in the sky confirms the same Hummer being waved into the ministry parking garage. We'll be waiting for Mukhamet to bolt."

Someone asked about the Calgary Five.

"Mad Igor may be crazy but he's not dumb," Clara said. "Dead hostages, no bargaining chips."

"And what about those poor women from Saskatchewan?"

Foreign Minister Sonja Dubjek passed around copies of a letter. "Dr. Svetlikoff just received this. From his wife, Jill. It was mailed from Kazakhstan, probably smuggled out, but it confirms the women were in Bhashyistan as of December first and in good health."

Thiessen was too sapped to follow much of this, but gathered the women were hiding out in a farm near Igorgrad. Something about bribing a Bhashyistan immigration officer and staying in a yurt. The letter ended, *We're sticking it out until peace has been declared,* which produced big sighs of relief.

"We'll pray for their continued safety," Gracey said. Then, with uncharacteristic fervour: "We are not going to be slapped around any more by some two-bit psychopathic tyrant. If any Canadians get touched, we'll bomb the crap out of Igorgrad." Cheers, people rising, applauding.

Thiessen was impressed by this new version of Clara Gracey, the Amazon warrior. But as discussion continued, he was assailed by mental flashes of Stonewell and the stripper and the hookah pipe. If it got out on the street, how would he ever explain it to his mother?

Suddenly he turned white, a spine-stiffening, anus-clenching surge powering him to his feet. He made a beeline to the door. "Sorry, not feeling too good. Forgot something. *Son of a bitch!*"

The tape recorder . . .

24

———

t was a hazy, grey Thursday morning as Arthur and DiPalma boarded the ferry to cross the mile of choppy blue water from the Greek holiday island of Corfu to the hardscrabble republic of Albania. DiPalma went below, away from the smokers, but Arthur stayed above with his phrasebook, packing burley into his pipe bowl, and was soon watching Corfu's tony villas fade into the mist.

After a three-day Greek layover, the adventure had begun, with Arthur feeling amazed at himself, at his spunk in undertaking so perilous an errand. But it had to be done – not just out of professional duty but for pride. *A Thirst for Justice* deserved a nobler ending than a nosedive into obscurity behind the ever-extending shadow of the hero's rookie M.P. wife.

Ray DiPalma was the catalyst for this, cockily sure he could worm his way into the confidence of Abzal Erzhan's keepers. Trust me, he kept insisting, eager for intrigue, eager to prove his global spying expertise. But for the moment, the poor fellow was doing battle below, conquering his pain, at the very nadir of nicotine withdrawal, though still on the patch.

The mainland loomed, the customs dock, a welter of tumbledown structures by the shoreline. Arthur tamped out his pipe as DiPalma, breathing heavily, burst outside and advanced toward the railing with cold determination.

Aghast, Arthur feared he was about to drown his misery by jumping, but it was the nicotine patch, ripped from his arm, that went overboard. DiPalma grimly pulled a pack of Greek cigarettes from a duty-free bag, refusing to meet Arthur's censorious eye. His first effort at ignition failed, either because of the breeze or his shaking hands. He squatted in a corner like a whipped dog and finally got a cigarette going, pulling on it ravenously.

~~~

By mid-afternoon, they were in the Gjirokaster Hills. Their clanking taxi made slow headway among the grunting transports and donkey carts and errant flocks of sheep. Arthur's impression was of a country bypassed by the modern world, so derelict as to seem barely recovered from the last world war.

But the sense of timelessness was lulling, and while DiPalma, fully re-addicted now, chain-smoked his foul-smelling cigarettes, Arthur sat back and enjoyed the views as they twisted up a tall range of hills to the town of Gjirokaster, a jumble of rectangular, slate-roofed Ottoman houses strewn haphazardly about steep, cobblestoned streets – a wonkily attractive town, crowned by a massive fortress.

They disembarked at the Gjirokaster Hotel, four storeys, a look of ill-restored elegance. It was opposite an empty plaza that, DiPalma explained, had once been dominated by a statue of Enver Hoxha, the despised native son of this town.

Free enterprisers had displaced the dictator – the plaza hosted a dozen hawkers and food vendors, the aromas from their braziers sending enticing greetings to Arthur's empty stomach. The nearest of them called out. "Very good lamb shish kebab. Beef, goat, chicken. Excellent price. Name is Djon. Speak English." Middle-aged with thick glasses, a paunch, and a Salvador Dali moustache. He waved a thickly laden skewer. "Here, try, on my house."

Arthur and DiPalma sent the porter into the hotel with their bags and crossed the street. The braised chunks of lamb looked delicious and the posted price ludicrously low.

"Also change dollars. Arrange excursions. Help with translation. Anything you want. Best prices for souvenirs. Girls also."

They ordered two lamb skewers to go. Djon held Arthur's ten-euro bill close to his astigmatic eyes, examining it for flaws. "Not able making change right now." When told he could keep the bill, he shook Arthur's hand powerfully.

The shish kebabs had been honestly advertised, and were gone by the time they entered the Turkish-style lobby. "Well coming in," said the clerk. "Best rooms for you top floor, only fifty dollars, includes satellite TV and hair blower. Sorry, no elevator working."

They were escorted up three flights to side-by-side rooms, baronial with carved wood ceilings, that rewarded with balcony views of twisting, serpentine streets, hillside forests, and promises of Ionian sunsets beyond the foothills.

It was too late to seek out Hanife Bejko. DiPalma planned to reconnoitre his neighbourhood the next day, then they might come calling in the evening. They'd speculated a lot about Bejko – had he shared a prison with Erzhan? As an enemy of the state? An Albanian mafia figure? A murderer now paroled?

They spent the remaining daylight hours puffing up and down the unforgiving cobblestones, then settled into a restaurant to try its specialty, yogurt soup and tongue of veal. DiPalma washed down his with a jug of wine, all the while flirting with a comely barmaid, who couldn't have been older than twenty and wasn't inhibited in response.

Sipping an after-dinner slivovitz, DiPalma adjusted his glasses to better view the young woman's bottom as she leaned over a counter. "God, she's hot." He butted his cigarette, and wandered over to engage her, winning a smile and a whispered word in his ear.

"Ledjina, entrancing name," DiPalma said on his return. "Speaks excellent English – she's taking day classes for a degree in tourism. She wants to practise on me tomorrow, show me around town."

~~~

The next day, while DiPalma went dallying off with Ledjina, Arthur explored Epirus's rocky coast and its preserved Greek and Roman temples – the Troy reborn so celebrated by the *Aeneid*. On wearily returning to his floor, he paused to rap on DiPalma's door. No response.

He lay down for a catnap, a refresher before the business planned for the evening, the Bejko visit, and in seconds was carried off by the Lethean current, past pillared shrines and palaces from which the shadowy figure of Abzal Erzhan flitted into view, then vanished in the mists.

It was already night when he was aroused by DiPalma's reverent roar from the next room. "Sweet Jesus!" That was followed by female laughter.

As Arthur rose to shower, he glanced at the bedside clock: eight-thirty. He'd slept three hours and missed dinner. They must head out directly – Hanife Bejko might be an early sleeper. He hammered the wall with a shoe, shouted a summons to meet in the lobby.

~~~

It was after nine as Arthur paced impatiently near the front entrance – DiPalma was taking an inordinate time parting from Ledjina. Grumbling under his breath, he stepped outside, lit his pipe. His stomach was vocalizing too, responding to the kebab vendor across the street: "You, friend. Best lamb, pork, chicken killed today, two-for-one Christmas special."

Arthur had developed a taste for these greasy, meaty morsels, and in short time was nibbling from a skewer, nodding or shaking his head in response to Djon's interrogation.

"Not American? Not English? Ah, Canadian, very good. Am giving deep regrets over your prime minister kicking bucket. Now you have lady like Maggie Thatcher, except more pretty. Djon Bajramovic is my name, student of politics, keep up with world, support Canada in war with Bhashyistan. You come as tourist? No? You look like professor. Wrong guess. Businessman then, what else is left? So what business?"

Arthur swallowed. "We build resorts." It was an uncomfortable lie. What was that false front of DiPalma's? Apex something.

"So is obvious you need translator, yes? Also I speak Italian and Greek, some Serbian. Many contacts, in Gjirokaster province, in capital city Tirana, whole country. Can get best property agents, best lawyers, help with bribes."

The multitalented Djon Bajramovic began a cheerful story of his decline and fall. "My father was partisan, good communist, never liquidated in purges. Yours truly also was big wheel in party, managed state farm after cultural revolution. Now Socialist Party is out, Democrats in. Now no government job, no work, because of bourgeois revanchists. But still many connections." He stroked his long curling moustache.

Here was DiPalma shuffling across the street, pausing to take some cellphone photos of the busy stalls, then to examine a vendor's array of handmade scarves and woollen caps. He finally presented himself, nonchalantly lighting a cigarette and ordering chicken with a side of cabbage.

Arthur took him aside. "I suggest we scrub Mr. Bejko. It's well after nine o'clock."

"Whoa, this town stays up late, that's when the important business is done. This is the best time, not so many people about." Contradicting himself, still in rut, his mind clouded.

Djon called: "Is done to perfection. Two for one, only fifty leks." Less than a dollar. "Anything else, I am faithful servant. Contacts in hotel industry, Adriatic resorts? I got. Djon Bajramovic has answer for every need. Can be dangerous here, maybe you need bodyguard."

DiPalma ate on the go as they strolled across the plaza, toward the old town. "One of your more engaging Albanian street swindlers," he said, his mouth full of cabbage. "I'm planning to meet Ledjina's parents tomorrow, if that's okay with you. She told them I'm head of Apex International Getaways – I gave her a copy of the brochure. I feel a little sneaky about it, but I'll straighten it out later."

Arthur was becoming impatient with his easily sidetracked companion. "You located Hanife Bejko's house?"

"A two-storey duplex. Nicely restored, balcony overhanging the street. I took pictures there this afternoon."

He pulled out his cellphone. The screen showed the last photo taken, Ledjina, bra askew, a breast bared, miming a puckered kiss. "Never mind." He stuffed the incriminating device back in his pocket, embarrassed, talking fast. "Anyway, his digs are across from an antique store. You might want to rummage in there – they've got some great carved furniture, some copperware Margaret might like, some handcrafted jewellery, but watch out, a lot of collectables here are fake."

"Any sign of activity at Bejko's house?"

"Yeah, his wife, I guess it was, a short, hefty woman, nice smile, she took a jaunt to a deli down the street, picked up some sausages."

A short walk took them to an area under restoration, scaffolding everywhere, tarps on windows. Some bars and tea rooms were busy, but the streets weren't. The several rectangular windows of Bejko's residence were curtained, upstairs and down, as was the glass in the front door. But lights were on within, and a bulb was burning outside, as if in welcome.

DiPalma drew Arthur into the shadows and whispered: "If something fouls up, we make like jackrabbits for that tavern over there."

This was unexpected and unnerving. "If what fouls up?"

"If this turns out to be a trick of some kind."

Arthur had no time to weigh that consideration because DiPalma was already at the door, poking a button that produced the unlikely sound of distant cowbells. No immediate answer, no other sounds from within.

"The good news is they've got no guard dog." DiPalma sounded the cowbells again, and after several seconds the curtain opened to reveal a sturdy, middle-aged woman, presumably Mrs. Bejko. DiPalma put on his politest face and showed her his passport. She looked confused until he laid a copy of Bejko's handwritten note flat against the glass.

She nodded, raised a finger: one minute. Soon a bony, greying man took his place behind the glass, his outstanding feature a bristle moustache that extended two inches from either cheek. DiPalma showed the note, then urged Arthur to the glass with passport, business card, a photo of Erzhan, another of his wife and children – if Bejko owned a television he ought to have seen, on CNN and elsewhere, some coverage of them.

The door opened. "I am Hanife. Come quick inside."

Arthur hadn't taken five steps into the house before it was confirmed that Bejko indeed owned a TV – in fact about a dozen of them, stacked around the living room, some boxed, some not, mostly high-end flat sets – along with several stereos and DVD players, a home theatre sticking from a crate, and a shiny new BMW motorcycle.

"Hanife the thief," DiPalma whispered.

Arthur, a connoisseur of thieves and receivers, was impressed. Bejko hurried them up a staircase, to an office that looked out over a clump of pine trees behind the house. More electronic goods here, smaller items: laptops, Blackberrys, cellphones. *No telfon here* – meaning, presumably, don't telephone me here.

Bejko waved them to a couple of plush armchairs and sat behind his carved walnut desk. Arthur introduced himself as Erzhan's lawyer, DiPalma as his assistant. All this in crude Albanian, an effort that caused Bejko's moustache tips to wiggle as he suppressed a smile.

"I sorry Pomeroy not come. Abzal, he very much love Mr. Pomeroy. He is the best."

"Mr. Pomeroy sent Mr. Beauchamp," DiPalma said. "He is second best."

"I am hoping honest lawyer, if so, first in history in Albania. They sell you for song. Abzal, he not do this thing, he is, how you say . . ."

"Scapegoat," Arthur ventured.

"Exactly. But I say nothing to no one, wait for you. I am in jail two months but meet Abzal only three days. Was drugged and put on plane, he says, and this I believe, so after I pay off warden to get back on street, I mail note to Mr. Pomeroy."

"Excellent," Arthur said. "And in business again so quickly. You put to shame my most valued clients."

Bejko beamed, threw an arm out expansively. "This? It is nothing. You should see in warehouse the cars, Lexus, Mercedes, Porsche, new, right off ship. But too many middlemen, too much overhead. Bribes alone eat half of profit. Is why I get arrest, not pay enough to police chief."

A bottle was produced, unlabelled, but when uncorked it smelled of a powerful brandy. Arthur said simply, unapologetically: "I don't drink."

"Bad luck. You, my friend, Mr. Ray, must make up for second-best lawyer." Bejko filled a glass and passed it to DiPalma, who choked on the first sip.

"Warms stomach, yes?" Bejko found a ginger ale for Arthur, and clicked glasses with them. "To freedom for Abzal." A second toast: "To great country you belonging, Canada." Bejko expanded on this tribute, extolling the Canadian military for emptying the Bhashyistan jail. "Smart move."

Bejko topped up DiPalma's brandy, then accepted a cigarette from him. DiPalma's hand trembled as he held his lighter, a typical Parkinson's effect. Increasingly often, Arthur had observed, DiPalma would keep his hands in his pockets or otherwise out of view.

Bejko blew out a gust of smoke, then described how he'd spent two months of a three-year term in an institution known simply as Prison 303. Half a day's drive from here, into the mountains between Korça and the Macedonian border.

Three days before Bejko's release, Erzhan had been thrown into an adjoining cell. "He looked like drugged. He demand, why am I here, I am simple teacher, Canadian citizen, and they beat him, but only use rubber cables."

He'd seen no Western agents, nor had Erzhan been taken away for questioning. The police laid into Abzal for two days, though to what purpose Bejko couldn't explain, other than, "Is standard procedure." By the third day, they'd tired of the sport. "No one is knowing this Erzhan, or why he in jail. No criminal charge, no lawyer, no nothing. Everyone confuse, even police, guards. No one have much English for talking him."

Black and blue but finally left in peace, Erzhan was able to tell his neighbour what he remembered of his abduction. A grey sedan pulled up and a front-seat passenger leaned out to ask directions to the nearest liquor store. Without waiting for an answer, that passenger got out of the car and another from the back. A sudden blow to the back of his neck, as if from the edge of a hand, paralyzed him. He fought for consciousness but all went blank as he was bundled into the vehicle.

This was in finer detail than Iqbal Zandoo's account, but despite losses in translation and Zandoo's distant perspective, the two versions meshed well. Arthur asked if Erzhan had described any of the three men.

The one who asked about the liquor store was tall, thin-faced. The one from the back seat, Erzhan's attacker, "looked like heavyweight boxer."

"And the driver?" Arthur asked.

"He not ever see."

He came to fifteen hours later, naked, groggy, in a police van, just as it was rolling into Prison 303 under a raised steel gate.

"What day was this?" Arthur asked.

Bejko rummaged in a drawer for an old desk calendar. "I am release November thirty. So three days before, on twenty-seven."

Arthur and DiPalma exchanged looks. That was the same day, Ottawa time, that an IED demolished the Bhashie limousine.

"When come home from Prison 303, I learn more from BBC news. Abzal, he is, how you say, inconvenient person because of bombing in Ottawa City. But is also famous former assassin. All confusing to me. But he not do bombing, not possible."

"Tell us about this warden," said DiPalma, who was chainsmoking. He'd warmed to the brandy by now, was on another refill.

"Hard bargainer. Hundred thousand leks to commuting my sentence, not take less. Hasran Chocoli, good communist in past life, but repent, kept job." Bejko studied Arthur's tailored dark suit, as if appraising its value. "Chocoli and me, we have mutual respect. Maybe I make contact for you. For token introducer fee."

"That would be very kind."

"Five thousand dollar is usual fee. For you, three thousand."

Arthur swallowed, but decided not to quibble, drew out his traveller's cheques.

"Chocoli is not so cheap, I must warn. He prefer leks, but maybe also take euros, dollars. Not traveller's cheques, too easy to trace."

~~~

Though a taxi had been hired for the morning, for the journey to Korça and the date with warden Hasran Chocoli, Arthur couldn't locate DiPalma. No one from the Gjirokaster Hotel had seen him leave. Everything was in order in his room, clothes hung, the washroom giving evidence he'd showered and shaved. His cellphone was still there.

After cancelling the taxi, Arthur scoured the neighbourhood in the hope, proven vain, that he might find him in a restaurant or bar or maybe a drugstore, seeking a remedy for his hangover.

I'm planning to meet Ledjina's parents tomorrow. But where were they to be found? The manager at her restaurant was unfriendly, claiming not to know her address or phone number, let alone those of her parents. She wasn't expected on duty until the dinner hour.

Arthur spent the afternoon seething – while either pacing or studying his phrasebook, trying to focus on the perplexing Albanian consonants. In a restless fury, he snapped the book shut and turned on his set to CNN. He was besieged by rolling shots of Christmas celebrations around the world. Bizarrely, depressingly, he was suddenly aware he was alone for Christmas in a strange land.

The newscast went to the day's headline story, a startling event: a Canadian raid last night on Igorgrad. CF-18s had taken out Bhashyistan's ground-to-air defences and blown up hangars holding several MiG interceptors. The Information Ministry had been razed flat. A missile had made shards of a yellow Hummer whose occupant was believed to be the infamous third son, the late Mukhamet Khan Ivanovich.

On screen now, trying not to smile, was a colonel from Canadian Forces Air Command, describing a "perfectly executed, surgical procedure with limited targets." All aircraft and personnel had returned safely to the U.S. base in Kyrgyzstan.

Arthur felt no joy in anyone's death, even Mukhamet's, but the man had authored his own downfall, courting disaster with his taunts.

Here, in clips from a press conference in Ottawa, was Clara Gracey, confident and commanding, praising the military, proclaiming that Canada would not be mocked by a tinpot dictator, instructing the Ultimate Leader to release the hostages to avoid further strikes, castigating UN members for their empty phrases of support, and announcing that Canada would single-handedly do what international justice demanded.

A reporter asked if she feared fallout because the raid was on Christmas Eve. "Certainly not. We're dealing with a country that denies Christians the right of free worship and perverts the true meaning of the great religion of Islam. The entire free world applauds what we have done."

A political tour de force. The prime minister could yet raise her party from the grave. She had embarked on a clever campaign, not against the official opposition but against a country far, far away.

Meanwhile, with exemplary bravado, Bhashyistan national radio was telling a different story: patriotic defenders had beaten off yet another invasion by the Western warmongers. A lie so pitiful that even in Muslim Albania it was likely to provoke only laughter.

It was three o'clock. His anger at DiPalma was being succeeded by concern for him.

25

For Charley Thiessen, this didn't seem a lot like Christmas. Yet everything was in place for it: the house festooned with decorations, the glowing angel reigning over a spruce dressed with sparkly icicles, carols pumping from the stereo, the rich greasy smell of a twenty-pound bird in the oven, Aunt Myrtle and Uncle Earl hunkered over the thousand-piece jigsaw that was a holiday tradition. Mom and wife in the kitchen, jabbering nonstop. The two boys trying out their new toboggan by the riverbank. The entire town of Flesherton prettily coated with five inches of newly fallen snow.

His mother had been constantly at him: "You going to sit there all day like a lump? What's eating you, anyway, Snarly Charley? It's a time of joy, for Christ's sake." His wife would chime in: "You with us or against us, Charley? Get off that stupid computer."

He'd been all day on his laptop, hiding behind the massive, blinking tree, surfing the news outlets for headlines he didn't want to see. Like, for instance: "Justice Minister's Smear Backfires." His head was aching and his insides were boiling from the stress accumulated over the last few days, ever since that gut-clenching horror show when he'd raced back to the Château to try to rescue the mini-recorder.

Scenes from that foiled mission kept replaying. Calling Stonewell's suite from a house phone, leaving an inane message:

"Guess you guys must've split, I'll keep trying." Then, taking no chances, racing up there. A moment of hope when he saw the "Do Not Disturb" – surely it meant they were sleeping it off. Rapping on the door, calling, "Yo, Robert, it's me." Shouting, hammering in vain as a housekeeper stared at him from down the hall. Returning to the elevator, feeling defeated.

Also bugging Charley was that his oldest, Joy, just turned eighteen, had come back from college for the holidays like the green avenger, carrying on about vanishing bears, whales, fish, forests, and coral reefs. She was doing a paper on greenhouse gas emissions. She'd forced him to watch a Suzuki documentary predicting scenarios he didn't need to hear about, coastal flooding, drowning cities. He had his own problems.

Uncle Earl passed by to refuel before attacking the jigsaw again. "Get you another toddy, Charley boy?"

Thiessen smiled wanly, nodded – another toddy would not hurt.

"Why so glum? We blasted the bejesus out of those Bhashies, best Christmas present the country's ever had."

"I'll bet it was your idea, Charley." His mom, joining in, wiping her hands on her apron. "Don't tell me. Cabinet secrecy. I may be just your dumb mother, but I know how things work." Then going after him again: "Such a perfect Christmas Day. Get in the spirit, Mr. Prime Minister."

Mr. Prime Minister. The concept was strange to him now, illusory. Maybe he'd been fooling himself thinking he was P.M. material, maybe DuWallup and the gnome had been having a private joke, encouraging the cabinet buffoon to think he was the party's prince-in-waiting. Maybe they thought he could be used, the way George W. Bush was.

He scanned the Canadian Press site: no bulletins from Garibaldi Island, no interviews with smirking staff at the Château, or its pompous desk clerk, Fortesque. He'd sidled up to him calmly, explained he'd dropped a gold cufflink in Mr. Stonewell's suite. The matter went all the way up to the hotel manager, who told Thiessen, with great aplomb, he was immeasurably pleased to help the honourable minister any way he could.

A surly security officer had accompanied Thiessen to the suite, breathing down his neck as he fumbled under the bugged table, pretending to look for the alleged cufflink. The mini-recorder hadn't dropped to the floor, nor was it still stuck to the underside of the table.

Frantic, he crawled about on his elbows and knees, checking under every piece of furniture. Gone. It was gone. Not found by housekeeping obviously, because the room hadn't been done yet. The security guy watched with narrowed eyes, saying nothing, unwilling to restrain the country's highest law officer from going through drawers, closet, wardrobe. Unable to suppress a grin as Thiessen got his prints all over the hookah pipe, then wiped them with his shirttail. He'd recoiled at the sight of a used, leaking condom beside the bed.

His quest failed, he'd fled the Château, entertaining images of Stonewell striding into the *Ottawa Citizen* newsroom, the political editor listening raptly to Thiessen's taped voice. *Boy, I'll bet you must know some stories about the old shyster.* Or worse, far, far worse: *Normally I don't toke up until after dinner.*

Thiessen had spent that afternoon in near paralysis, weighing options: should he hang around the hotel waiting for Stonewell? Then what – confront him? Or should he call Crumwell? Have one of their goons take Stonewell down in a back alley? In the end, he couldn't bear to see their incredulous faces, to hear their icy tones of contempt. In the end, he did nothing, because anything he tried would only make things worse.

So he simply prayed that these Gulf Island loadies would shrug the whole thing off, see it as a joke, garbage the device. He'd got along with Stonewell, hadn't he? He and his pal had been well looked after, they weren't the kind of guys to repay generosity by causing a stink. Surely if they felt otherwise, the story would have already broken. After all, three days had passed.

Maybe he'd skate through this. The national press could easily miss the story – the election had scattered them across the country, and they weren't doing much but collecting snippets about how prominents were spending Christmas. Charley Thiessen, for instance, would be at home "sharing this blessed time with my loved ones."

It *was* a blessed time, damn it. It was a good-news Christmas Day. Look at that job the flyboys had done in Igorgrad – they pitched a perfect game. Yes, sir, the Conservatives were back and the maple leaf flag was flapping proudly in the Thiessen front yard. Nothing to worry about.

His wife: "Charley, get off your lazy duff and sharpen the carving knife."

An overpowering aroma from the kitchen informed him they'd taken the turkey out. His stomach looped like a cresting wave. He bolted for the bathroom.

~~~

Bulked up with pillows, in a red suit smelling of mothballs and a beard you could hide a small human being inside, Abraham Makepeace was holding Stoney at bay. "This here government post office does not open on Christmas Day." To Stoney, this smacked of bureaucratic fanaticism. There it was in his box, the overnight Express Post envelope, just a reach away, but this Santa Claus masquerader was protecting it like it was his virgin daughter.

"Honest, I couldn't make it in yesterday, I got caught in the Christmas rush." Crush was more like it, at the Honker's annual all-day, all-night, wall-to-wall Christmas Eve ape-fest. Stoney finally managed to fight his way out of there today at noon, with Hamish McCoy, both still half in the bag, and they drove straight here to enjoy the shopkeeper's traditional Christmas ration of a few tots to thank his customers for letting him rip them off all year.

"Her Majesty does not work on the day of the Saviour's birth, and nor does her servant Abraham Makepeace."

This was wildly unreasonable. It wasn't as if the General Store was closed. The porch was packed, all the regulars plus the several survivors of Honk's drunkarama, as sleepless as Stoney, but just as game to make it through this festive day.

"It's the time of *giving*, Abraham."

"I am giving. Three kegs of aged rum. Organic, made locally with them sugar beets the Frannery boys are growing. Have another."

"Have a *heart*. I better explain. It's from my dear old granny in Ottawa, she promised to send me a locket with her picture in it. She ain't got much longer. Please, Abraham, please let me see her smiling face one more time." He wiped an eye. "Give me that for Christmas Day."

Makepeace jiggled his pillowed false front and went, "Ho, ho, ho. That's the best one I heard all year."

"I'll donate two days' free work on the new tavern."

"I'll give you this here package if you promise not to." He gave forth another ho-ho-ho and pulled out the fat, padded envelope.

Stoney scuttled off with it, pausing to lace his mug of rum with enough coffee to keep him ambulatory until the Reverend Al's annual punchbowl party. He put two fingers to his lips, a signal for McCoy to join him outside to sneak a joint. The old Newf was just back from his triumphal three-month tour of Berlin.

"Oi still got no grasp on why them Ottawa fellas gave you the keys to the city, and you ain't gonna persuade mesself you been recognized as a top business enervater. That's a load of hugger-mugger."

Stoney had told McCoy the whole story, the two nights as a guest of the government, how they were supposed to pick his brains about how to run the country. But that never happened. All that happened was some glad-hander calling himself Charley asked a lot of questions about Garibaldi, then took off after a couple of drinks, looking unstrung.

Stoney originally thought Charley was a lawyer, but the way Arthur Beauchamp's name kept coming up, he reckoned he might be a copper. A bon vivant with the chicks, he'd said, which led Stoney to worry he had something on Arthur, a sex crime. It was hard to see Arthur going to such extremes when he had his pick of the island's hotties.

He lit up, passed the bomber to McCoy. "Let's have a look at this gizmo." He began wrestling the tape off the package. "Man, if I hadn't tripped over the duffle bag, I wouldn't never have seen it, but I'm on my ass under the table, and there's this ugly black cock-roach, eh? Staring at me with a blinking green eye."

He and Dog had had been too wiped to figure out how the device worked. So they'd couriered it to Hot Air Holidays, Rural Route 1, Hopeless Bay.

It was obviously some kind of bugging device, so he and Dog assumed Charley was a narc, this was a sting, they'd been ratted on. They didn't go to the ballet that night, donated the hookah and the leftover ten pounds of dope to a grateful street person, cleaned up the room, and waited for Charley to lead in a SWAT team to take it apart. Yet that hadn't happened, or Stoney wouldn't be standing here on Christmas Day smoking a doob with Hamish McCoy.

He wished he wasn't so hammered. Events had turned all boogly-woogly, he was maximally confused. He'd hoped the weed would lead him to some inspired answers, but that wasn't happening.

He fiddled with the recorder. "See, I press rewind, then play, and nothing happens."

"I'm gonna tell you again, b'y, you wanna deep-six that there item, it's stolen government property. Them narcs are gonna be climbin' all over your arse, oi'm surprised they ain't already slapped the darbies on. You're askin' for heat, b'y. Meanwhile, oi'm freezing me nuts off."

He flipped the roach and went in. Stoney stayed outside awhile, contemplating McCoy's disagreeable scenario. No way was he going to let the paranoid little bugger get to him. On reflection, Charley couldn't have been a cop. He wasn't smart enough. Yeah, he was probably only a lawyer, making friendly talk, squeezing out a little gossip on a famous personage to pass on to his wife and mistress. After all, Stoney *had* been chosen as one of an elite group of small businessmen, he had paper to prove it, a government letterhead.

Buoyed by that more satisfying script, he sought out electronic expertise, honed in on the editor of the *Island Bleat,* who was at a long table, in front of a ton of nachos. Gomer Goulet was beside him, shit-faced, trying to get people to sing along with him. "Everbuddy. Good King Wensheslush."

"Yo, Nelson," Stoney said, drawing up a chair, shouting over Goulet, "you ain't interviewed me yet on my national award as achiever of the year."

"We only report the facts." Forbish slapped Stoney's hand as it hovered above the nachos. He was the island's champion eater, he pulled 320 pounds, fastened his belt twelve inches above his belly.

"As you probably heard, I just got back from Ottawa after being bestowed upon with this unique honour." Stoney wasn't going to tell him about the alternative concept, the hugger-muggery, but a little publicity never hurt business.

"We don't print rumours unless they're basically true."

Stoney produced, with a forgiving smile for the scornful newsman, the letter nominating him as B.C. entrepreneur of the year. Forbish frowned over it, rejected it. "I wasn't born yesterday."

The local news anchor was a crack hand with gadgetry, cameras, and computers, so Stoney moved the nacho bowl aside and placed the fat black cockroach in front of him. "You want more proof, it's all in here, but this here thing ain't user-friendly, it won't turn on."

Forbish held it to his eye, revolved it. "What we got here is some kind of digital recorder. I note the LED light won't turn on, therefore the battery's dead."

Stoney remembered now the green light; the recorder had probably been on when he couriered it. By now McCoy was squatting beside them, and others were leaning over their shoulders.

"They sure are making them new cellphones small," Ernie

Priposki said. "Look, it's got a suction cup so you can stick it on your forehead."

Stoney snapped his fingers, remembering Constable Ernst Pound's role as mailman. "Call Ernst right now, he was the deliverer of these glad tidings. Yes, boys, you're looking at the achiever of the year for British Columbia, right here."

"Buy an ad," Forbish said.

Gomer Goulet boomed from the next table: "Oh, what fun we had today! Laughing all the way! Come on, everbuddy, you all know this one."

"I got a spare nicad," Forbish said, peering into the battery compartment. "Where'd you steal this doodad from?"

Stoney yanked it from under his paw. "Okay, Mr. Doubting Thomas, you can cancel my subscription to the *Bleat*. And this is sensitive material, it ain't for public consumption. You ain't getting your hands on it until I talk to my lawyer."

That was the obvious course of action. Get some advice from his wily house counsel. If the old sharpie had somehow stuck his wire into the wrong socket, he had a right to know before the media got ahold of this. But maybe Arthur was on the run, because, mysteriously, he hadn't come home for Christmas.

~~~

Christmas Day.

Maxine, Ivy, me, and a hundred partisans are lounging around a Christmas tree in a mad dictator's winter palace in the foothills of the Altay Mountains. Atun went out with an axe last night as we were sleeping, and brought in this bushy ten-footer. Now it's all decorated with some surveyor's tape they found, and some painted ping pong balls from the rec room.

I started to laugh, but then found myself blubbering, imagining my family sitting around another tree, Hank and the kids, Mom, worrying, praying.

Ruslan Kolkov did his best to comfort me: "But you have family here too. We are all family, yes? – here are your brothers, here are your sisters. You come next year with your Hank and your beautiful daughters, to Igorgrad, when the statues of the mad god of Bhashyistan have been toppled, and we will celebrate the best Christmas, we will celebrate the gift of freedom."

He promised we will soon be able to contact the outside world by sat-phone – Canada, I mean, home – and Maxine and I have been absolutely tense with the prospect of doing so. ("Hi, Hank, we're sitting in Mad Igor's winter palace with a huge mob of revolutionaries armed to the teeth. What's up with you?") But the young man who left with the satellite phone in search of batteries hasn't returned, and we're worried for him.

Anyway, Ruslan and my family here (my brothers, my sisters) got what they wanted for Christmas. A huge cheer went up when we heard on the radio – reception is bad, but we get a Russian station in Omsk – that we, meaning us Canucks, knocked the poop out of Bhashyistan's military base and its airport and totalled the Information Ministry. A different official version from Igorgrad, though, which Ruslan called "a load of Ivanovich."

The raid had everyone dancing around and giving us hugs, and they broke open the liquor cabinet and there were so many toasts everyone got a little tipsy. Old Ilyich did something stupid, firing off a fusillade outside, and he's been demoted to dishwashing detail.

But there's also bad news, terrible news, from the western steppes, a peasant revolt put down, scores of them shot, hundreds of others forced to flee and regroup in the forested hills. The details were vague on Omsk radio, but we also heard about it from the people still straggling in. They say the government is trucking in troops to eliminate "subversives" hiding in the mountains, which means us.

"Now there will be great danger," Ruslan warned. "Now we cannot risk taking you to the border. We will be shooting ducks."

Atun was to have escorted us into the mountains, through a pass to Siberia. But that will be too dangerous, so we're better off staying with our protectors. Ivy is amazing, she greeted that almost with delight – she's found love. There's been a lot of steam rising from the hotsprings.

The new plan is to send scouts to find some safe route out of here, away from the advancing troops. We will break into groups, and descend into the pine forests. Snowshoes, winter tents, several layers of clothing to survive the biting weather. We're from Saskatchewan, we've known thirty below, that's what I keep telling myself.

The fighters will move west to join the partisans on the steppes, but the three of us will be led to a safe shelter – a friendly farm, a yurt, away from the action. We will be led by Aisulu the brave, who refused to be airlifted from the Igorgrad prison. So we will trust Aisulu, and trust in God.

26

—

As Arthur walked from the Gjirokaster Hotel into a snappy, bright winter afternoon, he was immediately seduced by the siren call of Djon Bajramovic and his sizzling *qebaps*. "You, mister resort developer, looking hungry, is lunchtime. Best food all Albania, proof is in pudding. Today starring premium lamb and goat."

Arthur opted for the lamb. "*Mirëdeta*, Djon," he said. "*Si ja kaloni?*"

Djon roared his approval. "*Mirë*, thank you, I am very good. Where you learn Albanian so fast? But not pronounce right. I give lessons, good teacher, fair price. How come you wearing suit today, you going church? I show you way."

"I'm looking for the police station."

That prompted a flurry of questions, to which Arthur responded candidly, telling of DiPalma's careless, gonad-driven pursuit of Ledjina, and his current status as a missing person.

Djon explained that a system of tight-knit clans was entrenched in Albania. Outsiders were distrusted. These clans tended to guard strictly the honour of their unmarried daughters. "Especially virgins. This girl, Ledjina, was virgin?"

"I doubt it."

"If so, he dead." He pointed across the plaza. "There is state police." A typical two-storey rectangle with inset windows. "Best you talk to chief, Kapitan Bizi. Sorry, he no friend, hates former communists, so I not going with you. Be ready for him asking gift for police recreation fund. Good luck. *Paç fat!*"

Arthur hurried across to the station, into a waiting room where several citizens, wearing the sad masks of crime victims, were filling out forms before taking their turns at the complaint desk, a long table manned by three bored officers. On a pedestal, overseeing all, was a senior officer. Several other police were drinking tea and gabbing.

Talk stopped as Arthur, in his dark suit, strode to the man on the stool, handed him his card, and asked, in Albanian, if he or anyone else could speak English, French, German, or Italian. No one spoke these languages. But when the name DiPalma was mentioned, the senior officer raised a finger in recognition. "Ah, *kanadez.*" Then he shook his head sadly. There came sighs from the cops drinking tea. One screwed up his face, wincing, as if demonstrating someone's great pain.

Struggling with his phrasebook Albanian, Arthur finally got his message through that he wished audience with their leader, Kapitan Bizi, and he was soon ushered upstairs to his office.

Rising from behind a desk was a robust, square-chinned man with a sweeping moustache, the requisite emblem of Albanian manhood. He greeted Arthur with a broad smile and an extended hand. The room was decorated with emblems: soccer, boxing, riflery.

Arthur was relieved to find Bizi had a fair knowledge of Italian. His opening words: "*Buon giorno,* Signor Beauchamp. I have been expecting you."

Arthur could barely hide his surprise – or his dread. "*Piacere,* Signor Kapitan."

"The situation with Mr. DiPalma is very difficult." In apologetic tones, Bizi explained that certain clans forbade outsiders from engaging in "adulterous activities with their young women," an unwritten law of which Signor Beauchamp's friend Mr. DiPalma had run afoul.

Arthur felt a chill. "What happened to him?"

"It seems the young lady introduced him to her father, Mr. Lushi, the family patriarch, as a developer of holiday resorts. I personally attended on Mr. Lushi earlier today – a good man, a foundry owner – and he gave me this."

Arthur's heart sank as Bizi showed him a glossy foldout from Apex International Getaways Corporation, advertising its properties worldwide.

"Mr. Lushi was suspicious of your friend, and he phoned the number that appears here, as I am doing now." Arthur put on his glasses so he could make out the area code: 514, Montreal. A few moments later, Bizi passed the phone to him. "It is ringing."

This is what Arthur heard: "Good morning, *bonjour,* Moishe's Bagel Bakery, hold the line a sec." Shouting to a customer: "Plain or sesame?"

Bizi retrieved the phone, set it in its cradle, and handed over DiPalma's wallet and cellphone. "These were taken from him at the hospital. You may wish to advise him to delete this photo." Ledjina half out of her bra, puckering her mouth. He then opened its picture folder to the photo of Janice. "Attractive woman, his wife."

"Former wife," Arthur said weakly, pocketing wallet and phone, rising. "I must get to the hospital."

Bizi stilled him with a raised hand. "There is no rush. He is under heavy sedation. Concussion, broken ribs, multiple bruises. Ledjina's brothers are well built, their work at the foundry is hard and physical. Please sit. Tell me what is going on. I am not a fool, Mr. Beauchamp."

"No, indeed you are not." Arthur retook his chair. A different approach was required, one that was unique, untried. Honesty.

He tapped his finger on the brochure. "This, Chief Bizi, is the disguise behind which Mr. DiPalma hides. Like you, *il mio amico,* he is a man of the law, but his work is unusual – he is an undercover police agent with the Canadian Security Intelligence Service, our CIA. We mean no disrespect to the Republic of Albania, but we are on a mission to rescue a Canadian citizen who has been illegally transported to your country. Abzal Erzhan. I am his lawyer." He was taking a chance: a call by Bizi to confirm this with, say, Anthony Crumwell would be counterproductive.

"Yes, I have heard of your intelligence service. But I must tell you that Canada is not viewed sympathetically in Tirana, because of your problems with a fellow Muslim country."

"I presume the name Krajzinski is familiar to you, sir. The Balkan wolf. The Serbian general who committed genocide upon a village of Kosovan Albanians."

Bizi turned and spat unerringly into his wastebasket. "Forty years. He should have his testicles stuffed down his throat and his body dragged through the streets."

"It is Ray DiPalma you must thank for General Krajzinski's arrest. It was his hired infiltrator who taped his incriminating boasts."

Bizi took a while to digest this. "Remarkable. Yes, I have heard there was a Canadian involved, it was widely rumoured. Ray DiPalma, you say. I shall check that out. If it is true, a dishonour has been done to him." He held his hands up, expansively. "He will get the best possible care."

Arthur prayed that DiPalma's injuries were not so serious as to demand an emergency call to the Canadian consul in Tirana, or even to CSIS in Ottawa. This rescue mission was in shambles, and he feared it might have to be aborted. "I really must run to the hospital."

"Yes, yes, you will see the surgeon, Dr. Muhbarren. I will arrange for it." Then his face contorted, as if with pain. "But, sadly, there is still the matter of his insult to this young girl's family. The situation is not entirely under my control. He will need to be guarded. And so will you – the Lushi family may regard you as in league with him."

Arthur was sure this was leading to nowhere good.

Bizi stroked his long moustache, thoughtfully. "This Canadian who was transported to our country – is that what prompted you to visit Hanife Bejko?"

Arthur managed not to flinch. "Ah, yes, Hanife. He was most helpful to Mr. DiPalma and me. A generous fellow." *Is why I get arrest, not pay enough to police chief.*

"He is not always so generous. Sometimes he has to be reminded." A broad smile. Bizi seemed not to mind sharing these corrupt intimacies with Arthur, who, as a lawyer, was presumed to be equally dishonourable. "Hanife spoke highly of you, Mr. Beauchamp. Indeed, he asked me to smooth the way for your meeting with the warden of Prison 303, Hasran Chocoli, also a friend. I can do this. I can offer a driver to take you to Korça."

"You are extremely kind."

"I can offer this service for three hundred thousand leks."

Arthur calculated: nearly three thousand dollars.

"As I say, you and Mr. DiPalma will need protection while you are guests in our town. There is much danger here, plus Serbian spies may seek revenge on the man who caused Krajzinski's downfall. Unfortunately, our resources are strained. Worse, the Gjirokaster police recreation fund is over budget on our new firing range."

This was a twist on the old protection racket. Arthur resigned himself to it, and ultimately they settled on an honorarium to the recreation fund of seven thousand dollars – Arthur would come by later with the traveller's cheques. After totalling all expenses and bribes, he would have less than a third left of his original twenty thousand.

Warden Chocoli would be even more rapacious, he assumed. But Bizi seemed to understand that, and graciously called the manager of a local bank, attesting for Arthur and arranging an appointment so a top-up could be wired from his law office in Vancouver. Now Arthur must steel himself for a call to Bullingham.

Bizi called Chocoli next. Arthur caught the words *një shok* and

Hanife. Translated: friend of Hanife. He also heard several times the word *dollars,* a word common to many languages.

~~~

DiPalma's crown was swaddled in a turban of bandages, and his purple swollen cheeks and blackened eyes gave him a raccoonlike look. Arthur could tell that the three cracked ribs caused him pain to breathe even shallowly. The only pleasure he took from seeing him flat on his back in a hospital ward was his pathetic, cringing look of contrition.

"I will personally take him by ambulance to Tirana," said Dr. Muhbarren, in excellent English. "He will have better facilities there, specialists. In the meantime, it is an honour to have him in our little provincial hospital." He turned to his patient. "You will also be safer in Tirana, Mr. DiPalma – you have too many enemies here."

He glanced at the two officers standing in the hallway, suggesting even they were not to be trusted. They had delivered Arthur here, on Bizi's orders. Another officer had been assigned to escort him to Korça the next day, Sunday. He had dismissed all thoughts of backing down, and was almost glad that the expert in all things Albanian would not be tagging along.

Dr. Muhbarren had urged Arthur to keep his visit brief – the concussion had not been a mild one. It would take weeks for his head to heal, months before his ribs mended. The doctor paused on exiting, with a salute. "To the Canadian James Bond, who trapped the Balkan wolf in his lair – our people thank you."

Arthur got close to DiPalma. "Are you alert enough to exchange a few words?"

"It only hurts when I laugh," he said hoarsely.

"I have outed you. You may forget Apex Getaways. Let us hope this escapade, and your sudden notoriety here, do not get back to Ottawa before I find Abzal."

"Carry on regardless. I'm washed up, I'm done."

Stoned talk, through the analgesic fog. "I will see you in Tirana. *Paç fat.*"

~~~

As of seven p.m., Arthur had done little else but make arrangements for a wire transfer from Canada, the local bank manager obligingly seeing to his needs on a weekend. For the rest of the time he attacked his phrasebook, waiting for the right hour to call Bullingham – too early and he would be dragging him out of bed, with calamitous consequences. But now it was mid-morning in Vancouver, when Bully ought not to be at his dyspeptic worst, breakfast tucked away, a relaxing Christmas Day to look forward to.

His housekeeper answered. Mr. Bullingham had left for the office an hour ago. Arthur remembered that the indefatigable nonagenarian often dropped into the shop on Christmas, a practice that served as a compelling example to the slaves on the lower floors. He dialed Bully's private line.

A curt "No, I do not accept the charges."

"Merry Christmas, Bully, it is I."

A weary "Oh, very well. Keep it short, Arthur."

"How wonderful, Bully, to hear your voice so clearly from afar." Great warmth and spirit. "I bring greetings from the wondrous strange land of Albania."

"I hope this is important and doesn't involve money. Do you have good tidings or bad?"

Arthur wasn't going to mention the DiPalma reversal. "We're closing in on the target. I expect to see him tomorrow." A deep breath. "Expenses have been heavy, Bully. If I may be blunt, they're robbing me blind."

"Who?"

"Officialdom."

"Then I suspect it's time to cut the losses. Whether or not your knight errantry proves successful, fairness surely demands you earn back the $29,850 that are currently on the books for this expedition. Not a problem, I think. A.J. Quilter and several high executives of Alta International have just been charged with authorizing corrupt payments to the Bhashyistan government. You're the counsel of choice, of course."

Stopping short of a promise, Arthur teased him with the hope he might take Quilter's case – he was, after all, quickly becoming a corruption specialist. Then he made his pitch: Tragger, Inglis could expect to earn a massive return on its investment. Erzhan's claim against the Canadian government would start at twelve million, plus all disbursements – including this long-distance call.

He could hear Bully's brain computing. Finally. "Give me a figure."

"To be safe, fifty thousand."

An indecipherable sound, like gasping. A clearing of throat that didn't clear it. "Fifty?" he rasped. "Fifty, did you say?" The long silence meant he'd calculated the odds as being favourable but was having trouble saying so. "Not a cent more. Tomorrow is Sunday. Monday is also a bank holiday."

"Do your best." The old boy not only had the bank manager's home number, he was on its board. "Trust me, Bully."

~~~

"Sunday breakfast special, eggs any way you like, scrambled, boiled, on pita bread. Best coffee in Europe." It was seven-thirty, the sun had barely dawned, and Djon Bajramovic was already at his stand. Did he never sleep?

Bizi's expensive chauffeur had yet to show up at the hotel, so Arthur ordered a coffee.

"I hear from friends about Mr. Ray. Too bad – but he survive, so lucky man. How you make out with shady head copper? Police recreation fund is richer?"

"Thank you for the advice. Yes, that has bought us some apparently needed police protection."

"Already you have adapted to local economy. You see how Djon Bajramovic can help business adventures here, he has been around the block a few times. But maybe you need protection from police protection. Also from kidnapping for ransom – Apex Getaways is very rich company, yes? My security service comes with personal guarantee, tough guys but cheap, work for tips."

"Let's talk about it later, Djon."

Pulling up was a four-wheel-drive van bearing the insignia of the Albanian State Police. Climbing out, a smiling bearded officer, who held open the passenger door for Arthur. Grigori was his name, and for the enjoyment of his patron, he chose a mountainous route, by the Greek border. They looped around hairpins that Grigori took with wide, heart-stopping turns to avoid potholes, then descended to valleys with raging streams under creaky wooden bridges that were another test of courage. But the views were stunning, and Arthur captured several on DiPalma's cellphone.

Occasionally, on emerging from scrub and pine forests, they entered areas of small holdings and dilapidated villages where grizzled locals stared after them in amazement, as if their passage were the highlight of the month. Grigori wasn't shy about using his siren to clear passage between horse carts and fleeing chickens and flocks of stubborn, grumpy goats. Finally, a sizable town, Korça, where they turned north.

Snow was clinging to the roadside as they crested a final high point and took a view of Lake Ohrid, a glassy blue expanse beyond which lay the isolated little Republic of Macedonia. A steep descent took them to a plateau upon which a twelve-foot-high wire fence enclosed a concrete structure with guard turrets at each corner.

Prison 303 resembled an industrial warehouse, featureless and flat, with barred windows, and was abutted by a shedlike administrative office. Some three hundred prisoners were housed here, said Grigori, many of whom he'd bussed in over the years. The gatekeeper recognized him, strapped on his submachine gun as he opened the gate.

Several yard guards lounged about, keeping an eye on the dozen prisoners shovelling snow from the driveway, picking up litter, and washing two prison service vehicles near the office. Grigori barked an order as he and Arthur alighted, and they started in on his muddy van.

A rat scurried under the office annex as Arthur approached its locked steel door. Clearly, he was expected, because he was admitted immediately by a secretary. Several others sat at desks, with the resigned look of underpaid civil servants. A group of uniformed guards was watching a soccer game on a small TV. Rifles and shotguns hanging on the walls.

The man standing at an office doorway had to be Hasran Chocoli. Saying nothing, sizing Arthur up. Birdlike, twitchy, hints of an anxiety disorder, all masked by another fine example of Albanian facial art, handlebars as thick and wide as a clothes brush.

"Come in, Mr. Beauchamp." In English, slightly accented.

The secretary followed them in with a tea tray, set it on a side table, and poured. The office was handsomely done, leafy plants, lounge chairs and ottomans, Turkish carpets, walls draped with fabric in Byzantine patterns. *Good communist in past life, but repent, kept job.*

"How do you take your tea? I usually prefer goat's milk. Very healthy."

"No question. I happen to raise goats."

"A goatkeeper and a lawyer, how unique."

Tea poured and stirred, they settled into soft chairs, testing each other in conversation. Arthur lied about how much he was enjoying Albania, and complimented Chocoli on his English. The warden said he'd improved it by studying abroad.

His hands were active, playing with his tie, his shirt buttons, his moustache. "I regret this meeting must be brief, Mr. Beauchamp. Abzal Erzhan is no longer in this facility. He was transferred two weeks ago."

Arthur showed no reaction.

"Here, let me show you." Chocoli went to his desk, returned with a leather-bound book. It was rather like a guest register, with dates and remarks written in pen after prisoners' names. Here was Erzhan crossed out, two weeks ago, Monday, December 13.

Arthur checked himself from asking why Chocoli hadn't mentioned this on the phone yesterday to Captain Bizi. Quickly, cellphone in hand, he snapped a picture of the page. The warden made a half-hearted effort to retrieve the book, but Arthur held on tight, flipping the pages back to late November, looking for Erzhan's name. Here he was, booked in on Saturday, November 27, ten a.m., confirming Bejko's account. He took another photo.

"It is not permitted to record government documents." Chocoli wrestled the register away while Arthur calmly pocketed the phone. The warden seemed uncertain whether to pursue the matter.

"And where was Mr. Erzhan taken?"

"That is a mystery. He was signed out by the State Border Police under warrant sealed by the director-general of prisons." A tight smile, though Arthur could barely make it out behind the foliage. "No forwarding address."

"May I see the documents relating to his transfer?"

"You must ask in Tirana for these."

"But you have copies, I assume?"

"I am not authorized." He straightened his tie.

"Help me, Warden, I'm confused. Hanife Bejko – you know him, of course?"

"In my official capacity here, yes, I have met him."

"A month ago, Hanife was in a cell adjoining Mr. Erzhan's. He observed him being beaten."

"That was not done. There were even discussions about his safety . . . Never mind. Hanife has a wayward tongue, he exaggerates."

Discussions about his safety? "I'm curious to know what my client was charged with."

Chocoli spread his hands. "It is a criminal offence to enter the country illegally. That is why the border police are involved, yes? I have no control over what they do. Maybe you should ask them. Or the prisons office in Tirana. It's not my job to keep track of fifteen thousand inmates in thirteen institutions, I am sorry." He shrugged.

"You were not aware Erzhan was flown secretly here from Canada? And that he was accused of a crime he could not have committed?"

"I know nothing about him. They come, they go, I don't even look at them." He was having trouble meeting Arthur's eye.

"Warden Chocoli, what is the usual penalty for illegal immigration?"

Chocoli drained his tea. "Fine, jail, deportation, there are many solutions."

"And how much must Mr. Erzhan pay in fines before I escort him out of the country?"

"That would be for decision by judicial authorities." Shifting in his chair.

A hard bargainer, Bejko said. "Would fifteen thousand dollars pay his debt to society?" To get Abzal out of the country safely and fast, Arthur would be prepared to pay well in excess of that.

Chocoli stood. "Mr. Beauchamp, I would be insulted if I thought you were offering a bribe. But surely you are not, because it is against the law. Now I must close this meeting. I have many things to do."

"I can arrange for thirty thousand in one or two days. Cash, of course."

"Cash . . ." Temptation was written on his face, but there was fear also; Arthur could see it in his eyes. "No, it is not possible." He indicated the door with a trembling hand.

Arthur calmly sipped his tea. "I am not satisfied with what I've been told, Warden. This is a matter with serious international implications. I can't believe you aren't aware of that."

"I have to ask you to leave." Holding the doorknob. "Please."

Arthur rose, returned his cup to the tray, then towered over his host for a silent moment, not threatening but demanding, forcing Chocoli to look squarely at him and reveal the mendacity in his eyes. *Vultus est index animi*. The face is the index of the soul.

Chocoli had broken into a sweat by now. He twitched again, and spoke softly: "I have instructions. There are other people involved, people in Tirana."

27

——

For the past couple of days, Charley Thiessen had been hanging at Hoffstutter Blane, the Tory ad agency, where a cluster of witty, bright-eyed women had taken him in charge, sprucing up his message, rehearsing him, dressing him, powdering him, perfecting his handsome, confident John Wayne grin.

His mother had come with him to Toronto, but they'd sent her packing on the first day, she having been considered a disruptive force, a distraction, and there'd been an unhappy scene around that. But the young ladies cooled him out, flattered him, insisting he had great camera presence. He guessed he didn't come off too bad on some of the takes, but he never felt he was speaking from the heart: these were somebody else's words, Gus Hoffstutter's words.

Some of the clips would go national, some just in Ontario, most in Grey County, where he'd also be playing live the next night, New Year's Eve, with a dozen soirées to visit.

Today's last taping, for national free-time radio, was important enough that the man himself was guiding him through it, Hoffstutter with his pink face and puckered smile. Several of his girls were here in the boardroom too, hovering about, practically swooning whenever their Einstein came up with another brilliancy.

"Bhashyistan, that's the ticket we ride to January twenty-four. How did we fare on *La Presse*'s poll, my darling?"

"We're up eight."

"And that's just in Quebec. Are we charting up with a bullet?" A chorus of agreement. "And do we know what caused that bump?"

"The raid on Igorgrad."

"Front of the class. We're riding to victory on the coattails of our air force heroes. I told Clara to get that on the street, and I'm telling you, Charley. Here's how we're deep-thinking this thing – if silencing Mukhamet has clawed back eight points, three more shots like that will send us off the grid. We hit them again, and hit them hard. Affirmative, Charley? You with me? Hello? You zoning out on us again?"

"I was just wondering if I should say something about, you know, the environment, capping carbon emissions." *Talk about what's really important, Dad.* Joy had been all over him about Big Oil, the stripping of the boreal forest, drowning him in numbers, charts, graphs projecting climate catastrophe. She'd embarrassed him by signing on as a Greenpeace volunteer.

Hoffstutter finished his latte, wiped the foam from his manicured moustache. "Get me another of those, dear. Okay, Charley, you're not going airy-fairy on us, I hope. That climate stuff only confuses people, scares them. No, you're going to talk about our brave boys in uniform, and you're going to talk about patriotism, national pride, heads held high. We're not waiting for those chickenshits at the UN to step in, we're not waiting for the rest of the world. We're setting an example, we're righteous warriors for democracy." Applause. "The Grits, needless to say, are to come off as cowering pantywaists. *Capiche,* Charley?"

"Yeah, I guess, okay."

"Remember Huck's rallying cry. What was it, Jackie?"

"Canada first!"

"Canada first, Charley. You're Captain Canada. Now you skedaddle out of here while we poop it up."

That gave Thiessen a chance to get some air. He went down to Queen Street, buttoned his coat against the chill, took an aimless walk, slowing as he passed a cocktail lounge, tempted but carrying on, knowing they'd smell it on his breath.

It was December 30, ten days after the debacle in the Château Laurier. Why wasn't *that* on the street? It had been an unbearable time, like waiting for the other shoe to drop. On his head, like a hobnailed boot.

But the long silence was giving him hope – there was a credible reason for it, obvious even. Robert Stonewell was a dope dealer, he didn't want to get involved, didn't want the heat. He'd chucked the recorder, deep-sixed it in the Ottawa River, and gone back to his hot-air balloon business. He probably smuggled his dope that way, with air drops.

So maybe all was good, maybe it was time to come up for air. Maybe his dreams hadn't been dashed – the big prize was still open, he could yet score the game-winning touchdown. The Tomato Juice Fiasco had finally slipped off YouTube's most-watched list, it would soon be forgotten. *To the great, adversity is a welcome challenge.* His mom's favourite fridge magnet.

He stopped at an array of newspaper boxes, bought the *National Post*, flipped through it. Only one reference to himself – which brought relief, not despair. Buried in a story headed SIX ALTA BRASS REMANDED ON BAIL, a mention of the fiat he'd signed, as attorney general, authorizing the bribery indictment.

Gracey and the PMO had pushed him hard to approve it – Quilter and his crew were probably as guilty as Judas, but the main idea was to get distance from Alta, to demonstrate that the rule of law prevailed without fear or favour – and, as a by-product, mollify the Bhashies. The Tories weren't expecting any campaign donations from Alta anyway.

He headed back up to the ad agency to record his jingoistic spiel. How had he let himself be cowed by Hoffstutter? How was he going to look Joy in the face?

~~~

"I come armed with vital dispatches." Percival Galbraith-Smythe, by Clara's bed, lowering a tray with coffee and a bowl of tastelessly healthy bran cereal – he seemed determined to keep her alive until the election. "It seems you had a rare old time last night. Doesn't hurt. Shows you're not some pinch-faced academic but a fun person, vital, still attractive to the dominant sex – though you might consider taking a few centimetres off those thighs."

She'd seen those thickening thighs on *Canada AM,* doing a kind of faux step dance on a Halifax stage at two in the morning, a New Year's Eve campaign kickoff party. The press was to have left early, but someone must have hung around with a minicam.

"What time is it?"

"First of all, do you know the day?"

"Saturday. New Year's Day."

"Correct. It is half past eleven in the morning. You are at 24 Sussex Drive. You arrived here four hours ago after a three-hour nap on the Challenger jet. You are ready to roll."

The iron lady found her gown and slippers. She'd pretty well blown *that* image, a stale, ill-fitting role foisted on her by Hoffstutter and the campaign team. Couldn't they at least call her the iron maiden? But the wartime prime minister image seemed to work. The successful air raid had ended the cyber attacks on businesses and boosted Conservative numbers.

She couldn't remember the name of that lovely young man from last night. Ralph something, a common surname, Harrison, Henderson. Campaign manager in Dartmouth. On waking at the call of her bladder, she'd been abashed to find, sleeping beside her, a man young enough to be her son. She'd fled for her plane at five a.m., abandoning him in her hotel suite. She hoped Percival wouldn't hear about it – he was so censorious.

Coffee and a cigarette aided the recuperative process, and soon she was showered and dressed. When she returned, Percival was at his laptop.

"I do have some good news, but first the bad, something that will not soothe your hangover."

On the YouTube screen, an entirely unwelcome face: Mukhamet Khan Ivanovich chortling: "He's back!"

Clara groaned as the lens widened to show him behind the wheel of a yellow Hummer. "Surprise, not so easy to pull out thorn in side, eh, Canada? So guess what, this most-watched news host has *five* Hummers, all same colour, for to confuse assassins. Now only four, and also one less innocent underling who you murder. So once again so-called advanced country is outwitted by emerging nation."

Fade to a country scene, a barn, livestock. "Just in, spontaneous demonstration by agricultural workers and wives." A throng of peasants, some holding farm and household items, pitchforks and rolling pins, chanting, in rehearsed English: "Death to Canada, death to Abzal Erzhan!" A horse reared as they set a maple leaf flag alight.

Fade back to Mukhamet, starting the Hummer's engine. "Stay tuned for more hot news. This is your roving reporter Mukhamet Khan Ivanovich signing off." He accepted the video camera from whoever was holding it, and his chubby face again filled the screen. "Canada goose, hah! We give *you* the goose."

Clara chained a cigarette. Her hangover was compounded by a migraine – they'd been coming more frequently. So much for the jump in the polls. "For God's sake, tell me the good news."

"Not yet. More bad. Bit of a row in Kyrgyzstan about our use of the American base. The Yanks want us to back off. They could lose their lease."

"Those faithless fucking faint-hearts, always looking out for number one –"

"Whoa . . . Listen up, my sweet." He wagged a finger to still her rant. "Last night, our embassy in Kazakhstan received a call by sat-phone from a partisan of the Bhashyistan Democratic Revolutionary

Front. Didn't leave a number. Announced himself in English as 'a friend to Canada.' The rest was in Russian." He passed her a memo with the translation.

"A dissident? Some are still on the loose?"

"Well, we did empty the jail, Clara. They seem to have developed an effective underground grapevine."

Clara put on her glasses. According to this informant, the Calgary Five were in the cells of a police station in a town called Özbeg, in the northern desert, near the Russian border. A company of Bhashyistan regulars was barracked there, protecting the nearby oil fields. "Very dangerous, but you will squash them like cockroaches. Good luck. God save the Queen."

Percival opened a file. "Özbeg, population twenty thousand. Aerial images place it approximately in the middle of nowhere. Hometown of one of the defectors from the Ilyushin crew, he helped the DoD pinpoint the police station. Buster Buchanan has a plan to pull the hostages out of there, fly them to our base in Kandahar. Total Canadian show, avoiding Kyrgyzstan."

"What if it's a trick, Percival?"

"Buster Buchanan is willing to gamble. What do we have to lose?"

"Lives. The election."

"It's also ours to win, pet." He looked at his watch. "High command will be here for lunch at twelve-thirty to seek milady's blessings. No time to brief the cabinet. They're spread all over the country anyway. It'll be your call."

This is what it was all about. This is what killed Huck Finnerty. Clara stared at her wan, haunted face in the dressing table mirror. Eyeshadow seemed well advised. "What else?"

"A.J. Quilter filed suit yesterday against Her Majesty for two billion dollars."

Clara snorted derisively. "Oh, dear, he must be smarting." The week before, Quilter and five executives had spent a night in the pokey while the RCMP took twenty boxes of paper from their offices. The PMO, meanwhile, had issued a press handout saying the government remained fully dedicated to the safe return of the Calgary Five.

"Will Mr. Crumwell also be joining us for lunch?"

"I expect so. He has rallied from his intestinal problems."

"Don't let him get away." He'd been avoiding her.

~~~

The testosterone was so thick in 24 Sussex's boardroom that Clara instructed an aide to open some windows, letting in a draft. Crumwell looked grumpy back there, bundled into a coat and scarf.

Everyone had seen Mukhamet's video, his triumphant return from the supposed dead. The mood was angry, vengeful.

Clara was also picking up a sense of suppressed disdain from the high commanders, with their military jargon, their assumptions she had no clue what they were talking about. Even their one woman officer, a colonel, had a contemptuous smile, a reverse sexist.

"Nothing handles unprepared runways like a Herc," an air force general was saying. "Exceptional STOL ability, she's the vehicle of choice."

STOL, Clara knew, meant short takeoff and landing. She also understood the Hercules turboprop was the force's workhorse. But she kept silent, reluctant to ask questions that might indeed show her up as a military naïf.

Buchanan raised a pointer at an aerial image of Özbeg, a cross-hatching of streets in the desert, the police station circled in red, a few scratchy lines depicting highways. "We could risk a run for the Russian border. But we've no idea what might welcome us there."

"We wouldn't want to rile the Russians." A Central Asian expert from Foreign Affairs. "But what if we simply have our commandos surrender to them? Make them look good." He began to wilt under Buchanan's fierce scowl, but struggled on. "Surely they'd simply deport our people to Canada."

"Surrender." Buchanan was having trouble digesting the word, he croaked it, struggling, his face red.

Clara finally spoke. "The concept offends me too. Summarize for us, Buster."

"Operation Wolverine. Named after the commando group that's going in, the Wolverine unit. Pound for pound, the toughest animal in the world, by the way."

"Okay, a step up from a beaver."

"Stage one, we airdrop a few personnel in the flat desert south of this burg, in darkness. They'll scout and prep a landing site, and do some snow clearing so we don't face an evac impediment. They'll set up flares, landing lights. Stage two, another Herc will nestle down two hours later, at five a.m., with the troops and three Humvees. A pre-dawn raid on Özbeg's police station. There may be a firefight, but we expect the hostiles will prove too cowardly and disorganized to engage effectively. Stage three, back to the C-130, and non-stop to home plate, Kandahar Airfield. We're at maximum turnaround range, that means in-flight tanking."

Aerial refuelling, Clara decided. "The timeline?"

"Target day is January tenth."

"Can't be sooner?"

"Too much prep, Prime Minister."

"What's our risk level?"

"Light to medium. I can't guarantee there won't be casualties."

Nor, she supposed, could he guarantee against calamity. She looked over at E.K. Boyes. "Nothing ventured," he said. Other advisers nodded. Unspoken was the fact that an election was in the balance.

"We had unreliable information for Eager Beaver." She looked at Crumwell, his cold, deadpan expression. "Buster, has there been any unusual activity in this town, or around their jail? Anything to suggest they might be expecting us?"

"Negative on that. Our drones are keeping a watchful eye."

Instinct told Clara to put off her decision, to tread with caution.

She'd been the one government voice urging thoughtful patience. But she had a week and a half to say go or no. Her headache was not abating. She kept seeing Mukhamet's hamlike face.

"I'm giving this a provisional green light. I'll want an update two days prior to the point of no return. Let's have lunch."

~~~

Crumwell had looked ready to eat and run, but his escape was thwarted by Percival, who ushered him into Clara's study with coat in hand. "You asked if I could stay behind, Prime Minister."

"Yes, sit down." She swivelled to the window, the forest of frozen hare-limbed trees that made the grounds seem spooky. She struggled to quell her distaste for the spymaster, his mask of competence, his paranoid mindset, his misogyny. "Anthony, I'm still waiting for that briefing note." Promised a week ago.

"Yes, I have that project on my desk. I haven't been feeling too tickety-boo."

"I'm very sorry. Well, brief me now. What's the latest on this threatened tar sands bombing?"

"We're waiting. We have eyes everywhere, but we're not sure of their timing."

"But you have someone in deep cover. What's his name – DiPalma."

"Ray DiPalma."

"And is he still out of contact?"

"It's been eleven days. I can't say we're not worried."

"You've no idea where he is?"

"Afraid not. He has befriended Zack Flett, whom you'll remember is posing as Ms. Blake's hired hand – though his real goal is to run around the country stirring up trouble. Flett's movements are known to us, but he's had no recent contact with Agent DiPalma, by telephone or otherwise. I should add that we have a judicial order to intercept the suspect's calls."

"Does that extend to Margaret Blake's home phone?"

"Indeed."

"Okay, I want that stopped. You are not to bug the line of a member of Parliament."

"Excuse me, madam, but that would seriously compromise our efforts."

"It could seriously blow up in our faces. Especially if it turns out your Mr. DiPalma has been fed a line of bull."

Crumwell looked shocked. "Agent DiPalma is a very capable operative."

Clara pulled a news clipping from a file. "This him? Left his laptop in an unlocked car in a shopping mall?"

"That was, uh, when he was having marital difficulties. Started off brilliantly . . . I did discuss all these matters with Minister Thiessen, but let me brief you."

"Please." She was in growing dread that a massive screw-up was afoot, a concern not allayed by Crumwell's narrative of nervous breakdown and wife-stalking. Astoundingly worse, it appeared DiPalma was quickly outed as a CSIS agent by his targets on Garibaldi Island.

"Sorry, I'm spinning. He is posing as a *traitor?*"

"He has artfully persuaded Zack Flett he is a convert to his cause."

"And Margaret Blake as well? And Arthur *Beauchamp?*" Unable to still her fury, she stood, her fists balled. "Do you think they're *idiots?* Are you saying Charley Thiessen did *not* put a stop-action on this?" Her voice cracked.

Crumwell stammered. "I, um, didn't see this as being so awkward, because, uh . . . the operation was also cleared by Gerry Lafayette . . ."

She sat with a thud, pinched herself. No, she was not asleep, this was not a nightmare.

"And now your incredibly talented Mr. DiPalma has vanished into thin air. Let's bloody hope we don't find his body floating down the Fraser River." She sighed wearily. "Anthony, tell me bluntly. Has anything else been going on I should know about?"

A massive clearing of throat. "Excuse me." He drank some water. His eyebrows scrunched in thought. "No, uh, no, nothing comes to mind."

28

O n this first day of the new year, Arthur had decidedly little to celebrate. He'd just returned to his hotel in Gjirokaster after six days of bureaucratic hell, so morose that he was fighting the seductive pull of the half-litre of cognac DiPalma had left behind.

Ray was still in Tirana – he'd been transferred from its National Trauma Centre to a Catholic clinic and hospice for recovery care. On his several visits Arthur had seen physical improvement but also emotional decline – DiPalma was oppressed by an intense sense of failure. Gone was the braggadocio, replaced by teary confessions of incompetence – not just in the field of espionage but in life generally. His inability to sustain a marriage or a love affair or any kind of deep friendship; this he blamed on the early loss of his mother, the disaffection of his father.

He'd entered an extreme depressive phase, said his physician, who was concerned that the concussion may have accelerated the symptoms of Parkinson's he'd observed. It was as likely, Arthur thought, that DiPalma no longer had the strength to hide the shakes. Adding hugely to the toll: he was battling addictions to alcohol and nicotine.

But Arthur too endured a sense of failure after his week in the Albanian capital. He'd been hung out to twist in the wind, shuffled from one prison official to another, his inquiries met with grins and shrugs. None were able to unearth records of Abzal's transfer from Prison 303. Arthur had made it as far as the assistant director-general of prisons. "If Warden Chocoli says he was taken away by the border police, then I'm sure he's correct." He professed to know nothing about Arthur's client; he had too many problems at work to follow the world news.

The border police had no evidence Abzal Erzhan had even entered the country – though they were aware, from Interpol bulletins, that a man by that name was wanted. "We escort prisoners into the jails, not out," said a senior officer who opened computer records showing they'd not visited Prison 303 on December 13 or any other day that month. He begged Arthur to believe Warden Chocoli had made an honest error – some other policing agency must have taken custody of Mr. Erzhan.

A bored clerk in the Justice Ministry asked him to come back in ten days while they checked on the matter. Immigration officers knew nothing. Doors of more senior officials were closed for the holidays.

Arthur refused to believe Abzal was lost within the labyrinthine oblivion of the country's jail system. This was a classic case of stonewalling, an effort by corrupt officials to hide their illegal role in a high-profile rendition. *There are other people involved, people in Tirana.* People who'd been paid a vaster sum than Arthur's laughable offer of thirty grand to Chocoli, their underling. He had a sick feeling that Abzal might have been disappeared permanently. A sham accident or suicide.

Arthur had never been inclined toward paranoia, but had sensed a strong whiff of it in Tirana. On every street he'd walked, he'd glanced back to see followers. Sometimes a man, sometimes two, sometimes a man and a woman – ducking into shadows or doorways. He stopped venturing from his hotel at night. In the day, he took taxis. Even then he sensed pursuit, felt danger. The message: don't get too close to the truth; you can disappear too.

The Gjirokaster had kept his room for him, and from its balcony he stared out at a fittingly dismal, wet day, murky clouds hanging low over the hills, the street vendors protecting their wares under umbrellas – among them Djon Bajramovic, wiping his thick glasses clear of the steam rising from his curbside cookery as he served two burly men in rain hoods.

He glanced back at that flagon of Skënderbeu *konjak,* but was rescued from temptation as much by firmness of will as by recall of the New Year's Eve revelry on the streets of Tirana, the hapless, roaming drunks, a fight spilling from a tavern. That morning, the driver of his minibus, dangerously hungover, had nearly skidded off the road.

To make matters worse, his cash reserves were down to five hundred dollars' worth of leks, and the local bank was closed for New Year's. Happily, Bully's fifty thousand was there – the bank manager had confirmed this by telephone. Unhappily, he could conceive of no useful way to spend it: he was at a dead end, his campaign beyond resurrection.

The money would stay in the bank for now – Arthur would feel very jittery carrying big sums around. Doubtless his contract with Chief Bizi for police security had expired – unless those two heavyweights munching Djon's *qebaps* and looking up at him were undercover police.

He returned inside, gave the operator the Blunder Bay phone number. Savannah answered with a poorly smothered yawn, and he realized it was five a.m. there.

"I'm sorry, I'm obviously quite discombobulated."

"Hey, I was going to get up anyway."

"Please don't wake Margaret. Tell her I'm returning to help with her campaign as soon as I can make arrangements. I'll call her later in the day."

"Where are you anyway? Somewhere exotic I heard, but nobody's saying."

"All will be known soon."

"Sounds like you're not having a happy new year."

"The most dismal I can recall."

Pride goeth before a fall. Reckless in his anger at Anthony Crumwell, Arthur had vowed to solve what that thief of privacy had been unable or unwilling to grapple with. He would look moronic on his return to Canada. Going cap in hand to the Foreign Ministry, to CSIS, seeking forgiveness for DiPalma, begging help to rescue Abzal.

He'd gathered some evidence to confirm the rendition, but would an infamous fence like Hanife Bejko be believed? Might Warden Chocoli spirit away the Prison 303 guest register? Arthur had photos of it, but the prospect of presenting such paltry proofs to Crumwell caused his stomach to clench.

That stomach would feel better filled. He put on his coat.

~~~

"For best customer all of Albania, unless you are observing Jew or Muslim, best buy today is pork. New Year special. Organic, from farmer friend, Christian like me. How is Mr. DiPalma?"

"He's very depressed."

"You also look not happy, Mr. Beauchamp."

"There is no easy way from the earth to the stars." Seneca's despairing cry.

"You not have success in Tirana? Did I warn you? Hire Djon Bajramovic, otherwise they jack you around."

"Djon, I am not a developer. I am a criminal lawyer."

"The truth is revealed." Djon passed him a thick nugget of braised pork. "You try, you like. Feast of gods."

"I am representing a client unlawfully detained in your country."

"Ah, yes, Abzal Erzhan. Why you not say so earlier?"

Arthur gagged on the meat. "What? What? You know about this?"

"Is secret? Not to Djon Bajramovic. Erzhan is well-known outlaw, famous in news. In Prison 303, north of Korça."

"He was there, but no longer. I talked to the warden."

"Chocoli? A scared mouse, he would lie to his mother to save ass."

"For God's sake, Djon, how did you learn about Erzhan?"

"I explain for umpteenth time, Djon Bajramovic have many contacts." A wink and a wide smile that copied the sweeping curl of his Dali moustache. "As example, friend who is in same clan as night-shift captain at Prison 303."

Arthur looked up to the heavens. It had stopped raining; the clouds were breaking up. The power of Djon. "Do you ever *not* work, my friend? You seem to be perpetually in this spot."

"Seven in morning to nine at night, with break for lunch."

Arthur handed him twenty thousand leks. "An initial retainer. You are hired."

Djon wiped his thick glasses, stared at the bills for a moment. "About time." He slipped them into a pocket.

"Why don't you pack up early, Djon, and come to my hotel room to talk?"

"Is maybe not safe. Not even safe here." A glance at the street, a silent message.

Nibbling on his kebab, Arthur turned casually, saw a one-ton truck cruise by, recognized Ledjina in the cab, looking miserable, sandwiched between two glowering men. The truck slowed near the hotel entrance, then moved on. They appeared not to have noticed Arthur on the plaza, but the two hefty men he'd seen from his balcony – Djon's customers, ugly customers – were still staring at him from down the street. Their rain hoods were off; one was hatless and bald, the other in a black toque.

"Not to worry, Djon has special today on accident insurance, especially for visiting famous lawyers. Lifetime guarantee." He laughed merrily, and slipped Arthur a card with an address and directions. "Close by, in old town, friendly club on second floor where comrades sometime gather. Ten o'clock not too late?"

"I shall meet you there. God willing."

Arthur considered returning to the hotel, but something in him rebelled at turning tail. Never let a dog sense your fear. In any event, he might be safer on the suddenly sunlit streets than alone in an insecure room. But he was unnerved when, as he began a steep climb up the cobbled streets, the two beefy toughs began to follow. But they were puffing, carrying too much weight, and by the time he attained the fortress summit they'd faded from the chase.

Resting at the barricades, he studied Djon's card. It translated, as best he could tell, as: "Fabian Branch, Albanian Socialist Party, Reading Room." An address near the main square – which was spread out below him, the cafés busy, music drifting up from the bars.

It was full sunlight now, the sky a deep afternoon blue. But the same wind that had whipped away the clouds was sharp on his face, and he was about to begin his descent when he saw the two followers – they'd ascended by a different route, like stealthy mountain goats, and were standing by the ramparts, smoking, watching. As he headed downhill, they followed, fifty paces behind. When he stopped, they stopped. The bald man offered a gap-toothed grin. The other was expressionless under his black toque.

But they kept their distance, and soon after, from his balcony, Arthur saw them enter a tavern. He watched the sun dip toward the hazy horizon, turned on his alarm for nine p.m., then worried himself to sleep.

~~~

As he set out from the hotel that night, he tried to reconstruct the morbid dream from which he'd awakened: a silent, medieval town, moustachioed giants in dark recesses reaching out for him, body snatchers. But as best he could tell, no one was stalking him now. It seemed foolish to take a taxi for a seven-minute walk, and the streets were well lit, the bars and cafés active.

As he entered a narrow street from the main square, he nearly jumped from his skin as a big man accelerated past him and pulled open a wide wooden door. "Happy New Year, comrade!" he roared. "Pliss to welcome in!" It took Arthur a moment to place him: his bald, gap-toothed follower. There was nowhere to flee – his friend in the black toque was hurrying toward him from across the street.

"Pliss to enter, *kanadez*," the bald man urged, holding the door. "Djon Bajramovic waits."

It came to Arthur, with a gasp of relief, that these weren't stalkers but bodyguards whom Djon had quietly placed in his service. *Tough guys but cheap, work for tips.* He gave them each a hundred dollars in leks, and winced with pain at the ferocity of their handshakes.

On the second floor, a doorway opened to a smoke-filled lounge in which a group was in loud debate around a table. A few others were reading or playing cards. Various Albanian heroes glared from the wall, along with Karl Marx, Che Guevara, and an Italian bequeather of a familiar place name, Giuseppe Garibaldi.

Curious looks were satisfied when Djon rose from a chess game and announced his guest, not by name but as "a comrade, good socialist from Canada." He abandoned his opponent, a young woman, and drew Arthur to a counter where they filled mugs with tea from an urn. Arthur contributed some of his last remaining leks into a collection jar.

"Come, my friend, a quiet corner." They settled on upholstered chairs near a desk computer and a magazine rack. Djon gestured to the group at the table. "Local party executive, our trusted brains . . . no, brain trust."

Arthur was uncomfortable in this coven of radicals. As a stranger in this country, he didn't want to be caught up in their political feuds and machinations.

"So. Is best I know everything, then bring resources to bear."

Arthur held nothing back, told him of the rendition, the bombing, the loose talk at CSIS headquarters, his suspicions about an oil giant's clandestine role, the information gleaned from Bejko and Chocoli, his failed expedition to Tirana, the stonewalling.

"Is junk food, what they feed you," Djon said. "Abzal Erzhan in isolation, Cellblock A, Prison 303." He raised a hand, as if to quell any doubts. "Is confirmed, we have ears everywhere."

His chess partner caught Arthur's eye and smiled: bespectacled, dark, an expression both serious and confident. She returned her attention to the board, plotting her next move. The brain trust was still in debate, but more muted – occasionally one or the other glanced at Arthur with encouraging smiles.

"And do you see any way to win his release?"

"Of course."

"Can it be so easy?"

"As I say, I have connection, night captain at 303. He too is former party member, but officially repent. Also corrupt but in good way. Already, I have plan. Tomorrow, I close up shop, we go to Korça in friend's car. You cross border to Macedonia, stay low in beautiful town of Ohrid, leave everything to Djon Bajramovic."

This all seemed too quick, too pat. He gave Djon a long, intense scrutiny, the bottle-thick glasses, the confident curl of moustache. During their several encounters, this student of world politics had engaged him pleasantly enough but all too insistently.

"I think, Djon, that you already knew who I was when we first met."

Djon sipped his tea, slowly lowered his mug, and spoke softly. "My turn to reveal truth." He reached over for the computer mouse, went online, and searched for "Arthur Beauchamp Canadian lawyer." From one of the dozens of hits, Arthur found himself looking at a network video of his press conference with Iqbal Zandoo. *I come not, friends, to steal away your hearts.*

Djon clicked forward, to the end, the tomato juice episode. "I always laugh."

"You suspected I might come here."

"So did central government – informers tell us this. So I set up shop near hotel you reserve, make friend of you, yes? Then wait for you come with tail between legs after runaround in Tirana."

"How could you possibly know I'd return here?"

"Because waiting in bank is fifty thousand smackers, less what you pay in bribes. Not much I don't know, many contacts from former secret police, the Sigurini, many friends still in service. Enough said."

Arthur picked up a sense of a shadowy past, and didn't care to pursue it. One vital element of Djon's stratagem remained unclear. "Dare I ask how much this will cost?"

That was greeted with a pained look, as if the subject were one that gentlemen did not raise. "First and also foremost, this I do for my country. Could scandal topple crooks in power? Maybe yes, worth a try."

Was Arthur finally dealing with an Albanian altruist, a rare angel not on the take? "You ask for no compensation?"

A shrug, a sly look. "I make offer, Mr. Beauchamp. If I fail, I want only thanks for trying." He looked at the ceiling, as if calculating. "But if I deliver Abzal Erzhan safely to your hotel in Ohrid . . . a million dollars."

There came an image of Roy Bullingham, red faced, collapsing with a coronary.

"Half for party, half for me and Dordana, danger pay."

"Dordana?"

Djon indicated his chess partner. "Party organizer, even better than me speaking English. Second-best chess player in entire province. You are looking at best. Also Dordana is fourth cousin of friendly night captain."

Arthur watched her inch a pawn forward. He felt out of his depth here. Was he expected to haggle? That might seem insulting, given the risky gamble Djon seemed ready to take. Finally, regretting he couldn't promise such a sum, he said Canadian authorities might offer an ex gratia payment for his aid in repatriating a citizen wrongly imprisoned.

"But Mr. Erzhan will earn many millions, yes? From the book he will write."

After much discussion about the travails of the book industry, it was agreed that should Ottawa not cough up the whole million, the balance would come from Erzhan's suit for damages. That left many loopholes, but Djon seemed satisfied.

"Now we must talk unavoidable expenses." Dordana's fourth cousin had expressed a need for a reliable car. His mortgage was in arrears. Silence of other, lesser participants must be bought. Out-of-pocket costs, something for emergencies. Rather suspiciously, the total came close to the $43,000 still sitting in the bank.

Arthur was distinctly uncomfortable with the notion of Djon wandering off with his entire poke. Was he to be trusted? Or was he the most skilled confidence trickster he'd ever met? He was certainly no idiot, and seemed to have a credible strategy. Faced with no viable alternative, Arthur threw caution to the wind, and the deal was secured with a clinking of mugs.

"Now Djon must return to game. Come, meet." He drew Arthur toward the chess table, introduced Comrade Dordana.

"A pleasure, Mr. Beauchamp. Here is the hotel where you will stay in Ohrid." She ripped a page from a pad. "Three days, no more, and Mr. Erzhan will come to you. Do not worry."

As Arthur shrugged into his coat, he paused at the door to watch Djon and Dordana settle at the table among their comrades. Nods, smiles, handshaking, revolutionary salutes.

29

———

Dear Journal,

January 5, I think. Some hurried notes, too pooped to write much. Still scared but more hopeful. Making better progress after a couple of our guys unburied the truck from where it was hidden in piled snow, plus supporters lent us other vehicles, one a big farm truck with fifty men and women packed in the back.

One encounter with a Bhashyistan army outpost, but they scattered like scared mice when we pulled in. Now we have three extra jeeps. Numbers swelling daily, men and women leaving their farms and villages to join our march to the Russian border.

Stayed in a snow cave last night. Maxine, Ivy, and I now waiting out the night in a yurt, our comrades camped outside. Not too cold in here but spare, the only decoration a framed photo of Abzal Erzhan (he's everywhere) who I found out had lost his parents to executioners. So sad. Little Hasran, only fifteen, says he is like a king to him, to all of Bhashyistan.

Aisulu has ordered lights out. Bedtime. I keep thinking that tomorrow I'll awake in my own bed, and this will all have been a nightmare.

~~~

As of noon on Friday, January 6, the eve of Orthodox Christmas in the Republic of Macedonia, Arthur had not heard from Dordana and Djon. Three days, they had promised – and if anything went awry they were to phone him here, in his assigned hotel on Lake Ohrid. But not a whisper. Five days had passed since that promise.

An ugly scenario haunted him – Arthur Ramsgate Beauchamp, Q.C., who had dealt with some of the most brilliant minds of criminality, had been sucked in by an Albanian grandmaster. *If I fail, I want only thanks for trying.* Arthur had eaten it up like a hungry dog. And now Djon and Dordana were off on a romp with $43,000 of his law firm's money.

How would he find the strength to face Bully? The jeers of Crumwell and Thiessen? His portrayal in the press as an innocent abroad?

He'd had qualms earlier, certainly at the beginning of the week, as he emptied his account. But those had settled when Djon and Dordana picked him up at nightfall as planned, in her Fiat compact. He'd even slept, a bumpy back-seat slumber as they drove up the winding road to Korça and beyond, his compatriots jabbering gaily away in Albanian.

At dawn, he was dropped off at the Macedonian border, on the shores of Lake Ohrid. He was quizzed by a distrustful immigration official unused to lone Canadian tourists showing up on foot in winter. Arthur's explanation – he was fulfilling a lifelong dream to see the beauties of the region – felt lame, but he got through.

Macedonia was a small landlocked country of two million, with a large Albanian minority, maybe less corrupt than its neighbour and slightly better off – as symbolized by its working ATMs. And there *was* beauty here, with its mild Mediterranean climate, the beaches and Byzantine churches and cobbled, hilly streets and red-tiled roofs.

His apartment in a lakeside hotel in the old town was clean and spacious, with a balcony overlooking the deep blue lake. Beyond, distantly, the snowy mountains of Albania. Somewhere over there were Djon and Dordana, enjoying their lucrative joke now that Arthur was out of their hair, out of their country.

He had spent the first few days in Ohrid touring by foot and taxi: its thousand-year-old churches, its castle, museum, Roman ruins, the palatial, peacock-patrolled grounds of the ninth-century Sveti Naum Monastery. But for the last two days it had rained, and he'd rarely ventured out, preferring to pace and fret or surf his TV's hundred satellite channels.

On his arrival, he'd called Margaret to say he was back on the trail. She was mainstreeting somewhere, crowd noises, horns beeping. The line was bad. A few words of cheer and affection were followed, confusingly, by, "Oh, thank you, they're lovely. Smell these, Arthur." Her little joke – someone had given her flowers.

He'd made no mention of DiPalma, and would have hedged had she asked about his health or whereabouts; there was no point upsetting her in the midst of a hectic campaign. He had promised to call her later, but buried under the rubble of growing depression he hadn't found the strength.

Arthur kept up with Canada and the world on his twenty-inch screen. Aside from the third son's resurrection, there'd not been a peep from Bhashyistan – all TV and radio services had been knocked off the air, and the national Internet server was down. The BBC was trying to confirm reports of widening unrest, protests, arrests, martial law.

That network also reported an unusual event outside the Bhashyistan embassy in London. Demonstrators, along with a couple of news crews, had witnessed two limousines pull up, a platoon of businessmen hastening in with their briefcases, avoiding shouted questions. It hadn't taken long to identify them as lawyers and board members of Anglo-Atlantic Energy.

Now, as Arthur quit his pacing and turned up the sound, a BBC expert was speculating as to what seemed obvious to Arthur: Anglo was about to get its hands on the oil reserves of a country in desperate financial need. A furor was expected. The interloping oil giant was already being widely condemned. The Russian president, Arkady Bulov, had brusquely announced the recall of his ambassador in Igorgrad for consultations.

Though grimly pleased that he could now settle on Anglo-Atlantic as the architect of a scheme of assassination and false incrimination, only one man, Abzal Erzhan, could identify its hirelings who had bundled him into that sedan. High-flying gangsters who'd come from careers as anti-terrorist agents: Arthur liked the irony of that theory. Experts at rendition, at assembling roadside bombs. Still unexplained was why they'd not dropped their kidnappee into the Atlantic Ocean.

The day was waning, the phone waiting, demanding an act of penance. Finally, he gritted his teeth and called the Catholic hospice in Tirana. They took the phone out to the courtyard, where DiPalma, bundled up against the cold, admitted he was working through his third pack of cigarettes that day.

When Arthur confessed to having been played the chump, DiPalma said, "You should never have trusted me." That seemed sardonic; there was a brittle quality to his voice, edgy, likely brought on by a drug they were feeding him. "Zykoril, it's a boutique mood elevator only licensed in a few backward countries like Albania. Gets you up faster and higher than top-shelf flake from the Alto Chapare." Bolivia, Arthur guessed. Maybe he ought not to have been surprised that DiPalma had such familiarity with quality cocaine.

"How are your ribs?"

"Prime and tender."

"More important, your head?"

"Fucked."

Arthur was astonished – he'd never heard this good Catholic utter a vulgarity.

When the rain began to slow, he took a pre-dinner stroll through the old town, gaily decorated for the Orthodox Christmas. There was music in the air, sprightly music that weakened his resolve to nurse his sour mood. Buskers, a violin-accordion duo, a trio with lute, bagpipes, and banjo, a quartet of shivering women in miniskirts setting up amplifier and microphones. Arthur had seen the posters: this resort town was about to host a holiday weekend music festival.

He paused at a travel agency, at a window in which were posted flight schedules from Ohrid with connections to the Americas. He was aching to return to Canada. But he could hardly leave DiPalma behind, in his condition, and it seemed unrealistic to flee the Balkans before alerting authorities in Ottawa – the RCMP, not CSIS, Ray had urged – to the evidence they'd obtained of Abzal's kidnapping.

Arthur walked down to the strand, gazed out at the boats at anchor, a few yachts among smaller pleasure craft and fishing boats. Distantly, a few sailboats were bending to the wind. A dinghy was idly motoring into the little harbour, with two fishermen in black Greek caps slouched unhappily over their empty catch baskets.

He perched on a low stone wall, pulled out his pipe, watched a bus disgorge festival-goers. Others were pulling in by car. From a nearby café, soulful Balkan folk music. From another, folk-jazz fusion. A television van marked "TV A-1, Skopje" prowled toward the buskers, who hurried to meet it, attracted like birds to a feeder.

Arthur knocked the duff from his pipe, watched the two luck-less fishers tie up their dinghy and stroll off in their rainslicks, heads bowed. He knew their pain, had often shared their sense of failure. He wondered if coho were running in Blunder Bay. That's where he ought to be today, on the *Blunderer*, trolling, doing what he did best.

He made his way up the street to watch the TV A-1 cameras bearing down on the four young women in miniskirts, two of them on flute, one with a two-sided drum, their leader belting out a wailing melody. After a few moments, he felt his foot tapping. Other onlookers were laughing, whooping, clapping in cadence with the beat. It was hard to maintain his comfort blanket of despair.

From behind him, close to his ear: "Nice voice. Nice legs also." He had a ludicrous delusional moment: Ray DiPalma, fully and mysteriously recovered, had just materialized from the ether. The face, beneath a black Greek fisher's cap, bore no such resemblance, but was oddly familiar. As was that of his companion, who had also pulled in on that dinghy.

"Like road sign say, sorry for delay. But mission accomplish." Djon Bajramovic wiped his thick glasses, set them on his face, grinning. His prize moustache was gone. A five-day stubble of beard. "Please now you meet famous revolutionary comrade."

Abzal Erzhan's hug took Arthur's breath away.

30

———

"Your town has a great future, Mayor." Charley Thiessen gathered it hadn't had a great past: your basic Main Street, not even a mall. But now it had a shiny new ethanol plant, thanks to the federal green initiative program. "Yessir, boom times ahead."

"Ay-yep," said the mayor, a man of few words, almost none.

"There's gold in them thar hills, eh, pardner? Liquid gold." The snow-covered cornfields, he meant.

"Ay-yep."

Charley had just cut the ribbon, the exclamation point to the day's festivities, which included a tour of the plant and a peppy speech while freezing his ass on a makeshift outdoors stage. But they ate it up, the good humble folk of this Ontario town whose name he kept forgetting.

Later in the day, he was off down to Middlesex County to help the local M.P. open a federal office building. Tomorrow, a stopover in Ottawa for a cabinet briefing, then back to his own riding, where last week he'd whomped the local lacklustre Liberal in an all-candidates debate. He'd got the crowd roaring with a string of lawyer jokes – people love a guy who can make fun of his own profession.

Also coming home for the weekend was his eighteen-year-old Greenpeacer, who was threatening not to vote for him. He expected a lecture about biofuels, about crops being diverted to fuel over-powered cars, all of which was somehow connected to starving people in Africa and food riots and God knows what.

It was impossible to argue with Joy; she didn't see reason. Global warming had brought the earth to the tipping point, she said – but look at the evidence, it was the coldest winter in years. No ice caps were melting here, snow was blowing relentlessly, almost a blizzard.

Despite the weather, despite the defecting daughter, he was in much better fettle than a couple of weeks ago, after the calamity with that doper from the Left Coast. As of this seventh day of a new year, there hadn't been a hint of fallout.

Politically too, things weren't looking too bad, thanks to Operation Snow Job and the demolition of the enemy's propaganda machine. All they had left was a clown posting videos on YouTube. Tomorrow's cabinet briefing was about something called Operation Wolverine, hush-hush, another go at rescuing the Calgary Five, and if that worked Canada might yet stay true to Conservative blue.

"Looks like we're in for a little weather, Mayor."

"Ay-yep."

His driver was urging him to get into the Lincoln van. He'd kept the engine running, thank God.

~~~

"Ready, Dog? Turn up them burners. I'm gonna loosen this here rope."

Dog was standing in the gondola like a zombie, the envelope of the balloon suspended limply above him from a high tree branch. He'd suited up in hockey gear, a helmet, a chest protector, leg pads, a ratty old Canadiens sweater reaching to his knees.

"Give it a burst," Stoney yelled.

No reaction. This was supposed to be dress rehearsal for next week's official launch, but it looked like Dog had stage fright, possibly induced by the presence of the trespassing media in the form of Nelson Forbish, perched on his ATV.

He'd been totally on Stoney's case, stalking him like some hippo from the wilds of Africa. It had been a mistake whetting Forbish's appetite about that recorder, a mistake compounded when he'd blurted out it had to do with Arthur Beauchamp.

He stomped over to confront the trespasser. "Official ceremonies are next week. This here preliminary event is closed to the public. We are in camera."

"After talking to Ernst, I see that I treated your high honours too light, and I've come here to apologize. I have a proposition. The *Bleat* is willing to put out a spread on you being West Coast entrepreneur of the year."

That put a different complexion on things. "Front page?"

"'Local Businessman Acclaimed in Ottawa.' Pictures and everything."

"I really ought to talk to Arthur."

"He hasn't been home for the holidays, and no one's seen him for a month almost. He could be dead for all we know. If there's something on that recorder you're worried about, I suggest we take it over to his best friend and spiritual adviser and play it for him." He pulled out a nicad battery.

Stoney called, "Take a break, Dog."

~~~

Al Noggins frowned over the letter from the Small Business Department. "You sure this is genuine?"

Even the local preacher was a non-believer – why did no one have faith in Stoney?

"This Charley fellow was a lawyer, you say."

"Or a cop." Stoney produced the bug, stuck its suction cup on Reverend Al's desk.

"Let's play it." Forbish was all antsy. They were in Al's cottage, the parlour, where they'd caught him searching a joke book to spice up his Sunday sermon.

"I want it on record that we're off the record," Stoney said.

"For now, okay." Forbish reached over and clicked it on. There was nothing for a few minutes, just background noises, a door closing.

Then: *What do I call you, Robert, Bob?*

Call me grateful, Charley.

Stoney listened to the opening skirmishing, in which Charley, instead of focusing on the award, waylaid him with questions about Garibaldi. Then a gap when the houseboy came in to restock the fridge. "This is where we tilted a couple back," Stoney explained. "Now I got to warn you, there's stuff here about Arthur, who, by the way, I'm kind of worried he's on the run."

Reverend Al looked shocked. "Nonsense, I'm sure he's out campaigning with Margaret. She's on Vancouver Island. I'll give her a call." He was campaign manager for her on Garibaldi, he'd pestered Stoney into staking a bunch of lawn signs.

Forbish impatiently pushed play. Here was where Arthur's name was used in vain: *A bon vivant with an eye for the chicks, they say . . . Boy, I'll bet you must know some stories about the old shyster.*

And that was about it. Charley blew the scene, then there were just the sounds of Stoney and Dog getting back in party mode.

Forbish looked resentful, like he'd been conned. "Well, that was a total letdown. Everybody knows Mr. Beauchamp has been acting up. Savannah Buckett, you told me yourself. I can't print this, I run a family newspaper."

"Can I hear the beginning again, please." Reverend Al had the expression you get when something in the back of the fridge has gone bad.

Forbish rewound until they got to: *I'm a no-bullshit country boy just like you. Charley gives you no blarney, that's my motto.*

"Stop right there," Al said. "Who's this Charley?"

"I got his note right here."

Reverend Al's mouth fell open as he looked at the brunch invitation, the note that had improved the attitude of Fortesque at the front desk. "Charley *Thiessen?*"

"Yeah, I guess that's his last name. Thiessen."

Reverend Al began rummaging through some clippings on his desk. Forbish, suddenly overexcited, tried to rise too, but his wooden armchair came with him. They were both talking at once. "Charley Thiessen? Whoa, hang on here. Thiessen? The minister of justice?"

Al came up with a photo – the same dweeb, red paint smeared all over his white shirt.

"Hey, yeah, that's him." Stoney never read the papers, so this was totally mystifying.

Forbish freed himself from the chair. "Hold the presses. This is gonna go national." He made a grab for the recorder, but Stoney whisked it away.

Reverend Al picked up the phone.

~~~

As her limousine sped from the airport, Clara Gracey lit her first cigarette of the morning, drew on it greedily. Beside her, Percival Galbraith-Smythe gave her a tsk-tsk, lowered the window a few inches. Snow blew in. "Went well?"

"Well enough," she said. They'd had to bus in an extra thousand supporters to help fill an arena in Gerard Lafayette's riding. She'd denounced him as a coward who'd fled his party and his responsibilities after bungling Eager Beaver. But unfortunately, his defection wasn't playing as poorly as she'd hoped among the tough-minded burghers of Montréal Nord, and expectations of unseating him were dimming.

"Your reference to him as a procurer of prostitutes is today's top sound bite."

She regretted that; she hadn't been able to restrain herself. Rally in Vancouver coming up, but if this storm didn't relent, her plane could be grounded. But she'd had to make this Ottawa pit stop to give audience – a confrontation, really – to emissaries of Anglo-Atlantic Energy. "Who are they sending?"

"Their board chairman from London, their CEO from New York, and their head of legal from Dallas. All by private jets. They don't want press, so we're smuggling them into the Langevin Block by a back door."

"We should put them behind bars for aiding and abetting the enemy. Hang them up by their heels and waterboard them." There were no boundaries to Clara's wrath. Greedy cowards. Sneaking behind Canada's back.

"We're not certain what they want. To grovel, perhaps, at the feet of our radiant chain-smoking ultimate leader. Or perhaps they will come bearing gifts of frankincense and myrrh and cheques made out to a campaign fund that's running on fumes." He batted away her own fumes, opened the window wider. "I've arranged an impromptu later with the Wolverine team. Mr. Crumwell has not been invited."

"Thank you. They're still set to go in three days?"

"Weather permitting. Forecast shows clearing skies over the Bhashyistan desert."

Unlike here. She couldn't find an ashtray, reached across him, flicked the butt from the window. "Warn the press we're flying out before this blast closes the runways. Mid-afternoon." Air Cleavage, they'd dubbed the party's chartered 737. She ought to have dressed less boldly but hated looking matronly, Thatcherish.

"What about this rumour Alta bribed Lafayette?" Clara had seen it on a popular blog, hints he'd been rewarded to smooth Alta's way into Bhashyistan.

"Oh, it's just a little thing we're spreading. Might even be true."

"I'm going to ask you to pull it, Percival. It's below the belt, even for that demagogue. He's become a minor player."

"Not. He's found scores of candidates. They're eroding our vote in some touch-and-go rural areas."

"History won't remember him. He'll be buried in the footnotes. I'd like to have a chat with the RCMP commissioner."

"Goodness, I hope not about our rumour . . ."

"No, something else." She wanted Commissioner Lessard's take on what Crumwell was up to – the business about the tar sands stank. "Do we have a complete slate of candidates?"

"All holes are filled, if you'll pardon the expression. Three losers in Quebec were nominated just before deadline, and one in Cow Islands." As Percival preferred to call Cowichan and the Islands.

"And who's our loser there?" She'd done a flip-flop, decided against running a star candidate against Margaret Blake. They could run Mother Teresa and still lose. Option B was infinitely better: free Blake from any worry about retaining her seat, get her out of her riding, barnstorming the country – the Greens were feeding off the opposition parties eight to one as against the Conservatives.

"Our contest in Cow Islands was between a bigoted evangelist and an alcoholic ex-professional wrestler. The wrestler won. Known to his fans as the Viking. We'll be lucky to keep our deposit."

Clara lit another cigarette, and Percival cracked open the window again. The Airport Parkway had become Bronson Avenue, and now they were looping onto Colonel By Drive, by Dow's Lake, the Rideau Canal. And, blurred by the whirling snow, the skaters' changing shack from which a roadside bomb had plunged Canada into a ludicrous war. Six weeks earlier, this had been the scene of charred bodies and twisted metal. She shivered.

~~~

By nine a.m., she was in a boardroom in the Langevin Block, the PMO's operations centre, across the street from the Hill. The three men from Anglo-Atlantic were on one side of the table, facing Clara and her crew: E.K. Boyes, plus the foreign affairs minister and her deputy.

"How long has this been going on?"

"Exactly what, Madam Prime Minister?" The CEO, Reaves, Anglo's designated hitter, oozing with false sincerity, refusing to wilt under her slit-eyed glare.

"Your negotiations with a repressive regime led by a psychopath who declared war on us."

"We've been courting Bhashyistan for several years – though perhaps not as aggressively as several other competitors, including Alta International." Reaves had been a senior adviser to an ill-regarded American vice-president. Pinch-faced, a circle of hair around a bald spot, like a slipped halo.

"And you secretly reopened discussions after five Canadian citizens were kidnapped by these barbarians. I consider that despicable, gentlemen. Bordering on treachery."

Reaves didn't bat an eye, but she could read his disdain for her, the leader of a minor player on the world stage. "I had hoped you would find our intentions benign. We are committed to securing freedom for those five brave men. That, as we have assured Bhashyistan, is non-negotiable. The declaration of war must be withdrawn, civility must be restored."

"Have they agreed to this?"

"They are sending clear signals to that effect. We expect to wrap it up within days."

"How many days?"

"In less than a week. I can't imagine the terrible conditions those men must be enduring."

"Mad Igor wants ten billion in ransom. He's not getting it from us. Is he getting it from you?"

Reaves exchanged looks with his chief counsel. "The financial package has yet to be fully determined."

"Sounds like the answer is yes."

"There is a theory being bruited about, gentlemen," E.K. said, "that your firm undertook deliberate efforts to scuttle Alta's deal with Bhashyistan."

Clara saw Reaves's facial muscles grow stiff. "Let us put that to rest," he said. "It is a gross slander."

That was all bluster. Clara had heard reports of major stock movement into Anglo a month ago. Investors with good instincts and better ears had jumped on board. Irwin Godswill, the West Coast tycoon.

Foreign Minister Dubjek took a turn: "Anglo-Atlantic has become a global pariah. The Russians are as outraged as we are. You have cheated the corporate citizens who are your competitors."

"Madam, Anglo-Atlantic is growing aggressively, and is outpacing those competitors. We are running a business, and we are running it to win."

"And trying to soften up Canadians for your backroom deal," Clara said.

"You're referring to?"

"Your lies. Your ad campaign." Full-page pledges to sustainable energy, solemn promises to build a greener Canada. Anglo didn't have much presence in Canada yet, some gas fields, a piece of the tar sands, exploration rights off Newfoundland.

"I would prefer to say we are preparing to deliver some happy news for Canadians. Certain other negotiations are under way. This is in absolute confidence, of course."

"You're buying out Alta International," Clara said.

All three of them looked surprised. A good guess – their unexpected solicitude toward the Calgary Five had inspired it.

Their chairman, thick-necked Lord Stokely-Finn, harrumphed. "Quite. Indeed. And when the two companies are integrated, some sizable capital investments will follow. We see a robust future in Canada, and intend to become a much bigger player here. A petrol station network will soon be in place, as well as a refinery in Sascratchewan –"

"Saskatchewan, sir." Their chief counsel. His Lordship went red, but, Clara suspected, more with annoyance than embarrassment.

He cleared his throat. "Let me assure you as well, Prime Minister, that we are solidly behind your party's program for prosperity and are prepared to support it by any means you care to suggest."

Clara was insulted, was tempted to tell them to stick their dirty money up their anus.

"All we ask is that your government take, shall we say, a fresh look at the criminal charges against Mr. Quilter and his associates."

"When the moon turns blue," Clara said. "This meeting is over."

~~~

"If I may interrupt your pacing, the Wolverine team is assembling." Percival shut the door of Clara's office, handed her some briefing notes. "Minutes of our session with those cheeky fellows from Anglo. I have copies for distribution. I was able to corral a dozen cabinet ministers. We're set up in the war room."

Clara stared bleakly out the window at a lone scraggly griever, out of step with the trying times, vainly seeking signatures to legalize LSD. "Tune out, turn out, drop out," said his hallucinogenically garbled placard.

Why hadn't she had the gumption to call in the RCMP, bust those three hypocritical quislings from Anglo? She'd checked the Criminal Code, it was in plain language: *Everyone commits high treason who, in Canada, assists an enemy at war with Canada.* They'd be the heroes, though, if they sprang the five Albertans, and she'd have egg on her face. How pompous of them to set themselves up as the engineers of peace. But how clever – the world would no longer hold them in opprobrium. She stayed at the window, not wanting her executive assistant to see her unmanned, as it were, struggling.

"I don't know what to do, Percival." To no one else would she admit such doubt. Anglo-Atlantic's unwelcome intervention offered freedom for the Calgary Five without bloodshed. Operation Wolverine was set to go in two days, on Monday. If it turned ugly, Clara Gracey would become a political untouchable.

"You will do the right thing as always. Not counting, of course, the time you confused the German ambassador with his chauffeur."

"Did you get hold of Commissioner Lessard?"

"He in turn seems more than eager to see you. I asked him to accompany you to the airport. He is on his way. Shall we invite him to join us in the war room?"

"Please." She pulled herself together and followed him there. Her entrance prompted several to rise, but she waved them down. In addition to the cabinet members, ten top staff, and half as many military brass.

She took her station at the midpoint of the long oval table, thumped her gavel lightly, mostly to get the attention of Charley Thiessen, who was joking with the defence deputy. "Okay, somebody fill us in on the current situation in Bhashyistan."

"There is fighting going on." An analyst from Foreign Affairs. "No idea how extensive. In the countryside, mostly. Friendly embassies report that Igorgrad is quiet, but, the French tell us, *comme une poudrière.*" A powder keg.

An air force general amplified: "We have aerial surveillance of troop carriers and tanks moving north toward the steppes and the mountains bordering Russia, and west toward the desert."

"Toward Özbeg?"

"In that direction, yes, ma'am. Three, maybe four companies."

"That's not good." Clara had a fleeting premonition of disaster.

"They're moving slowly, Prime Minister." Buster Buchanan. "We think they're getting sniper fire. They batten down each night, and that leaves them only eight daylight hours to work with. We don't expect them to reach Özbeg before we do."

"But you can't be sure."

"Our soldiers are ready to go, Prime Minister. At plus three hours Zulu time, in two days, six engineers will parachute to the desert with their flares to set up a safe landing site. Two hours later, the Herc will put our forces on the ground. We'll be in and out before the enemy can blink."

"That's the right stuff!" The recently demoted Dexter McPhee, pounding both fists on the table, none of his enthusiasm lost.

"Let's all take a moment to read something." Clara nodded to Percival, who rose and began passing out minutes of the Anglo-Atlantic meeting as she summarized: Anglo was claiming they could free the Calgarians within a week; if Wolverine were to back-fire, Anglo would go public with its offer.

In the stillness that followed, she studied the TV monitors, the silent talking heads. She looked down to see an array of sour faces absorbing the implications of Anglo's entry into the mix. Charley Thiessen looked up, grinning. "Sascratchewan? Is that near Brit-itch Columbia?"

He seemed back to his old corny self, after a bout of weirdness that Clara believed had been brought on by misgivings over letting Crumwell bug an M.P.'s home phone. Clara didn't know why she abided Charley. His looks, his boyish, clumsy innocence maybe. But he'd been too chummy with Crumwell, too easily taken in.

Commissioner Lessard showed up just then, and Clara took a few minutes to fill him in, then said, "Okay, let's bat this around. They're offering to bring our people home without risk."

The woman colonel seemed ready to lead an armed revolt were Clara to abort the mission. A force field emanated from the other veteran warriors, all scrutinizing her for backbone, maybe seeing her doubts behind her facade of barely maintained cool. But she was determined not to be cowed by them. She must do the right thing.

"I want an honest appraisal of our chances, General. Unquali-fied, unambiguous. Don't put a shine on it." Looking right into Buchanan's eyes, until he gave way, looked down at his hands.

"Nothing is guaranteed in the field of combat, Prime Minister. We may have losses. Light losses. Theirs will be twentyfold higher."

"How would you feel if we postponed this for a week?"

"I would not say betrayed, ma'am, but pretty close to it."

"That is much too harshly put." E.K., fiercely. "We are dealing with human lives. A brief delay while we assess alternative possibilities may waste time but won't cost lives."

"A brief delay, sir, means we may be confronting four additional companies of enemy troops in Özbeg."

"Let's go around the table." Enervated by her dilemma, Clara fiddled with the gavel while people talked over each other, pros and cons, options, the best and worst scenarios. Denunciations of Anglo-Atlantic, doubts about their probity, about whether they could deliver. Dexter McPhee was in full-throated support of "our boys over there," proclaiming himself ready, by God, to put on his uniform and join them.

Lessard sat intently but quietly through all this, impeccably attired in his civvies, a lean man with a high-domed forehead. Clara had seen his calm nod of satisfaction on observing that his rival, Crumwell, was no longer in the inner circle.

She had to swallow hard to admit it, but she wished Gerard Lafayette was here. His crafty mind, his eloquence, his occasional brilliance. She played with the thought of seeking his counsel, then almost gagged.

Opinion was divided equally, a failure of consensus. "At what point will it be too late to call back the Hercs, General?"

"Zulu minus seven."

"Give that to me in English."

"Almost exactly two days from now, five o'clock in the afternoon of Monday, January tenth, Ottawa time. Three a.m. the next day in Bhashyistan. Tuesday."

E.K., one of his rare smiles. "I don't believe they have a Tuesday. It's called Timur. Monday is called Genghis."

"We'll make a final decision on Genghis afternoon," Clara said.

~~~

Clara felt the coming of another migraine as she digested the proofs of CSIS incompetence served up by Luc Lessard, beside her in the limo. RCMP analysts had laughed off the tar sands plot; the spy agency had been buffaloed by eco-schemers.

Lessard had expressed these views to Crumwell only a few days before. "I assumed he would pass word to you through appropriate channels." Meaning, obviously, Security Minister Thiessen, the broken link in the chain of command.

Percival was also in the limo, facing them, making notes, deadpan. He'd urged her to back-bench Thiessen. She hadn't listened.

She wiped the condensation from the window. Snowplows were hard at work on the Airport Parkway, but barely making headway against the thick spew from the cloud-black sky. Clara's driver hewed to a narrow traffic lane, manoeuvring around stuck or abandoned vehicles.

Flights were still being cleared, and with God's blessing she wouldn't be late for her Vancouver event. Photo ops all next day, trawling among ethnic communities. On Sunday, a hopscotch tour of Vancouver Island, its scheduled low point a clasping of the musclebound hand of the Viking, her throwaway candidate in Cow Islands.

"I regret to burden you further, Prime Minister," Lessard said, "but one of our members has learned of an unusual visit last month by M. Thiessen to a suite in the Château Laurier."

Clara tightened with dread as Lessard explained that a hotel security officer, despite orders by management to still his tongue, had spilled everything but the beer he was sharing with an RCMP pal. Sex scandal, that was Clara's first thought.

The truth was more bizarre. For a quarter of an hour, Thiessen had crawled about that suite in apparent pursuit of a lost cufflink. The room appeared to have hosted a rowdy, lewd party, was littered with its detritus and reeked of marijuana. The minister of justice had been seen pawing at a hookah pipe.

Percival uttered a squeal of horror, his eyes wide with incredulity. Clara's brain whirled as she assessed the awful implications. Disaster loomed if this blew up before January 24.

Lessard wasn't through. "The registered guests of that suite have been determined to be two young gentlemen from British Columbia. They gave their address as Rural Route One, Garibaldi Island."

Margaret Blake's home base. What in bloody hell had Thiessen been up to? Clara shakily lit a cigarette, looked out again at the relentlessly falling snow. Maybe she would be lucky, spin off the road and die. Or go down in flames on Air Cleavage.

Using all the might she could muster, she affected an insouciance: did not a search for a cufflink seem innocent enough on the surface? Might Lessard agree that this silly-seeming business really didn't warrant any further inquiries?

Lessard wasn't buying that but offered a salve. "I assure you matters will remain confidential while we make such inquiries."

"And you'll have my government's complete cooperation. A sensitive matter. I'd imagine your investigation will take a while." Eighteen days, make it eighteen days.

"I can assure you, madam, that we have no wish to be accused of influencing the election's outcome."

She took relief from that offer of breathing room. A glance at Percival. His surreptitious nod. He will get on it, gag Charley, scrabble together an innocent-seeming scenario.

"Thank you for being so forthcoming, Commissioner."

"It's not the main reason I wished to see you, Prime Minister."

Now what? Clara closed her eyes.

"Abzal Erzhan has surfaced."

31

———

rthur had pulled rank on Superintendent McIlhargey, co-
opting the most sumptuous chair in this Ohrid chalet, a
goatskin-draped La-Z-Boy. Feet up, thirty degrees from the
horizontal, he was enjoying a feast of newsprint, a bundle of *Globes*
and *Citizens* that McIlhargey had brought from Ottawa. Unusually
thoughtful of the cranky bugger.

Arthur had rank on him because he'd won all but a handful of
trials in which McIlhargey had been senior investigator, back in
the days when Arthur was a lush, thirsting for gin and justice,
and Hugh McIlhargey a toiling detective with Serious Crimes at
E Division.

"This has made Luc's day," McIlhargey had confided on arrival
in Ohrid. Commissioner Lessard, he meant, bitter at having been
shunted to the sidelines by CSIS.

Arthur had never known McIlhargey to be a chess player –
maybe he'd learned the skill after being seconded to Ottawa – but
he was in the throes of a match with Djon Bajramovic. A break in
the interrogation of Abzal Erzhan, now napping upstairs, after
having kept Arthur awake all night in his hotel suite – fretting,
pacing, flipping through TV channels, seeking updates on the
unrest in his birth country. Finally, Arthur had retreated to his
room, leaving Abzal to find what sleep he could on the sofa bed.

The day before, Abzal had been exhilarated, at breathing the free air, at the prospect of soon being with his family. But that had quickly dampened, and he'd refused Arthur entry to his private, haunted thoughts. He was entitled to his black mood – and to far more, to revengeful passion, hatred. The beast of Bhashyistan had ordered the execution of his parents, the arrest of his two brothers and his sister, all tortured, the girl defiled. Arthur had been unable to find words enough of consolation.

Abzal's escape had been remarkable only for its simplicity. At dawn, after the shift change, the night captain had driven off with him in the trunk of his car. Dordana met them on a country byway, sped off with him to a lakeside village where Djon had already closed the deal on the dinghy. Resourceful Djon Bajramovic and his intrepid associate had earned their million dollars.

Dordana's distant cousin had got a lesser but substantial reward – there was little change left from the $43,000. The scuttlebutt from the night captain was harrowing: a couple of Albanian high officials had been paid a hefty sum by anonymous foreign donors to ensure that Erzhan would leave Prison 303 in a body bag. But timorous Warden Chocoli, entrusted with the deed, couldn't bring himself to perform it.

Arthur had initiated a series of phone calls late in the day to Ottawa, finally connecting with McIlhargey, who excitedly raced into Lessard's office and, as his reward for being Arthur's friend and confidant, earned the privilege of leading a team – two inspectors and a staff sergeant – to the southern Balkans.

They'd pulled in to the little local airport five hours earlier, bushed from the long flight via Frankfurt and Skopje but eager to get under way. With the Ohrid music festival in full swing, few rooms were available, but they'd done better: a private chalet, a half-hour walk from Arthur's hotel. Five bedrooms, richly furnished, by a lakeside grove of olive trees, the grounds protected by a spearpoint steel fence. All arranged through diplomatic channels. Macedonia's minister of security, eager to embarrass his unloved

Albanian neighbours, was also providing official cars, technical support, sentries at the villa gate. He'd promised that the RCMP's inquiries would be kept under wraps.

Arthur folded open a paper from Friday, with its headlines about Anglo-Atlantic's connivery and the many hostile reactions. Here were the latest poll results: the Tories had clawed their way to twelve points below the Liberals, whose campaign was faltering. The three main smaller parties were inching up, as was Lafayette's Progressive Reform, accelerating past the Marijuana Party.

Margaret Blake was quoted as blasting the Anglo-Atlantic deal – an item jarringly juxtaposed with that company's ad proclaiming its commitment to "green energy solutions." She was on Vancouver Island, soon to begin her cross-country whistle-stop tour. It was two o'clock here, four a.m. wherever she was abed. He'd phone at her breakfast hour.

The two inspectors, Fyfe and Longstreet, were bustling about, preparing to drive to Gjirokaster to interview Hanife Bejko, then to Tirana to bring the good news to DiPalma and to arrange for his safe exit from Albania. "Where is Dordana going to meet us?" Longstreet asked.

"At Sveti Naum border crossing," Djon said. "In case of prob- lems, chief of customs can be trusted. Also maybe you talk to nervous Nellie warden, Chocoli."

McIlhargey looked up from the board. "You might want to thank Mr. Chocoli for saving Abzal's life. Is that right, Djon, the warden should get a medal?" McIlhargey's hand hovered over a possibly lucrative pawn–bishop exchange.

"Thank him because he is true coward, no stomach for simple act of murder."

McIlhargey asked if he had any theories as to why the two Tirana colluders had passed the buck to Chocoli. "They must've got paid off pretty good to zap Abzal. Millions."

"Maybe hard to understand, but Albania mired in Third World, different than Canada, contracts not always honoured. You get nice bribe, you lose interest in deal. Plus Abzal Erzhan, he is good Muslim and also hero for bumping off hated dictator like clone of Enver Hoxha." Looking pleased with this analysis, Djon showed no dismay as he lost his bishop. "Mate in three," he said.

McIlhargey studied his position. "Jesus wept." He laid his king to rest on the board. "Nice sacrifice," he said gruffly, waving Fyfe and Longstreet out the door to their Land Cruiser.

"I not play for years so was lucky. Now start making special Christmas dinner." Djon went off to the kitchen. Arthur had encouraged him to show off his kebab prowess; it might put him in better stead with McIlhargey, who had a typical policeman's distrust of proselytizers of the left. The superintendent was equally uncomfortable with Abzal, a revolutionary, an acquitted assassin. But he was an honest cop. *Honi soit qui mal y pense.*

"Hugh, I'll want to escort my client back soon. He'll need his passport." McIlhargey had brought it, along with his certificate of citizenship, but wasn't releasing them until he wrapped up inquiries.

"We'll see how it goes, Counsellor. No one is wandering off anywhere for a while. We're trying to keep this operation covert." He snorted. "We'll see how long that lasts."

McIlhargey didn't trust the Macedonians. Communists had ruled here under Marshall Tito. The street outside was named after him, and his portrait, in a resplendent white uniform, dominated the entrance foyer of this house.

Arthur followed McIlhargey into the adjoining sunroom, which Staff-Sergeant Daphne Chow, a computer adept, had commandeered for her office. A miniature jungle of potted plants, a south-facing bank of windows overlooking patio and pool, stone steps spiralling to a craggy shoreline.

Chow was online now, sending encrypted updates to Ottawa, downloading from the RCMP's trove of classified files. "HQ says there's been some international traffic over this mission." She didn't look up from her screen. "Mostly from the Russians. They want confirmation that Mr. Erzhan is in Canadian hands in the southern Balkans."

McIlhargey swore. "I knew these bums wouldn't keep their yaps shut. Yeah, they had to boast to their pals the Russkies." Another distrusted populace. "Now we're going to have a swarm of press."

Chow's laser printer was coughing out head-and-shoulder shots of eighteen unsmiling men. Three pages, six to a sheet. "It was tricky getting these," McIlhargey said. "We had to go over some heads while we stayed below Crumwell's radar. Five are CSIS agents."

No one protested when Arthur picked them up – in return for his client's cooperation, nothing was to be kept from him. McIlhargey had balked at that, but Arthur wore him down.

"Which one is Sully Clugg?" he asked. The Christmas party crotch-grabber had been a long shot, now was a contender. Antoine Salzarro had learned that Blackwater sent Clugg home after he shot to death three members of a family who'd been acting suspiciously – they'd been pushing a stalled car toward the official limousine he was guarding, and had not stopped when ordered. Innocent civilians, it turned out. Though investigators saw Clugg as reckless, they'd deemed him to have been following regulations.

McIlhargey pointed to number nine, second page. The ex-Blackwater martial arts master was in a suit, staring bull-like at the camera. Abzal had described a big man, broad forehead, a thick neck, for which Clugg qualified.

"Number eighteen, that's Clugg's buddy, Rod Klein."

He was younger and taller than Clugg, a thin, lopsided face. According to the RCMP's trusted sources at CSIS, the two men, loose on whiskey and cocaine, had been overheard at the CSIS Christmas party joshing about their first ghost flight.

Abzal had risen – he could be heard talking to Djon.

"Let's do this," McIlhargey said. Arthur followed him to the kitchen, where Djon was slicing meat into strips. Abzal was staring out the window at the bare-limbed olive trees. His hair was wet and gleaming from a shower, and he was dressed in newly bought casual clothes.

He was more thin waisted than in the photos Arthur had seen, most of them from fifteen years ago, from his arrest, his trial for murder. His chest had filled out, but he still had the wiry look of a marathon runner. Dark, intelligent eyes with a smile he bestowed infrequently, but full and bright when it came, creasing his bronzed, sculpted face.

But now he seemed lost in his thoughts, and he started when Arthur spoke his name. "I'm not quite oriented here, Mr. Beauchamp." The only accent Arthur could detect was French.

"Your mind was elsewhere, Abzal."

"With my people, the patriots of Bhashyistan. I've sat silent for too many years, and now my people are being hunted and murdered. I'm still doing nothing and I can barely live with myself."

My people. There was pride of self in the way he said that. Arthur suspected this former soldier was very much a hero among the oppressed of his former homeland. He had wanted Arthur to know that the Turkic name Erzhan meant soul of a hero.

"Liberate Bhashyistan from fascist tyranny!" Djon shouted.

McIlhargey's face darkened. "We're ready to go."

Arthur told Abzal he was wanted for a photo lineup. "Study each man carefully before committing yourself."

Back in the sunroom, they directed Abzal to a table on which were arrayed the three pages of headshots. Arthur watched tensely as Abzal perused them.

"No," he said, rejecting the first page. Then he stabbed a finger at number nine, second page. "This guy." Clugg.

Arthur cautioned him. "Wait, Abzal. Look at them all."

"No, it's him! This bruiser, the first one out of the car. He's the bastard who chopped me across the neck." He quickly scanned the others. "No, no, not this one, no one even close . . ." Then another finger stab, this time landing on Klein, number eighteen. "Yeah, this is the other one. With the thin face and cold eyes. He's the guy who asked about a liquor store."

"How tall was he?" McIlhargey asked.

"About 190 centimetres. Six-foot-two, I'd say."

McIlhargey looked more taken aback than impressed. Klein's official height was 187 centimetres.

"I carried these faces in my head for forty days," Abzal said.

McIlhargey handed him a pad. "Write the numbers down, son, and sign."

~~~

Arthur burned up the adrenalin of triumph with a shoreline jaunt, enjoying a lazy winter sun that flirted with the clouds and dappled the water with swatches of reflected light. Matters were moving ahead quite nicely; he was in a celebratory mood – after all, it was the Orthodox Christmas here in Macedonia, the land where Alexander's conquests had begun twenty-three centuries ago. Arthur had conquered too, in his small way.

Yes, the Green leader's consort had proved himself to be more than a decoration. It wouldn't hurt her campaign to have such a celebrated fellow at her side. Not hogging the spotlight, of course, just hanging about humbly in the background. Though pleased with himself (and making rather much of it), he also felt an odd sense of ennui, of letdown, like a hangover after the party. The excellent adventures of Arthur and Ray had ended except for the credits.

Transcriptions of Abzal's long recorded interviews were already on their way to RCMP headquarters. McIlhargey had telephoned an overview to Lessard. Surveillance had begun on Clugg and Klein, search and arrest warrants issued. Clugg might have thought it clever to have misled DiPalma with his "good intel" about a shadowy London group of former British, German, and Soviet agents, but this seemed a homegrown show, the three kidnappers presumably aided only by Anglo-Atlantic operatives.

Arthur pressed on to town, to enjoy the Christmas celebrations, stopping awhile at the Culture Theatre, where instrumentalists entertained in traditional costume. Many on the streets were similarly dressed, some more outlandishly: buskers in Santa suits or military jackets with braid, an operatic singer dressed as a weeping Pagliacci, an Elvis impersonator. Others with green-spiked hair and face paint.

Arthur watched as a camera from the Skopje TV van took in a panorama of street activity. He thought of offering them a scoop. It would hit the news anyway, given the Macedonian government was such a leaky vessel. And the news would make Russia's case that its petroleum monolith, Gazprom, was tricked out of the former puppet's oil and gas reserves.

He threw leks into musicians' baskets and hats as he made his way to his hotel, wishing all a merry Christmas. He must get back to the villa for dinner, but now it was breakfast time in Fanny Bay or Oyster River or wherever Margaret's tour had taken her. He hurried off to his hotel.

He'd promised McIlhargey on penalty of everlasting fire that he would not speak of Abzal's rescue to anyone outside their small circle, especially on insecure phone lines. "That includes your wife, your mistress, and Agent DiPalma." Margaret would intuit the news anyway, from his cheery tone.

In his bedroom, he made an operator-assisted call to her in Blunder Bay. It was answered, confusingly, by Nelson Forbish, who said, "Put him on, please."

There came sounds of a tussle.

Margaret: "Give me that phone."

Forbish: "Arthur, explain to your censorious spouse about the Charter of Rights. This is a free-press issue. The *Bleat* is going out today."

Margaret: "Pierètte, grab the phone."

"Special to the *Bleat*," Forbish shouted, like a corner newsboy from a fifties movie. "'Smear Try Backfires Against Prominent Islander.' That's you, Mr. Beauchamp. 'Top Tory Caught on Tape.'"

Margaret, from a distance: "Make him another omelette."

"You may talk to her, Mr. Beauchamp, but this is going out today. The *Bleat* will not be muzzled."

Margaret finally retrieved the phone, breathless. "Thank God. I've been calling your hotel all day. Nelson has stacks of his extra edition sitting out on his ATV. We're trying to stall him with food. Arthur, we need your consent for this, we want to get it out to the public – it's hilarious but it could cause you some embarrassment." That was too much to say in one gulp, and she caught her breath. "I'm sorry, are you all right?"

"All is going splendidly here. I can say no more. But I am fascinated to know about this backfiring scandal."

The history she related was a farrago of absurdity, Bob Stonewell on a government-sponsored lark to Ottawa, Charley Thiessen pumping him for dirt about the reputed Lothario of Garibaldi Island. Margaret's efforts at relating all this were frustrated by her succumbing to mirth, and the phone was rendered to Pierètte.

"This is totally nuts, Arthur, but I'll start from the top."

It took him a while to digest her more coherent account, after which he found himself in a quandary whether to feel insulted or tickled. *A ladies' man. An eye for the chicks.* He felt a rare welling of affection for Stoney – his refusal to take the bait entitled him to forgiveness for many past sins.

This foul-up had surely been inspired by the craftwork of Ray DiPalma, who had recounted the rumours of Arthur's sexual profligacy to the impertinent spymaster. Obviously, the story had gone up the line to Thiessen, who'd speared himself with his own weapon of revenge.

"I hope you're okay with this, Arthur," Pierètte said, "because the sumo wrestler out there is about to finish his omelette and we're running out of eggs. If you can live with it, we're ready to email the transcript to our media list, with a voice clip. I mean, how can we not?" Imitating Thiessen: "'Hey, man, normally I don't toke up until after dinner.'"

"Fire away." Arthur would somehow endure the roguish reputation foisted on him. He tried it out. Bon vivant. Sounded good.

~~~

Djon's Christmas kebabs had won the stomach, heart, and mind of Hugh McIlhargey, and they were at the chessboard again, working through a bottle of prime Vranec wine. The security minister had sent a case as a gift.

As McIlhargey answered his cellphone, Djon laboured over his move, shrugged, pushed one of his last surviving pawns. He seemed content to let the superintendent win this one – he'd won the bigger game, his daring but well-calculated bet with Arthur, and he hadn't been shy with reminders. "Work hard for good causes all life, finally in clover. No hurry, I wait."

After speaking guardedly with his two men in Gjirokaster, McIlhargey announced that statements were in hand from Dordana and Hanife Bejko, though Warden Chocoli had rendered himself unavailable by going on a hasty holiday somewhere. Inspectors Fyfe and Longstreet were proceeding on to Tirana. If DiPalma hadn't smoked himself to death and was well enough to travel – their news might be the magical cure-all he needed – they would fetch him to Ohrid.

McIlhargey went back to the board, looking pleased at what he saw. "Sorry, Djon, that little fellow's going nowhere." He snaffled a pawn.

Arthur abandoned his newspapers to check on Abzal – he was in the communications room with Sergeant Chow, searching news outlets on her high-end laptop. He'd not found much from Bhashyistan, but a streamed broadcast from Moscow told of flare-ups near their border. Abzal translated with ease; Russian was his native land's second tongue.

According to this broadcast, Russian troop carriers were streaming toward south-central Siberia – an ominous development, given an accelerated risk facing the eight Canadians trapped in Bhashyistan.

Abzal suddenly sat up. "Can we look at this YouTube clip they're discussing?"

Chow brought it up. Peering over their heads, Arthur saw Mukhamet Khan Ivanovich miked up in front of an architectural monstrosity, a five-storey wedding cake. "Almost live, we are outside culture palace for major address to nation." On the steps, in full military regalia, was Mad Igor, addressing a crowd cheering half-heartedly – they were corralled within a cordon of armed police.

"Father of country, and also of me, here is Igor Muckhali Ivanovich, immortal supreme leader for life, saying, Canada, we cook your goose. Also denouncing false rumours of discontent. His people are the most happiest on planet, he is saying, except for gang of terrorists hiding in mountains who are being hunted down like dogs."

"I'll be at your hanging, Mukhamet," Abzal said.

~~~

Abzal had been offered a bedroom in the villa, but Arthur wanted to keep close watch on his client, now in a sullen, silent fury – he'd slammed from the room after watching that video. As they hiked off for the hotel that night, Arthur could barely keep up with his athletic client's relentless stride.

At the edge of town, he pleaded with Abzal to slow down, and they rested on an overlook, in silent contemplation, watching a bright moon spangle the lake, listening to the jumbled strains of music from festive Ohrid.

"Has anything been heard from Mr. Pomeroy?" His first words in the last hour.

"Not for months, I'm afraid." Arthur had already told him of Brian's breakdown, the divorce, the cocaine, his collapse in court. His attempt to go native in the Subarctic, his bizarre and perilous trek across the Barrens in supposed search for buried gold.

"In Bhashyistan, we say that men on journeys to the steppes are in quest for their souls. I hope he can conquer his demons."

Concerns about his fallen hero had added to his bag of dark emotions. According to Vana, he'd rarely talked about his youthful years in Bhashyistan, but his homeland now seemed almost obsessively with him. It was as if a love of country, long suppressed, had burst free.

"I suppose you're eager to get back to Chambly, your wife and children."

"I miss them, God only knows how much." It aggrieved him that McIlhargey hadn't let him call them. "But I won't be going to Canada for a while."

"We'll hurry things along. No reason Hugh can't wrap up before Wednesday. I'll take you back then."

"I'm not sure I want to go so soon. I may be called upon."

Abzal strode off, Arthur scrambling after him. "What the devil are you talking about?"

"Canada has given me a home. I'm grateful for that. But I have another home."

Arthur thought he heard the siren call of destiny that throughout history has afflicted would-be heroes. Soul of a hero. He was in stunned dismay as he followed Abzal to the old town, to the hotel. His vengeful charge was dreaming if he was entertaining some fancy noble notion of jetting off to join the Bhashyistan insurgents. At any rate, he was going nowhere without a passport, nowhere but home to his family.

As they neared the hotel, a man came running toward them –

not with seeming hostility, but Abzal took up a defensive stand in front of Arthur.

"Abzal Erzhan, I presume. How are you relishing your freedom, sir?"

"Who are you?" Arthur demanded.

Out came a press card. "Rushton, Athens desk, Reuters. Can we have a few minutes, Mr. Beauchamp?"

The cat was out of the bag. Several cats, for others were hurrying toward them, including the camera-toting team from Skopje.

"Olivia Guillard, Agence France-Press," a breathless reporter said.

"Vlad Mishin, *Izvestia*," said another, who rattled off some words in Russian to Abzal as he took his photo.

Arthur grabbed his client's arm, led him through the encircling pack. "Gentlemen, ladies, please. There will be a press conference in due course, authorities willing. Not now, I'm afraid."

He retreated to the hotel door, brushing off questions like flies. They pursued them into the lobby, where the Russian, Mishin, flattered him in British-accented English: "Truly spectacular work, Mr. Beauchamp. Might we bother you for a few comments, sir." Arthur smiled his thanks, and led Abzal to the stairs.

When Mishin spoke another few words in Russian, Abzal stalled, turned to him with a cynical look, and then briskly carried on up the stairs.

32

___

It was Sunday, and Clara Gracey was in a B.C. town called Hope – an ironic name, given her mounting lack of it – listening to a United Church minister apply a love-thy-enemies parable to international politics.

Which enemies must she love? Mad Igor Ivanovich? His insolent, pestering third son, the immortal Mukhamet? Maybe Anthony Crumwell, though the only cheek she'd be tempted to turn to him was the one she was sitting on. Damn him. Damn Charley Thiessen.

She fought an impulse to stand up and shout: "You think it's so easy, you take over." She'd be tempted to walk out on this pacifist preacher and his simple recipes were not so many cameras lurking outside the church.

So she just stuck it out, fighting a headache, feeling crushed by the weight of fast-rushing world events. The clock ticking for Operation Wolverine. Bhashyistan troops plodding toward the frontier, Russians massing on the other side. Abzal Erzhan popping out of nowhere, creating myriad, unaccountable repercussions.

And Charley Thiessen going off the rails, an act of madness that threatened to take the Tory train crashing into the gully with him. . . .

She fled the church as swiftly and politely as she could, given the press of congregants eager to shake her hand. Others avoided eye contact, as if embarrassed for her. Reporters shouted questions about Abzal Erzhan, Bhashyistan, Thiessen. Clara deflected them with a frozen sunny smile, promising full briefings after all facts were in.

Unable to bear the sullen faces of her campaign staff, she had ordered them to stay in Vancouver. Nor had she wanted to rush back there by plane – she needed time with Percival, needed his solace, his assurance that she was not the paranoid target of a vast international conspiracy to drive her mad.

"Wonderful service," said the wife of the local M.P. They were leading Clara to Percival's rented sedan, manoeuvring through the crowds.

"Scintillating sermon," said Clara. "We're going to pull this one out, Ed. Give 'em hell."

She scrambled in beside Percival, who closed up his phone, started the engine.

"Okay, how are we spinning it?" she asked.

"Total mental breakdown. A prominent head doctor has been retained. He will say Charley suffered a near psychotic episode that erupted as a response to an acute stress disorder with severe hypo-manic symptoms. But for this to wash, the shrink has actually got to meet and assess him. Charley's up in Yellowknife – he's speaking there tonight."

"Don't let him *near* a platform. I want him flown down here strapped to a gurney."

"Senator DuWallup has confirmed he will take back the reins for the nonce. Tomorrow, he will appoint a commissioner to review the entire mess. It would be improper for you to comment until he or she reports, so you will be bound to silence."

A rap on the window, a supporter. Clara opened it to greet a toddler held out for show. "Oh, aren't you lovely in your Sunday dress. Thank you all, don't forget to vote." Window up, she said, "Let's get the hell out of here."

She was exhausted: two hoarse speeches the day before, two hours of sleep that night. A recurring migraine. She truly thought she might crash under the pressure. After her defeat, a period of recovery, then back to writing equations on a chalkboard about aggregate demand for goods and services. She could hear the taunts: *Gracey just wasn't the man for the job.*

She must suck it up and muddle through. She is the iron maiden.

"I don't suppose we can cancel lunch."

"It's the women's professional club, pet, you can't afford to." Percival pulled into the traffic, toward the Trans-Canada.

"Give me something for my head, for Christ's sake." She shook out a cigarette. "I'm sorry, I'm feeling very brittle."

"Look in my bag. There's Tylenol and some mild antidepressant."

What she really wanted was hard drink, but she settled for two tabs of painkiller and the Sunday *Post*. The fiasco in the Château got second billing – under headlines from Macedonia – but featured Charley's smiling mug and continued with a full page of interviews with hotel staff and Margaret Blake, plus a speculative sidebar about a mysterious government program to honour unknown entrepreneurs. Another item was about the no-comment stance of the P.M. and her cabinet, including Thiessen himself, playing hard to get in the Northwest Territories.

"What the latest from Lessard?"

"Erzhan has fingered a couple of CSIS agents. Moonlighting as mercenaries, a private-enterprise rendition. Sully Clugg, a thug – Blackwater Worldwide let him go over an issue involving dead Iraqi civilians. Rod Klein, a senior analyst, lost his shirt when the mortgage market collapsed. Whether they planted the IED remains moot, but Clugg had been trained in how to detect and dismantle them. They are under surveillance."

"The third man?"

"Believed to be out of the jurisdiction. Likely ex-CIA or FBI, presumably a rendition expert, and with Albanian links."

"And links to Anglo-Atlantic Energy."

"One infers. I suspect we'll never prove it."

"I don't care. I want those oily assholes brought before our criminal courts." Their CEO, Reaves, that priggish patronizer, and the flatulent Lord Blowhard.

The highway rose above the Fraser River, ponderous, grey, and thick with winter rains, a tree shorn at the trunk floating by. Her headache was finally lessening. "Operation Wolverine?"

"It hasn't been disclosed to the Russians, but they must know something is up. Dip notes are bouncing back and forth like tennis balls. Moscow feels its southern border isn't secure, but they assure us they have no plans to invade."

"Set up a call to the Russian president."

She had until maybe two the next afternoon, Pacific time, to pull the commandos back. Lives were at stake, her nation's reputation, an election in the balance.

Percival, as usual, was reading her thoughts. "History either condemns or acquits, but the verdict often doesn't come in for decades. I read that somewhere. It's tempting to do the popular thing, Clara, braver to do the honourable thing."

She realized she'd been thinking like a politician, not a leader. It would be wrong to gamble against harsh odds just to win an election. Obscenely wrong.

"Thank you, Percival."

~~~

A full bladder aroused Charley Thiessen from his hotel bed on Sunday morning, and he padded off to the bathroom in the grip of a mighty hangover. His watch said half past ten, and he was pretty sure he was still in Yellowknife.

Sitting on the can, ignoring a ringing phone, clutching a head that felt as big as a basketball, he trawled for recent memory. There'd been an aboriginal ceremony in the afternoon, which went off okay, but then the Château tape was aired nationally, and everything fell apart. At the campaign rally, they'd sat on their hands, embarrassed for him. His lawyer jokes fell flat.

He'd fled into the night, into the bitter cold, by a back door, avoiding a small hunting pack of reporters. Hiding his face in the fur cowl of his parka, he'd found his way into Old Town, into a tavern full of boisterous hardrock miners, nobody giving him a hoot, nobody caring about the city dude slouched in a corner, ordering doubles.

And as he stumbled out at closing . . . yes, that's when he saw the aurora borealis dancing like God's fingers in the sky. That's when he'd made a major life-changing resolution . . : but what was it? Not simply to escape the political life, though that was now a given. Something more all-encompassing. Starting over. Never going back home. Never having to look them in the eye. His mom.

He could open a practice here in Yellowknife, do good things, defend the poor on legal aid. Start a new life in the coldest city in Canada, median winter temperature thirty below. There was a masochistic feel of penance to that, somehow satisfying.

He surrendered to the persistent phone. "I think you've missed your flight, sir."

Thiessen almost said, "Call me Charley," but realized that's not who he was any more. Not the same old Charley. Different.

~~~

Dear Dr. Hank,

Colonel Letvinov says we'll have access to a telephone and fax when we get to Omsk, so I will have talked to you by now and sent this off. (Am I making sense?) I know I'm going to sound garbled on the phone, and it will take hours to explain everything, so that's why I need to fax, it'll fill in some of the details.

So what you are reading is a short letter with an appendix (it's inflamed but don't remove it!). The appendix consists of copies of entries from a journal I was half-heartedly keeping. You should read them first, so the rest of this makes sense. (Did you get any of my letters?)

Driving to Omsk may take a few days, because traffic is going only one way, trucks pulling in full of soldiers, they're setting up for God knows what, maybe an invasion, a war, and we can't contact the Canadian embassy because there's a communications blackout, except for military radio.

Colonel Letvinov doesn't seem to know what to do with us, Maxine, Ivy, and yours truly. I don't think we were in his plans, whatever they are. So he's keeping us "sequestered" until he gets permission to pack us off to Omsk and civilization.

But we're safe, and unless I sounded incoherently hysterical with relief on the phone call we haven't yet had, you know how that came about. I'm still pinching myself. Delirious at the thought I'll soon be with you and Ratle and Cassie and Jessie. I feel conflicted, though, as I fret about the safety of my many friends here, my comrades and saviours. More on that coming up . . .

The weird thing was how easy it was to get to the Russian side. We just dashed across the border (no fence, no guard posts, just rolling steppes), Ruslan and Atun in the lead, our company of resisters behind them – they've grown to about four hundred men and fifty women – plus Maxine, Ivy, and me (hearts in throat). Right into the arms of the Russian army. They'd been waiting for us, watching our progress, I guess, from one of those aircraft that had been dipping their wings at us and dropping supplies, food, gear.

Colonel Letvinov, their commander, greeted Ruslan with a bear hug, like an old friend. (Turns out he is an old friend. That big old red-bearded pirate has been keeping secrets from us – now we have serious doubts about who he was really working for all this time.)

Anyway, we've been transported to a Siberian border town whose main feature is a restored wooden fort, once a fur-trading post, and that's where we're barracked, the three of us, a heavy-timbered suite with a stinky bear rug. Atun is here too, so protective, he sleeps just outside the door. I'll tell you about him and Ivy on the phone, it's unbelievable. He proposed! They're engaged! (She didn't mull long over it.) After overthrowing the Ultimate

Cockroach he's going to fetch Ivy to be his Canadian princess and they will live happily ever after.

Right now I'm at the window looking down at some of our Revolutionary Front irregulars behind the palisade walls. They're getting basic training from a Russian drill major who spends most of his time shouting and stamping his feet with exasperation. It would be comical if we weren't afraid Russia has plans to use them somehow. As sacrificial lambs, maybe, to foment a terrible, full-scale civil war.

When we warned Atun he should not trust the Russians, he shrugged. "They are generous. Every fighter will have a Kalashnikov." That's what's making us nervous, talk like that.

Our fort is on a rise five hundred metres from a village on the Bhashyistan side that's even smaller than Canora, but a lot scarier. There are a couple of customs buildings at the border, which has a swing gate but no fence unless you count a few useless strands of barbed wire. But you can't say it's undefended. Brown-uniformed soldiers have been pulling in since dawn, in trucks or on foot, looking bedraggled when you see them through Atun's binocs. There have to be a thousand of them over there. I don't know much about military strategy, but it doesn't make much sense for them to be digging trenches in the desert.

Beyond the border, in the distance, are some deserted oil derricks, and farther away, clinging to the horizon, is a commercial centre called Özbeg. Atun says it's a strategic target, they're going to liberate it first.

Above, I see three unbroken contrails in the still afternoon sky. Russian MiGs.

My nightmares have stopped, Hank. Now I only dream of you and the girls. Love to all, and Mom, and all our friends.

XOXO, Jill

33

On Sunday, Arthur sought to entertain his melancholy client at the Olmid festival's closing events, but they were hounded everywhere by a tagalong team of reporters. The Russian, Vlad Mishin, was not one of them – he'd last been seen smiling and waving at them as he lined up for a rock concert.

"Maybe he has given up trying to get his Russian-language exclusive," Abzal said. "We owe the Russians nothing. We were their colony, and instead of granting us freedom they turned us over to their trained goons."

It was always "we" when he talked of his home – he was losing his Canadianness. He hadn't stopped lamenting about Bhashyistan, about his years of felt inadequacy, but at least he'd quit making veiled threats to disappear. Mostly, he was morose, tense, and silent.

Tired of insisting to the press, however pleasantly, on their right to remain silent, they finally retreated to the refuge of the RCMP's villa and its guarded gate. The press corps followed, but by afternoon's end had dwindled to a hard core shivering by the road in the cold, crisp evening air. Abzal carried on down to the basement fitness room, to try burning off his surplus of nervous energy.

McIlhargey and Djon were again at the chessboard – they'd been at it for three hours, off and on. It would be their last game; Djon planned to leave for Albania that evening. He'd already cleared out his room – accommodation was tight, and the two inspectors were soon due back from Tirana.

With them, hopefully, would be Ray DiPalma, sole medical casualty of Operation Erzhan. Arthur had talked to him the night before – he felt well enough to leave his care facility, but hadn't sounded enthusiastic. In fact, the news of Abzal's emergence in Macedonia seemed almost to have added to his melancholia. "Congratulations, Arthur," he'd said in a dry and weary monotone. "You pulled it off in spite of me." He was either off his boutique mood elevator or it was working in reverse. Like cocaine, Arthur suspected, it rewarded with extreme highs and punished with brutal lows.

"Offering draw," said Djon. He'd been defeated only once, a courtesy loss.

"Not yet, comrade."

McIlhargey rose to the summons of Sergeant Chow in the sunroom, now dimly lit by a desk lamp and a pair of glowing computer screens. The printer was humming, pages rolling from it. Chow said, "It's a wrap," and announced that Ottawa was sending an executive jet tomorrow to fetch everyone home.

McIlhargey sat, read through the printouts, handed Arthur a report from the Montreal RCMP.

The stilted, over-precise law enforcement jargon, when reduced to common English, disclosed that after twenty-four hours of surveillance and intercepted phone calls, Sully Clugg and Rod Klein had been arrested at the Montreal airport, carrying false passports and last-minute tickets to Mexico. The FBI had been asked to trace a call Clugg had made to an unlisted number in Dallas in which he'd warned, in poorly coded language, of a "blowback," spy jargon for alarming news.

Arthur assumed Clugg and Klein hadn't opened their mouths except to demand counsel. Law enforcers, traditionally contemptuous of criminal lawyers, tended to run to them with more haste than the average evildoer. So it would be difficult to identify other conspirators – the driver of the kidnap car, Anglo-Atlantic's operatives – or to trace secret bank accounts. Harder to nail these mercenaries for the ten murders on Colonel By Drive. But the kidnapping case seemed solid, especially with the panicky attempt to flee to refuge in Mexico.

Arthur expressed these thoughts to McIlhargey, who seemed torn between continuing this conversation or resuming his chess game.

"Let me ask you, Counsellor, how would you defend them?"

"I wouldn't."

"Don't play high and mighty, you've acted for the worst scum on the West Coast. Let's say these turkeys had retained you – what would you advise them?"

The answer seemed easy. "Any competent lawyer would plea-bargain for a minimum sentence, tendering their clients as Crown witnesses on their agreement to implicate Anglo-Atlantic. Clugg seems enough of a sociopath to roll over on friends and allies, especially if tens of millions are sitting in a numbered account in Freeport or the Caymans."

McIlhargey's grunt seemed to express admiration, but it might have been scepticism. A wrap, Chow had said. Yet much seemed unresolved, the entire backwash from the assassinations of November 26: the farcical mini-war with Bhashyistan, the perils facing the Canadians trapped there, the tumult in that country, Anglo-Atlantic's oil grab, the Russian bear at the border.

Arthur would let the politicians sort that out. He couldn't do everything.

"Again I offer draw," said Djon.

McIlhargey mulled over the end game, frowning, but then rose and took his hand. "Accepted. Next time we meet, I'll want revenge. Get out of here." His punch on the arm was intended as jocular, but must have smarted – Djon was rubbing it as he went upstairs for his bag. McIlhargey muttered, "I had a winner going."

Chow called again from the sunroom: "Mr. Bullingham, returning your call."

A few perfunctory words of congratulation, then: "I talked to McRory last night. Told him we're starting at twelve million for Erzhan. I expect he'll appoint a commission with subpoena powers and a wide-ranging mandate. I persuaded him that a good old-fashioned fault-finding inquisition will bury the Tories in opposition for the next twenty years."

"All very well, Bully, but the Liberals aren't in power."

"Only if the Almighty himself intervenes will they not be. With the justice minister gone crackers and this CSIS scandal, the Tories are hovering above single digits. You'll be the star of the show as counsel for Erzhan. The state will pay your fees, of course – I'll run some numbers by them tomorrow – and I'll try to get them to throw in an able young researcher."

"Bully, I pray you have not somehow committed me to an interminable commission hearing in Ottawa. I have a farm to run."

The voice sweetened. "Arthur, my dear, dear friend, have I mentioned I was thinking of modernizing the firm's name? Never did like the concept of dead people on a letterhead. Bullingham, Beauchamp – sounds more compelling, don't you think?"

Arthur told himself not to falter. "Bully, I am fully and finally retired."

He could hear Bully's wheezing laughter as they disconnected.

Djon came down, shouldering his bag. "Now I return to Albania to shake foundations of crumbling government." He took both of Arthur's hands, held them tight. "First item of business, we proclaiming you official hero of Albanian Socialist Party. Comes with framed certificate which I bring you when coming to Canada to collect on bet. So don't worry, not getting rid of old Djon yet."

Arthur invited him to visit him on Garibaldi Island, Dordana too. He felt a little damp of eye as they hugged – no one more deserved the title of hero than this wily, short-sighted, recently de-moustached gentleman of many talents.

He stood aside as Abzal, freshly showered, came forward and

clenched with Djon as a wrestler might, pinning his arms, kissing both cheeks. "May God always be at your side, Djon Bajramovic. You're my friend for life, for the life I will owe you forever."

They went out together to Djon's taxi, Abzal's arm around his skinny shoulders. Easily embarrassed by emotion – especially his own – Arthur made his way to the washroom for a Kleenex and privacy.

~~~

Arthur had nodded off in the La-Z-Boy and hadn't heard the Land Cruiser enter the compound, but he was startled to wakefulness as Inspector Fyfe charged inside. Fuzzy with sleep, Arthur watched him speed to the bar, pour himself a half tumbler of whisky, and down it in two gulps.

Arthur looked at his watch: ten o'clock. He'd expected to be back in his hotel by now, in bed. He started to struggle up, confused by Fyfe's inexplicable distress.

"Don't get up yet," Fyfe said. "Take a breath."

Longstreet came in now, alone. Arthur subsided back on the chair, his heart racing with the adrenalin of dread.

"He's dead, Arthur," Longstreet said. "When we showed up at his hospice, they had just cut him down."

~~~

Three a.m., and still Arthur had not slept, though he'd slid under the covers almost three hours earlier, upon his return to the apartment. The meagre details known of Ray DiPalma's suicide – if that's what it was – played an endless loop in his mind.

Fyfe and Longstreet had been told only this: at DiPalma's request, the hospice staff brought dinner to his room at six. When an attendant returned an hour later for the tray, she found him hanging from a beam, a chair tipped over. If the lead detective was to be believed, there'd been no sign of a struggle, no despairing note left behind. DiPalma's dinner had been untouched.

The state police were sour with the inspectors, almost openly hostile, questioning their role, their presence in the country. A reputed Albanian connection to Abzal's rendition was already big news in Tirana, and the death of a Canadian intelligence officer threatened a deluge of unwanted attention, so the inspectors contacted Canadian consular officials to attend to further arrangements, and proceeded on their way.

Arthur's door was open a crack and he could hear Abzal snoring on the sofa bed, a restorative sleep at last for one whose hungering for justice and vengeance had denied him rest the last two nights. Arthur supposed he was inured to tragedy – the death of one ill-fated agent was merely a sad digression from the bloody events of Bhashyistan.

But for Arthur, the impact was barely endurable. Ray DiPalma, the shape-shifting spy who never came in from the cold. Despite himself, Arthur had made an emotional investment in the fellow, had learned not merely to abide him but to tolerate his quirkiness and feel empathy over his many plights. He'd not admired his impetuosity, but it had fascinated him, as had his boozy, convoluted logic. *Crumwell thinks you think I'm on your side. Which is true. The last part, I mean.*

However much Arthur prided himself on his ability to read the psyche of others, it had taken him an inordinate time to be satisfied of this double agent's sincerity. Soon, proof of his good intent – an accusation against Crumwell but also a confession – would be removed from a safe in the Tragger, Inglis office and released to the media.

Arthur doubted he would ever be satisfied that DiPalma hanged himself. The indicators of suicide had been there: the overwhelming sense of failure and unworthiness, the shame of achieving celebrity not as a rogue but a dolt, his incurable nervous-system affliction, his alcoholism. Yet possible malefactors abounded.

Assassins hired by the renderers of Abzal Erzhan. Serbians seeking vengeance for the downfall of Krajzinski. Ledjina's brothers.

He rolled over, tried counting sheep. When they balked at the fence, he tried goats . . .

~~~

"I fool you," says a disembodied voice. Arthur sees only folk dancers on the cobbled streets, then looks up, and there's Ray DiPalma, hovering in the air. "I did it for you," he calls, drifting away. "I love you." Arthur pulls hard at a tether rope but the gondola rises higher and higher, until he can no longer see DiPalma waving.

That image propelled Arthur to consciousness, and he lay there awhile, orienting himself. He was in the bedroom of his Ohrid apartment, and morning mist was rising from the lake. He scanned the sky through a tall window, as if expecting to see Ray still floating toward the heavens. All he saw were dark clouds, and they were shedding snow, and the beach and the streets were turning white.

It was Monday, an important day, the end of something . . . Yes, he was to return to Canada that afternoon. He was going home. That prospect helped lessen his gloom, and he allowed himself a spate of longing for his funky, fuddled island. Margaret had been no devotee of DiPalma, but she would understand his need to mourn and rebound before joining her on the road.

He hoped the simple routines of farm life would assuage tragedy's pain, the health-giving chores, the communion of his boisterous farmhands and his many other friends. He will stoically endure the joshing repartee over his nationally advertised role as the bon vivant of Garibaldi. He must not miss the official launch of Hot Air Holidays – that seemed an important message from his dream.

He slipped into the main room – quietly so as not to arouse Abzal – and filled the coffee maker with water. "Damn," he said, too loud, as his packet of ground coffee broke open and spilled. Oddly, that didn't cause Abzal to stir – not the slightest motion or sound came from the sofa bed.

"Abzal?"

Closer inspection revealed that the bulge beneath the blankets was fashioned by cushions and pillows.

34

――――

"**R**oad to Victory!" proclaimed the banner on Clara's Winnebago. "Join the Conservative Bandwagon." Outside, five old-timers – boaters, braces, and brass instruments – were playing Dixieland, a genre Clara thought had died in the last century.

Advance scouts had done a methodically inept job of hiring local talent for each stop on this West Coast tour – yesterday's jug band had been bad enough, but the Dixiecrats betrayed her party as seeming old and out of touch.

Clara had awakened to their sounds with a bang, bringing her alive to the innumerable crises from which sleep had given fitful release. She was now hurriedly dressing in the confined space that was her bedroom in this heartland-friendly Winnebago – the strategy was to portray Clara Gracey, Ph.D., as down to earth, just one of the folks.

She peered out a window. The Dixiecrats were outside an old movie house – the Palace, according to a marquee blazing bright in the dim morning light. "Remind me, Percival, where are we?"

"Oyster Flats."

"And what are we doing here?"

"You are about to flip pancakes."

She saw grills being set up near the press bus. Eight o'clock, locals streaming in, enough to make it a respectable show. She was in Margaret Blake's constituency, a pit stop to show the flag in the Viking's home town.

A jolt of black coffee swept clear the last cobwebs of sleep. No headache today, that was a mercy.

"Where will I take the Moscow call?" Arkady Bulov, the Russian president, was due on the line in about forty-five minutes. She'd met him once, at an economics summit in Lucerne. An unstuffy Harvard-trained M.B.A.

"A secure line is being set up in that theatre over there – it's now the town's recreation centre. After that, four quick stops before lunch, at which time we will connect you with General Buchanan."

Operation Wolverine. As of two o'clock, she must tell Air Command to proceed or back out. Her divided cabinet, after wrangling through a long conference call, had thrown the whole load on her. She had never felt more alone, or more overwhelmed.

"Did Buster express any second thoughts?"

"He remains gung-ho."

Clara opened the curtain of another window. A frost on the ground, but snowless. She'd had it with snow; somebody had lied about global warming. Her view was of framed country houses on large, well-kept lots – a neighbourhood that ought to be Tory blue, but the only lawn signs were Green, three of them. No matter. Clara had practically gifted the riding to Blake, whose brand of direct talk and unyielding idealism was playing surprisingly well across the country.

The Greens had gained two points in a weekend poll, only six behind the Conservatives, sitting at an anorexic eighteen per cent. The brief euphoria of Operation Snow Job had evaporated after Canada got the goose from Mukhamet.

The former justice minister had added exponentially to the bleeding. Thiessen was still holed up in the Subarctic, hiding from the medical team sent to fetch him. Clara would love to tie

Crumwell into the charade at the Château, but he was claiming ignorance. The only Burton on staff at the Small Business Ministry was a twenty-year-old female clerk.

Meanwhile, Thiessen's name remained on the ballot like a curse – it was too late to slot in someone else. The party was no longer staying on message in admitting he'd gone off on a wild tangent. Somehow, his mother had got through to Clara on the weekend: her Charley had been set up, the victim of a Liberal plot, none of it was true.

Confusing matters was last night's news that Abzal Erzhan had disappeared again. All Macedonian border posts and airports were being watched, but he hadn't been sighted. Clara didn't know what to make of that, how it might play out politically. Not to the government's advantage, obviously. Had he been kidnapped, murdered – who knew? Or was this some kind of political ploy by his wily lawyer?

The arrests of two CSIS agents, the utter incompetence shown by Crumwell, the unaccountable death in Albania of one of his agents (DiPalma, the screw-up – what was *that* about?) . . . she was almost drowning. But, strangely, still no headache. *Do the honourable thing.* Percival's calm advice was the lifesaver keeping her afloat.

"The Viking awaits your gracious presence at the flapjack table."

The local throwaway candidate. She saw him out there, mixing a batch, a bearded leviathan wearing a gag hat with horns. A few dozen wrestling fans had gathered to gape and schmooze, while his election workers stood by listlessly, like shipwrecked sailors waiting for rescue.

Clara's campaign staff, crowded like penguins in this vehicle's midsection, cowered as she emerged from her room. "Pancakes!" she shouted. "Dixieland! A fucking Winnebago! I want the head of whoever came up with this loony backwoods theme." A moment of recovery as she squeezed past them. "Sorry, wrong side of the bed."

Outside, she put on her happy face as she waved at an assembly of meekly applauding supporters, about as dutiful in their enthusiasm as the cheering section she'd seen on YouTube corralled at the feet of the Ultimate Leader.

In exuberant contrast was the Viking, who was handing out DVDs with highlights of his televised matches. "I grew up here, everyone knows me," he confided as she joined him. "There's an undercurrent of support you don't see on the surface. Don't be surprised if I whomp the pants off the sitting member."

That image almost caused her clenched smile to come unglued. She endured a photo op, her hand swallowed in the Viking's forklift grip, then donned an apron, posturing for the press, bantering with the folks lined up with their plastic plates and cutlery. "It's so nice to be here in Oyster Flats, you're so lucky to live in such a lovely town, thank you for your support. A big fat one for you, little man."

~~~

Despite renovations, the Palace had retained the faded ambience of a movie house – complete with popcorn machine – but the stage had been extended. A yoga class was in progress there, young women stretching and curling, non-attendees of the pancake breakfast. Those thin, lithe thighs – maybe Clara ought to take up yoga after she goes down in flames on January 24.

An office at the front afforded little privacy – glassed interior walls, a window to the street, the Dixiecrats still blaring away. Clara and Percival were there with a communications technician, her campaign crew on the other side of the glass, whispering, speculating about this top-secret call. The Viking was also out there, grinning, such an awful presence that she turned her back to him.

"All set. Good luck." The technician placed the phone in front of her and slipped away. She started when it rang, but it was only E. K. Boyes. "President Bulov will be on at the count of ten. I shall quietly monitor. His English is excellent, so no interpreters to slow things up, and you won't notice the split-second encryption delays."

The president was bold and cheerful in greeting, tempting the bounds of sexism by telling her how radiant she'd looked on a recent cover of *The Economist*. She said he must not have been wearing his glasses. He laughed.

"We have a very clear line, Prime Minister, it's as if you're right beside me." He carried on with a weather report: a Siberian front, twenty below, Moscow buried in snow. "But you are no stranger to snow in Ottawa."

"Actually I'm on the West Coast. Much milder."

"Pacific climate. Like Vladivostok. And what is the time there?"

"Half past nine. I suppose it is late in Moscow, so I hope this is no terrible inconvenience."

"Not at all – we're having a few friends over for a late meal. But it is breakfast hour for you?"

"I've just indulged in a little ritual called a pancake breakfast."

"Like blintzes, except you use maple syrup. With us it is cream cheese filling, a famous Russian treat . . . What is that music? Dixieland? I love Dixieland."

"Part of the hoopla of an election campaign."

"An election. Another great Canadian ritual." He laughed to tell her he was joking. "I hope it goes well for you, Prime Minister. A tough one, yes? But as the saying goes, it's not over until the fat lady sings."

Clara wondered if Bulov had had a cocktail or two. She looked at Percival, listening on headphones. He shrugged.

"President Bulov . . ."

"Arkady. We are neighbours, after all, along with the great governor of Alaska, sharing the Arctic vastness."

Clara didn't like the sound of that. The Russians were always encroaching up there. "Call me Clara, then." This seemed an over-cozy game: both knew their respective staffs were listening in. "I'm glad you seem in such generous spirits, Arkady, because I'm hoping we can work together on this Bhashyistan matter."

"A shared concern. We are both having some bother with that cranky, belligerent state."

For a while they danced about the subject, keeping it light, like a family joke. Bulov characterized Bhashyistan as the juvenile delinquent in a world of otherwise grown-up nations. Clara told him of their psychological profiling, Mad Igor's failure to find closure after his father's death. Chuckles.

Then a sigh sounded across the ten thousand miles from Moscow to Oyster Flats. "A shocking business, Clara, with your two agents being arrested. A kidnapping, a foreign rendition – and is there not a likelihood these men committed your terrorist bombing? I pray that does not severely complicate things for you."

Clara felt she was being needled, and she cut through the fat, bluntly telling him plans were under way to effect a rescue of the Calgary Five.

"Yet another attempt?" More than a tinge of sarcasm.

Clara took a deep breath – this was turning edgy. But she must stick to the game plan: be candid, free from pretense, let the Russians know Canadian forces proposed to attack the Özbeg jail. Express reasoned concerns about Russian troop movements at the border.

Bulov listened without comment to her careful summary of Operation Wolverine, then to her polite entreaty that Russia respect these confidences and not put the Canadian sortie at risk.

He spoke with a slow, calculated firmness, dropping his mask of bonhomie. "The position of the Russian government, Clara, is that we shall do nothing vis-à-vis the Bhashyistanis unless provoked. We have no intentions to trespass upon their borders, but fully intend to guard ours from any spillover from the skirmishing there. We view Bhashyistan's internal unrest as a matter for them alone to resolve. We do not, like certain other great powers, assume to be policemen to the world."

That was one of Russia's practised mantras. Clara took it at face value – she was sure they had something up their sleeve, a view affirmed when Bulov added: "However, it cannot go unnoticed that a major Western oil conglomerate has taken advantage of your dispute with Bhashyistan to make a deal behind our respective backs. We have substantial economic interests there. We intend to protect them."

Clara assumed he regarded the former Soviet republic as not merely in their sphere of influence but a kind of protectorate. She thanked him for his directness and repeated that her main concern was the safety of the Canadians, those in uniform, the five in the Özbeg jail, and the three women in hiding. When asked if his sources had any knowledge of the latter's whereabouts, he made no direct answer – which Clara found both curious and foreboding.

"Rest assured, Clara, that we do not intend to expose your nationals to any increased danger that is not of their own making. But given the turmoil in Bhashyistan, our government cannot give you our blessings for your Operation Wolverine."

That was about as good as she expected to get. They carried on for a few minutes more, in their earlier relaxed manner, Bulov thanking her for the Dixieland music, and belting out an off-key stanza of "When the Saints Go Marching In." Clara ventured that he'd obviously had voice training at the Bolshoi. Both laughed, and concluded with hopes for continued good relations.

"What do you make of that?" she asked Percival.

"They're giving us a window to go in, but it's our problem if we trip over own feet."

"He's really quite clever, isn't he, in his Machiavellian way. Couldn't help treating me like a dumb blonde, though."

"My dear, you *did* look radiant. Canada's cover girl."

"I'll bet he actually wants us to go in, to precipitate a crisis, give them an excuse for intervention."

"Goodness. Maybe you're not a dumb blonde."

~~~

Behind schedule after the long recess at Oyster Flats, Clara gave brief, desperately hearty orations at the other stops, and affected delight at entertainments from a barbershop quartet with accordion backup, a square-dance ensemble, and two pipe bands.

Finally, in Comox, just after one, she was ushered into an operations room of Nineteen Wing, Air Command's West Coast base. The colonel in charge had been briefed on Wolverine, so she invited him to hook into the line. Percival slipped on another headset.

From National Defence Headquarters, Clara heard a babble, the echoing of many men on a speakerphone. E.K. Boyes and his advisers would be there, facing off with senior military staff. Clara assumed the heavy breathing on the line emanated from Buster Buchanan, unaware they were connected.

"Good afternoon, General."

"Prime Minister?"

"Let's get right into this, General Buchanan – what's our current situation?" More heavy breathing, like a horse pulling a load. "Shoot, General."

"Two CF-18s are currently airborne, Prime Minister. The Herc with the attacking force has just lifted off from Kandahar field. The advance aircraft is nearing Bhashyistan air space, and in twenty minutes will drop crew and equipment – "

"Twenty minutes! I thought we had an hour."

When Buchanan didn't respond immediately, one of his staff broke in. "They had a strong tailwind."

"Is that twenty minutes exactly, General Montpelier?" Buchanan asked.

"Nineteen and a half, sir, give or take –"

"Never mind!" Clara fought another attack of the furies – they were carrying on as if she wasn't there. "Continue, General Buchanan."

"The drop will be to an uninhabited plateau fifteen miles south of Özbeg – aerial surveillance has confirmed this to be a choice landing site."

Buchanan's composed tone, his slow, measured words, warned Clara that he was stalling until it was too late to turn back. Hard puffing by high command had produced the strong tailwind; they'd launched early.

"Let's zip it along. The situation on the ground?"

"The enemy is focused on the border north of Özbeg – that's where its main positions are set up."

"How many troops?" Clara asked.

"Four companies."

"Stationed how far from Özbeg?"

"Twenty-five kilometres of bad road. Not a real problem, Prime Minister, because the Özbeg garrison hasn't been beefed up. We will be in and out within the hour."

"General, only two days ago you assured us that the Bhashyistan troops were poking along too slowly to pose a problem. Now we find they got there well ahead of our ETA."

"They put on a spurt when they reached the flat country."

"Nor was it anticipated, when designing Wolverine, that the Russian army would become a major presence twenty-five kilometres north of Özbeg."

"We've been given to understand they won't intervene."

"So they say."

"General Montpelier here, Prime Minister. We have factored in the Russian presence, and I assure you it's to our advantage. They have so many planes flying around that the enemy is unlikely to notice our airdrop and landing."

Buchanan took over, continuing to pound the drums for Wolverine, a fait accompli, inexorable, unalterable. Subdued by this rhetoric, E.K. and his crew were as mute as cowering rabbits. And now it was ten minutes to airdrop.

"General, your enthusiasm is commendable, but now hear me. My take is we're being played like pawns in an old-fashioned great powers coup."

"Madam Prime Minister, I beg to differ." Buchanan, volume up. "This is about Canadian honour."

"This is all about oil, gentlemen, and nothing about honour. You'll go in there, and there'll be a firefight – and let's not pretend lives won't be lost – and the Russians will have their excuse to invade. While you're factoring in the Russian presence, add the Yanks and Brits – Anglo-Atlantic is their shared brat. Canada will be caught in the international crossfire. I will not see our country play the helpless stooge."

From Ottawa, a sullen silence.

"I am ordering you to abort."

~~~

Dear Hank,

By my watch it is almost five a.m. I guess it was an airplane that awoke me, because I can still hear the drone of distant propellers to the south, over Bhashyistan.

I've scurried to the window but can't see any aircraft, no lights moving in that cloudless sky. The sound is dimming, gone.

The excitement of making it to Siberia and freedom (a sort of freedom) is paling, and I'm feeling tension over what awaits our friends and rescuers camped below. Add to that the agony of waiting to get out of here, and waiting, waiting. We will be escorted to Omsk imminently, Colonel Letvinov keeps promising, then continues to ignore us.

Maxine and Ivy sleep on, but I am bundled into a quilt, staring out at the snowy barrens. They look so haunted and desolate under the silvery moon. Fires are burning in the Bhashyistan encampment. An occasional flick of a lighter below, where Russian sentries smoke and murmur.

Far away on the Siberian steppes, something else is sending darts of light – headlights, it looks like, a vehicle coming down the dusty road from Omsk.

I've nudged the window open, and I can hear the purr of its engine. Maybe someone has finally come to fetch us. Soon, Colonel Letvinov said. Soon. With repetition, that no longer seems a comforting word.

The vehicle has taken shape, a big black Lada, maybe a staff car . . . It has just rolled into the encampment, and . . . wow, it's causing a huge stirring among the tents of the Bhashyistan resistance army . . .

Okay, a couple of men have got out of the car, and one of them is going toward the men and women pouring out of the tents. A huge commotion! A shout, repeated. "Abzal! Abzal!"

It has become a chorus. They are thronging him. "Abzal! Abzal! Abzal!"

~~~

Dear Hank (continued),

Eight a.m., a cold winter sun is rising over the snowbound eastern plains. In the tent village of the Revolutionary Front, the partisans are dipping bowls into a huge pot of, I guess, porridge. Abzal Erzhan is still moving among them, hugging, shaking the hands that are not pummelling him on the back. "Abzal! Abzal!" Where had he come from? No one is saying.

We have just returned from breakfast downstairs in the officers' mess, where we met a very engaging journalist, Vlad Mishin. The card he gave us says he's with Izvestia. He arrived with Abzal Erzhan, I guess, though he didn't say so. No one will talk about Mr. Erzhan, we just get shrugs. I find his presence here a little unnerving. A hero of the resistance, and a Canadian citizen to boot, but isn't he also an assassin?

Anyway, Mr. Mishin wants to interview Maxine, Ivy, and me, and we're game for that, anything that will get word out that we're alive and well. He's the only journalist here, and seems to have privileges, talking and joking with the colonel and his *staff – they've probably ordered him to put the right slant on this story. Cynical me . . .*

Abzal Erzhan has just entered the palisade gate, a Kalashnikov over his shoulder, and has joined red-bearded Ruslan and Atun and Colonel Letvinov, and they're poring over maps down there. I've read history. Sometimes the big powers don't directly invade the little ones. They use surrogates. At the Bay of Pigs the surrogates got trounced.

Through the binoculars Atun left with us, I see cook fires burning in the Bhashyistan army encampment. Their efforts at trenching have been abandoned – I think they struck hardpan over there. You don't see any civilians on the village's streets, it's like a ghost town. Sometimes you hear a shot, accidental or caused by nerves. If you believe Atun, it's deserters being executed.

The air seems prickly with anticipation. I know I should get away from the window, but I can't. It's nerve-racking, though, what if one of those rifles sends a bullet my way? Or a missile. I have an eerie sense the Russians might not mind, they'd have their excuse to go to war, which it looks like they're itching to do.

~~~

Hello again, darling. It's a couple of hours later. I'll try to relate this as plainly as possible, though I'm absolutely shaking.

First of all, there was a plane, a small one, Russian, I guess, and it flew right above us, low, over the border, and you could see the Bhashyistan soldiers scampering off, like they were under attack, but the plane only dropped leaflets, it was like a snowfall of paper.

As this was going on, Ruslan was leading about a hundred partisans south, and Atun was taking another hundred to the west, a pincer manoeuvre, said Mishin. I'd better explain. Vlad Mishin has come up to our suite to do his interviews, and we all got distracted when the plane passed over. Vlad had his own binocs (and a satellite phone, by the way), and Maxine and Ivy and I were fighting over the other pair.

So Bhashyistan officers were running about, ordering their soldiers back to their positions, and you could see them, officers and infantry, mulling over the leaflets. They're from the Bhashyistan Revolutionary Front, Vlad said, with a picture of Abzal Erzhan and a message urging the army to put down their guns and join the resistance.

While that was going on, Abzal Erzhan led the main body of partisans straight toward the little customs houses, and as they approached, there was wild activity on the Bhashyistan side, with most of the officers piling into army trucks and speeding off.

Some of the foot soldiers followed, bounding off like jackrabbits, but most began throwing rifles into a pile, raising their arms in surrender. By this time, Abzal Erzhan's contingent had crossed the border. Not a shot fired! They simply took over the village, and the townspeople finally emerged from their homes. You could hear their chanting from the half a mile that separates us. "Abzal! Abzal! Abzal!" Even the soldiers who'd surrendered were calling his name.

Meanwhile, Vlad Mishin has been on his satellite phone, to his editor in Moscow, relating his scoop. Somehow, the communications blackout doesn't apply to him. He looks really pleased with himself as he concludes his call . . . Oh, boy, he wants to know if I'd like to call home.

~~~

The girls had finally gone to bed, and Dr. Hank Svetlikoff was contemplating the risks of doing the same, of suffering through another tormented night.

He was slow to answer the phone, fearful of what he might hear – eleven o'clock on a Monday night seemed a good time for bad news. By the time he got to it, Katie had already picked up the extension, and was screaming wildly, nonsensically.

"Who is this?" he demanded.

"Just me, dear."

35

"'How like a winter hath my absence been. What freez-ings have I felt, what dark days seen.'" Apt lines from a favourite sonnet, recited with rumbling brio as Arthur warmed his buttocks by the blazing phony fireplace – a break from the gratifying task of vacating his unloved tenth-floor Ottawa flat.

No longer would he have to endure this thin-walled sound box, whose lessor was soon to resume his Ottawa professorship. No more Handel, no more theatrics, no more weekend revels deto-nating through walls and floors. Almost all his belongings were now bagged and boxed, and what wasn't ready for storage would travel with him. Westward ho!

The four days since his return from Europe had been hectic: wearying sessions with police, politicians, and press, the constant nagging of the phone. Among the worst perpetrators: the deadline-bedevilled chronicler, Wentworth Chance – whose title for the final chapter, "A Balkan Odyssey," hinted of ponderous prose throughout.

Newspapers had devoted vast columns of ink to Abzal's rescue and his secret journey to his homeland, ultimately dwarfing the sadder story of DiPalma's travails and death. Arthur had largely abided by RCMP pleas to withhold details so as not to compromise the case against the renegade CSIS agents, but he'd balked at keeping back the DiPalma tape. *I'll swear on a stack of Bibles about how CSIS's top spy tried to engineer a vicious slander campaign.*

The media trumpeted the tape as confirmation that Crumwell and Thiessen were co-sponsors of l'affaire Château Laurier – a journalist had already traced the hotel's billing charges to an unspecified government account. CSIS issued its standard vague disclaimer: "The Service does not comment on investigations it may or may not be pursuing."

Nor had it commented on DiPalma's death, though it was the subject of massive speculation. His demise was still heavy on Arthur's mind, his shrouded figure shuffling energetically through his dreams.

"The play's the thing!" A bellow from the hallway, as the theatre major unlocked his door. He sounded in fine fettle, well recovered from the critical flop of "Marital Bonds." Inhuman screeches sounded from the rock fan's flat below, a skirl of amplified guitar, the thump-thump of bass. A woman's shout: "Turn that damn thing down!" How pleasant it was to be facing imminent eviction.

It was Thursday, and tonight he would lay over in his Vancouver club before taking a weekend of recuperation on Garibaldi Island, a respite too brief. Then he would join Margaret on her cross-country campaign train. Manitoba maybe, Northern Ontario.

Margaret must regain her voice for that. She'd been hoarse on the line that morning, but cheery: the Greens, at fourteen, were a point behind the Tories. But the Liberals were poised to sweep, riding a tidal wave of disgust at a government perceived as ineffective in crisis and with its foreign intelligence service in disarray.

It was hard not to feel sympathy for Clara Gracey. Her strategy of caution, however wise, had not won plaudits. *Nihil est incertius vulgo.* Nothing is more uncertain than the favour of the crowd, snorted that wily counsel Cicero. A leader more foolhardy than Gracey might have led Canada into a disaster, but she'd had the wisdom to back off. Arthur honoured her for her restraint.

Prime-Minister-in-Waiting McRory had already announced that

the Bhashyistan imbroglio would go to royal commission – a banquet of delights for participating barristers: treachery, bribery, kidnapping, assassination, the death of a spy, and now a growing rebellion in Bhashyistan. A spectacular opportunity for the lucky man or woman who'd be working Abzal's corner – whoever that might be. And it wouldn't be Arthur Ramsgate Beauchamp, Q.C. But how to explain this to Abzal? He could imagine his look of astonishment and betrayal at being forsaken for goats, garlic, and prize pumpkins.

Unless . . . a glimmer of hope. If Brian Pomeroy were suddenly to appear out of the cold Arctic blue, showing himself reasonably sane, the client would be more than mollified. Arthur must get back on Pomeroy's trail.

He strapped his suitcases shut, paused to review his packing list: books, CDs, a hand-sewn quilt from Ohrid, Margaret's Christmas gift. He was pestered by the thought he'd forgotten to do some tedious task, something routine but which he couldn't identify. Never mind – he phoned for a taxi.

As he manoeuvred his three bags past apartment 10C, he heard a favourite line: "'Let the candied tongue lick absurd pomp.'" Hamlet! The neighbourhood thespian had raised the level of his art.

"'And crook the pregnant hinges of the knee!'" Arthur shouted back as he headed to the elevator.

~~~

The Mishin Statement
A Blog by Vlad Mishin – Version: English
Dateline: Thursday, January 6. Somewhere Inside Bhashyistan

Welcome to the only unfiltered, uncensored reportage of events that are electrifying the world, as this veteran war correspondent is still the sole representative of the free press to have attained entry into this isolated, troubled land.

Our dramatic story continues again in Bhashyistan's cold northern barrens, a war zone unlike any other I have covered in my twenty years as international journalist. A war zone in which a small force of rebels marches resolutely forward, and a vast army flees like stampeding caribou.

As those who have followed my articles in *Izvestia* [see sponsored links] know, I am imbedded, along with camera and technical assistants, in the newly created First Battalion of the Bhashyistan Democratic Revolutionary Front. This fighting force has grown to nearly 700 men and women, spectacularly led by a former Bhashyistan soldier who has returned to his beloved homeland after years of exile in Quebec and Canada: Abzal Erzhan, [click to enlarge] whom I am proud to call a friend, having bonded with him during our night flight to Omsk in *Izvestia*'s executive jet. [click on Farewell to Macedonia]

As you may know from my posting three days ago [click here], the BDRF were guardian angels to three Canadian women with Russian roots whom they smuggled to freedom, protecting them as fiercely as if they'd been their sisters. Now these brave women are happily winging their way to Moscow for a special welcome by President Bulov before flying home first class to their loved ones, courtesy of the Russian government. (And hello to you beautiful women, Jill and Maxine and Ivy, and to Dr. Hank whose words of thanks still ring joyfully in my ears. Happy reunion!)

Soon they will be joined by other homecoming Canadians, not so heroic in my humble opinion. Here is where we pick up the story from Tuesday when I crossed into Bhashyistan.

Friendly arms pulled me onto a military lorry that the insurgents had seized from fleeing government soldiers, and in no time we were on the outskirts of Özbeg, a small but important administrative centre. [Search "oil fields," click on Özbeg] I was nervous, it cannot be denied, because I expected artillery fire from the garrison protecting the town.

But advance scouts soon returned to say that the official army had deserted. Even so, Abzal Erzhan was cautious as he led us toward the city square. Then suddenly hundreds of happy men, women, and children poured from their homes and boarded-up shops with great cheers of Abzal! Abzal! coming from every street.

Your correspondent got many hugs too because Russians are seen as sympathetic to their struggle for freedom – though like good international citizens we respect our neighbours' borders. I was swept up by the cheering crowd as they led Abzal to the city jail, which had been left unguarded except for one old man. A poignant moment occurred then, because after he surrendered the keys to the cells he went to his knees sobbing not to be executed.

Of course he will not be! Abzal assured him he is a man of compassion. His army is an army of compassion.

Keys rattled and doors clanged, and I hurried forward to join Abzal so I could capture faces of the five Canadians languishing in the cells. When they saw the guns they were petrified at first [click here], but as the dawn rose for them, that gave way to this: ☺☺☺☺☺.

"Gentlemen, you are free to return home," said Abzal, in English as impeccable as my own. It gave me ironic pleasure to see these high-rolling North Americans, who had tried to bribe their way into the oil fields [go to www.izvestia.com, search "Revenge of Revered Mother"] supplicating themselves before this self-effacing saviour who refuses to be known as anything but a simple soldier, teacher, and patriot. More Ghandi than Genghis Khan.

So as our humbled Calgarians (I mean no insult to Calgary, home of the famous stampede and the revered Flames) journeyed north to the freedom and safety of Mother Russia, we began our trek east, toward Igorgrad.

And now it is Thursday and so far the BDRF has met little resistance. The battalion's three prongs, led respectively by comrades Abzal, Ruslan, and Atun, are sweeping across the plains like reapers, harvesting eager recruits, men and women leaving farms and towns to take up arms against their fascist enslavers.

We are a day's march from the capital, where the President's elite guard, fiercely loyal to the Ultimate Leader (and, sadly, Russian-trained), stand ready to fight to the death . . .

Comments   Email   Print   Share

Read more Izvestia Blogs here → → →

~~~

Arthur arrived at the Vancouver airport suffering flight guilt – a phenomenon unknown to him pre-Blake but which had begun to plague him in recent weeks. He vowed to abstain from these gas-gulping journeys; he'd been soiling planet Earth with his massive carbon footprint. A train next time – if there was to be a return journey.

At the arrivals level, Augustina Sage gave him a kiss and a hug, and helped stuff his three bulging suitcases into her small car. As they were under way, she peppered him with questions about his Balkan exploits and the spectacular events in Bhashyistan. That continued over prawns and noodles in Chinatown. Finally, Arthur was able to ask if her former partner, gone native, had sent her any smoke signals.

"The good news, if you can call it that, is Brian is still alive. Somehow, he made it over the Nahanni Range to the Mackenzie Highway. This news comes from the RCMP in Fort Simpson, who called wanting to know if a haggard prospector found eating snow-shoe-rabbit stew in a trapper's cabin was actually a lawyer."

"And?"

"I asked them to hold him, arrest him for something, anything, a trumped-up charge. They just laughed. I asked them to have him call me collect, but he hasn't had the courtesy or courage to do that. This was three days ago. I was booking a flight up there when they phoned again to say he'd joined some First Nations people driving to Fort Providence, on Great Slave Lake. He could be anywhere."

Arthur couldn't believe that Pomeroy, having re-emerged into the human community, could be unaware of world events or that his favourite former client was on course to liberate Bhashyistan. Surely, the gold claim his clients had presumably assigned to him was an illusory fee. He would find more gold in Ottawa – if appointed to represent Abzal, he could earn several thousand tax-payers' dollars a day.

~~~

The next morning, Arthur got up early at his club to meet Roy Bullingham in the dining room. As he waited over coffee and a soft-boiled egg, he watched the wall screen, where talking heads were reciting the obvious about Bhashyistan. The received wisdom was that the Russian army was calmly waiting at the border for its invitation from the new regime to help with reconstruction. An army of Gazprom engineers would not be far behind.

Canada AM lingered lovingly for several minutes on happy faces in a Kremlin reception hall, where President Bulov toasted the three Prairie heroines and posed with them, arms linked. The love-in did not include the five Calgarians – who'd been very bad boys in Moscow's estimation. Military police had held them for eight hours of questioning before deporting them on an Air Canada flight.

Journalists continued to be held up at the Russian and Kazakhstan borders, so the only person filing reports was the Russian spy and intriguer Vlad Mishin, whose tendentious blog was widely read and profitably smothered in ads. Arthur hadn't realized, when he'd met Mishin in Ohrid, that *Izvestia* was owned by the Gazprom Media Holding Company.

Nothing new today from him, but his videotaped sequence from the day before was replayed: a statue of Mad Igor being toppled in a newly occupied town. Otherwise, there were unconfirmed reports that Igor and his family were seeking refuge in Turkmenistan, ruled by an almost equally despotic regime.

Here came Bully, frolicsome as an April lamb, briefly stopping to needle a former Conservative revenue minister, then taking a few moments to commiserate with Irwin Godswill, a few tables down, whose sour expression intimated he hadn't got out of Anglo-Atlantic before its stock plummeted.

Bully settled beside him. "Before you rush off to your bucolic sanctuary, I hope we can chat about a few opportunities. Quilter and his crowd are still desperate to retain you. Then there's that DeCameron matter, with all those mouth-watering hot tub orgies."

"Neither tempt this simple farmer."

"Nonsense." A waiter hurried over with Bully's morning oatmeal. He took a spoon to it, blew on it. "Now, as to Erzhan, precedent restrains McRory's team from offering more than eight million dollars, but they'll pay the bulk of your Albanian helpmates' fees and a fair per diem for representing Erzhan at the royal commission – five thousand a day, and they'll throw in junior counsel."

"For reasons of my personal health and sanity, Margaret and I have agreed I shan't return to the nation's capital. She will find an Ottawa bed-sitter and I will keep the home fires burning."

"I can see you are overwrought, Arthur. Hard to blame you – it's been a tense and difficult time. Your dubious friend DiPalma, murdered, was he? Never mind, tell me no secrets. Yes, a few days sopping up the rustic pleasures of your island home, then you'll be ready to take on the world again. Bullingham, Beauchamp. Reverberates with power and prestige, does it not?"

He went back to his oatmeal. Arthur couldn't finish his egg, stared balefully at the TV screen – a news flash: Turkmenistan had just rejected a request for safe haven from Bhashyistan's ruling family.

~~~

Once aboard the *Queen of Prince George,* Arthur turned his mind to the problem of getting from the ferry dock to home. He'd called ahead to Blunder Bay, drawing Savannah from a strategy session of the Inter-island Roadside Bicycle Path Coalition. To his dismay, Arthur learned she and Zack had yet to retrieve the Fargo from Stoney, despite cajolery and threats. Their guests could offer no help – they'd come on mountain bikes.

Arthur was unsurprised when his next call, to Garibaldi Taxi Service and Hot Air Holidays, went unanswered.

His quest for a local whose vehicle might accommodate his luggage won quick success, even gushing insistence from Mookie Schloss, who insisted her Land Rover had *gobs* of room. She'd be *awed* to drop him off.

Not forthcoming, however, was a renewed invitation to her cozy cottage on Sunrise Cove – but soon an unsavoury reason for that joined them from the outer deck: the poetaster Cudworth Brown, who'd just finished a smoke. He snuggled beside Mookie, snaked a proprietary arm about her waist.

"Watch out for loverboy here," Cud said, "he's left a trail of broken hearts."

Mookie slapped Cud lightly. "He's an absolute *gentle*man – not like you."

"Man, I feel a sad poem coming on. Broken hearts, it still smarts when Cupid's darts miss their marks and only prick the private parts."

"You are *so* not normal," Mookie said.

Afterwards, on the car deck, Cud winced as he tried to heft Arthur's bags. "What have you got in there, gold bricks?" His back was acting up, so Arthur manhandled them into the Rover.

With Mookie at the wheel, Cud beside her, the absolute gentleman in the back, they rolled from the landing ramp into the welcoming arms of Garibaldi Island, a moment that never failed to gladden Arthur. By the time they conquered Ferryboat Knoll, he'd begun to laugh at himself, freed from the insupportable burden of his false role as loverboy, so wrongly earned, so quickly doused.

~~~

As they began the steep descent on Centre Road, past Breadloaf Hill, Arthur saw that Santa and his reindeer were still raring to take off from the Shewfelts' asphalt roof. Historically, they tended to remain aloft until Groundhog Day. The lawn ornaments, three-foot versions of Santa's elves that more resembled Snow White's dwarfs, would often hang around until replaced by Easter bunnies and duckies.

On the neighbouring acreage: a blighted landscape of rusting cars and trucks. If he wasn't mistaken, that was Stoney by his garage, with a camera crew – he could see their van, a Global TV logo. And parked nearby, silently seeking rescue from its abductor: Arthur's extraordinarily rendered Fargo.

"Mookie, please stop behind that big arbutus and let me out. I see my truck."

As they drove off, he toted his bags to a grassy lay-by, then slipped from behind tree cover and up a mossy path behind Stoney's garage. The hot-air balloon, deflated but suspended by ropes from tree limbs, afforded a blind. After further advance, he could hear Stoney crowing behind the TV van.

"I figured early on this was a phony set-up, so I decided to play him along."

A woman interviewer: "Charley Thiessen, you mean?"

"It didn't click who he was right away. I figured him for some lowly underling."

"And at what point did you realize it was a set-up?"

"Well, between me and you, I got real suspicious when he wouldn't take a toke."

Arthur finally found his way to his truck, ducking behind the cab. The tires were up, the hood warm, and the keys on the dash.

Not far away, Stoney was struggling with his recall of the mystery man, Burton. "Dude with a goatee is all I remember. I'd just crawled out of the sack, so everything was kind of out of focus, eh."

"Okay, Bob, can we get a picture of you in front of your cool truck?"

As they approached, Arthur bent so low he could see Stoney's untied sneakers by the wheel wells.

"Yeah, this here's my sweetheart, my honeybun. Forty years in service, still street legal."

"That's a great shot. Kiss it again."

Camera lights blazed. As they sauntered off, Stoney pitched them about Hot Air Holidays' balloon launch. "Test run to Ponsonby Island, winds permitting, otherwise we go wherever they take us. Gala event, a spectacle you don't want to miss. It's BYOB. you can score your party juice at the General Store."

Arthur slipped in behind the wheel. As the engine came quickly to life, Stoney turned, startled, but the Fargo was already pulling around the garage, down the driveway, out the open gate. A quick stop to retrieve his luggage and he was on his way.

A perfectly executed freedom ride. Ray DiPalma would have been proud.

~~~

At home, he was greeted with muddy-pawed exuberance by Homer and a weary nuzzle from old Barney's muzzle. The two mousers, Underfoot and Shiftless, tangled themselves in his legs by way of hello, then wandered off, already bored with him.

The Fargo locked in the garage, its keys secreted in the back of the pantry, Arthur accepted Zack Flett's tight, sinewy grip and Savannah's enveloping arms, and exchanged greetings with the roadside bike-path boosters sprawled about the parlour. Then he changed into his grubs and let Homer take him on a tour of the farm.

Fences were sturdy, the barn in excellent repair, solar panels added to the roof of Margaret's neighbouring house – Zack and

Savannah were almost ready to move into it, minimizing the threat of awkward sleepwalking incursions.

He spent the rest of that day in the fields and the garden, in the greenhouse and the goat corral, and felt the turmoil of recent weeks slip away. Yes, he must come up with some impregnable plan to avoid that royal commission hearing. Could he persuade Abzal and Bully he was too close to critical events? Yes, an excellent solution – he'd explain he was a potential witness. One can't be both counsel and witness.

Pleased with this solution, he settled into his club chair and turned on the set for the six o'clock news, while his housemates sparred in the kitchen over who ought to dispose of a dead shrew, Underfoot's gift. *Nullus est instar domus.* There is no place like home.

Arthur enjoyed several minutes of Jill Svetlikoff and her sister and niece rejoining their families in a clamorous welcome at the Regina airport that had the news anchor wiping his eyes. This was interrupted by a bulletin.

"The Bhashyistan government has fallen," the announcer said. "Russian media has advised that President Ivanovich, his family, and advisers are surrounded in the presidential palace, seeking to negotiate terms of surrender."

~~~

The Mishin Statement
A Blog by Vlad Mishin – Version: English
Dateline: Saturday, January 8. From the Steps of the Number Two Imperial Palace of the Former Ultimate Leader for Life.

Good evening, readers and fans. And thank you for making the Mishin Statement the most popular blog of the new year. My front-page *Izvestia* dispatches have been picked up around the world by now [click for list], but as usual it is time for reflections from one

who has had the fortune to be at the centre of the whirlwind –
though a whirlwind that, as Catherine the Great complained to her
husband, "petered out."

That's bad, isn't it. Forgive me.

Anyway, it turned out that the dreaded elite guard were cowards
to a man, and when their colonel told Igor Muckhali Ivanovich
they weren't willing to die for him, that's when the negotiations
began. The Mishin Statement is now able to confirm that Mad
Igor and his retinue will face trial, but because they spared bloodshed by surrendering, the provisional government has agreed not
to put them against the wall. (You read it here first. There was a
lively debate over that one among the provisional leadership.)

Ex-President for Life Ivanovich remains with his family and
advisers in the main palace [click to enlarge] which will be their
prison until the BDRF decides where to put them.

Meanwhile, there is dancing in the streets, and hugging and
kissing, and the Stolichnaya is flowing. (Expect a high birth rate in
nine months!) Never have I seen such joy since the election of
President Putin in my own country. Check out the podcast below
where you will see Vlad Mishin flailing helplessly, being carried on
the shoulders of revelling students.

Behind me, as I write, is the number two imperial palace [click
here], in which the provisional government is quartered for the
time being. I have just returned from there after a few interesting
words with Abzal Erzhan, who has been named chair of the provisional council. He told me he is determined to create a democracy
in a land that has never known one. Many, including your faithful
correspondent, hope that is not a naive goal.

"Not everyone agrees," my friend confided, "but I favour the
British system, a house of the common people."

Yours truly is neither a politician nor a great student of history,
merely a recorder of events, but I humbly pressed our own
Russian model on him, recalling Lenin's line: "It is true that liberty

is precious — so precious that it must be rationed." Jesting right along with me, Abzal quoted the even more famous line from Churchill: "Democracy is the worst form of government except all the others."

I question whether that will hold true in the cauldron of the future.

Comments   Email   Print   Share

Read more Izvestia Blogs here →→→

36

———

On Saturday, Arthur bundled up against a rare coastal snowfall to head off to the General Store, a welcome return to his hiking regime. The coffee lounge was sparsely populated, with just a couple of carpenters on break from roofing the new bar.

Abraham Makepeace was in the grocery aisles, helping the cantankerous island centenarian, Winnie Gillicuddy. "If I want your advice about fat-free yogurt, I'll ask for it. Don't treat me like I'm helpless."

The frazzled postmaster joined Arthur at the mail counter and offered the most cursory of greetings: "Welcome back to the rock." He tossed a thick bundle onto the counter. "Bunch of magazines waiting for you. Political flyers. Catalogue from a publisher, your picture's in it. Invitation to the Starkers Cove shindig this afternoon, family fun in the afternoon, followed by a dance featuring a rock and roll band called Skunkweed."

Arthur would take a pass on that, saving his strength for the next day's balloon launch.

"A couple of interesting postcards. This one's from Capri – that's in Italy. You can read it yourself."

"Why, thank you, Abraham."

In carefully printed letters: *Greetings, Comrade Arthur. Albania not so safe right now for Djon Bajramovic, so having holiday until heat dies. Sorry about sidekick Ray. Maybe Mafia rubout hit. Talk to you when coming soon Canada, looking forward. Solidarity!*

"This here other one is addressed to Margaret, postmarked Albania. Guess things weren't going too good when you sent it. I got depressed just reading it."

Arthur sat down with a coffee, glanced at the publisher's catalogue, the spring list, Arthur's eagle beak in inglorious profile on the cover of *A Thirst for Justice*. He hid it under the pile. The political bumf included an exhortation from the Progressive Reform Party, Gerard Lafayette standing proudly by a maple leaf flag. The right-wing renegade was suddenly polling well; he'd reaped a harvest of Tory malcontents. Margaret had sounded a little flattened on the phone the night before – with the election ten days away, the Greens had hit an electoral ceiling, were scrambling for leftovers with the other small parties. Progressive Reform was coming up the middle of the pack.

Makepeace came by with the portable phone. "Normally, as you know, this establishment frowns on personal calls, but this here is from a foreign dignitary."

"Who?"

"President pro-tem, he calls himself, of Bhashyistan. Don't tie it up all day."

Arthur was slow to recover from the shock of hearing, from halfway around the world, the liquid-clear voice of Abzal Erzhan apologizing, of all things, for this intrusion. "Forgive me, Arthur, but someone at your house said you could be reached here."

"Good lord, is that you? Truly?"

"Weary but more at peace than when we shared our last adventure. I apologize for deserting you in the night, but you can appreciate the reasons."

Arthur recovered sufficiently to ask after his family.

"I just got off the line with Vana. She's well, the kids are in excellent health and spirits. I expect they'll join me here after their school year. Hopefully, things will have settled down by then."

He'd reunited with his siblings, who were also well – "all things considered." His bitterness at the tyrant who had tortured them and murdered his parents seemed somewhat mollified by his easy, triumphant victory. "There has been enough blood, Arthur. Better that Ivanovich and his bootlicks spend the rest of their lives in solitary contemplating the hatred the nation feels for them. Oh, incidentally, our technologically savvy friend Mukhamet has denounced his *père* – thinking to save his skin – so he may be a useful tool."

Arthur could hardly believe he was hearing these unguarded, confident words from a man who'd seemed congenitally moody and taciturn. It struck him that he'd not got his true measure during their few days together.

"There'll be elections, of course?"

"When we're ready." That was too ambivalent. Arthur was reluctant to ask about the ominous influence of the Russians. He feared that this educator, however well intentioned, despite his impressive show of leadership, might prove unschooled in the politics of power.

Abzal asked after Brian Pomeroy, and Arthur was able to tell him the lawyer-turned-goldseeker had been reported alive and reasonably well.

"It will be too much to ask you, but maybe Brian Pomeroy – We'll need help organizing a justice system."

"An invitation to serve as adviser to the Bhashyistan minister of justice might tempt him to emerge from hiding."

"And Djon Bajramovic, have you heard from him?"

"He's on holiday in southern Italy."

"Well earned. I'm sorry I never had a chance to meet Mr. DiPalma before his sad end."

Makepeace was wagging an impatient finger. There would be time enough to tell Abzal of the eight million dollars negotiated on his behalf. "Tied up as you are with affairs of state, you obviously have little reason to come back."

"Oh, no, I'm looking forward to watching you in action at the commission hearing. Very important to see justice done."

Arthur stifled a groan.

~~~

Parking was tight when he arrived late at the Hot Air Holidays proving grounds, so he left the Fargo by the gate, deep-pocketing the keys. It was a cold, crisp day, the sun unable to muster the energy to melt the leavings of yesterday's snow clouds. These had deposited a white film on roofs and untrampled foliage, making Stoney's car lot less homely. The ribbons, banners, and helium balloons – a clever touch – along with the swollen, red-striped airship, gave the feel of an inelegant amusement park.

Stoney's cronies were all present, along with the bulk of the Centre Road neighbourhood – though not the next-door Shewfelts, who were constantly at daggers drawn with Stoney, dragging him to court under the Unsightly Premises Bylaw. No sign of Constable Pound, who'd likely found the ballooning regulations too complex to be enforceable.

When Baldy Johansson offered a swig from his hip flask, Arthur looked at him severely.

"Oh, yeah, I forgot, you're AA."

"So are you."

"Had to take a break from them meetings, I get too emotional. Besides, it's the year's biggest social weekend. How late did you stay at that Starkers Cove ring-dang-do?"

"I wasn't there."

"I'd of sworn you was in the hot tub with us. Man, they had half a steer on the spit. Kegs of beer, enough to fill a bathtub, wine galore, not from kits either, the real stuff. Live music, Skunkweed from Port Alberni, played all night until their lead singer passed out. Everything kinda died out around four."

Arthur thanked him for this update, and carried on to join the folks massing by the balloon. It was tethered to a stripped-down chassis, the propane burners on low burn in the gondola, an over-sized basket. Stoney was in there, doing last-minute checks, Dog standing beside him, looking decidedly ill at ease in his hockey regalia.

Stoney turned to the eager watchers, grinning. "Houston, do you read? All systems are go." His own system, however, seemed less primed. Crawling over the basket's guardrail, he floundered and fell, losing one of his untied sneakers. He brushed himself off, weaved over to the tether rope, slurring: "Ladies and genermen, you are about to observe hishtory in the making."

The Starkers event had clearly done him severe damage. Arthur could only hope that Dog wasn't similarly challenged. His impulse was to demand a halt to this, but he hesitated, not wanting to act the wet blanket.

"Turn up the burner, Dog!" Then: "We have liftoff!"

As the balloon suddenly rose, Stoney followed. Somehow, in the process of untying the tether rope, he had looped it around his wrist. His ground crew, led by Hamish McCoy, led a dash to catch him by his remaining sneaker, but it came off in their hands. Stoney spiralled into the sky, clutching the rope, caterwauling: "Turn down the burner, Dog! Turn *down* that burner! Move! Open the vent!"

The test pilot was immobile, staring down at him over the rim of the basket, but he finally came out of his fugue and set frantically to his task. By this time, they were floating above the Shewfelts' roof. Sheep were stampeding in the pasture across the road.

"Turn the burner *down*, I said! Not *off!*" This final instruction came too late: the balloon quickly went limp, and in seconds Stoney was entangled in plastic hooves and antlers, the entire rooftop display collapsing, with Rudolph going stiff-legged over the edge, plummeting to the Shewfelts' walkway and shattering into shards of plastic. The gondola came to rest on Santa's sleigh, Dog crawl-ing from under the fabric of the balloon.

Mrs. Shewfelt ran from the house screaming, and her husband came barrelling out after her, knocking over lawn elves like bowling pins as he bolted to the safety of the road.

Everyone watched, stunned and silent, until Stoney rose in a tangle of Christmas lights, barefoot and dishevelled. Then they all whooped and cheered.

37

———

"You got troubles, partner?"

Thiessen's reddened eyes rose from contemplation of his pint of ale and sought focus on the weather-beaten face of the character on the adjoining barstool, a trapper maybe, or a prospector.

"I got troubles," Thiessen said.

"Wife?"

"Not yet. But those are coming." The bar was called Gold Diggers, a log structure in Yellowknife's Old Town, poorly lit, good for hiding in. His searchers hadn't found him here, nor in his new digs at Captain Ron's Bed and Breakfast. They'd finally given up, fled back to Ottawa.

"With me, it was wife," said the grizzled man. "Kicked me out on my patoot." Late forties, fifties, it was hard to tell. Salt-and-pepper hair, a full set of whiskers, his nose and earlobes scarred from frostbite. "Things went downhill from there."

"With me . . ." Thiessen shrugged. "I just blew it." He was sporting a five-day stubble. He'd put away his suits – he wasn't Charley any more – and clad himself in newly bought work clothes, a floppy hat to shade his eyes. Longjohns. He was determined to survive up here.

"You new in town?" the stranger asked.

"Yeah. Getting my bearings."

"I just rode in myself. So what's going on in the world? Haven't seen a paper in months."

"Not much."

"You on the run?"

"Guess you could say. Starting over." Thiessen took a gulp from his pint, wiped his lips, saw that the other guy only had a coffee. "Buy you something stronger?"

"Wouldn't mind. I am currently resource depleted, as they say in the prospecting business." He called the bartender. "Same as my buddy here." To Thiessen: "Starting over? At what?"

"Thought I might open a law practice."

The prospector grunted, a kind of laugh. "What's the difference between a lawyer and a rooster?"

Thiessen canvassed his wide inventory of lawyer jokes. No roosters. "I give up."

"When a rooster wakes up in the morning, its primal urge is to cluck defiance."

Thiessen laughed when he finally got it.

"UBC, class of eighty-seven," the prospector said.

"You're *also* a lawyer?"

"Was. Where'd you practice? You look familiar."

"Ontario. Stint in Ottawa. Made the mistake of getting into politics." Thiessen sensed he was getting a physical once-over, his broad shoulders, his thick, pink fingers.

"Those hands ever seen a pick and shovel?"

"Not for a while."

"You look like you played a little football in your time."

"Winning tackle in the Vanier Cup, 1990."

"Shouldn't take long to shape you up."

"Doing what?"

"I've got rights to an assload of gold, a registered claim up by Nanacho Lake. The project needs a small cash infusion. I'm looking for the right kind of partner."

Maybe it was empty talk, but sometimes you stumble into things.

Thiessen wasn't going to hand over any blank cheques, but this could be the new life foretold by those dancing northern lights, God's portent, a divination.

His new friend stuck out his hand. "Brian Pomeroy."

"Call me Chuck."

~~~

After dinner, his blood still racing from the hot-air disaster movie, Arthur took to his club chair with a pile of unread magazines. But he couldn't concentrate. Not because of the sniping from the living room over a game of Boggle, but a feeling, still plaguing him, that one of his regular, tedious duties had gone ignored since his return from Europe. Some odious task, like cleaning the toilet or disposing of dead mice . . .

It came to him he hadn't looked at his emails for almost three weeks; a prospect so dreadful he'd repressed it. In Arthur's view, the world had been more civilized before electronic mail, less threatening – who knew when some clicking error would unleash a penis-enhancing deluge, or viruses or worms or adware or whatever they call those things that broadcast your every taste and inclination.

Surely if something was important, the concerned party would phone.

But to dampen the niggling worry that some message of worth was craving attention in his in-box, he rose with a sigh and slumped into his desk chair and turned on the computer and watched his creaky old monitor display a series of accusatory messages – impossible to get rid of – complaining of files not found.

Finally, the computer let him open his mail program. He was dismayed by the flood pouring in, as if from a burst dam. Uncaught spam whirled by, news updates, notes from lawyers, friends, acquaintances barely remembered, plaintive pleas from Wentworth Chance.

When the storm finally let up, he grappled with the thought of adjourning this task until the morning, when he'd have more vigour. But as he idly scrolled through the bulging account, a sender caught his eye: DiPalma078@hotmail.com. It rolled past, and he feared he'd lost it, but finally zeroed in on it. It had arrived two weeks ago, Sunday, January 2, at just after eight in the morning here. Five p.m. in Tirana. An hour before DiPalma was found hanging from a beam.

Arthur felt a little wobbly, and before opening the message he went to the kitchen and poured himself a cup of the spicy herbal tea that Savannah kept in a thermos. On his return, as he passed by the living room, she and Zack looked up from their Boggle game. "You okay?" she asked.

"Me? Oh, fine, yes. No problem."

He quietly shut the parlour door, and clicked on the wrong message, from Cinny who wanted to meet him. Finally, DiPalma's letter came up on the screen. He printed out its several pages and retreated with his tea to his club chair, adjusted the lamp, and began reading . . .

~~~

Yo, Arthur, I know you hardly ever check your mail, so by the time you get this I'll be in heaven or hell or whatever is out there, and you'll probably be on Garibaldi, just back from squeezing teats in the goat shed. I didn't want to leave you confused and worried about whether I got snuffed. I only have one real enemy who dislikes me enough to do that. Guy named Ray DiPalma.

Remember that little Internet café around the corner from my hospice? Well, it's not just a café – they also serve something to liven your spirits. Skënderbeu konjak, nectar of the gods. I was working on a jug of it in Gjirokaster, whatever happened to it? Goes pretty good with the

Zykoril. Which they're threatening to stop giving me, they don't like my moods when it wears off. Man, when it does, you're ready to kill for more.

Latest medical news: they did a brain scan, and they won't confirm or deny but – how did the neurosurgeon put it? The risk of permanent brain damage cannot be eliminated. Brain damage. Well, Ray DiPalma declines to spend the rest of his life on head meds. Not this shitty life.

Remember that lecture you gave me in your Ottawa office? It's stayed with me. Solicitor-client communications remain privileged, you said, even after the client pegs out. So it looks like you're stuck to the end of time with keeping my secrets. Funny how that works. Privilege outlasts death. So it's just you and me, Arthur, unless someone pirated your password and infiltrated your in-box – and if they have, well, fuck them. I bet you never thought that word was in my vocabulary. I actually had to bite my tongue a lot while I was hanging with you and Margaret. Appearances, appearances.

I didn't need a high-powered receiver to pick up Margaret's distrust. She suspected the klutzy thing was an act, didn't she? The blatant following, the shuffling and stumbling. She was right. I think she's got an innate sense about people. She always made me feel skittish around her, exposed. Not you, Arthur, not you, never you. You wanted me to be who I wasn't, you wanted that badly.

The Parkinson's thing too, that was part of my legend. The greening of Ray DiPalma? That was a little harder, couldn't get totally into character. But, hey, I'm green, you're green, today we're all green. The planet's going to shit. Another good reason to attrit myself.

The God thing was a problem too. I tried believing . . .

The nervous breakdown? Probably real. Hard to tell, I'd never had one before. But, yeah, I was kind of screwed up. But I figure I deserved an Oscar as the neurotic spy. Hope you agree.

Here's what came naturally: nicotine and booze. I *wish* the lush thing had been a put-on, I wouldn't have buggered up so many times. I get just one digit wrong, and suddenly Ledjina's father is calling Moishe's Bagel Bakery on Rue St. Laurent.

You're supposed to think with your cortex not your testosterone in this job, but I never figured out how to do that. Telling a girl from Gjirokaster you're a multimillionaire developer and offering to take her to Canada, object matrimony — these are not the kind of mistakes that make you want to live.

Wife-swapping, nudist clubs, sex with a slight freaky edge — all that would come out in the public hearings that are as sure to come as death and taxes. The open-marriage experiment never really worked for Janice, not in the end. Blame me, not the other woman. Janet, I mean. Anyway, I don't intend to testify before some sneering commissioner about my sordid social life, okay? I don't want to deal with it. I would die of embarrassment.

I'm rambling. That's another quirky thing about me, I'm the spy who can't stop talking. Can't stop acting.

It's funny how things worked out. Crumwell figured it would be a good test for me to target Margaret, a chance to show my stuff again after my marital trauma. I was supposed to do follows on her, tie her into a conspiracy with Zack and Savannah, that was the idea.

I walked out of Crumwell's office wondering if he'd flipped. After an hour of open-source intel I was sure he had — I came away from my research wanting to ask Margaret for her autograph. I think the old man has this paranoid thing about environmentalists. He wants all life on the planet to suffer the way he has.

I had no idea our connection was going to play out the way it did. To my advantage. Well, sort of, because I was able to parlay my role as Margaret's official follower into being friend and confidant to both of you. You particularly, Arthur. I was good, wasn't I? "I shall need absolution from you. Trust me. I'm on your side."

You were the key to finding out what Vana Erzhan knew, what Iqbal Zandoo knew. The idea was to entice you to act for them, and the bait I set out was my good intel – alleged good intel – that Abzal had been snatched. The fact that Julien Chambleau was their M.P. smoothed the connection, but you'd have probably gone for it anyway – you were hungry, I could tell. Hungry to show you could still rock and roll.

The other stuff I fed you, from Aretha-May, about Abzal being rendered . . . What can I say? There's no Aretha-May. I wouldn't be caught dead making out with someone called Aretha-May. Doesn't change the fact that he *was* rendered. Never mind. Let me collect my thoughts . . .

Pausing for a refill here. That's got to be the one for the road, I don't want the nuns to see me staggering back to my room. Excuse me for a moment while I cycle through the news sites. No flashes, nothing new on the bust of Clugg and Klein. Have they ratted on anyone yet? They will, to save their skins. I know those guys.

I've got to remember to delete these musings from the sent box, we don't want them floating around in the Internet cloud, do we? Because you know what, Arthur? I hate to say this, but you're going to look like a donkey if this gets out. The tomato juice will be on *your* shirt, a stain upon your spotless career. Yes, sir, folks, the brilliant lawyer whose thrilling cross-examinations leap from the pages of *A Thirst for Justice* bought it hook, line, and sinker from a fucked-up spy.

I'm sorry about that because something touched me, Arthur, something about you. You're a sweet guy, kind of stuffy yet lovable, like an old teddy bear. But full of some weird residual guilt. I'll bet you had lousy parenting too. So full of self-doubt that I started doubting you too, to the point I underestimated you. I'm still not clear how you sneaked Abzal out of that jail. I'm sorry I missed him.

Moving right along. The Zandoo connection. It was like a purgative, sort of like having your first bowel movement in five days, when you confirmed that Zandoo never saw the driver. So that left Abzal . . .

~~~

Arthur sped to the washroom off the back veranda, thinking he was going to puke. But slowly the nausea dissipated, until he could perch on the toilet seat, his head in his hands, and conquer his shakes. An image intruded: the bottle of rum his housemates kept on the upper shelf, second to the right, next to the dishwasher. Half-full, last time it encountered his eye.

"You all right, Arthur?" Savannah, at the door.

"Splendid. Reading a copy of the *Anarchist News* someone left here."

~~~

You've figured it out by now, right? Yeah, I'm the third man, the wheel man. I actually played with confessing to that priest, it was one of those impulses that hit you when you're screwed up on booze and coke. Mostly coke that day, I don't think I'd had a drink yet.

A lot of this came about from too much of the white stuff. We had our own Operation Snow Job going. Rod Klein was the blow-meister, he had a Colombian girlfriend. Sully liked to get shit-faced liquidly too, like me – he didn't need so much coke, he already came pre-packaged as a dominant, a doer, an ego-fucking-maniac. He was a prick, still is. But you can't repeat that, Arthur, your tongue is tied.

Did Abzal ever ID me back on Nov. 26? I never got that straight. I was doing lookout, not watching him. But he must've ogled Sully and Klein pretty good, given only a couple of hours ago they got busted in the security line for a Transat flight to Mexico. Their next stop would've been Panama, but how they expected to access the account without my signature, *yo no entiendo.*

Pause for a peek at Google News, at Reuters, to see if they've ratted on the wheel man yet . . . If they have, the horsemen ain't saying. But they wouldn't grass on their old pal Ray, would they? There's a code of honour among spies, isn't there?

Not.

Like I say, I know those guys. They've already rolled over on me, haven't they? That's why those two RCMP brass are on their way here, isn't it? I've got no place to hide. I'm maxed on my cards and so broke I can't afford a bus out of town. But the main reason I want to join the eternal chorus is they don't prescribe Zykoril to lifers in the Kingston Pen.

E.O., Arthur, as we say in the service. Eyes only. Here's where I foist everything on you, make you haul around my sack of woe and guilt for the rest of your life. Because I have to unload. I can't bear taking it to the grave.

The story thus far: Klein had a friend in Dallas who'd learned that Alta International had Mad Igor in their hip pocket. This friend visited Klein in October, after learning some of Igor's cronies were to be red-carpeted in Ottawa. Klein spoke to Clugg. They spoke to me. The three musketeers. Okay, the three greedy, fucked-up malcontents.

The London security company with the ex-KGBers? Created from the same raw materials, booze and blow.

Klein worked with the customers, the guys in Dallas (they kill presidents, don't they?), and made arrangements for the Lear. I had the Albanian contacts, so I took a break from tailing Margaret for a week in early November to go to Tirana to set up Abzal's reception centre. Clugg did the easy part (easy for him). After a final double-check of the Bhashie cavalcade's exit route, he stuck his IED in the skate shack at four a.m. and triggered it six hours later from fifty metres away with a modified garage-door remote.

Albania. I never dreamed you'd agree to go with me. I was heading back there anyway, to make sure my acquaintances in the Security Ministry followed through on their commitments before I paid the final instalment. Enter Hanife Bejko with his, "Abzal Erzhan, he say pliss help." That's when I burned my finger, reading that note. Those assholes had stiffed me. Stiffed our customers, anyway. My idea was to wander away from you at some point, come up here to Tirana, and tell them to finish the job. Never thought I'd be going by ambulance with busted ribs and possible perpetual brain damage. Never thought I'd die here. That wasn't part of the master plan.

You enjoy your life, Arthur. You earned it.

Confidentially yours till the end of time,

Ray

P.S. I forgot to mention the little detailing touch that would have made the whole thing credible had those shufflers in Tirana done their job. "No problem," they said, "we learn at CIA school all best enhanced interrogation methods." I forget the exact wording we'd agreed on for Abzal's note, something like this: "My darling Vana, how sad I am that I can never return to you and my beautiful children. I must stay in hiding forever. I love you, and will always remember you. I did it for my country. For both my countries, Bhashyistan and Canada." Then after they terminated him, we'd mail that goodbye kiss from some international haven for escapees, crooks, and deadbeats, like Costa Rica.

P.P.S. Somewhere along the line, expect to bump into a guy named Vlad Mishin, he's one of the best. He's so fucking transparent, though, I don't know how he gets away with it.

~~~

Arthur added more logs to the fire, and fed the pages into it, then wandered off to join Savannah and Zack. They were laughing, not fighting, over some obscure and improbable word, *gruffish*. Arthur studied the Boggle cubes. "You could have added 'ible' to 'gull,'" he said.

"Son of a bitch," said Zack. "I missed it."

"So did I," said Savannah.

"So did I," said Arthur, and went out to feed the goats.

38

─────

Gerard Laurier Lafayette bent low into the wintry blast as he followed a snow blower to the Centre Block steps. On this third Tuesday of March, Ottawa's enduring winter seemed bent on eclipsing the thirty-year snowfall record, 175 inches. "Three inches to go!" trumpeted the *Ottawa Sun*. The headline smacked of lewdness, reminded him of penis-extension spam.

Only two protesters had ventured out today. "Global warming is a Lie," proclaimed one sign. "You're an Idiot," said an opposing view.

As Lafayette gained the front portals, a parliamentary officer, a supporter of Nouvelle Réforme, greeted him with inordinate enthusiasm. "Give 'em hell in there today, sir. The whole country's behind you."

Perhaps an exaggeration. Arguably, thirteen seats failed to demonstrate massive public approval, particularly since five had been filled by post-election crossovers from the Conservative Party. But enough to confer on Lafayette, to the astonishment of all, including himself, the title of Leader of the Official Opposition.

The Tories, leaderless and floundering, had eleven members now, tied with the NDP and Bloc. The Greens had outpolled them all, but lacking a regional base gleaned only four seats – a respectable showing, however, for Madam Blake, her reward a front-bench desk to the Speaker's left. Dominating Parliament was a faceless swarm of 258 Liberals, in flood across both sides of the chamber.

Lafayette was confident those numbers would halve after four years of Cloudy McRory's wayward efforts to govern. A patient scholar of politics, Lafayette would wait for the inevitable turning of the tide.

He was met in the foyer by several of his aides, who formed a phalanx to guide him through the mobs seeking entry into 253-D, where the Royal Commission on Issues Relating to the Dispute with Bhashyistan had been in boisterous session for the last three weeks. Lafayette might pop in if time permitted – today's sitting promised some sport: Beauchamp was on the stand.

As he doffed his coat in his office, his chief political adviser swivelled a computer monitor toward him. "You may find some material here for Question Period, boss."

YouTube, with its library of fatuous visual collectibles. "A production from Bhashyistan Revolutionary Front Studios," proclaimed the intro, which dissolved into a familiar pulpy face, the insufferable Mukhamet Ivanovich.

"Welcome, all freedom-loving people, to new, improved version of beautiful Bhashyistan. Today, we are showing President Erzhan in action, praise Allah, may he long reign." Erzhan had recently got a hero's welcome in Ottawa, his testimony before the royal commission marked by a fawning display of solicitude from his interlocutors. After an exchange of consuls, he'd spirited his family back to Igorgrad.

"Here is President Erzhan cutting ribbon for friendly military base near Igorgrad to protect borders from foreign interlopers." Various views of the country's new leader shaking hands with Russian officers and Gazprom apparatchiks amid wild applause from onlookers, then moving to a microphone to laud "friends too long ignored."

"Here also sharing spotlight is Prime Minister Ruslan Kolkov, long may he also reign." A red-bearded giant from the Siberian steppes, favourite son of his Kremlin overseers. Thus had that miserable nation been restored to its historic role of satellite.

Clara Gracey's timidity over Bhashyistan had deservedly pink-slipped her to political oblivion – she'd lost her seat and nearly her deposit. McRory had expressed his gratitude by posting her to lead Canada's delegation to the World Economic Forum. Politics had never suited her – she was too . . . was *principled* the word? Too ingenuous for the rough-and-tumble.

"And now we conclude with stirring tribute to our dear friends from Bonavista to Vancouver Island. No hard feelings, Canada, over recent trobbles. God willing, always be glorious and free like us."

Cut to a motley band playing the classic former theme to *Hockey Night in Canada*.

Lafayette felt a hint of nausea as he observed one of his aides blinking back tears.

~~~

Arthur settled himself into the witness chair under the black, unforgiving glare of his long-time nemesis, Wilbur Kroop, retired chief justice of the B.C. Supreme Court. How he had ended up chairing the Royal Commission on Bhashyistan was a distressing mystery, the final appointment of the imploding Conservative government. Maybe it was intentional. Get Beauchamp.

C.P.G. Barclay, the commission counsel, rose and carried on in his unflappable manner, taking up where he'd left off the day before. "Mr. Beauchamp, you have conceded that on January fifteenth, two months ago, you received, posthumously, an email from Mr. DiPalma."

"I have not hidden the fact." One has to be honest.

"As I understand the law, Mr. Beauchamp, death terminates solicitor-client privilege under special circumstances."

"Only when disclosure may prevent imminent harm. That is not the case here. Alive or dead, Mr. DiPalma and his reputation are entitled to my silence and protection."

Clugg and Klein weren't talking either, though Arthur could hardly feel he was in good company. Morbid irony resided in DiPalma's suicide – an act encouraged by his certainty they would sell him out. Arthur too had expected they'd dump everything on DiPalma. They might yet, subject to advice of counsel, of course.

Meanwhile, their former boss, Crumwell, had been fired without even a nominal golden handshake, and was in the Seychelles, avoiding subpoena.

"I will ask once again that you reveal the contents of Mr. DiPalma's email."

"And I will refuse again, Mr. Barclay." How could Arthur possibly assent to a precedent that could loosen the bonds of confidence between lawyer and client? How could he live with himself?

"I hesitate to remind a barrister of your reputation of the consequences."

Commissioner Kroop, who'd been staring at Arthur like a hungry vulture, finally lost patience with this gentlemanly discourse. "The sender of that email is *dead*. Dead as a doornail."

Arthur looked unflinchingly into the black tar pits of his sunken eyes. "The sender of that email was a client who had entrusted me with his words. An ancient code of ethics demands I honour that trust. Need I add that the solicitor-client relationship, unlike a marriage, doesn't end when death us do part?"

A ripple of laughter, but there was also a nervous sucking of breath in this packed hearing room, with its electric air of tension.

"Dead as a dodo bird! There was a state funeral! Posthumous honours!"

"Privilege outlasts death." Quoting none other than the heroic deceased himself, his last words.

The retired chief was seething, red spots glowing on his cheeks and jowls. But he found control, began with measured words. "Mr. Beauchamp, I have been granted special power to hold witnesses in contempt of court. I would be saddened to have to do so here."

But why that tiny, pursed, evil smile? It would not be the first time Kroop had held Arthur in contempt – he'd jailed him back in the old days, over some unremembered drunken insult. After a few days in the slammer, Arthur had gone nearly mad with thirst, had practically crawled on his knees for forgiveness. He'd sworn he would never again so debase himself.

"Should I find you in contempt, Mr. Beauchamp, I warn you . . ." Kroop's voice began rising. "No, I *promise* you, that you will enjoy the hospitality of Her Majesty for as long as it takes *for your contempt to be purged!*" A shout that rattled the hanging portrait of that very queen.

Kroop must have guessed – all too correctly – that there was something in DiPalma's email that was bound to embarrass Arthur. *You're going to look like a donkey if this gets out . . . this time the tomato juice will be on* your *shirt.* But of course it was the principle that mattered.

Again, with what seemed enormous effort, Kroop regained control, but the veins on his scalp were engorged and throbbing. "Very well, Mr. Beauchamp, your silence leaves me with no alternative but to try you for contempt, and it is with extreme anguish I do so."

"I'm sorry to cause you so much pain, Mr. Commissioner."

Kroop's face grew redder and redder, until it seemed about to explode . . .